P9-DXG-579

Sarah Vincent has two grown up children and lives in the South Shropshire countryside with her husband and her Jack Russell terrier, Beryl. She writes in a converted coal shed at the back of the house.

In the early days she juggled writing with various jobs as a care assistant, school dinner lady and museum guide. For the past twelve years she has worked as an editor for two leading Literary Consultancies. She also teaches Creative Writing online, and gets a buzz out of helping new writers achieve their goals.

She loves world music, and visiting art galleries when she's in town. Her greatest thrill though is going off-grid for a few days, and camping in remote places in her tiny caravan.

www.sarahkvincent.co.uk

CALGARY PUBLIC LIBRARY

JUL - - 2015

THE TESTAMENT OF VIDA TREMAYNE

SARAH VINCENT

THREE HARES PUBLISHING

Published by Three Hares Publishing 2014

Copyright © Sarah Vincent 2014

The right of Sarah Vincent to be identified as the author of this work has been asserted by her in accordance with the Copyright, Designs and Patents Act 1988.

This book is sold subject to the condition that it shall not, by way of trade or otherwise, be lent, resold, hired out, or otherwise circulated without the publisher's prior consent in any form of binding or cover other than that in which it is published and without similar condition, including this condition, being imposed on the subsequent purchaser.

This is a work of fiction. The characters, incidents, and dialogues are products of the author's imagination and are not to be construed as real. Any resemblance to actual events or persons, living or dead, is entirely coincidental.

First published in Great Britain in 2014
www.threeharespublishing.com

Three Hares Publishing Ltd Reg. No 8531198
Registered address: Suite 201, Berkshire House,
39-51 High Street,
Ascot, Berkshire, SL5 7HY

ISBN: 978-1-910153-10-9

For 'M'

23RD JANUARY

DORY

In the gloom of a late January afternoon, the house has an accusing look. It's as if it knows already of her treachery, Dory thinks. She can't face getting out of the car just yet. She lights a cigarette and frowns at the smug curves of the thatch through a haze of smoke. The thatch is crammed low over walls fringed with the dusty skeletons of those purple spiky things she can't remember the name of. She's not into flowers like Vida is. Like Vida *was*, rather. As for the trees, there are too damn many of them, huddled like mourners at a funeral. Chestnuts, she thinks, or maybe poplars, grown huge, fed from those murky underground streams that flow down from the hills. Too close to the house, that's for sure. She's told Vida before, nightmare stories from her clients about roots worming beneath the foundations, sending up cracks and fissures, buckling walls.

Don't digress. You're not here to fell trees. You're here to pick up the threads of your mother's life and sort out her affairs. There's no one else, is there?

It's the moment of arrival she's been dreading the most. She's often cursed the three-mile-long

1

track to the house; cursed it for its jay-walking pheasants and canyon-deep cracks which flood in winter, but this afternoon it hasn't seemed nearly long enough. Just the thought of pulling up outside the empty house made her feel sick. But here it is. End of the road. She's reached her destination.

'Home again!' How Vida had trilled this whenever they returned from a trip away, as if she couldn't wait to scuttle back to her study. But 'home' was in London then. If only it still was, things would have been a lot easier. Her parents couldn't have been in their right minds to move to this godforsaken place. The Shropshire-Welsh border, a no-man's land of misty horizons fit only for sheep. And now it's Vida who isn't in her right mind.

Dory's throat contracts and she coughs into the silence. The woman she's just left in the hospital *looks* like her mother, it's true, but it's as if there is no one at home. Only Vida's fingers had seemed alive, feeling blindly along the edge of the turned-down sheet, as if eternally searching for something.

'Okay, let's get this over.' Bracing herself she climbs from the car and heaves her bags from the boot. She considers coldly, does the cottage have what you'd call "Kerb Appeal"? Apart from the fact that there is no kerb, of course. Well, she'd knock this porch down for a start. It serves no purpose and the dark green blistering paintwork is more shabby than shabby-chic. Bamboo wind-chimes brush the back of her neck as she stoops to find her key. Kicking aside a basket of pine cones, she bangs her ankle on the iron mud-scraper. Sod that stupid thing! It might have been placed there for the very purpose of crippling her. Her hand trembles as she slides the key into the lock. She almost expects that it won't work, that the house will refuse her entrance, so rarely has she visited. But it does yield eventually, sticking a bit as doors do in old houses, the wood swelling and contracting with passing seasons. The door opens onto the square low-ceilinged room which serves as an entrance hall, woven rugs scattered over stone tiled floor, the coat stand with Vida's favourite purple cord jacket still dangling there, boots and trunks, and telephone.

Mum? She almost calls out like a child home from school, but swallows the word back just in time. Part of her stands aside, appalled at this sense of loss. It's just that Vida was always home, tapping away in her study. You always knew where to find her.

The hallway is stuffy as if no one has opened a window for a long time. She breathes in the dreary scent of old cooking, sprouting onions and damp umbrellas. It's her job to walk into empty houses. She's never been one to sense things. As far as she's concerned a house is a space to arrange furniture in, although some of the decor she's seen would be enough to scare a poltergeist. But this time she does feel something. There's a tension, a kind of expectancy in the air. This is ridiculous, she tells herself. She's behaving like her least favourite clients, the kind who blather on about the "energy not being right", when energy, as any reasonable person knows, is something you get from a bowl of muesli. Yet there *is* something. Beyond the tick of the hall clock the silence is taut and strained. She glares at the umbrellas, static, mock-innocent in the hallstand. The octagonal mirror in which Vida used to peer to straighten her woolly hat reflects nothing but dust. And yet something is not right. She can't say what. Ahead of her, the kitchen door stands slightly ajar. She throws the house keys on the hall table and coughs loudly, a warning to the empty house that she's here now, she's in charge. Almost immediately there's an answering creak of floorboards from somewhere above her.

'Dorothea?'

At the sound of her name, that *old* name no one ever uses, her heart plummets. She turns. There's a woman. Some damn strange woman is standing at the top of the stairs peering down over the stair rail at her.

'What? Who are you?' Her voice startles out of her throat, hoarse, almost unrecognizable.

'You must be Dorothea… Vida's daughter?' The woman is tramping down the wooden stairs that Vida always refused to carpet, saying they were "country" stairs. She is wide-hipped and heavy-footed in those ghastly knitted slipper things with crocheted daisies on the toes. Her cord skirt dips just short of her ankles. 'I am so, so sorry. I didn't mean to frighten you.'

'I'm Dory,' Dory corrects her. 'I wasn't expecting to find anyone here. You are…?'

She takes in the gypsy hair and homebody hand-knits. The woman looks the kind who would paint henna patterns on her hands and caper about at festivals in nothing but a pair of star-spangled wellies.

'Oh, I'm your mother's friend. She might have mentioned me? Rhiannon, Rhiannon Townsend. Look, I'm really so sorry, I must've scared you half to death.'

'Yes, you did actually.' Is she supposed to shake hands? The woman is holding out her arms as if she expects her to collapse into her embrace. Dory stiffens, taken aback at the idea of Vida having a friend: Vida who lived like a hermit, always buried in the latest book. But why shouldn't she have a friend? God knows she'd need someone out here in the middle of nowhere.

'I've been staying with Vida for a while. It must have been a terrible shock for you.'

'At first, yes, but I'm all right...' She endures the hug, battening her arms rigid at her sides. 'I'm all right. Really, I'm fine.'

The woman takes the hint and releases her. 'You've been to the hospital?'

'I'm just back from there.' She's about to recount how she found Vida four weeks ago, right here in the kitchen on her hands and knees, with the quarry tiles littered in mud and blood and feathers but she stops herself just in time. She'd rather not think about that. And it's not the kind of thing one blabs about to a stranger. At least Vida is now lying safe and clean in a hospital bed. She's being treated, looked after.

'After it happened, well, I had to dash back to London to sort a few things out first.'

The friend nods. Thankfully she doesn't enquire what the "things" were. It's pointless explaining her business concerns to a woman like this, how she had several property viewings to steer her clients through, and a couple of big deals to clinch. The period coming up to Christmas was always crazy with everyone wanting to move at once. January usually brought a lull. She should be thankful for that at least. Suddenly she feels numb, as if she'd like to just lie down in the snow Eskimo-style and quietly go to sleep forever.

She turns to the woman. 'Vida never mentioned she had someone staying with her.'

It comes out a bit snappy, but after all, what does she know about this person? And she's in no mood for chitchat. She just wants to dump her bags, collapse onto that big oak-framed bed with the squashy mattress in the better of the spare rooms and sleep.

The woman explains in her north London twang that she and Vida are very close.

'I moved in, let's see, it must've been three months ago. Sadly I wasn't here when your mother had her breakdown. When I got word, of course, I came straight back.'

Moved in? *Thanks, mother.* So now she has a sitting tenant to get shot of before she can put the wretched place up for sale.

'You got word from…?'

The woman smiles. 'Word spreads fast in a place like this.'

'So when you say you've moved in...?' There's no way of putting the question tactfully.

'Oh, I don't mean permanently. I just came to help Vida out a bit; she was having some problems with her work. She's been going through such a difficult patch. When I heard she'd been taken into the unit at Cregaron, I thought I'd come back just to look after things, her mail and so on, sort out her clothes and toiletries that she needs. I tried to ring you. I left a couple of messages on your answer phone, but perhaps you didn't get them. If I'd known you were coming...'

Dory cuts in on the slow emphatic speech, her own voice shrill like a child. 'Of course I'd be coming. I just told you, I had a few things to sort out. I have a business in London to run. I have clients, employees. I can't just dump everything at a moment's notice.'

The woman nods, her eyes brimming with sympathy. 'I understand. Vida told me how busy you are with your agency, how hard it is for you to get away.'

'I *am* her daughter. I can get away if it's an emergency.' She hears the crack in her voice, on the edge of hysteria.

No wonder this woman lays a hand on her arm. 'You look all in. Have you eaten?'

No, she hasn't and Vida's friend has soup on the simmer. Dory follows her into the kitchen, her mother's kitchen, just as she remembers. Mismatched chairs around the huge heavily scored wooden table, the blackened Rayburn smelling of coal dust, the grimy terracotta floor tiles. She remembers the last time, before that terrible day with the blood feathers, the day she was here with Dan, how Vida prattled on nervously and insisted they eat some stale old cake from the freezer, which gave her indigestion.

'Sit down. I hope you like Butternut squash. Not everyone does.'

It seems odd, a stranger offering her hospitality in her mother's house. It gives her an uneasy feeling.

'That's fine, thanks.' She shrugs off the black military style woollen coat with some reluctance. Vida's house is never quite warm enough for her, too many draughts and chilly corners for someone used to under-floor heating, and she's been known to sit out an entire visit in her outdoor clothes. Now she tugs the cashmere cardy down over her wrists and sneaks a glance at Rhiannon's back view as she turns to stir the soup. Her droopy skirt is the colour of pomegranates, with tights to match. She looks quite at home here, bangles chinking at her wrists as she stirs. Not the kind of friend you meet for coffee then. Close friends rather. Bosom buddies. A live-in friend, a confidante. Has Vida unburdened herself to this woman, talked about her, Dory, the cold daughter who never visits? Along with the pang of shame, she feels at a disadvantage. Rhiannon will have a weight of knowledge, of insights about Vida's illness, while she, Dory is in the dark.

'Sorry if I sounded edgy. It's just all been a bit wild. I mean when I found my mother, you know, *like that*, it was a bolt from the blue.' She pauses.

'We'd been talking about plans for Christmas and everything on the telephone. She was a bit vague, a bit weird at the time. But it's odd that she never mentioned you were staying with her.'

'Did she not? I can't really account for that.' Rhiannon stops stirring for a moment and half turns from the stove. 'Sadly, poor Vida was retreating into her own world by that stage.'

'But if you were staying here, you must've seen some signs. Do you have any idea how it – the illness, I mean – how it came on?'

Vida's friend clamps a lid on the pan and draws up a chair. She has that faintly yearning, empathic expression on her face that Dory identifies with counsellors. Not that she's had much to do with counsellors; well, only that time when she was trying to give up smoking. A lot of help that had been.

'She was trying to write something new for the publishers. You know they wanted her to be another Ella de Vile?' The woman leans forward confidentially. 'Incredible, isn't it? We're talking about the author of *The Gingerbread House*, the winner of the Peccadill Prize churning out trashy horror novels.' She hesitates as if waiting for a reaction.

Dory refuses to oblige. How many times have people quoted that title at her? It's the title Vida is famous for, the title that picked up the awards, and bought this house re-named for the book. She's not a fan. It still rankles that her mother used her for one of the main characters, Hetty Jackson: spoiled, selfish, a thoroughly nasty piece of work with few redeeming features. As for de Vile, the name means nothing to her.

Vida's friend continues. 'Your mother is an artist. Well, of course you know that. An artist can't just write herself into a little box for the sake of some stupid category.'

Dory's head is starting to ache. Vida's artistic struggles have no relevance in her life.

'So, have you known my mother for long?'

The friend calculates. 'About three months, I think. It feels like forever, though. I'd been a fan of Vida's work long before we met. You know how it is. When you admire someone's work, you feel you know them through their fiction.'

Dory turns away slightly and lights a cigarette. She's about to ask if she minds her smoking but decides against it. It's her mother's house, after all, and the woman is beginning to annoy her. She imagines the two of them sitting around talking about novels all day.

Through a plume of smoke she announces, 'I'm afraid I don't read fiction. I prefer facts.'

'No need to apologize. There's no shame in that.' It's the non-judgmental response you might expect from a counsellor. Perhaps she *is* one. Dory could do, say something completely outrageous and this woman would hardly flinch.

'Some people would think my not reading fiction is a crime.' She's seen people visibly recoil when she's said that before. Vida Tremayne's daughter doesn't read fiction? Doesn't even read her mother's work? Shocking!

But Rhiannon doesn't appear to find it so. She murmurs some homily about children being individuals, having their own paths, their own journeys to make.

'Did you meet Vida at one of her book signings?' Dory flicks ash into a potted cyclamen. Its leaves are yellowing anyway, so it hardly matters.

'Not a signing. Let's just say we started up a correspondence. It grew from there.'

'I see.' Actually she doesn't "see" at all. 'So, are you a writer as well then?'

'Sadly I haven't been blessed with that talent. But I do understand the creative process.'

'So er, what *do* you do?'

Rhiannon smiles; it's an indulgent smile, the smile one gives to a child who has asked where babies come from.

'What do I *do*?' She repeats the question as if it amuses her. 'I tend to think of myself as "*being*" rather than "doing", you know. A human *being*.'

Oh please, come on. Dory almost grinds her teeth together. 'It doesn't pay the mortgage though, does it, just *being*?'

Rhiannon says she doesn't have a mortgage; she rents a place in London.

'Huh, well rent... mortgage, not much difference, the price of rents these days. Whereabouts in London? Excuse me if that sounds nosy, but I'm always interested in where people live. Houses are my business.' This is true; she knows every square inch of the capital intimately: not in a romantic, historical sense, but in terms of property values, at least.

Rhiannon's smile looks a little stretched. It's north London apparently, somewhere near Palmers Green, but then she's moved around a lot. She gets up at this point to set out bowls and spoons.

'Ah, which street would that be then? Is it near Broomfield Park? We found a house for some clients there last summer.'

A spoon clatters to the tiles. Rhiannon bends to pick it up, so that Dory just catches her muffled response. Farringdon Avenue, not a street she's familiar with.

'Ah, doesn't ring any bells. So do you live alone then? You're not married?' There's no wedding ring, and she doesn't look the married sort, but you never know.

'No.' Rhiannon seems quite emphatic on that point at least. She says fondly, 'I have Caliban. He's more than enough for me.'

'Caliban?'

'My cat. A neighbour is very kindly feeding him so he'll be fine.'

Dory restrains a groan. She presses on. 'So, are you between jobs at the moment, or do you normally work from home? Forgive me, but it's tough on you giving up your time to be...'

'Not tough at all, it's a privilege to be able to help.' Rhiannon sits down again, facing her. There's something solid, implacable about her gaze that makes Dory's fidgets seem almost an affectation.

'I do most of my work from home, you're right, but my work moves around with me, and my clients are not especially demanding at the moment.'

'Well, lucky you.' Dory thinks of her own clients who rarely give her a moment's peace. But then she's never sought peace. Peace would drive her crazy. 'There aren't many businesses I can think of with undemanding clients. At least not *successful* ones.'

Rhiannon smiles and says it depends what you term as success. 'My line of work is very different to yours, Dory. I suppose if you really want to label it, you could call it Creative Therapy. I work with artists, writers... *creatives,* people who are blocked for various reasons. I like to think of myself as a facilitator more than anything.'

Dory nods, but really this isn't her field. It all sounds a bit deep for her. But yes, she supposes this is exactly the sort of woman that Vida would want as a pal. And she has to admit this friend is a relief in a way, someone else who knows Vida, who appears to care so much about her welfare. She says almost grudgingly, 'Well, I expect my mother was glad to have you with her. It's lonely out here. I never got why she and Dad moved here in the first place.'

Rhiannon says that people are like plants, only flourishing in the right spot.

'Vida needed solitude to create, but you're a city girl, you like to be where the action is, I can see that. Vida told me all about your apartment. She was looking forward to seeing it.'

Dory fidgets with her ring, twisting it over her bony knuckle and back again until the knuckle smarts. Her mother has never seen the flat, although she'd dropped enough hints about longing to see it. She'd meant to invite her. Dan, in the short time he was living there, was always nagging about it. 'Why not invite your mum? I'll cook. I'll take her around town if you're working.' Dan was into families. He never really understood how clients must always come first if you want to survive. That was the main reason they broke up.

'The flat's fine.' She can't quite look Rhiannon in the eye as she says this. 'To be honest I'm hardly ever there. My assistant Harvey takes care of things at the office mainly. The house-searches take me all over the country. I hardly ever get a free weekend and anyway, Mother doesn't come to London much. She's always in the middle of a book. And I've been working 24/7. You can't let people down. If you take your eye off the ball for a minute, you'll get trashed on Twitter and that's it, game over.'

Thinking of work, she wonders what kind of house she would find for this woman if she were a client. A yurt probably, or one of those converted shepherd's hut jobs, or an off-grid hovel in an eco-collective.

Rhiannon sympathizes. It takes time to build a reputation, she says, to build trust. She's not such a bad sort it seems. Dory allows her defences to drop. She gives way to the exhaustion she's been fighting ever since she heard the news.

'Look, I should thank you for taking care of my mother, sorting her stuff for the hospital, all that.'

Rhiannon waves away her gratitude. It's been an honour to look after Vida's interests. In fact, if Dory needs to get back to London urgently, she'd be more than happy to take care of things here. She folds her arms beneath her breasts: huge breasts, Dory notes with a twinge of envy, the breasts of a flipping fertility goddess.

'I could visit Vida while she's in hospital, and keep you posted on how she is. If there's any change you could come up...'

'Oh, thank you, but no, I mean I have to be here for a bit.' Part of her wants to grab the offer and run, but it's odd how when someone offers you a way out, some perverse urge to self-sacrifice kicks in. 'I need to think about what to do with the house. I spoke to Mum's doctor briefly last week, and it doesn't look as if she is going to... well, he can't say how soon... you know...' She stumbles over her words. She knows nothing of mental health apart from Gothic visions of straitjackets, chains, asylums of lunatics howling at the moon. 'I'll be seeing him again on my next visit. Now that they've had a chance to assess her properly, I really need some answers.'

Rhiannon grimaces. 'Consultants don't know everything. They're an arrogant breed, talking down to us mortals as if we're children.'

'Actually he was quite kind...' Dory has to admit that. Dr. Saleem was, however, infuriatingly non-committal. He couldn't say how long, or perhaps wouldn't say.

'But how long?' she'd wanted to know. She needed confirmation; dates, times, forecasts. 'Can you give me some idea? Are we talking weeks or months?' Her mind flitting to her diary, please let her mother be normal again soon, before spring at least, when the housing market went into overdrive. The doctor began to outline treatment.

'We're going to put her on a course of drugs to begin with, and see how she responds.'

'Drugs? But how long do they usually take?'

His voice was gentle when he told her they had no way of knowing. It could be weeks, months... it could be... He didn't actually say "years" but the implication of the tailing-off sentence was clear. It could be... *forever.* To her shame her first thoughts had been selfish. Why her? Why did her mother have to do this to her, and at such a time, when she was so damn busy, and now there was no one else, no one that is but...

Rhiannon gets up to attend to the soup. 'I'm glad you found him kind. In any case it's too soon for you to make decisions. You need nourishment. At least have something to eat first.'

Nourishment. It's an odd choice of word. Or maybe it's a comment on her figure, which is all angles, broad bony shoulders and knees, big knuckled hands and size 8 feet.

'Thanks.'

The soup has bits in it she can't identify. She doesn't like bits in soup; she likes it blended smooth, but she has to admit this stuff tastes okay. Only when she's finished does she wonder about the sleeping arrangements. How long is this Rhiannon planning to stay? She can't very well kick her out on this first evening. As if reading her mind, Rhiannon spreads her fingers over her upper chest as if in apology. 'I'm not sure which room you usually sleep in when you stay over, Dory? Vida told me to take the bigger room at the front of the house. I hope that's okay?'

Damn. The room with the double bed which she wanted to spread herself across and sleep in for a thousand years. It's the official spare room, with the patchwork quilt and a view of the forest. In this bed Vida's writer friends, in the days when she had them, have dreamed their next novels.

'Of course. Fine.' She can hardly lay claim to the room when she has never ever "stayed over", as Rhiannon puts it, in her mother's house, not even that Christmas before last when Vida had practically begged her. She'd always had an excuse to get away before nightfall.

'Are you sure, because I can move my things into the back bedroom if you like.'

'No, no, stay where you are please, it doesn't matter where I sleep. Actually, if you don't mind, I think I'll go up now. It's been a long day. We can talk about things in the morning.'

❖ ❖ ❖

Rhiannon bids her good night with almost motherly concern. Will she be comfortable enough? Would she like a hot water bottle? Yes she will, and no she wouldn't like a hot water bottle. She hasn't had one of those since she was ten and had the flu. But later, when she's made up the bed with sheets from the airing cupboard, she wishes she'd taken up the offer. The room is freezing. No wonder. As she draws the curtains she sees that the window-frames are practically rotten, shrinking away from the glass like diseased gums. Such civilized comforts as double glazing and central heating are unknown to Vida, who tended to hole herself up in her study in the fug of an electric convector heater, while throughout the rest of the house ice would form on the inside of the windows.

Dory sinks onto the single bed. Hardly anyone has slept on this bed. It's just a prop for cushions, awful crafty crocheted things that Vida used to fiddle with between novels. Decor wise, it's a nightmare. It's a room where all those items Vida was too superstitious about chucking out, yet couldn't bear to look at, are gathered. This includes the portrait of herself, Dory, as a teenager.

It is this portrait she finds herself focussing on as she climbs, at this ridiculously early hour, into bed. Her father's artist friend Mikhail Chalnachick had drawn it, mainly to swell the material for one of his solo exhibitions. In the event, no one bought it, and it ended up hanging in her parents' hall, where it greeted guests with a glower.

It was around nineteen years ago, yet she remembers sitting for this as if it were yesterday. Everyone agreed that the mood sketch, dashed off in smoky charcoals, captured her personality. The girl in the picture is sulky, listless and flirtatious. Dory recalls how painful it was sitting motionless for over two hours. How impossible. How she had wriggled and yawned.

Little Miss Fidget Bum, Dad's friend had called her. It was the kind of pet name her great aunt Jean might use, yet how different it sounded in Mikhail's sexy East European accent! Two years later when she turned eighteen, he painted her again, this time without either her parents' knowledge or her clothes.

Dory scatters crocheted cushions as she squeezes herself into the too small bed. Sex. This is what she needs right now, the quick release. It's the only thing that works when she's really wound up, the only thing that takes her out of herself. She thinks of Dan. Dan was never the most expert of her lovers, but he was eager to oblige – that is, before they had that god-awful row and he walked out.

Little Miss Fidget Bum smirks down at her, as if she can hardly believe what she's turned into. What's wrong with her? Why has nothing ever been right? How come she's still alone when she's officially middle-aged, and practically on her way to cronedom?

And now she has to worry about her mother. Just before she slides down into sleep she wonders why Vida stuck the picture up in this cupboard-sized room with the sloping ceiling that no one ever goes in.

Vida's Diary

Tuesday 2nd September

It's Market Day in Cregaron. This is the highlight of my week since Jonathan left. It's become almost an Occasion. In honour of such, I washed my hair this morning, and even put in a couple of rollers to give my limp grey-blonde locks some bounce. They quickly unravelled in the autumn drizzle. I trundled about the stalls. Even the vegetables had a wilted look. In the hotel where lank-haired girls serve dusty scones to walkers, I sipped my coffee and pondered on why we ever moved here.

Cregaron's attraction for me then, twelve years ago, was that it *had* no attractions, nothing beyond some faded Victorian grandeur, the stone clock tower, the memorial plinth, the funny little shops selling the kind of junk and trinkets no one ever buys. The library of yellow brick so soft it might crumble like cheese, with its damp papery scent and jaunty assistants.

It was my mistake this morning to go into the library.

'We haven't seen you for a while, Vida.' Janice, who organized my talk three years back, swiped my card past the scanner. This is true. The reason I rarely darken the doors is because Janice is forever pressing me to join their book group. To have "a real live author" as a member would be a real boost to morale apparently.

No, I said, I was afraid I seemed to be very busy of late. I managed not to say – Time Flies. That would be a lie, when time doesn't fly but crawls on its belly with an almost supernatural lethargy, as if some universal law has been overturned without anyone yet noticing.

'Still writing are we?'

I almost cringed at this. Janice is not the type to lower her voice to church whispers. Her southern vowels, so foreign to this region where voices are quiet, soporific, running out of steam halfway through a sentence, drilled through the silence. She thumped *Time of Your Life!* across the desk to me. The book was something of an embarrassment, but as I haven't had a period in three months, it struck me it might come in useful.

Her look was conspiratorial, as if we were both in on a state secret. 'Working on something new then?'

'Yes.' I managed to force a smile. 'Something new.'

⚜ ⚜ ⚜

Outside I bundled myself into the car, and drove smartly out of town. Something new. The only thing I've written since Jon left is this journal. I keep saying since he left, which implies a scene: slammed doors, emptied wardrobes and the wife of thirty-six years abandoned sobbing on the drive. That's not how it was. We had, as they say, been drifting apart for years. While I sat grinding out my turgid prose, he was spending more and more time in London.

'It'll be better for you; you'll have nothing to distract you from your work without me cluttering up the place. It's what you always wanted, wasn't it, peace and quiet?'

This is how he put it, as if leaving was a charitable act, a sacrifice to my art. I didn't know then that he'd met Millie, the woman he now lives with in the Dordogne.

"Quiet" is not necessarily peaceful. Driving back from Cregaron through the dun-coloured uplands, the forests that hug the contours of the land like corporation carpet, my mind fretted over the same old question. What am I doing, living here in the middle of nowhere? Why don't I admit defeat and move back to town, find a proper job, pick up with my old friends, *meet* people again?

Back in my driveway, I sat for a moment, gazing at my house with a stranger's eye. The thatch needs repairing. Great tufts of straw loosened from last winter's storms straggle over the dormer windows, blocking out what remains of the light. At night I lie awake and listen to the mice scrabbling away. Dory says a thatched roof is a cliché and a costly one at that, but when we first stumbled upon the place, I was in love and blind to any such defects.

'It's "*The Gingerbread House*",' I told Jon, 'just as I imagined it in my book, as if it's been sitting here waiting for us to find it.'

I loved it all: the warped green-painted window-frames, the rickety porch, and inside the jumble of low-ceilinged rooms, even the 1950s extension at the back, with its plastic ridged roof and acrid tang of geraniums: the extension which Dory says is a horror, and which Jon intended to do something about, but never did.

It was a kind of voluntary exile. I imagined we would tramp off about the hills, and in between the words would spill out endlessly into the silence. Let the editors and journalists and fans come beating a path to my door if they must. *The Gingerbread House* royalties were still flowing in then. Dory was busy with her agency, and would hardly miss us.

That was *then*. Today as I opened the front door, the silence pressed against me like a living thing, the way a cat winds itself about your legs when it wants feeding. It had a swish to it, like silk. I paused, listened. What I would have given to hear Jon's tuneless whistling right then. I nearly tripped over the rug in my rush to switch on Radio 4, as I always do, just for the comfort of hearing a human voice. When I dumped the menopause book on the kitchen table, the woman on the cover, a toned fifty-something, beamed up at me. *Hormones*, she seemed to be saying. *It's just hormones, making you edgy.*

Wednesday 4th September

I wish I hadn't got this book. That beaming woman on the front cover was entirely misleading. There's a whole section on diseases of the middle-aged; fallen wombs, gallstones, crumbling spines. The diagram shows a woman whose breasts are slumped like old pillows; her waist is the same thickness as her hips. She is a sad androgynous creature. She is like a tree, stolid, enduring, with no curves or undulations.

Am I like that? Peeling off my clothes at bedtime, I tighten my tummy muscles and strike a pose in front of the mirror. At least I still have a waist. Hands on hips, I turn this way, that way, and yes, I am still recognizably woman-shaped. But my face without makeup is the face of a haggard schoolgirl. Why bother with makeup when there is absolutely no one to see you?

Thursday 5th September

Moped around all day yesterday gazing out of windows. I meant to work, but nothing came. Then I went for a walk, and stumbled in a ditch and wrenched my knee. I had a moment of panic when it happened. Supposing I'd broken something? Who would I call? Who would come to my rescue? This is one of the perils of living alone. The fixation with keeping well, keeping safe so as not to burden anyone. My risk avoidance strategies are getting out of hand. Soon I won't venture out of the door without knee-guards and a helmet.

One hour later – Cindy just rang. 'Vida! Did you get my book in the post? No? Oh sorry, must've forgotten to send it, so many people after their freebie. I'll bring it when I come down. How are you fixed for next week? Vida, if I don't get away from London

I shall go bananas, and anyway I've got this fabulous idea for you to think about...'

Cindy has plenty to gush about; she has managed to clone herself into no less than six heroines, their names plastered across the sweetie-coloured covers... Georgia, Jemima, Daisy May... I forget the other two. Oh yes, the latest one is called 'Arabella'.

We first met at some Authors' Society do, and I was flattered then at how Cindy just seemed to latch onto me. She'd loved *The Gingerbread House*, she said, even though it was so different to her own work. We hadn't mingled much, just giggled and gossiped for the rest of the evening over the canapés and white wine.

When I put the phone down the silence was louder than ever. I gave the house a good blast of Dylan, then rushed to switch it off. It's as if I'm scared his *Baby Blue* will wake something; as if I had a baby sleeping in the house, a tyrannical child that once woken will never rest.

I can't go on with this entry. Must *do* something. Bake a cake. Make up the bed in the guest room for Cindy.

Friday 6th September

Yesterday I typed one page. A single page, which I printed in triumph, then threw on the fire. It's perverse of me I know. What I would have given for this solitude in my thirties when Dory was small, and Jon always bringing his pals home for meals, and the phone ringing nonstop.

Speak of the devil. Twenty minutes later, and interrupted by a call from Dory.

'I just heard from Dad.' Her voice is tight with accusation. 'He tells me he's staying in France with this Millie woman. I thought he was there for work. I thought you said it was only temporary. I didn't know he'd actually *bought* a place down there.'

Dory is outraged. Who is this girl, and where did Jon meet her for God's sake?

'I should have thought he was past it. I mean it's too disgusting to think about. Why didn't you tell me? I am *only* your daughter, but I would have thought I had a right to know what my parents are up to.'

Yes, she does have a perfect right. But this was Jon's idea. 'We don't want to tell Dory and upset her just yet.'

'Oh Dory, I was going to ring this week some time. Sorry. I just didn't want to burden you, when you're busy with work.'

'Oh for goodness sake, Mum, why do you have to be such a martyr?' She adds reluctantly, 'Are you all right? It's hell here at the moment, but I suppose I could try and come down.'

'That's sweet of you, but I'm fine, love, really.'

I say this because it is what she needs me to say.

'But what are you doing with yourself? You'll go mad down there in the middle of the nowhere, on your own.'

'No, really, I'm fine. I've just started work on a new book.'

'Oh.'

Wrong thing to say, I know it at once from the silence. Dory has a way with silences; they are far more eloquent than her conversation. After a while she continues in a small piqued voice:

'Yes… well…'

'Yes, well?'

'Sorry, Mother, but Dad isn't coming back. *Ever.* And all you can think of is the next book?'

'Dory… I need… I have to deal with this in the only way I know how. And anyway, I've just been talking to Cindy, and she's coming down next week. You know Cindy… she…'

'Well, I'd better not hold you up any more then.'

'Dear, you're not holding …'

Slam! She's gone. Just like the old days, slamming doors and telephone receivers on me. She's upset, of course, who wouldn't be? I should ring her back, but I can't. I'll call her tonight and try to smooth things over. I'd love her to come down, I'd love it if we could just sit and talk it all over face to face.

My eyes burn momentarily, but tears fail to come. What went wrong between us? I wish I could pinpoint a pivotal moment, some incident I could apologize for, but there doesn't seem to be one.

On my desk is the photo of Dory aged eight, showing off the new roller boots that were all the rage that year, practising her curves and spins in the park. Her wonky-toothed grin is unguarded, and there's something touching about the way her knee socks have rolled down over her calves.

They talk a lot about hyperactive children these days. I don't believe Dory was hyperactive exactly, but she was eternally clamouring for trips to skating rinks, theme parks, cinemas, it seemed to me then: always nagging for friends to come for sleepovers. It was as if she hated her own company. I remember finding this hard to understand, wishing she was more like I'd been as a child, nose in a book, or drawing pictures, or making up stories for my dolls. I imagined all only children were like that.

'Can't you find something to do?' That was my constant refrain, especially if I was trying to meet a deadline during school holidays. Or, *'Why can't you read your book if you're bored? You haven't even tried it yet. You haven't even read the first page.'*

'I *have* read the first page, and it's boring!' That must have been the time she threw the new Roald Dahl I'd bought her across the kitchen. The mug of coffee was right in its flight path. I can see the book now clearly, sprawling face down on the tiles, the cover with the Quentin Blake drawing of Matilda, turning into a brown mulch. That was my snapping point. I slapped Dory then, just once, hard across the forearm and we both ended up in tears. The slap left a red mark on her arm for days.

That wasn't good. No, I can see that now. Maybe in my exasperation, I got a bit screechy at times. Clearly I wasn't as much fun as the mothers of her friends, with their casual, riotous households, which was probably why she opted to spend more and more time away from home.

I give myself a shake. Really I should know better than this. Digging up the past, looking for reasons. I could do with a walk, but it's still raining, sloshing in puddles beneath the Damson tree, blotting out the hills.

Monday 12th September

No chance to write in here, with Cindy staying this past week. I just waved her off with mixed feelings. Relief mostly, mixed with dread at the thought of the silence she's left behind.

She arrived six days ago in the red convertible bought with her last advance, with several bottles of champagne stuffed in the boot, shocking me as she always does with the realization that she is about the same age as Dory. Yet how different she is, with her froth of angelic curls, and her fierce hilarity, gripping my shoulders, planting kisses on my cheeks.

'Can you play Pictionary?'

'What?'

'I've brought loads of silly games. Don't worry, I'll teach you. We must have games. We must celebrate.' Like a lot of childless women, she is *childlike*, windmilling her arms around in the dank autumnal air. 'I can't tell you, Vida… I am soo…ooo ready for this break, it's been manic lately.'

Cindy won every game, of course. She wiped the board with me each night after dinner. I must admit I got a bit drunk on the champagne. I laughed so much my stomach ached. On her last night, Cindy got around to her crazy idea that I should open a Creative Writing School.

I did my best to laugh it off. 'You've got to be joking. How would I ever get any work done?'

Cindy just poured more champagne. 'I'm serious, Vida, practically the entire literate nation is writing a novel, and you've got all these empty rooms going to waste. You've got to make a living now you're on your own. You did say that sales hadn't been great lately.'

'Well, I...' This is an understatement when only one of my books remains in print.

'I could always come and be your guest-author, you need a Big Name to get them hooked in, remember.'

'Thanks for the advice, Cindy,' I said. 'I'll think about it. No, really. I promise.'

I have no intention of opening a creative writing school. I told her that to shut her up. I know she means well. She's just off to the States, where *Arabella* is already flying off the shelves. I might have been jealous once, but now I am pleased for her, truly, as I wave her off.

But now I come back to my desk, and the creaking silence of this house, and think of all my books now out of print. Only *The Gingerbread House* lingers on in the darkest corners of provincial bookshops, dribbling out a few royalties. When did I last hear from my editors at Nelson and Hargrave? As for my agent, I've almost forgotten she exists. The vibrant young woman who signed me originally is long gone.

I think she went off to have a baby and never returned. I was "inherited" as they say, by one of her colleagues, Fee Moody, a woman with a terrifying barky sort of voice who deals mainly with cookery and crime. I've only spoken to her once on the telephone when she first took me on. For all she knows I could be dead. Still, at least she's never tried to persuade me to write a cookbook. For that I should be grateful.

Tuesday 13th September

Funny I should mention the publishers yesterday. Today the post brings a package with their stamp, enclosing the first fan letter I've had in an age. When *The Gingerbread House* won the award, I had sackloads of them. .

Dear Ms. Tremayne, I just want to say how much I enjoyed your book. I'd love to know where you get your ideas. I write a bit myself, for my sins. I know you must be very busy but I wonder if you could find time to look at something… etc etc…

This one is different. No mention of that dusty manuscript in a drawer she wants an opinion on. She doesn't even ask where I get from my ideas from. Instead she gives a flattering account of *The Gingerbread House,* endowing it with all kinds of mystical significance I never dreamed of in the writing. She apologizes that several years after publication she has only just "discovered" it.

'*I am only sorry that I didn't come across it before, but you know, I do believe it's a case of when the pupil is ready, the Master appears. The right book falls into your hands at the right time. Serendipity.'* On and on she goes. I read the adjectives, my breath tight in my chest... *'Totemic, powerful, liberating.'*

She finishes:

'I am currently writing a paper on the power of the unconscious and alchemical symbolism in the contemporary novel. I'm sure you must be very busy, but would it be possible for us to meet? I feel we could learn a lot from each other.

With all good wishes, Rhiannon Townsend'

I have no idea what she means by "alchemical symbolism". I wonder if *she* even knows. At one time, I would have shredded a letter like this. Now as I listen to the sheep bleating, and the distant growl of a tractor taking their feed in the rain, I anchor it on my desk with a paperweight. I savour the word "totemic". Perhaps I will write to this Rhiannon, maybe tomorrow.

27TH JANUARY

DORY

Vida is slumped in her chair in what they call the Day Room. Her head lolls forward, occasionally righting itself, like someone dozing on a long train journey, jerked to semi-consciousness with a sudden snore. Thank God she's sleeping. The first time Dory visited, that terrible blank stare had chilled her to the bone.

'Hallo. How are you feeling?'

No answer. Dory doesn't expect one, but they've told her to talk to Vida as if everything is normal. It's ludicrous. What is she supposed to say? Is she supposed to witter on about the weather, when her every instinct is to run howling from the ward without a backwards glance?

She makes another stab at one-sided conversation. 'It's warm in here, isn't it? They could do with opening a window...' She tails off. With her head bowed, Vida looks smaller than Dory remembers, shrunken. Her hair was never that grey before, surely? Someone has clipped it back off her face, giving her the look of an ageing schoolgirl.

'I'm glad you're having a nice sleep.' She feels foolish, yakking away to herself, not that anyone would notice. They all talk to themselves in here. In the far corner, a woman wearing a denim mini-skirt and fluffy hamster-face slippers is hooting merrily at someone on daytime TV; a girl so stick-thin she looks as if she might snap in two rocks endlessly on her chair by the window, back and forth, back and forth. The creaking of worn springs nearly drives Dory wild.

'I've met your friend Rhiannon back at the house.' Dory hovers by the chair, feeling like a giant-ess as she stoops awkwardly over her mother's bob-bing head. 'She seems all right. Helpful. Kind of her to look after you, visit you, I mean.'

Vida's head lifts just slightly. This time her eyelids flicker open just long enough for Dory to notice the complete absence of any kind of light in her eyes. Chilled, she takes a step backwards. It's like staring into the void.

Somehow she finds her voice. 'Sorry, I can't stay with you long. I've got an appointment to see your psychiatrist. Dr. Saleem. He wants to talk about you, about how they're going to help you. We've got to get you better, haven't we? Get you better and out of here.'

The rocking girl by the window is staring oddly at her. Time to move.

'Well, I'd better go and see what the doctor says. I'll be back in a day or two.'

She reaches out a tentative hand towards her mother's head, then swiftly withdraws it, the way you'd pull back from a creature that might bite. What is she afraid of? That she might get contaminated by Vida's madness? Catch something? Really she wants to get down on her knees and shake her mother by the shoulders, plead with her to wake up, beg her to be normal again. But all she says is, 'Goodbye then,' and turns on her heels.

❊ ❊ ❊

The psychiatrist's office is adjacent to the ward. She knocks twice and a soft voice invites her to come in. Dr. Saleem rises from his desk to shake her hand. He gestures at the chair. 'Please, sit down.' His brown eyes on hers are so gentle, she almost wishes she was one of his patients.

'You have seen her just now, yes?'

She nods. 'Yes.'

He seems to intuit just how she's feeling. 'It's distressing to see her like that, I understand.'

She draws a breath. 'What exactly is wrong with her? I mean why is she not responding to anything?'

'Your mother is in what we would call a catatonic state.' Dr. Saleem settles back in his chair, steeples his fingers together.

'Catatonic? I thought that was a kind of shock.'

'It can be the result of a shock, yes. We refer to it as Post Traumatic Stress Syndrome.' He explains that Catatonia can manifest in various ways. Some patients may repeat meaningless phrases. Others withdraw from the world and appear to be in a kind of stupor.

'This has happened in your mother's case. Mutism is common in such cases unfortunately. Your mother hasn't spoken a word since she came to the ward. Neither does she make eye contact. However it doesn't mean her brain is not active. We can't know, of course, what she is thinking. She may see and hear perfectly well. She is managing to eat a little and this is a hopeful sign.'

Dory forces down a rising panic. 'But why? Why now? She's never had anything like this before.'

The doctor says this is what they need to find out. 'That's why I'm hoping a little chat will throw some light on what triggered the breakdown.' He pauses. 'Firstly I should just check. We have you down as next of kin. I take it you have no siblings; you are Vida's only child?'

'Yes I am.' She bites the soft inside of her lower lip so hard it hurts. What a curse it is to be the only lonely child! How she could have done with an elder sister right now, some mumsy type who would take on the caring role without a second thought. Clearly Vida and her father had not cared to repeat the experiment after having her. She'd overheard her mother once discussing her post-natal depression with a friend, telling how *she, Dory*, had been a colicky baby, grizzling her way through her first three years of life, and how Vida had barely slept a wink. There was a family joke that they had once nicknamed her Grizzelda. She has a vague memory of her father coming home from work and tossing her high in the air. 'Now what's my Grizzelda been up to today?'

'That's fine,' soothes the doctor, as if being an only child is not her fault. 'And did you notice anything unusual about your mother's behaviour prior to the collapse?'

She doesn't want to think about the collapse. Yet it comes to her anyway, a vision of Vida crawling about the kitchen in some tatty old fur coat; the bones, the feathers, the weird animal noises that still freeze her blood.

Dory distracts herself by staring at the framed photograph on Dr. Saleem's desk, a slender woman in a blue hijab, with two beaming children. Next to a box of pink tissues stands a jug of blood-red dahlias. She shifts uneasily. This is not what she bargained for. Shouldn't *she* be the one asking the questions?

'I can't tell you much about her behaviour. I'm afraid I hadn't seen much of my mother before her illness. I run a business in London, and it's hard to get away.'

'Of course. But perhaps you spoke to her on the telephone? Did she mention any concerns, any worries, anything that might be bothering her?'

Did she? If so Dory hadn't noticed. 'Well, my mother is a writer. She's always lived in her own little world. When I last spoke to her, though, she did seem a bit vaguer than usual. She kept calling me Dorothy, which she's never done before. That was a bit, well... odd to say the least. I was worried about her being there alone. I tried to discuss her selling the house, moving closer to London.'

'I see.' He bends to his notes. 'But she didn't like the idea?'

'No.' She feels that twinge of resentment again. If only Vida had behaved like any normal person and lived among civilization, instead of hiding away like a damned hermit, this might never have happened. Possibly she'd go mad herself if she was left alone in that place too long. She might begin to hear things that weren't there. *See* things. She suppresses a shiver.

'She did have an estate agent to give a valuation on the house, but she's always loved the country...' She tails off, hoping she doesn't sound pushy, mercenary.

'So, do you think your mother felt pressured about moving?' It's hardly an accusation. Dr. Saleem's voice is so soothing it's almost soporific. But when those brown eyes graze hers she wants to cry.

'No. I don't think so. Not at all. I mean *I* didn't pressure her.'

He tries a different tack. 'And your mother lived alone for how long, would you say?'

'Not that long. My father left just over a year ago.'

He remains silent, waiting for her to elaborate.

'He's living in France now, with his... girlfriend.' She almost chokes over the word.

'I see. And how did your mother take this, when it first happened? Was she depressed? Did she confide her feelings to you?'

'No. I didn't even know about it until months later. To be honest, we don't confide in each other much. I don't think she was exactly crushed if that's what you're suggesting. She was too wrapped up in her work. I mean, I think it was amicable and everything. They didn't fight. They were still in contact with each other.'

'But your father hasn't come to visit.'

'No. We've talked of course. I've kept him informed. He's concerned. But he and... Millie, well, they're running a smallholding apparently and Millie's pregnant, so he can't leave right now.'

Recalling that first call to her father she flushes with anger. It wouldn't have hurt him to fly over, at least offer some support, but there he was going on about bloody goats and chickens, and how Millie was suffering terribly from morning sickness, which was frankly way too much information. They'd had a few harsh words. It was too bad of him to leave her in the front line like this.

She looks directly at Dr. Saleem; 'He made it quite clear he can't come back.' Let him put *that* in the notes. Why should *she* take all the flack? Why not let the finger of blame be pointed at her father?

The pen skims over the page: more writing, surely, than the bald facts she's delivered demand? Is he describing her, she wonders, as she sits tugging her skirt over her knees: her attitude, her body language? She hates being scrutinized, even by those gently probing eyes.

'And is there a history of mental illness in your family?'

'No. Nothing like that. At least, not as far as I know.' It's a terrible thought. Supposing this kind of thing is genetic? Supposing Vida has passed on some defective gene to her, a time bomb waiting for her to hit the menopause and reduce her to a zombie?

'I don't know much about my grandparents. My maternal grandmother died not long after I was born. Sorry I can't tell you any more.'

That's fine, he says; perhaps if she does recall anything of relevance later she can let them know.

'Yes, yes, I will, of course. Dr. Saleem, what are you going to do for my mother? Are you planning to keep her sedated?'

He tells her they are keeping her on Benzodiazepines for the time being until they can assess her state a little more.

'There are the anti-psychotic drugs of course, but they can have an adverse affect; we use them as a last resort. Some patients do respond well to Electric Convulsive Therapy, but that's not something we use lightly, you understand.'

She nods. The ECT sounds barbaric, like something out of a medieval torture chamber. No, she doesn't want Vida subjected to that whatever happens. Dr. Saleem is rising from his chair. She wants to ask, '*How long? Please tell me how long?*' But the meeting is over.

❧ ❧ ❧

'How is poor Vida?' Rhiannon is sitting at the kitchen table when she gets back.

'She's... oh, you're not leaving *today*, are you?' Dory stops short, observing the bags gathered at Rhiannon's feet. The red poncho-style coat hangs ready over the back of the chair. Part of her is relieved. Having to make chitchat to Vida's devoted fan would have been hard to stomach for very much longer. It's just the thought of being alone here that gives her a jolt suddenly. She loosens the top button of her coat but doesn't take it off. After the warmth and lights of the hospital the Gingerbread House seems dingier than ever.

Rhiannon pushes the hair from her face, frowning. 'Sorry I have to run out on you like this. I heard from my neighbour. It's Caliban. He's refusing to eat.'

Caliban? Oh yes, the cat. God, how she wishes that was her only problem.

'He's eighteen,' Rhiannon chunters on in a funereal voice, 'a good age for a cat, but if he should go... well, I want to be with him.'

'Of course.'

'I'm just waiting for the Hill-Hopper. There's one in ten minutes. If you hadn't come back I would have waited for the next one at three o'clock, although it'll be dark by then.'

Dory moves to the stove. The warmth from the hotplate lids seeps up through her palms. Without Rhiannon here, she realizes, it will be her job to keep the wretched thing stoked up. She fills her in briefly about the Post Traumatic Stress.

'Dr. Saleem asked me if I could think of something that might have triggered it. Seems like a stupid question. I mean it must have been my dad. When your husband goes off with a woman half your age, well, it's enough to send anyone over the edge. Unless you know of…?'

Rhiannon rummages in a bag for something. Maybe, she says, as she hunts deep in its musty interior, she should tell him about the way the publishers treated her mother. She starts on about Vida's agent, Fee Moody.

'I was in the study when Vida took a call from her one day. Whatever that woman said it wounded her deeply. It took a while for me to get her back on track after that.'

'Oh.' Dory sighs. Not the tragic career stuff again.

'You'll be all right on your own?' Rhiannon peers at her. 'I've left my address and phone number on the kitchen table in case you need it.'

Dory assures her she'll be fine. She manages a few words of thanks for taking care of things. Yet it's strange how abandoned she feels when the Hopper bus driver hoots outside. The thought of being left here alone, in sole charge of Vida's affairs, triggers an uncharacteristic neediness. She resists an impulse to tug on this woman's skirts like a child dumped at the school gates and plead with her to stay.

❧ ❧ ❧

Later on, however, when she goes upstairs to shift her things into the bigger guest bedroom, she discovers a canvas hold-all stuffed full of belongings, and a turquoise kimono spread across the bed. The musky scent is nauseating: some cloying hippy-ish mixture of sick cat and patchouli. She wrinkles her nose. So her mother's friend intends to return? Odd that she hasn't mentioned this. When though? And for how long? She doesn't know whether to be reassured or irritated as she sits on the edge of the bed, feeling the give of the soft mattress beneath her weight, and comparing it to that hard single bed she's tossed and turned on all that night. Better to stay in the single room though. She can't be bothered changing sheets. And anyway, if she can just focus on getting this house ready to sell, she might not need to stay for too long.

※ ※ ※

The next couple of days pass in a blur of hospital visits, and aborted attempts at work. Work is proving trickier than she imagined. The sound of the rain, drumming on the galvanized roof of the lean-to as she hunches over her laptop, is like Chinese torture. The rain out here is different to London rain, she thinks. It batters the windows, pooling in through cracks in the frames; it turns potholes in the drive into minor lakes in minutes. Once it starts, it never stops, and now, wouldn't you know it, the connection is down again.

Dory bites into the Maple and Pecan Danish fresh from its paper bag; she brushes pastry crumbs from the folds of her pashmina. The Cornish Tin-Worker's Cottage flickers from the screen, leaving a vague impression of a velour suite and surfeit of horse-brasses. Would her clients see past the decor? Possibly if the grounds are generous enough, but how can she tell?

She lights up a cigarette and gazes through the kitchen window at the blurring afternoon.

In theory she should be able to run her business anywhere in the civilized world, emailing clients, researching locations, trawling through estate agents' websites; this is mostly what she does in the office anyway. Or she *could* if the broadband wasn't running at zero speed. So far this morning, she's had to abort around six emails, and the few tweets she managed to spit out were moronic even by Twitter standards. No wonder she's losing followers.

She grabs her smart-phone and drops it again. What's the point? She can't get a signal anywhere in the house, not even hanging out of the upstairs bedroom window. The landline is also hopeless. Every time it rains, the line hisses and whistles like the soundtrack to an exorcism movie.

She casts an eye over the debris scattered around her. The big adventure this morning was driving to Cregaron to pick up paint charts and agents' details.

'The market's a bit sticky at the moment.' The agent had a red bobbly Adam's apple, and a vicarish look. 'I'd be happy to come and give you a valuation of course.'

She told him thanks, she'd let him know. She's not a fool. She's not going to get a valuation until the place has had a complete makeover.

That tap dripping is driving her nuts. She gets up and wrenches it so hard her wrist hurts. At the same time she notices the greenish mould furring the cracks between the tiles. Reaching for her pad, she scribbles: *Washers, Re-tiling kitchen*. In the sitting room, she ponders the quarry tiles, the bits not covered by Vida's colourful assortment of rugs. They are glazed with a chalky deposit that rubs off on her fingers. Is that damp? Oh dear God, no damp course either. That's more expense.

This is the only way she can deal with this situation, viewing the property with an objective eye. Pretending this is work. Okay, she could just lock up this place, and let Vida's papers gather dust in the study. But soon Vida will need long-term nursing care. Who is going to pay for it?

She listens. Outside something is banging with monotonous regularity: a door perhaps, or the roof of one of those sinister outbuildings which Vida should have converted or knocked down years ago, leaning constructions of galvanized metal and asbestos and rotting wood. The kind of place you expect to find someone hanging from the end of a rope in. She hardly dares peer in them for fear of rats. Rats are one of the few things that scare her.

She turns on Radio 4. It's Woman's Hour, and Jenni Murray is discussing how to recognize the onset of Alzheimers with an expert. She switches it off and tries the office again. Predictably enough the display flashes: *Service Unavailable*.

Right, there's nothing for it but to go outside, climb a hill if necessary; there must be somewhere in this techno-forsaken dump that she can get a signal. If she waits for the rain to stop, it'll be dark. She pulls on her coat and stabs her feet into a pair of floral Hunters.

✤ ✤ ✤

Outside, is well… *outside*. But so much more outside than she feels in London streets. A lane leading nowhere. Fields. Sheep. Hills patched with dead bracken and gorse, vanishing into the mist.

Try again. *Service Unavailable*. She crosses the lane, pushes at a gate that won't budge, and breaks a fingernail trying to wrench back the bolt. What is the bloody point of a gate that won't open? Cursing the farmer who put it there in the first place she stumps a foot on the third bar and hoists her legs over into the squelch of mud below. This is the first time the Hunters have seen real mud and they don't look too happy about it. Halfway up the hill on a sheep path that snakes beneath twisted hawthorns, the service becomes mysteriously available, and she gets through to Harvey.

Her heart lifts at the sound of a human voice. 'Sorry, Harve, you won't believe where I've had to climb to make this call. I'll keep it brief because it's pissing down and this raincoat is not exactly doing its job. I hope you're coping without me?'

'Darling, I am working my butt off to keep the punters happy. I told you not to worry, didn't I? I am looking after the clients like a mother.'

'I thought you were off to Devon this week with our empty-nesters?'

'I was. The empty-nesters are having a little re-think. Don't want to be too far from their grown-up chicks, bless them.'

This doesn't sound good. Can she really trust Harvey to handle things, or should she dash back to London for a few days?

'Harvey, you have to persuade them the bloody chicks don't need them any more. They should move to Devon, and pig out on clotted cream and scones and enjoy themselves before they snuff it. We'd lined up at least five viewings for them.'

'Yes, well two of those viewings have been taken off the market. It's a bit sticky down there appar-ently. In fact it's sticky all over.' Harvey emphasizes the "sticky" with relish.

'Oh please, sticky is a word I so don't want to hear.'

'And what objections do you have to the word "sticky". sweetie?'

'Sticky is not a long way from stuck, and I can't afford to get stuck with *this* bloody house, that's my objection.'

'Poor you!' Harvey sympathizes. 'Still, it must have its compensations down there. What about those Welsh Male Voice Choirs?'

'What about them? There is no welcome in the hillsides, if that's what you're thinking. Listen, Harvey, can you put Lucy on for a moment?' Lucy is their dreamy-faced assistant who comes in to water plants and make tea one day a week. 'I was wondering if you might spare her for a few days; she could help out with the painting.'

'No can do, sweetie. She's just taken maternity leave.'

'But maternity leave... I didn't know she was pregnant.'

'She kept it well hidden. Anyway, much as I'd love to shoot the breeze...'

'Okay, but look, if you come across any clients looking for a Writer's Retreat, you know romantic sorts, whatever, keep them in line for...' She is cut short by the sound of phones ringing in the background, and Harvey's breathless goodbyes.

Struggling back down the hill, she envies Harvey the buzz, the sweet talk, the hard sell, the last-minute deals that make your palms sweat and your heart pound, and probably cut whole years off your life. This is why she has to get out of here. She has to find a builder to give her an estimate. Like, yesterday.

⚜ ⚜ ⚜

At least the landline behaves itself when she gets back to the house. In the encroaching gloom of the afternoon, Dory lights lamps, switches on extra heaters, then settles herself on the lumpy Chesterfield with the Yellow Pages.

Builders... builders... none of them seem to be particularly local. Most are the other side of Ludlow, and anyway, all she gets are their answer phones. In one case, a suspicious wife treats her as if she's a rival, not a potential customer. A surly chap with bad mobile reception, who sounds as if he's lying scrunched up beneath somebody's bath, says he has a big job on and won't be free until spring. What's the matter with builders around here? Don't they want the work? Determined, Dory leaves messages on answer phones around the county.

'This is Dory Tremayne speaking. That's T-r-e-m-a-y-n-e, *Tremayne*. I need an estimate for some restoration work on an old cottage. The job is urgent. I really need someone immediately.'

You have to be assertive with workmen, she's found in the past; it's the only way.

❖   ❖   ❖

The afternoon passes in this way: slowly, but it passes. At four o'clock she draws the toile de joy on the dusk. There are no wintry sunsets here, just a thickening of mist as it swallows up the remains of the day. Rooks cluster like black rags in the umbrella pines at the boundary. The earth makes sucking noises like a sponge.

At six, she can bear it no longer. Broadband kicks in and she checks her emails. There are three. One from Harvey tells her the empty nesters have dropped out altogether. The second tells her how to maintain an erection. The third is an auto-reply from Pansy, a designer acquaintance she was hoping to invite down, saying she's in Tuscany until the end of January but will get back on her return.

Nothing. Today she has achieved nothing, except to find out that the market is "sticky".

The prospect of another useless evening drives her across the hall to what is essentially a dining room, which Vida used as her study. What's to lose? She might as well make a start here while she's waiting for the builders to get back to her. There will be papers, books to sort out. It's no use getting sentimental about it when Vida is lying flat on her back staring up at the hospital ceiling.

Pushing open the door she feels a slight resistance. So slight you'd hardly notice. Except that she *has* noticed. Her breath catches in her throat. What is this? Stiff hinges probably, yes, she makes a mental note adding this to her Repair List. However, as she stands there in what Dad used to jokingly call "The Nerve Centre", the resistance is still there. It has a fluidity about it, like the pressure of water in a stopped sink as if the room itself doesn't want her in there. Or Vida doesn't. She takes in the room, the oak veneered dining table upon which no one has ever dined, and where Vida's computer squats alongside her beloved typewriter. The damson-painted walls are hung with portraits, not of ancestors or even distant relations but odd pictures Vida used to pick up in junk shops, saying they gave her inspiration for characters. In pride of place above the black-leaded Victorian fireplace hangs an enlarged print of the cover for *The Gingerbread House,* a faux naïve collage design of a cottage with a fox leaving a trail of prints in the foreground. Everyone raved over that cover. Personally Dory thought it looked more like a kid's novel, but what did she know?

The sight of Vida's empty chair gives her a jolt. She almost expects it to swivel round to face her. It's as if her mother is there, looking at her over the top of her reading glasses. 'Oh darling, it's you. You're home early.'

The bright smile of welcome never fooled her.

'Mummy, can I make a story, Mummy?' She strokes the keyboard of Vida's desktop. She used not to be so gentle. She remembers her pudgy fingers battering on the old typewriter keys, wanting to break something, wanting to break the made-up people. They'd bought her a little typewriter of her own with different colour print ribbons and sheathes of bright paper. But she didn't want her own typewriter. It was Vida's she wanted. Bang, bang, crashing the keys, as if she would make holes in the paper, until she was dragged off, Vida's hand gripping her arm, 'Why are you such a horrid little girl?'

Vida looked genuinely perplexed as she said this, as if she could hardly believe she'd given birth to Dory. The memory of her mother's face, the look of sorrow in her eyes, pierces her suddenly as if it were yesterday.

She sinks into the chair. She's remembering that nursery rhyme Vida used to read aloud from *Lavender's Blue. There was a little girl who had a little curl, right in the middle of her forehead. When she was good, she was very very good, but when she was bad, she was **horrid.***

How they used to chorus that last word together almost as if in triumph. She can hear herself saying, 'But I haven't got a curl in my forehead, have I, Mummy?' And Vida assuring her no, no sign of a curl, smoothing her fine fair hair straight beneath her palm. The remembrance of her mother's hand on her head now, the reassuring weight of it, is almost like a blessing.

Now, taking in the heaps of papers, the drawers buckled with old manuscripts, the shelves of books, she thinks that maybe after all she can leave this job for another day. Creeping out, she closes the door so quietly you'd hardly notice, just as Vida would have wished. Outside she pauses. There's a sense of something shifting, sighing as if with relief at her departure, just as Vida might have done years ago. Or perhaps she just imagined it, the swift resumption of tapping the moment her back was turned. Supposing she were to hear it now, the tap of the keyboard echoing from behind the door, following her down the hall, tap... tap... tap... what would she do? But that's stupid; she shakes herself. Even if she believed in ghosts, which she doesn't, it's not as if Vida is dead. How can a house possibly be haunted by someone who is still alive?

Vida's Diary

15th September

I am summoned to London. Kate, my old editor at Nelson and Hargrave, wants to take me to lunch. At first I think it's some mistake, but here is Kate gushing breathily at me: *how am I?* It's been an age! And we really must do lunch and discuss my next book, throw some ideas around. She speaks as if the gap of five years is nothing, as if not "doing lunch" or communicating in any way has been merely a matter of finding a space in the diary.

'Would it be an awful bore for you to come down to London?' Kate names a date towards the end of the month. 'I understand it's quite a trek from your neck of the woods.'

'No… no…' I have to clear my throat, adopt a steadier tone. 'No, actually that will fit in very well, as I have one or two other engagements in town that week.'

Engagements! When I've put down the phone, I marvel at my cool. Then I panic. What on earth am I going to wear?

16th September

Thinking about the trip to London last night, and where would I stay? Then I thought of Dory. I've never even visited the new flat. It's one of those converted warehouse apartments overlooking the docks.

'You must come once I'm straight.' Dory said this a couple of times after informing me of the new address. That was over a year ago, and since then Dan has moved in.

I ring, heart in my throat as if I'm calling a lover.

'Oh, hallo.' Cold, her voice is so cold. I might be anyone, a cold caller trying to sell her a Stannah Stairlift.

'How are you? Are you well? How's the flat?' I twitter like a demented sparrow.

'It's fine....' There's a pause. 'Actually, Mum, you've caught me at an awkward time. There's a crowd of us here, and we're just about to go to a gallery opening.'

'Oh. That sounds fun. I won't keep you'. I can hear voices in the background, the roar of male laughter. I tell her about my trip to town: perhaps I could come over, or we could go shopping – or maybe just a coffee if she's busy?

'I'm in Amsterdam that week, sorry.' She sounds surprised, hesitant. Then, grudgingly, 'Perhaps your editor could make it the week before?'

I say this might be difficult, editors being busy people. There is a sharp intake of breath at the other end:

'Well, look, if your editor can reschedule or something, let me know. But give me plenty of warning, because to be honest, I'm really up against it right now...'

Crying before bedtime is never a good idea. It makes breathing through one's nose impossible. As I lie in bed snuffling into a tissue, I tell myself I should be pleased that my daughter has a lively social life, a boyfriend, a crowd of friends to go about with. But I can't help feeling excluded. It would be so lovely to meet at least *some* of them, to have Dory introduce me… 'This is my mum, Mum, this is…' like other people do. Like any normal mother and her grown-up daughter. Then I think of those sleepovers and pizza parties which I valiantly tried to curtail when Dory was young and I was working years ago. It's my fault; yes, I can see it's my fault. Dory hasn't forgotten my failings as a mother. This is payback time.

I fall asleep eventually with my mouth open, an invitation to one of the seven spiders you are statistically likely to swallow in a year. When I wake up, my eyes are burning slits. Thank God there's no one to see me.

17th September

Today I get up and my bones click like castanets. A mad wind is hurling hailstones against the windows. It feels like the whole world is coming apart; nothing fits properly, things rot and warp and rattle, as if they are holding on by a thread, a whisker. Like me. Everything feels so *precarious*.

Living out here, I've let myself go. My mother used to use that phrase about certain women she knew, *'She's let herself go'*, in an ominous undertone. She believed in corsets, in armoured bras and stiff upper lips (whisker-free). One drop in standards

and everything would come spilling out... whoosh...
exposed, sliding downhill to the grave.

Like me, belly slack in tracksuit bottoms, my
breasts that no one has touched in an age flopping beneath a sloppy sweater. There's a hole in my
tights, and my big toe jabs through as I slip my feet
into trainers. I peer in the mirror. The contours of
my face are blurred, indistinct from last night's sobbing. My hair is lank. I've done nothing, but I feel so
tired I could sleep for a year.

I face myself, frankly.

'Look at you, Vida,' I snap, 'how can you go to
London in this state? You're not fit to be seen.'

Maybe I'll cancel. At least down here I can be
mad as I like, wear crochet hats, take in stray cats,
eat out of tins, and grow my dust-dry hair to my waist
if I want to.

18th September

Reading yesterday's entry makes me cringe. What
maudlin, self-pitying drivel! It occurs to me over my
morning porridge that I should at least let my agent
Fee Moody know about this latest development. I
dread talking to her, but it's only right to keep her
informed. I take a deep breath, and call her office.

'Vida? Vida who...?' There is that barky voice I
remember from years ago. If anything it's become
even barkier, whether from smoking too much, or
sheer pressure of work I have no idea. My heart thuds
in an agony of embarrassment as I'm asked to repeat

my name. I've already announced my name three times, once to the receptionist, then to an assistant and finally a sub-agent before getting through to the great lady herself.

'Oh, Vida Tremayne…' I can tell she's struggling to remember who on earth I am, even as she speaks. 'How can I help you? I don't want to rush you, but actually I'm just off to a meeting and…'

When I tell her about the lunch she seems in less of a hurry. The voice softens a fraction. 'And do you have any idea what they want to talk to you about?'

'None at all, I'm afraid.'

'Ah. Well. *Interesting.* Well, do go along to the meeting and let me know how it goes, will you? I would come with you, but I'm in New York next week with Jakob Yang; he's up for the Pulitzer. Have you read *Wilderness?* Wonderful book. Charming man, thoroughly well deserved…'

After a few more words about the amazing Yang, whom I've never heard of, she says goodbye and thanks for letting her know, and is gone before I've even put down the receiver.

I'm not going to let this crush me. I refuse to allow it. Outside the wind has dropped, and all is calm. I lift my face to the sun, and march down the track, fringed with withered couch grass and cow parsley to the postbox. Nothing but junk as usual. Oh, and another letter from *her,* Rhiannon Townsend. I weigh it in my hand, feeling its ominous fatness. In her recent letters she has moved on from *The Gingerbread House* and read every one of my books. She endows them with a significance they hardly deserve. She asks me what I am working on, and then in the same breath begs me not to tell, saying the process is a mystery and must remain so or lose its power. I have my tea on the back terrace in the autumn sunshine, and tear open my letter.

Dear Vida,

In your last letter, you mentioned that you are going to London to meet with your editors and will do the trip in a day. I can well understand your dislike of hotels. A hotel room is a reservoir of stale energy; all those one-night stands, the sad affairs, the stressed-out homesick business-men. Believe me that stuff worms its way right into the fibres of a room and can make a person seriously sick.

I have an idea. Why don't you stay over with me? My housemate will be away that week, and the tube station is just around the corner.

She continues as if I've already agreed to the plan, asking if I have any special dietary requirements. She used to be a vegan, apparently, but switched to vegetarian because of zinc deficiency. I shall write back and thank her, of course, but will make up some excuse. It's kind of her, but I don't want to feel obliged. Not to a fan anyway. Yet it seems extraordinary that I have a devoted fan after such a long silence. My heart, trampled only a moment ago by Fee Moody's indifference, stirs back into life. Just knowing that someone out there cares fortifies me for next week's trip.

Tuesday 21st September

I write this in my hotel room, after coming back from the lunch. It seems strange to be writing at a different desk, one of those beech veneer jobs, with computer connection, and a room service menu with lurid photographs of the Full English. The hotel's all right, modestly priced, bed a bit hard, situated near Paddington Station, one of those wide streets of grubby Georgian terraces.

I can't help thinking though of what Rhiannon Townsend said in her letter about stale energies. I never noticed before, but now as I sit facing Regency-striped curtains so bulky they entirely muffle the buzz of traffic, I can feel it: something sad like slept-in sheets. The air, over-heated, conditioned, filtered and regulated, has a fuzziness to it that gives me quite a headache.

So, the lunch. I found the restaurant all right, a dark little place in Bloomsbury near the British Museum. The three Kates were there. Not just my editor Kate, but two new Kates from Sales and Publicity. All three are butter-fleshed blondes with a polleny bloom and I felt old enough to be their grandmother, smoothing the linen skirt bought hastily in Cregaron over my hips as I sat down. I had to give up squinting over the menu and put my reading glasses on. Finally I settled for some kind of salad, with sun-dried tomatoes and feta cheese.

I couldn't help thinking of that other lunch when *The Gingerbread House* won the prize: the prospect of a tour of the States and TV appearances, neither of which materialized. And Jonathan skulking around the corner in Starbucks, the froth cooling on his cappuccino, wanting to know why on earth a mere lunch should take so long?

Then the critics, slamming the sequel. '*A whiff of old lace and mothballs*', sniped one male reviewer, and '*Vida Tremayne has turned out one from her bottom drawer*', said another. There was no more champagne after that.

This time we had white wine, and the Kates put forward their plan. *The Gingerbread House* was still, as they put it, "holding up", which was fantastic after so many years. They had noticed a sinister undercurrent in the book that might be taken a step or two further.

'Don't get me wrong,' Kate from Editorial soothed, 'TGH was fabulous, just a little bit too subtle, maybe, for most people.'

Kate from Sales came straight to the point. 'We were thinking "horror" actually, Vida.'

'Horror?'

I must have looked fairly horrified as I said this, but it was something of a shock. Kate from Publicity blotted scarlet lips on a napkin. 'And sex, the horrific kind mostly. People love to be scared... excuse me... out of their pants. And Vida, we think you could do it.'

It seems Marshall and Nelson's best-selling horror diva, Ella de Vile, she of the crow-black pageboy and Cleopatra eyes, has laid down her pen and become a born-again Christian.

Kate from Sales sighed. 'It's all rather a blow to her millions of fans, as you can imagine. They feel they've been abandoned, let down.'

Kate from Publicity who looked hardly old enough to have left school chipped in. 'It's bad enough when your favourite author dies, isn't it. You feel kind of bereft for a while. But fans understand death. I mean they accept the situation.'

'Oh... yes, I suppose so.' They could hardly do otherwise. I was lost for words, trying to imagine what it must be like having millions of fans. My mind drifted to Rhiannon Townsend and her oddly morale-boosting letters. Ms de Vile presumably received such letters by the sackload.

'Have you read any of Ella's work, Vida?' Editor Kate was casually topping up my glass.

'No.' I paused to take a sip. 'I can't say I have.'

There was a silence. I could feel a kind of bristling around the table as the three Kates focused intently upon me.

'Oh you must try her. I know horror isn't for everyone, but Ella wrote for the upper end of the market. She's good. Or rather she *was* good.'

Kate from Publicity added with a giggle, 'As long as you don't read them when you're alone. They're *so...oo* scary. Her last one kept me up all night; I had to keep the lights on, because my boyfriend was away...'

I was just smiling at the self-assurance of youth, the certainty of always having company, when Editor Kate moved in for the kill. She gazed at me, her blue eyes frank. 'Vida, we think you could be *her*. We think you could be the next Ella de Vile.'

It took a while for this to sink in. What a fool I'd been to imagine they wanted another *Gingerbread House*, that they wanted another Vida Tremayne! So this was what I was here for, to fill a de Vile shaped hole, pick up all those cast-off fans like so many stitches on a knitting needle and keep the tills rattling.

Editor Kate was holding up her hand. 'Now we don't expect you to make a decision right away, Vida. You'll need to think about it, of course. We've brought one of her books for you to look at, just to give you an idea.'

'I have it right here, in fact.' Publicity Kate dived into her satchel bag and slid the book across the table to land beside my plate. 'It's her last one actually, quite a page-turner.'

'Fab reviews,' echoed Sales Kate.

I gazed at the cover in something of a daze, my vision blurring momentarily as if in sympathy with my emotions. I had an impression of black, gold and crimson; red lips, gold mask, and the name de Vile in gold lettering almost dwarfing the title: *The Curdling*. Superimposed upon this was the cover of *The Gingerbread House*, swimming unbidden into focus. For once I'd felt the artist had actually read my book, had done it justice. I'd loved it at first sight: the house with the crazy-paved path crouched behind spidery Monet-like branches, the fox trailing paw prints in the bottom right-hand corner. It was at once innocent and sinister, with its childlike collage effect. The colours were smoky, autumnal, enticing. I blinked back what felt ridiculously like a tear, and at once the red, gold and black of *The Curdling* blazed back into focus.

'Well,' I struggled to keep the dismay out of my voice, 'if you think I can do it...'

All three chorused at once. 'Of course you can do it, we know you can! We have faith in you, Vida.'

All through the next two courses they talked of their scheme. It would be such a hoot. I could stretch my imagination to the limit. Best to avoid vampires though, tittered Publicity Kate; they had rather been "done to death" just lately. In retrospect I'm not sure how I got through the fish course, and even the tiramisu seemed to stick in my throat. Yet, by the ecstatic expressions on the Kates' faces, all had been decided. I had agreed to their plan. Result.

As I got up to leave, Editor Kate bestowed a kiss on either cheek, gave me a long hard look and said, 'It would mean re-branding, of course. New cover design. A new *you* really, Vida.'

So now here I am, gazing at myself in the hotel mirror. I can't do it. I can't do what they ask, be someone I'm not. I would like to go home now, catch the next train back to oblivion. But I've arranged to meet this Rhiannon woman at the British Museum for coffee tomorrow and I can't let her down.

Thursday 23rd September

Back home. Or is it? Home is where someone waits for you with the kettle on, eager to hear your news. How did it go? What did they say? I miss that. In the old days Jonathan would have loved hearing about the Kates, and their new vision for my career. Would I have told him about my fan though? I doubt it. He was suspicious of fans, concerned that they might become potential stalkers, I think. Wanting to protect me. No, I probably would have kept quiet about Rhiannon Townsend.

When I opened the door this afternoon, the house smelled as if it had been shut up for months. Then I lit the stove and there was a rush of soot in the chimney and a smell of cinders. It took me hours to warm the place up and now it's already nine p.m. Too tired to finish this now... will pick up tomorrow....

Friday 24th September

After my lunch with the Kates, I was in no mood to talk to anyone about books, certainly not *my* books. But there it was. Arrangements made. It would have been churlish to let down my only fan.

I had trouble locating the café and ended up racing blindly through Ancient Greece like some philistine Time Tourist. The Cyclades, the Parthenon, the Acropolis were all a blur, until crossing into Assyria I found the sign – **Gallery Refreshments.**

Climbing the stairs, I made a promise to myself: if she turned out to be a mad-looking woman with a tie-dye turban, I would pass on by. Then I leant against the swing doors and there she was, sitting at a table to my right. I knew it was her. *The Gingerbread House* was the clue, held high enough to almost obscure her face. As though sensing me watching, she lowered the book, and stood up to greet me. No tie-dye, no turban, but a tumble of brown hair and a rust-coloured vintage-style dress, worn over those ubiquitous black leggings that girls all seem to wear these days. Except that she's not a girl, of course. Closer to, I guessed her to be in her late thirties, with a wide jaw and amber-flecked eyes. Attractive despite her complexion, which I couldn't help noticing. It had the faintly pitted look of weatherworn terracotta, as if from old acne scars.

I held out my hand. 'Sorry I'm late. You must be Rhiannon.'

'Vida. It's very good to meet you.' She didn't smile, but her eyes fastened on mine as if she'd been waiting not just a few minutes, but her entire life. Her hand, small and dry in mine, seemed reluctant to let go. She dropped it at last and went off to the counter to get us both drinks. While her back was turned I glanced at my book lying next to the sugar bowl, and couldn't believe it had anything to do with me.

'I hope you haven't been waiting long,' I said as she returned with coffee.

She hadn't noticed the time apparently, being utterly absorbed by my book.

'Oh? But I thought you'd already read it.'

'I've read it twice. This is the third reading.' She stroked the cover as she spoke, her short silver-ringed fingers caressing it with what I could only describe as reverence. It might have been a sacred text. Apparently it was Rudolf Steiner's belief that you should read a book seven times to fully absorb the finer levels of meaning.

'I believe that to be true. Every time I read your novel I find something new in it, something that I hadn't noticed before.'

I didn't question the Steiner reference. It seemed to me though that his incomprehensible metaphysical works have little to do with fiction. The book certainly looked well-thumbed: the covers flared at the corners, the spine bulged, yellow post-it notes fluttered from the pages like prayer flags. As she continued to sing its praises, I hardly knew where to look. All I could think about was the previous day with the Kates, the black and gold paperback nestling in my bag like an impostor. My fan might be ridiculing me the way I felt right now.

'I'm so glad you're enjoying it.'

She met this platitude with a look almost of agony. 'It's not about enjoyment though. I mean this seriously, every word. This book means so much, I can't tell you.'

'Really? Well, everyone gets something different from it, I expect.'

She spread her fingers across the cover almost protectively. An earthy practical hand, it looked to me, despite the battery of silver rings and the fingernails painted the colour of ripe damsons. It looked like the kind of hand that would turn a good pot, or nurture the seedlings of rare plants to maturity.

She attempted to explain. 'It's like the book is speaking to me directly, on an unconscious level. Books do speak, don't they? The ones with integrity do. They make a connection with their readers. That's the measure of the true artist.'

I shifted uncomfortably in my seat. 'Didn't you say you're a counsellor?' I was determined to deflect back the spotlight. 'That must be so rewarding, helping people that is, doing something useful.'

'It's a kind of counselling, yes. Not in the way most people understand.' From her dismissive tone, clearly her work was off topic. She paused, shifting her chair aside slightly as a woman struggling with one of those enormous twin pushchairs squeezed past.

'But let's talk about *you*.' She was resolved, tapping the book cover with those damson nails. 'I can't believe I'm finally sitting opposite the author of *The Gingerbread House*. I'll have to pinch myself. I want to know all about you.'

I noticed the man at the next table was giving her a covert glance as she talked. He caught my eye and looked guiltily back at his museum map. Clearly she was attractive to men. I wondered if she had a lover.

'I'm afraid I will disappoint you.' I emptied the paper tube of Demerara sugar into my cup and gave it a good stir. 'Authors are actually quite boring people. We live vicariously, if we live at all.'

'I hear what you're saying. Absolutely. It's the *inner* life that matters.' She was pressing her middle finger to that spot between the eyes, which Hindus mark with a red dot. 'It's all in here, in the locked room where ordinary mortals are afraid to enter. The artist goes into the locked room, she roots around in the forbidden boxes, the shadowy corners, she excavates her own unconscious.'

A gaggle of Japanese schoolgirls tripped past us, and we both had to shuffle our chairs aside.

This was all getting a bit heavy. I gave a short self-deprecating laugh. 'But sometimes there is nothing in the locked room when you look there.' My tone was light enough, but at once I saw from her expression that I'd said too much.

Her face clouded. 'How did your lunch go with the publishers? You don't mind me asking? I'm just so interested in your work.'

Should an author discuss publishers with a fan? Something told me not.

'It was fine, thank you.'

'I hope they realize how lucky they are to have you. You must be one of their brightest stars.'

Stars? I didn't know whether to laugh or cry at this.

'What have I said? Are you all right?'

'Yes. We just discussed some ideas, that's all.'

'Ideas for your next book?' Clasping her hands beneath her chin she begged me to let her in on the secret. 'That's if you don't mind. I'm dying to know what it's all about.'

'It's not about anything.' Then, fatally, I added, 'they want me to try a new genre actually. Horror. Have you heard of Ella de Vile? Yes, of course you have. Well, like her.'

She shrank back into her chair as if from a blow. 'They can't be serious.'

According to her, Ella and I are not in the same league, should not be mentioned in the same breath. My publishers must be total fools.

'I mean, where are they coming from?' she despaired.

I tried to explain a little about the industry, how moving to a new genre might not be so bad, and how writers shouldn't be precious about their work.

'But that's exactly what your work is. *Precious.*' She seized upon the word with such ferocity I drew back a little from the table. 'Every single word is precious. You are an artist, Vida. A true artist bleeds, she offers up her life, gives up flesh and bones and blood for others to feed upon.'

'Well, I'm not sure…'.

'Tell me you're not going to agree to their plan?'

I managed a faint smile. Flattering though this was to my ego, I wasn't going to sit here all day defending my publishers' motives. I'd said far too much already.

I glanced at my watch; 'It's good of you to take such an interest in my work, but you know, I should make a move. I've got to pick up my bags at the hotel before I catch my train, and I'd rather get out of town well before the rush hour.'

Dismay registered briefly on her face. 'You're not rushing off so soon? I was hoping we might spend the rest of the day together. There's a fabulous exhibition in the Egyptian galleries at the moment.'

When I assured her I couldn't stay another minute, she thrust her copy of *The Gingerbread House* at me. 'Please. Before you go.'

'Oh yes, glad to.' I could sign the book for her at least. I whisked out my pen and wrote, my hands trembling slightly:

To Rhiannon with very best wishes, Vida Tremayne

The pages were slightly wrinkled, almost every margin marked with an asterix, endless notes and underlinings.

'Thank you so so much.' Greedily she read my inscription. I could see she was disappointed by the formality and felt suddenly mean. Perhaps I should have been generous and signed it "love".

The act of signing my prize-winning book with the wrinkled, scribbled-on margins depressed me. Didn't I owe this woman something? Couldn't I squeeze one more gem out of the locked room?

'Well, it's been very nice meeting you.' I pushed back my chair.

She stood so abruptly for a moment I thought she was coming with me. Then she extended her hand, and I could feel the cool chunkiness of her rings against my palm.

'Until the next time, Vida.' Her small lipstick-less mouth twitched briefly into something approximating a smile. 'This might sound wacky, but I believe we're destined to help each other, you and I. You will let me know if you need me?'

Again her eyes fastened on my face in that searching yet disconcerting way that I suppose must come with her profession. I must have nodded, murmured thank you, and reeled off a few more platitudes as I made my escape. Now I'm back home, I think about her parting words...

Need her? I can't think why I would need her, yet I confess I'm touched by her warmth and concern. I can't help thinking that here is someone who understands my work, who truly appreciates it. What more can any novelist ask of her fans?

30TH JANUARY
DORY

'Oh, you've had your hair done. It looks nice. Who did that for you?'

Actually Vida's new hairstyle looks terrible. It's some kind of institutional bob, an apology of a hairstyle for someone past caring about appearances. Better surely if they'd let her hair grow as mad as she is, wild and grey and down to her knees; at least that would be honest.

Dory feels sick. She should bend and kiss Vida. Any normal daughter would do as much. All she can manage is a forced compliment or two.

'Where did that blouse come from? I don't think it's one of yours, is it?'

Neither are the stretchy green leggings, or those awful slippers. Vida wasn't exactly a fashionista but she did have an eye for quality. Is it possible the staff snaffle up the good stuff when no one is looking and replace them with charity cast-offs? Dory looks suspiciously at the nurse pushing the drugs trolley. There is only this one nurse and a white-coated volunteer showing two dazed-looking women how to make collages from old Christmas cards. On the wall the cork message-board is covered with postcards and thank you notes from former patients.

To all in Beatrice Ward, thank you for looking after me so well.

At least this is proof of an outside world; of escape, of recovery.

She draws up a chair. Not too close.

'Sorry I haven't been to see you much this week. I've been so busy, with the house and...' She breaks off to cough, chest hurting from the half pack of cigarettes she was forced to smoke before driving here this morning.

'What are you reading then? Good book, is it?'

Vida's eyes lift briefly from the page, but Vida is not there behind them. Instantly, Dory has that vision of mother at her desk, lifting her glasses to peer at the child in her study.

'Who is it by, then? Oh watch out, it's slipping off your lap.'

Dory bends to retrieve it from the floor and replaces it carefully on her mother's knees.

'Oh, it's *your* book, it's *The Gingerbread House.*'

She winces at the false brightness of her voice, the voice she uses on her clients' children when they turn up at a viewing. She's had some real stinkers: kids who bounce around on other people's furniture, or set up such a whinge the parents blame it on the house. It's ludicrous how many screaming toddlers have been deal-breakers. But here she is thinking of work again, when she should be concentrating on her mother.

'I didn't recognize it without the cover.'

The book has been covered in a crimson velvety material. It's a neat job, as if done by loving hands, as if the book is treasured by someone. She wonders briefly where it has come from. Vida's own copies, the ones she keeps by her to give away to friends or local charities, are still on the study bookshelves. Perhaps one of the nurses is a fan, and brought it in to jog her memory?

'Would you like me to bring you some more books in?' she suggests. The bookshelves offer a dreary selection of romances, spines slumped against one another on the few shelves, like the patients themselves.

No answer. Vida stares intently at the contents page of her book as if it contains some vital piece of information.

'So, you've got everything you want?' Stupid question, but what else can she say?

'Oh dear, you've dropped it again.' Automatically she retrieves the book and replaces it on her mother's knees where it slides inexorably to the floor. When she sets it on the table Vida becomes agitated, patting her empty lap in dismay. This is a game that might go on forever. Suddenly Vida is hard work, like a baby who has just discovered the power of throwing a toy from its pram and yelling for its recovery, only to repeat the exercise. Vida is not yelling, thank heaven: not so you can hear anyway.

Dory is at a loss. She has never been good with children, beggars, outcasts, the homeless, people who don't play to the usual social rules... *mad* people. It's not that she doesn't sympathize with them, more that she feels like an actor without a script, in freefall, making it up as she goes along. And when that person is her mother, Vida, who has demanded nothing from her before, but has always accommodated *her*, Dory's moods, endlessly sympathizing with others, often in her view to a sickening degree, the transformation is just too much to stomach. She swallows back the sense of panic rising in her gut.

'That's no way to treat a book is it?' She is horribly aware that this was Vida's constant refrain from her childhood. Vida would rather she had tortured small furry creatures than tear pages and injure spines. This she frequently did, deliberately hurling books across the room. 'Borr...ring!'

The memory of this induces a flicker of guilt. Was she really such a brat?

'Excuse me, can you tell me the way out?'

A grey-faced, emaciated girl with horrific scars on her arms has drifted over.

'I need to go now,' the girl says. 'I'll be late for the wedding if I don't go now.'

'Sorry, I, er...' The doors here all seem to be open. No need for bars when most patients are drugged stupid, she supposes. 'You'd better ask the nurse.'

The girl leans closer. She hisses confidentially, her breath smelling of mouldy cheese, 'She won't tell me. They're keeping me prisoner. They've got guard dogs.'

'Oh, right. Well, sorry I can't help you.' She could do with the way out herself.

As soon as the girl has drifted away to pester the volunteer, Dory pats Vida's elbow and heads for the exit. There are no proper grounds in this hospital, just a network of pathways between the buildings, along which nurses scurry.

Dory sits on a bench beneath a tree with white berries, and lights a cigarette. That's better. Even that raw scraping in her lungs is pleasurable, the act of coughing a kind of release. She's debating whether to go straight back to the house, now she's done the duty visit. Or should she try to talk seriously? Maybe there is something going on behind the blank mask. *Listen Mother,* she needs to say, *we could get you somewhere nice, with lovely grounds to stroll in, but we'll have to sell the house.* It's just a question of getting through, pressing the right buzzer. The enormity of her burden suddenly hits her.

'Why now? I can bloody do without this...' She groans aloud.

A couple leaving the visitors' car park dart her a quick nervous glance, then scurry on past. They think she's one of the patients. She grinds out the cigarette in the gravel, and heads back to the ward to say a quick goodbye.

In the doorway of the Day Room, Dory hesitates. Someone is leaning over Vida's chair. She can't see much from this angle but the back view is unmistakable. A mass of reddish-brown hair obscures her mother's head, the coat that looks like it's been run up out of some old granny's velvet curtains bunches across ample hips. It's a dried blood colour, the colour of scabs. She imagines it being home-dyed from the skins of red onions, from poisonous berries, splish splosh, crushed by feet, grubby, exotic with toe rings and ankle chains.

Rhiannon.

'You're back! I didn't know you were…'

Rhiannon turns to look at her: 'Caliban's time had come, you know? I had to have him put down. I couldn't bear to see him suffer.'

'Oh really? I'm sorry to hear that.'

'He'll be quite happy. We've had a little word or two since he passed over to the astral plane.'

Dory decides not to pursue this subject. It's just too off the wall. She's still struggling with the idea that this woman is back. Why didn't she ring at least and warn her? It seems odd just to appear out of the blue like this.

'There. That's better.' Rhiannon huffs with effort as she heaves Vida forward in the chair to tuck a shawl around her shoulders. She adjusts a pillow behind Vida's neck. 'Her head was hanging over the book, poor love. You'll get a stiff neck like that, won't you sweetheart.'

'Ah, did you bring that?'

The shawl is the same turquoise colour of that kimono on the bed, hand-knitted in a rough textured yarn. Vida's face bobs ghost-pale above the collar. Rhiannon explains that her train got into Cregaron early this morning.

'I thought I'd call in and see Vida before catching the Hopper. She looked chilly so I popped back into town. They had the shawls in a sale in Ridgeleys.' Rhiannon shifts her attention to Dory. 'What about you? Have you been all right at the house? How are you coping?'

'Perfectly well thanks. I'm a bit surprised to see you back here to be honest.'

Rhiannon shakes her head as if saddened by this lack of trust. 'I'd never desert Vida. That's not my way. I never run out on people in times of trouble. And I know you say you can cope, but you need emotional support at a time like this.' Rhiannon has pulled up the only spare chair close to Vida's, so Dory has no choice but to stand.

'Sorry I snapped. I'm a bit on edge. It's just so awful to see her like this. I don't know what to say to her. She doesn't know me. She doesn't hear anything I say.'

'Oh but she does, don't you, Vida? She hears you on a level we don't understand.'

'That's kind, but I don't think so.'

Vida has nodded off to sleep in the midst of all this, her head nudging forwards, the book finally resting on her feet. The sight of those stupid slippers gives Dory an unexpected pang of sorrow. She bends to retrieve the book for the third time. As she does so, it falls open at the flyleaf and she reads the inscription:

For Rhiannon, all best wishes, Vida Tremayne.

'Oh. Your copy?'

'I thought she'd like it by her. To remind her of the person she once was, her writer-self.'

'Ah.'

Why didn't she think of anything like that? The book, the shawl. All she'd brought was a clean nightdress she'd found in a chest, and a bottle of Pomegranate fizz stuff that no doubt one of the nurses will guzzle.

Rhiannon says, 'I'm really glad Vida's got you at last.'

'Got me? I'm not sure what you mean.'

'That you're close to her now. She talked about you such a lot.'

'Did she?'

'Yes she did. She was proud of your success, your flair for business.'

Dory flushes. She'd always believed Vida would have preferred a creative daughter, if not another writer, an artist, a musician. There's so little she understands. And here is Rhiannon with her chair drawn close and, goddammit, holding Vida's hand! Why hasn't *she* done that? Why isn't it *her* holding her mother's hand? She resists an impulse to snatch it away, like a child jealous of a sibling. This odd friendship may turn out to be a blessing. At least there's someone apart from her who cares about Vida's welfare, someone to take a share of the worry, the burden. Does it actually matter that Rhiannon Townsend isn't family? She could be the older sister Dory regretted not having only a few days ago.

'If you want to go on home, and catch up with work, I can stay here with Vida if you like.' Rhiannon might be reading her thoughts.

'Oh... well, do you think there's any point in either of us staying? I mean, she's asleep again. It must be all that dope they've got her on. Anyway, I can give you a lift back.'

'I'd like to stay if you don't mind, for when she wakes. Don't worry about the lift. I can catch the Hopper back later this afternoon. There's one at about three.'

'Are you sure?' She should at least make a display of reluctance. Rhiannon is not to know she'd been about to dash off in any case. She can get a lot of work done if the connection holds.

'I wouldn't offer if I wasn't sure, now would I. I can catch up with my knitting.' Rhiannon releases Vida's hand and humps her bag onto the bed beside her. The tapestry bag looks sinister as if it might hold a live chicken, or a severed head. From it she withdraws a hank of tweedy-looking yarn and knitting needles that look like they're carved out of small tree trunks. What is it with the fad for knitting? It's an old lady's game in Dory's book. Still, it seems Rhiannon's quite happy to click away all day in this awful, frankly smelly ward just to keep a barely conscious woman company.

'That's good of you. I do have quite a lot of stuff to get through.' Dory hovers by the bed. 'I'll, er... see you later back at the house then?'

Rhiannon nods.

'Goodbye then.' Dory addresses Vida's bowed head. 'I'll see you later.' The head is lolling almost to her knees, too low even for a quick peck, and anyway, she can't kiss her mother on the head, that would be ludicrous. Aware of Rhiannon watching her, she reaches out and pats the mother who is no longer her mother awkwardly on the shoulder, then turns and almost slams into a ward assistant in her anxiety to escape.

⚜ ⚜ ⚜

Back in the car park, Dory punches out the number to her office. Harvey's voice shrills over the auto-message. *Very sorry, there's no one in the office right now. Please leave a message and we'll get back to you as soon as possible.* Damn it, he must have gone out on a view-ing. The thought of the office being unmanned on a weekday unnerves her. She tries his mobile, but he's not answering that either.

She leaves a message after the tone. 'Harvey, where the hell are you? I could be a potential client. People don't want to be fobbed off with bloody auto-replies, Harve, they want to talk to a real live human being. That's assuming you *are* still alive, and don't tell me they can email because that's not good enough!'

Harvey is used to her rants, but this time she means it. How can she trust anyone? If she doesn't get back to work soon, there won't be a business left. The business she's given up everything for, includ-ing friends, lovers, and especially Dan.

Hurtling back along the lanes she nearly mulches a pheasant on the track to the cottage. The stupid bird launches itself into the air with a rattled squawk, wings whirring slowly as if from a clockwork mechanism which is winding down. Everything here, even the damn birds seem to move at a geriatric pace, and she can't stand *SLOW*. But the moment she lets herself into the cottage she wonders what all the rush to get back here was about. The slamming of the front door seems a violation. The whole house shudders as if she's disturbed its very foundations, disturbed something better left sleeping. There is a strange bristling quality to the silence that follows, a kind of static energy, as if a cat had brushed itself against her legs. For one moment she almost expects Vida's study door to open, for Vida to poke her head out and say in that gently despairing voice she always used, 'Is there any *real* need to slam the front door like that, Dory? Can't you be a bit quieter? I'm trying to work.'

Trying to work. Yes, exactly. The irony of the situation hits her as she makes her way to the kitchen and switches on the kettle. It's all very well for Rhiannon fussing about Vida. She has no idea what it was like to grow up with her. Here she, Dory, is, putting her mother's needs first. Did Vida ever do that for her? Not that she remembers. Always there was a deadline to meet, and even when the wretched manuscript was delivered, she'd be away in her head thinking about the next book.

That was how Murphy her pet rabbit had died.

'You won't forget to feed him, Mum, will you? Promise you won't forget?'

She was eleven. First year at comprehensive, and the other girls were organizing a "we all hate Dory Tremayne" campaign. She'd been too ashamed to tell Vida. Vida had no idea why she didn't want to go on the school trip to Paris. Why she practically begged Vida to let her stay at home. It would be such fun, Vida said. It was the kind of thing Dory loved.

'You'll be bored here with just me,' Vida said. 'You know I'm bogged down with work right now. You'd much rather be with all your friends.'

How could she tell her mother that she *had* no friends in that first year, that they all hated her? Vida would want to know why, what happened, and then she might go up to the school wearing that funny purple coat of hers and make everything worse. That was why Murphy was so important to her.

'Promise you won't forget, he needs fresh greens as well as the dry food.'

'Of course I won't forget Murphy,' Vida had said as she waved her off outside the school gates where her enemies were already making faces at her through the coach windows. But she'd seen that dreamy look in her mother's eyes, heard her pacing about downstairs in the middle of the night, heard Dad go down to persuade Vida to come back to bed. She was having trouble with a plot and that always made her more than usually vacant. If only Dad had been around, she could've asked him to feed Murphy, but he was away a lot then. Perhaps he was playing around even then. And who could blame him?

Thinking of it now, she forgets to blow on her coffee to cool it and it scalds her tongue. She flips open her laptop and sits at the table. Still she can't stop thinking of Murphy. She remembers how she loved the ritual of chasing him around the garden every night to put him back in the hutch. When she cradled him in her hands, he was like warm black silk and she'd marvelled at the feel of his little heart beating against her palms.

It was the first thing she'd done on her return, race down the garden to say hallo to Murphy. But there was no Murphy. Just an empty hutch with one yellowing cabbage leaf withering in a bed of dirty-looking straw. Vida spent ages helping her look for him. She couldn't explain what happened.

'I went down to give him his greens like you said, darling. I'm absolutely sure I closed the door properly. I'm sure I did. I can't think how he got out.'

Eventually even Vida had to agree that Murphy wasn't an escape artist, that it was her fault, that it was all due to her negligence.

They concluded that Murphy must've been got at by the urban foxes that were beginning to infiltrate the neighbourhood.

'I'm so sorry, love. We'll get you another rabbit.'

Dory hadn't wanted another one. There was only one Murphy.

✤ ✤ ✤

The laptop screen lights up and Dory flicks onto *TREMAYNE'S HOMESEARCH*. There are nine queries. She runs through the first Wish List and sighs. People's expectations seem to get more unrealistic by the day. When she first started up, the average house-hunters were happy enough with a garage and a conservatory; now they absolutely must have an Italian marble kitchen and a roller disco in the basement.

No matter. Whatever the punters want the punters get. Or do they? It may be the dead doldrums of winter in this godforsaken hole, but back in London the market is already buzzing. Even as she types in her response assuring Mr and Mrs. Hogg-Patterson of her ability to tick even the boxes they haven't yet thought of, she seethes with frustration. She needs to be on the spot, lining up viewings, *pressing the flesh* as Harvey loves to put it.

What use is she here, faffing about in the Gingerbread House waiting for Vida to rise completely sane from her bed and resume her life? She should face it: miracles *don't* happen. She could rot away here, while her business collapsed along with her entire life. Is that fair? Isn't that too much to ask of anyone? Just because she's Vida's flesh and blood, that doesn't mean she owes her. It doesn't mean she should sacrifice everything for her. As she thinks back over the disappointments of her childhood, her resolve hardens along with her heart. If her mother's friend is so keen to take on the odious task of visiting, then why not let her? The realization that she does have a way out after all makes the afternoon just about bearable as it ticks slowly away. After all, what does it really matter to Vida? Vida won't even notice she's gone.

Vida's Diary

Monday 27th September

Dear Vida,

I know you must be very busy with your new book right now, but I can't help thinking of our conversation in the museum the other day. You mentioned 'going into the room and finding it empty'. Vida, the room is never empty, although it might seem so. Have you ever used lucid dreams to guide the creative process? Just a thought. Perhaps you would like to meditate upon Isis the Awakener. May the goddess be your inspiration.

Please remember Vida, I am here if you want me, at your service... Rhiannon

The letter arrives in today's post. I know nothing of lucid dreams. As for *Isis the Awakener,* she sounds like some kind of video game character, but I'm touched by my fan's eagerness to help. I file the letter with all her others she's sent me. There's quite a little pile by now. I suppose keeping them at all proves I still have a shred of ego left. Just knowing there's at least one discerning, intelligent reader who can hardly wait for the next book is a hard thing to shrug off. But she's wrong about the empty room of course. Sometimes the more you look, the emptier it seems.

Throughout the day, as I prune back the dead honeysuckle on the porch, and make myself scrambled eggs for lunch, I find myself thinking of the letter. It's as if she *knows*, can see how I sit for hours, trying to capture Ella de Vile's formula, how I try to conjure them up, vampires, gremlins, werewolves, the Fey. Taps drip blood, and bats wheel about. It's all such a cliché. This is the really horrific thing, far more terrifying than werewolves: the fact that I can't do it. I can't write like Ella de Vile. I can't even write like *me* for heaven's sake.

Tuesday 28th September

It's three o'clock in the afternoon, and I have been scribbling like a demon all day. A strange thing happened last night. I woke around midnight, convinced that something was lying on the bed. It seemed like a great weight, breathing on me just as an animal might do, a huge dog or a cat. I don't know how long I lay there. It might have been five minutes or an hour. I didn't dare to move, not even to twitch a muscle. I wasn't even sure if I *could*. There was a dead sensation in my limbs, as if I'd been drugged and the normal flight or fight reaction immobilized. Only my mind raced, keeping pace with my heart, painfully alert to danger. The creature, whatever it might be, seemed to be stretched across my body, oblivious, as if dreaming its own primitive dreams: dreams of the chase, the hunt, of the crunch of an old woman's bones in its teeth perhaps. I lay trapped, barely daring to breathe. One twitch and the beast would stir. It would sniff out the fear trickling in the folds and hollows of my flesh. This was the one thing

I had no control over: sweat. Basted in perspiration I stilled my breath to a whisper. I imagined a great tongue seeking, relishing the salty slick of my sweat at first, then teeth... then... Just as I was beginning to feel I'd suffocate, that I could bear it no more, my body revived. I yelled, a kind of muffled furious cry, and kicked out so hard the quilt slithered in a heap to the floor.

There *was* no animal. How could there be? Only the quilt, humped on the floor where I'd kicked it. Stupid of me. If that was an animal it was in submission, belly up, panting. I sat awhile in the darkness, and realized the weight was not outside but *inside* me. Not entirely unpleasant. Lighter now, like a butterfly beating its wings. There was a strong scent of burning in the room, a kind of sulphuric smell. I remembered reading somewhere that this particular scent was associated with the devil. Of course I had to go downstairs to check, drifting about the house in my nightdress. Was the grill still on? Had the Rayburn chimney caught fire?

But there was nothing, only a jab in my ovaries and a spurt of blood, brownish, mucky, but blood all the same. The moon loomed full at my window as I rummaged deep in my drawers for that relic of the past, a sanitary towel. Strange how comforting it was, the bulk of that towel between my legs.

I feel exhausted now, but triumphant. I have written. I have written two whole chapters.

Wednesday 29th September

The blood has dried up, and with it the ink. Perhaps just as well. After breakfast, I'd been reading through my efforts of the past couple of days, and was appalled. Dreadful, lurid ravings, the kind of thing my students used to pour out when I taught Creative Writing years ago. I fed the Rayburn with the pages, and opened my study window wide to the sun. Suddenly I was in such desperate haste to be in the fresh air that I tugged on my old green leggings and shoved my feet into a pair of gardening clogs without a thought for how I might look. The last thing I expected was visitors. I was forking couch grass out of a dusty tangle of Nepeta in the front flowerbed when there was a scrape of wheels on the track, and a car pulled up. Dory stepped out and looked impatiently at the sky as if she doubted the sun would shine for a minute longer. Then she looked at me, and her mouth twitched in a smile. 'Mother, you look completely wild!'

Flustered, I tried to tug off my gloves and smooth my hair at the same time. 'Why didn't you ring? I would have... well, I would have...'

I would have had my hair done, made a cake, something. In fact, we hadn't spoken since that tetchy phone call about Jonathan when she cut me off. Had she come to talk about her father, I wondered, persuade me to try and cajole him into coming back?

'Please don't fuss.' Dory yielded stiffly to my embrace. 'We can't stay long, I'm afraid. I'm meeting up with some clients who want to relocate to Wales of all places. They must be mad. I wouldn't normally do this in person, but they are seriously loaded.' She broke off as the driver of the car joined us. 'Dan, this is my mother, Vida.'

'Vida, how are you? I've been looking forward to meeting you.' Dan clasped my hand in a warm handshake. People say this all the time, but few sound as if they mean it. Dan did. He is not at all what I expected. He is lovely; huge, blond, genial, like a golden retriever but with just a hint of shyness in his eyes, which makes me fear for him. Dory had mentioned during one of her brief calls that he'd moved in with her a month or two ago. What had she said exactly? 'It's early days, so don't go buying the hat, Mother.' I prayed silently, *please let this be the one.*

Dory glanced about the garden fretfully. 'God, this is a jungle. How are you going to cope with it all? You should get a gardener, or think about moving or something.'

She continued the theme over tea and crumbly scones I found in the freezer and quickly defrosted.

'How can you live in this place? It was all right when Dad was here, I suppose, but... well, if he's not coming back, it's different, isn't it. When did you last go anywhere? Meet anyone?'

I smiled, 'Well, as it happens, I do go out. Of course I do.' I thanked God for my date next week, because I don't want this Dan to think I'm a recluse. 'I've got an engagement for next week as a matter of fact.'

'An engagement?'

'The local W.I. have invited me to give a talk.'

Strange but true. The speaker they'd arranged to give a talk about his travels in the Arctic tundra had let them down, and Janice at the library had given them my name instead.

Dory groaned. 'What on, jungle management? The early stages of lunacy?'

I laughed. 'My books, I think.'

'Oh, those.' She turned away to check her mobile for messages, while Dan asked me more about my work.

'I didn't know you were an author. Dotty only told me on the way here, didn't you, Dot. I'm a bit of a crime-thriller junkie myself... Dot thinks...'

'Oh, don't get her started on books.' Dory glared at her mobile and snapped it back in her bag. 'We'll be here all night.' She changed the subject to decor, and I know she's something of an expert on this. 'I can't think what possessed you to choose those curtains, mother. They're straight out of the Nightmare Zone.'

As she stood up wincing at my appalling taste, I observed her with a kind of bewildered pride. She looked so elegant, my daughter, with her golden hair swept up in a chignon, the pencil skirt and peplum jacket showing off her slender waist.

'And that wall paper! What is it, bohemian-gothic or something?'

I heard Dan groan softly. 'Go easy, Dot, taste is personal, right? I think it looks great, Vida, really. I mean it fits with the cottage.'

The wallpaper she despises is rich brocade, patterned with unicorns and strutting peacocks. Dory continued unabashed; I should sell this house, and buy myself a little apartment in West London or somewhere, so she won't have to travel so far to see me.

'You'll have to paint it white before you put it on the market. People want space and light these days; they want the wow-factor. If I were you, I'd just get the decorators in. Well, you can afford it, can't you? Why are you looking at me like that?'

'Like what? Sorry, I was thinking how nice you look in that outfit.'

'Do I? Thanks, but we're supposed to be discussing your plans for the house, not my outfit. Have you been listening to *anything* I've said, Mother?'

I asked Dan if he'd like to see more of the garden at this point, so off we trooped in a threesome, he with his arm looped about Dory's waist. The sun was already low, gilding grass and shrubs, burnishing the thatch roof of the cottage. A blackbird with grey feathers in its neck picked its way among the greengages smashed from the trees in last week's storms. Blood-dark butterflies feasted on the Michaelmas daisies, their raggedy petals flaming hot pink against the old brick walls. My fingers plucked and fussed automatically as we drifted about, deadheading, rolling the seeds in my palm as if they were prayer beads. I could smell winter on the air. Normally, I'm not one of those people who dread the approach of the winter, but today the thought of those long dark nights to come chilled me. I reasoned that it must be that nightmare I'd had a couple of nights back. I could still feel the weight of that beast breathing on top of me, the sheer physical horror of the sensation, even as the three of us stood there chattering in the deepening toffee-gold light. Far above us a buzzard fluted a melancholy note, as if seeking something it would never find.

Dan strained his head back to the sky. 'Is that an eagle?'

'Not quite an eagle, we're not that far north. Haven't you seen a buzzard before, Dan?'

He shook his head. 'We only get pigeons where we live.'

'I didn't know you were a birdie.' Dory rolled her eyes.

I laughed, wishing they could stay with me for a bit longer. In Dan's company Dory seemed softened, less brittle. Only Dan would get away with calling her 'Dot' for one thing. 'Doro' she had been at one time, then 'Thea', before finally settling for 'Dory'. Anything but Dorothea. 'Why did you ever give me that stupid old lady name?' she had railed at me as a teenager. I must have been crazy to name her after some dried-up old heroine in a novel. In fact I'd been re-reading *Middlemarch* all through that pregnancy. When I held her in my arms, and gazed into that solemn little face, crowned with a fuzz of the softest blonde hair, it seemed to me she could be none other than Dorothea. My only child would grow up to be a kind-hearted, principled young woman, bookish and scholarly. I was wrong to burden my daughter with such expectations, I see that now. Today's parents are more sensible, naming their daughters after flowers: Daisy or Poppy or Lily.

'We should go.' Dory's voice, suddenly business-like, broke into my musings. 'We don't want to get snarled up in these lanes behind some old coot in a tractor.'

Dan turned to me with that open confiding look. 'Do you come down to London much, Vida? Dory, why don't you fix a date for your mum to visit?'

Dory frowned. Her voice had an edge to it as she said, 'Yes, Dan, arrange my social diary for me, why don't you. No offence, Mum, but Dan has a habit of inviting the world and his wife over at the drop of a hat, when he *knows* I'm up against it. And Dan has all the time in the world of course, because he's between jobs at the moment.'

Dan said nothing, but his hand dropped from Dory's shoulder. I noticed his lips pressed tight together, a wounded look in his eyes. So he wasn't working? And whatever he did for a living, his easygoing charm was already beginning to pall. When it came to her work, Dory wouldn't tolerate any distractions.

'We'll arrange something soon. It's pretty full on at the moment.' She was fidgeting with her smartphone again: 'I'm either in the office or on the road.'

Fighting back my sense of being irrelevance I said, 'Just let me know when you get a space, dear, and I'll come.'

Dory flashed me a look, then realizing no sarcasm was meant, her face relaxed.

'I will. It's usually quieter in November, maybe then.' This time she met my eyes properly and smiled. 'Bye then.'

Dan's goodbye was warm, but even as he climbed in the car next to Dory, I knew in my heart that I wouldn't see him again.

30th September

My fan has sent me a book. It's called *The Power of the Goddess in Everywoman.* It is her own personal copy, she says, for me to keep. She hopes it will inspire me to write. It's kind of her but writing suddenly feels like a dry, self-indulgent occupation. I wish Dory and Dan could have stayed longer. The house seems emptier than ever after their visit. I flick through the book with a growing sense of panic. The pages are well-thumbed, wafting a scent of herbs and old velvets. The goddess is here in all her guises. Here she is as an Egyptian, raising her arms to the orange-black globe of the sun, and here again as an Indian yogini, full-breasted, legs akimbo, with an owl's head covering her vulva. There is something lewd and foul about this version which makes my skin creep, if skin can be said to be creeping. I can see how something like this might inspire Ella de Vile, but what has it to do with me? I slip the book back into its brown paper wrapping. I can't write. I can't even face my study. And now I have to give this silly talk to a lot of silly women in two days time, about the Literary Life.

1st October

Hallo Vida

I'm just checking that you received my parcel safely. The post is so unreliable lately. I hate to take up your time, but if you could just confirm receipt, I would be grateful. The copy I sent is of great personal value to me, but I had an impulse that it absolutely must find its way into your hands.

I shall wait to hear,

Blessings as ever, Rhiannon

This is puzzling. I don't remember giving Rhiannon Townsend my email address, but I must have. Maybe I slipped her my card without thinking. It's not as if I even use email very much. I check them about twice a week, just to see if the Kates have left a message. Sometimes Jonathan will send a round robin from the Dordogne, something about the goats or a fox getting the chickens, mostly. The connection here is so precarious that I've learned not to depend on this method of communication. I reply, of course.

Dear Rhiannon

Yes, I received the book yesterday, thank you. It's kind of you to think of me. I shall look forward to reading it as soon as I get a moment.

I hope you are well.

Kind regards

Vida

This is feeble, but I have no wish to get caught up in the mysteries of the goddess just now.

2nd October

This morning I receive an email from Fee Moody in response to my brief update. She seems very excited about the Ella de Vile idea. She suggests that I make the book a Crime-Horror, introduce a female detective, and set it in America with an eye on US sales. I shouldn't think in terms of a stand-alone novel either. Everyone wants a series these days. Also it would be good to have a heroine who is physically damaged in some way. Facial deformity is hot right now. Meanwhile, she's going to contact the Kates and see if she can get something more concrete in terms of deadlines and advances.

I shudder as I read the words "something more concrete". Perhaps I should tell her to hold back until I've written something at least?

But there's no time to sit shuddering like a fool. I spend most of the morning rummaging through my wardrobe. Every outfit tells a story. There is my red blouse, the one I always wore for book signings in the heady days of *The Gingerbread House*, because red makes a lasting impression. I forget where I read that. Some article called "Dress for Success" as I recall. When I struggled into it this morning, I just looked washed-out. I hurl them all onto the bed, the vintage prints, the flowing scarves and skirts in which I used to drift about. They may have looked arty at one time, now I just look like a frump. What should one wear for a W.I. talk anyway? Finally I settle on a black silk shirt and grey trousers.

Six o'clock and I've just opened a carton of Covent Garden Soup for my dinner. Tomato. I can't face much else. I do so wish I hadn't agreed to do this talk. It's raining. Perhaps the lane will flood and I won't be able to drive.

3rd October

I should have obeyed my intuition yesterday and rung to cancel. I am not well. The feverish feeling came on as soon as I got back last night. This is what happens when I come out of my isolation, I catch things. I go down with things. I get contaminated.

It's six pm now and almost dusk. I'm huddled in front of the Rayburn, laying down my pen to feed the burner with bits of wood, warming my icy hands upon its cast-iron flanks as if it's a living thing, a friendly comforting beast. What will happen if I'm really ill, and haven't the energy to carry in logs from the woodpile? I'll freeze, that's what will happen. It sounds ridiculous, but I'm sure it's to do with the Lemon Meringues I had to sample. The W.I. were having a contest, and as the visiting speaker and honoured guest, I was asked to help judge the entries. It makes me nauseous just thinking of it now, the poorly set meringue toppings, the squishy bright lemon fillings. How I wish I'd never gone. All those smug village women, gazing warily at me as I read a passage from *The Gingerbread House* as if I were trying to convert them to some strange religion. After the talk, a woman with fierce eyebrows came over and asked if I could put in a word for her with my publisher, as she'd just completed her Life Story. When I murmured excuses she became quite aggressive, assuring me that she'd "had a very interesting life". Later I heard her telling someone that anyone could write a book, *if they had the luxury of time.*

I sold just one of the six hardback copies I had with me, to Mrs. Calder, their president, only because she'd invited me in the first place. She assured me she couldn't wait to read it.

I really don't care if she does read it or not.

I shrug the shawl closer around my throat. It's dark outside, and my shivering bouts are growing more protracted. I'll go to bed, and sweat it out beneath the quilt, and tomorrow I'll be absolutely fine.

Looking up from this page, I notice Rhiannon Townsend's book on the table, still half-wrapped in its brown paper covers. The book nags at me as I pass it to fetch a glass of water, as if beckoning me to read. A vision comes to me of that picture, the goddess astride the owl; there is something foul about the owl's face, its big moony eyes and curved beak. The owl is a symbol of death. Is that what the goddess represents, I wonder, the triumph of life over death?

I slide the book back in its wrappings, so I can't see the cover any more. My head feels woolly, confused. I resolve that as soon as I'm better, I shall donate it to a charity bookshop, along with the Ella de Vile tome. This horror idea must be getting to me. I doubt I shall ever write another book. There. I've said it. And even though there is no one to hear me, it makes me feel lighter somehow.

7TH FEBRUARY
DORY

Dory wakes with a groan. She's slept badly, thanks in part to her feet, which were like a couple of ice blocks all night. It's no fun sleeping alone. In the short time Dan was living with her, she'd grown used to warming her feet on some part of his anatomy. He never objected. He's one of those people whose blood seems to pump eternally hot, his flesh toasty to the touch. He used to tease her about her body temperature, saying she needed someone to turn up her thermostat. He'd take her feet between his hands and chafe them gently until her blood warmed. She thinks of the empty bed at home, that state of the art Memory Foam mattress that will now have only *one* body, *one* set of contours to mould itself to. Hers. She's heard nothing from Dan since he walked out. No doubt he's already found someone else, someone with warm feet, and a heart to match. Someone nicer, kinder, altogether worthier of his love than she is.

She sweeps back the covers, and listens. Rhiannon must be up and about. At least there's no snoring from down the hallway. Dory throws a sweater on over her pyjamas and tramps downstairs. God but she feels a wreck. She'll have to fake it and paste on a smile for Rhiannon though. She'll have to force herself to be nice. There's no sense in alienating Vida's only friend, not when she's hoping to pack her bags after a decent interval and leg it back home. She won't say anything just yet though. She needs to make some decisions about the house first. And perhaps she should corner Dr. Saleem one last time and see if she can force him into a more definite prognosis for Vida.

Rhiannon is munching her way through a bowl of porridge and banana. 'Morning, my love, how did you sleep?' She pauses, spoon poised halfway to her mouth. 'I heard you in the night, walking about.'

'Did you?' Dory heaps coffee into the percolator, wishing she was home and could nip out to the deli-bakers on the corner for a couple of Danish pastries. 'Sorry if I disturbed you. I was a bit cold, so I made myself a hot drink.'

'The temperature does tend to plunge in the night. Why didn't you take some extra blankets from the chest? You look absolutely bushed.'

'Oh… I didn't think.' Such intense scrutiny combined with the slow methodical spooning of porridge sets her nerves on edge. So she looks as knackered as she feels? Great! Does she have eye-bags? Does she look like a hag? She doesn't want to be scrutinized, and certainly not pitied at this time in the morning.

'Never worry about disturbing my sleep.' Rhiannon wipes a blob of stray porridge from her cloud of hair. 'I sleep like the dead, thanks to my Valerian pills.'

'Valerian?'

'It subdues the sympathetic nervous system. I can recommend it. You're welcome to help yourself to some of mine any time.'

'Cheers. Not sure I want to sleep like the dead though.' Dory's attempt at laughter turns into a pro-tracted bout of coughing. She downs the last of the coffee dregs and lights a cigarette. 'It's the silence that does my head in. It doesn't feel natural to me.'

'Ah, you're a town mouse.' With one practiced hand, Rhiannon sweeps back her hair, twirling it up into a loose knot at the back of her head. The loose bits tumble in burnished tendrils disguising old acne blemishes that Dory has noted with something between pity and contempt. Rhiannon cherishes the silence, she says. She goes on about how rare and precious a thing true silence is, like true darkness.

'Without the darkness we wouldn't be able to see the stars. It's the same with silence. We're afraid of what we might hear.'

Who is this 'we'? Speak for yourself, Dory thinks, but lets her drone on just the same. She disagrees. Last night the absolute stillness felt solid enough to cut through like cheese. When she did finally drift off she dreamt that the thatched roof had grown overnight like hair, weaving its tresses about the beams, wiggling in through the cracks between glass and windowpane, smothering everything in its wake. She woke at one point, gasping for breath, in a panic, before realizing it was her own hair that had tangled across her face as she slept. She would love to mention Rhiannon's snoring, reverberating through the house like the purring of a great cat. In the end she'd convinced herself it *was* a cat purring, the monotonous rhythm eventually coaxing her into a light sleep.

Rhiannon has been back for three days now. Since Caliban passed over to the great Cat Home in the sky, she seems content to make her stay open-ended. Ambling over to the sink to wash up her bowl, she offers to put on another saucepan of porridge. Oats are also nature's tranquilizers apparently, along with Hops and Valerian.

'Yes, but I don't want to sleep now, I have too much to do.'

'Were you thinking of visiting Vida?'

'Er… well, I…'

It might not hurt to give hospital a miss today. Her visit yesterday had hardly been a success. She'd arrived clutching a carton of Pineapple Smoothie and a bunch of tulips to find the curtains drawn around Vida's bed. At first she'd panicked but the nurse told her they were just 'freshening Vida up a bit'. She'd had to pace around in reception for half an hour while they finished. When she finally got to the bedside, Vida was half propped up in bed, head flopping like a rag doll and emitting strange little snores that made Dory's blood curdle.

She'd made the usual inane one-sided conversation about the weather. After which she'd fallen silent and just sat there gazing at her mother's sleeping face. Was the real Vida in there somewhere? It was weird how seeing this cold, inert, comatose Vida fired her memories of the living one. Incidents she hadn't thought about for years, like the time Vida forgot to make her fancy-dress in time for the school parade, and had ended up sticking crepe-paper hearts over a disgusting pink nylon dress at the eleventh hour, giving her a paper plate with Mr. Kipling tarts on and calling her the *Queen of Hearts*. She remembered the parade taking place around the playground, the paper hearts peeling off the dress and withering like autumn leaves as she marched along. Then she'd managed to drop the tarts in a puddle. Even at the age of seven it had been a gross humiliation.

She'd said almost without thinking, 'D'you remember that outfit you made me for the fancy-dress, Mum? It was a disaster.'

Then it seemed a tad unfair to bring up her mother's deficiencies when she couldn't even defend herself. She'd shrugged. 'Well, you never did like needlework. Neither did I, come to that. That's something we had in common anyway.'

She'd sat by the bedside for a while longer, flicking through an old copy of *Good Housekeeping* she'd found in reception, eyes glazed over recipes for chutney, and a feature about a woman who went trekking in the Himalayas to raise money for maltreated donkeys. Twenty minutes of this was all she could stand before making her escape.

❖ ❖ ❖

'Why don't you take a day off? I'm happy to visit if you like.' Rhiannon wipes down the worktops with a cloth. She looks absolutely at home as she does so. Mistress of the house.

'But are you sure? You were with her for ages the day before yesterday. You must be bored stiff.'

It's a tempting offer. She needs to check on how Harvey is coping. Then there are builders to organize before she goes back to London.

'I'm never bored. I have my knitting, and the book I'm working with at the moment. I can catch up on reading for my next course.'

'Ah. Well, okay then, if you're sure you don't mind. Thanks.' Dory has noticed the book lying about – *The Power of the Goddess in Everywoman* – new age tosh. She won't ask about the course. Too much information. Still she feels she should make a show of gratitude.

'Listen, why don't you drive Mum's car to the hospital, rather than sending for the Hopper?'

Rhiannon considers this. She peers out of the window where the clouds are massing, dark, swollen. It would save her hanging about in the cold, waiting for bus times, she says, and it looks like more rain. So, if Dory is sure.

'Course I'm sure. Mum's hardly going to use the car in the state she's in, is she. There's no sense in it just sitting here rusting away while the battery goes flat.'

❧ ❧ ❧

As soon as Rhiannon has chugged away in Vida's battered KA, she calls Harvey.

'How are we doing, Harve? Have we got any viewings in this neck of the woods? Anywhere west of Oxford, in fact, I could take care of.'

There are a couple of possibilities. Harvey gives the locations and she promises to do the searches.

'I'll round up the estate agents today.'

'If you can, darling, there's only so much ground one man can cover.'

'Sorry, Harve. I'm doing my utmost to sort things out here.'

'Any idea when you'll be back?' Harvey's attempt to sound unconcerned fails to convince. Desperation pitches his voice to a whine. 'How is your mother?'

'Not good. And I can't get a word of sense out of the doctors. She might be like this for... Anyway, I can't give you a date just yet, I'm sorry. It's an impossible situation. I've got the house to sort out, and I can't just leave her... although...'

'Although?'

'Well, there is this woman staying here, a friend of my mother's apparently. She's a bit heavy-going, but devoted to Vida. Seems happy to do all the hospital visits, in fact she's there as we speak. She's offered to take care of things at this end, if I have to race back.' Her tone is casual, yet as she says this the enormity of the offer hits her. She visualizes Rhiannon sitting companionably by the dumb hulk of her mother, and puzzles a moment. Despite her insistence that she can use the time usefully, it must be deadly for her all day in that depressing place. How can she stand it? An hour is the very most Dory can tolerate. She feels a pang of guilt. It should be *her*, surely. It should be *her* sitting there, coaxing Vida back into life.

Harvey tries out one of his theatrical sighs. 'Darling, I don't mean to sound heartless but this is music to my ears.'

'Yes, well, don't get too excited. There are things to sort out. I haven't decided anything yet.'

❧ ❧ ❧

It's true, she hardly feels capable of making a decision right now. She spends the next couple of hours rounding up properties for the Gillespies before calling a few more builders. All she gets are answer-phones. Finally she reaches a man called Vince Evans who says he'll have a look at the job, but he's not promising anything before next autumn. His speech is so halting she thinks he's fallen asleep mid-sentence.

Rather than sit around chewing her fingernails, she might as well make a start herself. A quick rummage in her father's old toolbox yields up some basic tools. Soon she is balancing on a ladder in the entrance hall dashing away with the scraper. The William Morris print with its jungle of brown and orange leaves and birds has been giving her the creeps for too long. Now she carves tracks in the labyrinth of leaves, until the paper draggles off in dusty strands. Better to do this while Rhiannon is out of the way. Her mother's friend treads softly among Vida's possessions as if every object is sacrosanct. She might not *say* anything, but her watchful presence would make Dory feel like a Brazilian planter despoiling the rain forest to plant cash crops. It's all very well for her, but Vida is not her responsibility. Dory has no choice but to harden her heart. White walls sell houses, and that's a fact: a neutral space for people to stamp their mark on.

Unfortunately, quite a lot of the wall comes off with the paper. Damn. She breaks off to light a cigarette, and views her handiwork from a distance. What does she know about plastering? Not a lot.

At the sound of a vehicle pulling up, her heart sinks a little. She'd hoped that Rhiannon would stay longer at the hospital, long enough for her to get the worst of the destruction over at least. Yet, squinting through the porch window, she sees it's not Rhiannon, but a man climbing out of a Land Rover, a man who looks like he might be a builder.

'You must be Vince.' She flings open the door before he even has a chance to knock. 'Come in, Vince, your timing couldn't be more perfect. I was just about to tear my hair out... oh...' The man is looking somewhat taken aback. 'Do you mind Vince, or should I call you Mr. Evans?'

He seems to consider this. Clearly she is not what he's expecting, not what he came for at all. His eyes flicker past her, and over the scarred walls.

'You are Vince Evans, the man I spoke to earlier this morning?'

He shakes his head. Yes, he is a builder, but his name is Brendan, Brendan Riley. Of course, she can see now that he isn't Mr. Evans, who sounded ancient, while this man must be in his late thirties. She takes in his stocky dark looks, the check shirt bagging over combats that make him look shorter than he probably is.

'Is Mrs. Tremayne at home?'

This gives her a jolt, as if she'd forgotten for a moment this is Vida's house.

'I'm afraid my mother's away at the moment. Can I give her a message?'

'Your mother? Ah...' He lifts a hand to scratch his neck. She notices darkly pelted forearms, wrists encircled by a couple of leather friendship bracelets.

'She won't be back for quite a while. She's...' She hesitates. 'Sorry, what is your connection with my mother?'

'I just did some work for Mrs. Tremayne a few weeks back.'

'Oh yes? What kind of work?'

He starts telling her something about a walnut tree and Vida's bedroom window needing replacing. She didn't even know there *was* a walnut tree.

He looks uncomfortable. 'Do you, er, know when she's likely to get back?'

'No, no I'm afraid I don't.' If only she did! She considers a moment. 'Actually, my mother's in hospital right now. Look, why don't you come in?' He is after all some kind of builder. It would be stupid to let him escape that easily.

She takes him through to the kitchen, talking as she goes.

'That's why I want to give this place a makeover. Vida is so wrapped up in her writing, I mean she was... she'd barely notice if the ceiling caved in, I'm afraid. I mean, just look at those skanky tiles around the sink; they make my toes curl. Sit down. Would you like a drink – tea, coffee, something stronger?'

He hesitates in the doorway. 'I won't hold you up. I'm sorry to hear about your mother. It's not serious?'

Dory shrugs. 'I don't know. It's not physical.' Something in his face makes her trust him enough to say, 'Look, if I tell you she's ill, she's had a breakdown, I trust it won't go any further. I know how word travels in these places.'

His expression as he digests the news is inscrutable. She can't tell if he's shocked, or even if he cares, and why should he care about some ageing woman whose bedroom window he once fixed? This lack of expression says it all. He won't talk. He's a man of few words, clearly not the type to gossip.

To fill the silence, she says, 'Yes, well. It's all a bit of a shock, to be honest.'

He's glancing about the room the way builders do when they're assessing costs, man hours. 'The window was an urgent job, but there was a fence coming down out the back. I said I'd look at that for her.'

Apparently there is the little matter of an unpaid bill for the work done. 'But if your mother's not well… don't worry, it can wait.' She can see now that he does genuinely care about Vida's condition. How odd. Probably she baked scones for him, made gallons of tea when he was working there. Vida always had a way of making dull people feel important, something she'd found irritating as a child.

'Tell her when you see her – tell her I hope she gets better soon.' His tone is sombre. He has that respectful cast to his features that people who are not emotionally involved adopt at funerals. He makes a move to leave.

'No, wait. How much do we owe you? I can take care of it right now.'

It's quite sweet, really, how he's almost embarrassed to name the amount. She whips out her cheque book straight away, and scribbles in the figure: £759.00.

'Thank you.'

'No problem. Actually you couldn't have come at a better time. I need to sort this place out.' Some instinct prevents her telling him about her plans to sell. 'How are you with general repairs?' She casts a glance at the crumbling walls behind her. 'A bit of plastering? Painting, decorating. Basically I want a bit of TLC, touching up – I mean, the *house* wants it.' The cheeky cockney chappies she normally deals with would have had a field day with that one, but this man lets it drift past him. She runs through the list of jobs to be done. 'It may take a while.'

He shrugs. That's fine. It's usually quiet at this time of year.

'So, do you live nearby?'

He comes and goes. Right now he's staying in a caravan on a friend's land, on the road to Beguildy.

'Caravan?' she enthuses. 'That sounds fun.' She'd envisaged some kind of hobbit house, or straw-bale hut, but a caravan! It sounds dire. But come to think of it, she can imagine him washing his socks along with his pots in some greasy plastic bowl, eating his cornflakes at one of those folding formica-top tables. The rusting hulks of caravans are familiar sights in this landscape. Often, passing out-lying farms, she's shuddered at graveyards of twisted metal, idle tractors, the huddles of broken-down huts and hutches, of rotting barns. This is a place of ne'er do wells and odd bods, rubbing up alongside the spruce bungalows of the retired.

She leads him to the door. 'Brendan, thanks. You have absolutely saved my life. I was beginning to think I'd have to roll up my sleeves myself.'

Clearly her charm offensive is lost on this guy. Still he doesn't smile. It seems he's even more spar-ing with his smiles than she is. He nods at the walls she's made a mess of, and says, 'I'll start on the hall then.'

'Yes,' she says, 'yes, please. If you can make it for next Monday that would be great. And shall we say an early start, before nine if possible?'

❧ ❧ ❧

When he's gone, she remembers what he said about mending a fence. The morning's hard rain has fizzled out to a soft persistent drizzle. She pulls on the hideous waterproof she found lurking in the utility room, and tramps out the back, through the waste of dead nettles and mud to the sheds.

She stands shivering. Gardens are really not her thing. She prefers them contained, instant. The exotic shrubs on her balcony at home are absurdly expensive. She thinks of them as conversation pieces rather than living things. At the first sign of wilt, shrivel or droop, she chucks them out for the garbage men. She doesn't have time for all that spraying and feeding, and stroking the leaves, to nurse things back to life, no thank you.

But now she needs to get to grips with this sprawling mess Vida's left behind. She really needs to sort out the boundaries. There is no definition, just bits of fence and barbed wire buried in amongst the shrubs.

Where does plot end, and where does the land around begin? She ventures farther, thankful that none of her friends can see her tramping around like some old yokel. Pulling up the hood, she is partially deafened by the drum of rain on plastic. She's not sure if it's the hood crackling or her eardrums. Also, it's so vast it practically gives her tunnel vision. From within its confines she stares straight ahead at the whiskery fields, which rear up beyond the garden, to the beetling brow of forest. To her left is a neglected vegetable patch where there is nothing but weeds and the rotten stumps of cabbages. In the summer, there are masses of flowers, none of which she can identify. She only knows those monster-sized waxen lilies she gets from the florists, which fill her living room with a heavy burnt rubbery scent.

The rain beats harder. The wind is getting up too. Better have a quick look in the shed. The door already hangs open on one rusty hinge. She breathes in the smell of rotting potatoes and bits of old sacking. She considers descriptions: Studio-Workshop? Garden Retreat? A shed is never just a shed, after all.

Well, whoever buys this place will have to use their bloody imagination. She ducks back through the doorway, and glances over her shoulder at the steep slope of the land. How might she describe that view in a blurb? It's not exactly uplifting in any way. There is something oppressive, even claustrophobic about it. As she stares, the wind catches the hood from behind, tugging it down over her brow, so that for a second she's plunged into a crackly darkness.

This is how she explains it to herself later, the dark shape she sees, long and low and swift, moving towards the trees at the very edge of her vision. There is something intent about its progress that rivets her attention. When it pauses for a moment, her heart catches. She squints against the rain. Does she see or imagine a great muzzle lifted to the sky, scenting the air? For one horrible moment she has the crazy idea that it's turned its head towards the garden, that it's *her* scent, her sweat, her blood beating in her veins that the thing is sifting, assessing. But even as the thought strikes her it's on the move again, slinking away towards the trees.

She stands for a while rubbing her eyes, as if there might be something in them, a bit of dirt or grit blurring her sight. But no, a creature it definitely is, a moving patch of darkness against the grey distance. It could be anything, she reasons. Somebody's dog, perhaps: a big dog for sure but some of the breeds people have nowadays are monstrous. She shudders. This is one more good reason not to walk in those damn woods, if there are dogs of that size on the loose.

Back inside the house, she has to admit there was nothing dog-like about that shape; it was too sleek, too swift, too feline. You might say if you didn't know any better that it was some kind of cat.

Vida's Diary

4th October

I hate being ill on my own. Jonathan wasn't the greatest nurse, but he always did his best. At least he was around to fetch a glass of water and stroke the hair back from my face if I was sick. I want to cry thinking of this, but that will only make me feel worse. It's only a little bug, I tell myself, as I lie in bed listening to the house breathing around me. You're a grown woman of fifty-four, Vida. It's only some silly virus, a cold coming on perhaps... *you'll be fine by the morning.* I tell myself this over and over like a mantra.

The deep absolute silence of the country has never bothered me at night, indeed I've always relished it, but now it whispers such things in my ear... terrible things. *You are ill, Vida,* it whispers to me. *Don't kid yourself you can shake this one off. You are ill. Who will come? Who will look after you now Jonathan is gone? Why did you let him go, Vida? Why does your daughter despise you? Why are your friends all gone? You are alone, alone, alone. You will die here alone and no one will know.*

Sleep comes in snatches, dreams of ordure, of clouds of flies. I dream of a goddess with breasts ripe with milk and an owl between her thighs. What is her name? It seems important that I know her name, but the owl won't say. He only hoots... hooting me awake into a grey dawn. Morning but no sign of the

119

sun. At least I'm still here. It's morning at last. Thank God for morning.

Then, stumbling to the window, I see that garden, trees, hills have vanished into the mist like a child's pencil drawing, all grubbed out with a dirty rubber. There is no horizon. Nothing stirs. Not a breath of air. The house might be cling-wrapped, and me sealed tight within it, sealed in with nothing but my dream. The dream leaves a taint, an odour of something faintly remembered. It's perverse of me, masochistic even to try and summon it back, yet I must. I sit on the edge of my bed. Did the goddess speak to me? Did she leave a message? I shake myself and grope my way downstairs where I manage to prepare toast with a scrape of Marmite, and take it to my study.

There is one email in my inbox.

Good morning Vida
I hope you won't mind, but I tuned into your energy from a distance last night and sensed some blocks in your sacral chakra. The sacral as you may know is the source of all creativity. I have been meditating on the goddess on your behalf, and it seems she has spoken. Please let me know how your new book goes, and I will be working at this end to keep it flowing. Blessings, Rhiannon

I stop chewing, toast halfway to my mouth. The goddess has spoken? Is that why I dreamt of her last night? A cool sweat slicks at the back of my neck, between my breasts. Then I think to myself, at least someone *cares*. I don't understand what she means by 'tuning in to my energy' but it makes me feel less alone. I might have laughed at her 'blessings' once. Now I feel comforted by them. At the same time, I can't let her go on believing I'm writing. It makes me feel like a fraud. I hit reply:

Dear Rhiannon
You are very kind, but I have to tell you honestly that I am not writing at the moment. It has been my plan to retire for some months now. There is so much to do around the house and garden so I have plenty to keep me occupied. I do appreciate you sending the book, and all your kind thoughts and energy on my behalf. However I would not like to mislead or disappoint you. Please let me know if you'd like me to return your book. I'm sure you may find a worthier recipient!
Kind Regards
Vida

Once I've hit send, I go off to have a shower, but even though the water is scalding I'm shivering. I try an affirmation... *I am not ill. All is well. I am not ill.* Even so it seems prudent to check the fridge and cupboards for those invalid essentials: toilet rolls, tissues, drinks, tinned soup, yoghurts, Paracetamol. I toy with the idea of driving to Cregaron, partly to stock up on things like yoghurt but also just to be among people, people shopping, and going about their business. I put on my coat and then take it off again and sink into a chair. Truth is I don't have the energy to do anything. I creep back to my study, and see that a new email has boomeranged back into the inbox.

Dear Vida,

I can't quite believe what I'm hearing from you. Retire? Tend gardens? An artist never retires. The world needs more of your books, Vida. *I* need them.

No matter. I think the goddess has sent you to me, Vida. Let me explain.

I'm sure I mentioned before the work I do with Creative Artists? Recently, I've developed a programme specifically designed for removing such blocks to creativity, which I believe is unique. At the moment it's in the trial stages. You know, it's like a learning process on both sides. I will be straight with you. What I really need is a subject, a true Creative, someone who will give themselves up entirely to my programme.

I know it could free you, Vida. I wait for your response.

With love and blessings, Rhiannon.

An artist never retires. I might have been flattered by this once. Now I'm simply too tired to give it any more thought. I switch my computer off, and crawl back to bed to write up this journal.

5th October

It's around mid-morning as I write, but it might as well be midnight. I'm huddled at my desk in a huge sweater and the Mexican shawl Jonathan gave me draped around my shoulders. The bug, whatever it is my body's been nurturing these past days, has finally got a hold. I must be running a temperature although I can't check, as I haven't seen a thermometer in the house since Dory was a child. Come to think of it, perhaps I should just email Dory, let her know I'm not feeling so good. She might be up this way to visit another client, and be able to call in.

I haven't checked my emails since yesterday. Now my heart jolts as I switch on the computer, as if it knows what's waiting there. There are two new messages in my inbox, one from my local MP about a Save our hospital campaign, and one from my fan.

Vida, I think it better if we talk face to face about how I might help you. Am catching the 11 am train from Paddington.

Should be with you by early afternoon. Don't worry, I located your house with Google maps. I'll get a taxi from the station. Blessings, Rhiannon xx

I read this once, twice, three times. I can hardly take it in. I sag back in my chair as if from a blow. How she might help me? Come down? Here, to this house? It seems extraordinary. What kind of fan simply invites herself to an author's house on the basis of one coffee and an exchange of a few letters and emails? What can I do? I don't have her phone number, no mobile, nothing. There is no way I can contact her. And anyway, it's eleven fifteen; she's already on the train.

My fingers are frozen as I write this, and my heart skitters as if it's thinking about stopping altogether. All I want is to crawl back into bed and stay there. The thought of even normal visitors fills me with weariness, but a stranger!

8th October

At least I think it's the 8th. The past couple of days have been a blur. I must catch up now as I sit in bed, cradled by a nest of pillows that she has plumped and pounded to ensure my every comfort. I can hardly believe she has somehow become my nurse. But I race ahead. Let me pick up where I left off.

Reading back over my last entry, I see I must have drifted off pen in hand. I was woken by a knock at the door. My first thought was, dear God, how could I have slept that long? I rose shakily to my feet. Everything, walls, floor, furniture tilted sideways as I swayed across the hall.

'You can't come in.' I managed to open the front door a crack, enough to see the bags, plump and zipped, leaning up against fur-trimmed boots. 'Sorry, sorry you've had a wasted journey, but I can't see anyone now.' I waved her away as if I were a plague victim. 'I've got something. I'm sick. I'll only give it to you.'

She said stoutly, 'I'm not afraid of illness.' I believed her. She looked like someone who is never ill with her rosy cheeks and that mass of hair springing out from below a woolly hat. She peered past me into the hallway.

'Are you alone? Or have you got someone here to look after you?'

'No... I mean, yes. I'm calling a friend. Someone will be here soon.'

'I can't leave you alone like this.' She was inside before I could stop her. 'You look like death. Get to bed, and I'll ring for your doctor. Just give me the number.'

Her face was blurring as she spoke. She appeared to tilt, this way, that way, upside down; I wished she wouldn't keep moving like that. Then everything came adrift and I was falling. An arm clamped around my waist, breath huffed warm in my face. 'I've got you, you're okay... I've got you... come on, let's get you up to bed.'

When I opened my eyes again I was in bed and the world had stopped turning. The room was still. A woman was telling me she'd rung the doctor.

'I found the number in your telephone book. She's diagnosed flu. She says the entire area is down with it. You should stay in bed and keep warm.'

I struggled to understand for a moment what she was doing here. Then I remembered the email... **I'm catching the 11 am train from Paddington.** This was my fan, Rhiannon Townsend; the woman who wrote to me, who sent me the *Power of the Goddess* *in Everywoman,* which still lurks in its brown paper wrappings on the kitchen table, the woman I met in the café briefly. So she *did* catch that train. It seemed extraordinary. She'd come all this way to see me and I was too ill to do more than gawp like a goldfish as she stood there, vowing that my illness was a form of cleansing, a purge and nothing to do with viruses.

'Flu.' She sniffed at this diagnosis. 'It's a get-out when doctors can't be bothered to make home visits. Not that we need her. It's not flu. I would say it's a cleansing. You're clearing some emotional block. This is how it works. I don't think it's any accident that I arrived when I did.'

'I think,' I managed to croak,' I think I need to be sick.'

Perhaps she's right, perhaps it is no accident. All I know is I was so grateful to have her there, as I dozed between bouts of vomiting. It's amazing how she simply took charge of everything, bringing fresh water, helping me to the loo.

'You must be an angel of mercy,' I said as she held the glass to my lips. Her hair tickled my nose as she shook her head.

'No angel. The universe sent me. I knew there had to be a reason when I booked that train. You just rest. Don't worry about me. It's horrible to be ill alone.'

She fluffed my pillows, smoothed covers like my mother used to when I was small.

'If you like I could always send for your daughter?'

'Oh no, no, I don't want to bother Dory! She's so far away, and so busy.'

She asked, would I like her to read me something?

'Yes, yes, thank you, it's years since I was read to, but I think I would like that very much.'

I closed my eyes, and when I opened them again, there she was beside the bed with a volume of Sylvia Plath's poetry open in her lap.

'I found it on the shelves in your study; I hope you don't mind my looking in there? There didn't seem to be any books in your sitting room.'

I murmured something. Even turning my head to look at her made me nauseous. Illness is a kind of surrender I guess, a giving in, an allowing of things to happen, perhaps incredible and unexpected things.

Her voice was pitched low. She recited in reverent tones, something about a milk van and a cat lapping its grey paw.

There was more but my eyelids drooped. I drifted back to hear her talking about how Plath wrote in a kind of delirium.

'I read about it in her Journals. Have you read them? You must have. They're awe-inspiring, aren't they? A fascinating insight into the creative drive. She would scribble all through the night while her temperature raged. It was as if the illness somehow unleashed something. And it wasn't just stream of consciousness rambling, but beautifully crafted poetry.'

I didn't answer, just let her voice drone and drift like the bobbing motion of a boat in a harbour.

Then I heard her asking me if I felt an urge to put something down.

'I could fetch your notebook and pen if you like.'

'No... no... I don't want to write.' I turned my head away. The very thought of writing made me want to vomit again. I closed my eyes. She agreed it was far more sensible to rest.

'That was the problem with Sylvia; she was at the mercy of her muse, enslaved by her talent. That's why she burned out so quickly. We won't let that happen to you, Vida. You sleep now. I'll read some more, shall I?'

I remember being aware of her weight at the end of my bed, tightening the covers around me, pinning me. The musky reek of her perfume, the glint of silver at her wrist as she turned a page, the husky voice sending me back into fevered sleep.

9th October

Writing that last entry yesterday must have tired me out. It's awful the way I keep nodding off over the page like some very old woman. I'm still writing this in bed, but I'm feeling much brighter today. There is lemonade in a tall glass at my side, a jug full of Michaelmas daisies on the windowsill. From here, with the door wide open, I can hear her singing from the kitchen, some folksong about a carpenter's wife who runs off with a prince. Her voice is husky, the rise and fall of notes almost lulling me back to sleep. What is she making me? Last night it was soup, Leek and Carrot with a bite of lemon.

Oh, must put this away, strict instructions not to over-tire myself, and here she is, bringing me a lightly boiled egg, with little triangles of brown bread and butter; how spoiled I am!

10th October

I'm better, thank God. I'm dressed, and back in my study writing this. I feel weak but oddly clear-sighted, as if someone has just steam-cleaned the inside of my head, and left me empty. This room feels different. She must have been in here, dusting surfaces, rearranging my books. I could swear Cindy's new blockbuster was on the top shelf, its sugar-pink cover glowing next to my second-hand copy of *The Golden Bough*. Now it's on the bottom, lying flat and rejected on top of *The Writers' Yearbook*. There, I'll move it back again, pride of place, top shelf.

'Vida, I've just been admiring your herb patch.' She comes in without knocking, waving a ragged posy of thyme, lemon balm and rosemary at me.

'Oh!' I jump, feeling guilty for some reason about moving Cindy's book.

'I was just sorting through some papers...' I won't mention this journal, or she'll wonder why I'm wasting my time, and not writing the next book.

'Well, don't tire yourself.' She's going to rustle up a herb salad. Good for cleansing the blood, apparently.

'Thank you, and Rhiannon…'

'Yes?'

'I have to ask you. What made you decide to come down here? Your message, it sounded so urgent. I could have been away somewhere, I mean we hadn't discussed anything…'

'I came because you needed me. I told you I was at your service.'

'But… I don't quite understand. How did you know I was ill?'

'I knew.'

'But… I hadn't said anything.'

'*You* hadn't but your chakras did, they told me all I need to know.' She doesn't smile much, but when she does like now, I see how tiny her teeth are, like a baby's first teeth. Together with the rosy cheeks and mass of curls it's somehow endearing. Unsmiling she is quite a different person.

'My chakras?'

'It's a Hindu word for the seven wheels of energy along your spine. Sometimes the energy stops flowing, becomes stagnant and the chakras get out of balance.'

I know what chakras are. This is the New Age after all.

'So, my chakras have been talking behind my back.'

Quite a witticism, I think, considering my convalescent state. I'm disappointed when it fails to trigger that smile again.

'Your sacral chakra is stagnant; in fact it's virtually locked. No wonder your life force has been draining away.' Her manner is matter-of-fact, as if there is nothing exceptional about this diagnosis, nothing unusual about dumping her life to hurtle west on a three-hour train journey for this strange intuitive mission of mercy.

'But…' I continue, 'I'm a stranger to you. Why would you drop everything to race down to a stranger's bedside? I still don't quite get it.'

'Vida.' She shakes her head. 'You're not a stranger to me. You must learn to value yourself more. I told you before; I came to you because you *needed* me. The universe answered your need, and sent me along, and that's all there is to it.'

'Well…' To avoid the intensity of her gaze, I fiddle with some papers. 'It was very generous of the universe. I don't know what I'd have done without you.'

She demurs but I can see this pleases her.

How long is she planning to stay? That's the other thing I've wanted to ask, but it sounds downright rude. I don't mind if she stays another day or two. God knows I have few enough friends. I reason that such devotion wouldn't have been so unusual in past centuries when men of words routinely attracted disciples, people so devoted to their art they would willingly take care of the domestic side of things. Even so, her belief in me is a kind of pressure. I feel as if by *not* writing, I am letting her down.

8th October

It's almost ten, a cold still night and the moon bright at my study window. I must get this down while

Rhiannon makes us a hot Carob drink. I woke up this morning, resolved to ask how long she was staying. Not that I mind, but it would be useful to know. All through breakfast I kept dropping hints... how well I felt now... actually I was thinking about visiting my daughter for a few days in London, now I was better, and so on. I suggested that her clients would be missing her.

'I mustn't keep you from your work a moment longer.'

At this she took both of my hands in hers in ceremonial fashion, the way circle dancers do when they're waiting for the music to signal the first gallop. She gave me that grave shake of her head, saying I should think of myself for once.

'I'm touched that you should worry about my work, Vida, truly, but it's not your concern. Anyway, whenever I need the business, I just ask the universe to send me more clients. It's a question of tapping into the universal flow. It never fails me.'

With that, she went off to wash up the breakfast things. I pushed her gently to one side. 'No, really, I can do my own washing up, you mustn't pamper me. Actually, it's my shopping day today, so I'll just do this and then I must pop into town.'

She looked at me. 'Do you ever shop in Ludlow? I've always wanted to visit there. I had a glimpse of the castle from the train.'

⚜ ⚜ ⚜

So, Ludlow it was. Escorting her around town seemed the very least I could do after the fuss she'd made of me. But, as we wandered down King Street towards the Buttercross, Rhiannon exclaiming over every cobble and leaded windowpane, it was hard to focus on everyday things like bread and bananas. A damp wind funnelled through the narrow streets, which seem always to lie in shadow. Outside St. Lawrence's Church, I suggested she go and look at the famous Misericords. 'They're very fine. I'll just be in the square over by the farmers' stalls.'

She was reluctant to leave me, but I explained that I'm not keen on church interiors, which is true. While she was gone, I mooched half-heartedly about the market stalls, my only purchase a half dozen free-range eggs, my thoughts so blurred I could barely count out my change to pay for them. Then I saw her, flouncing across the square towards me, her expression fierce. Was something wrong?

'The Misericords. Dunking stools and witches, and nagging wives, all that post St. Augustine misogyny.' She glanced over her shoulder in the direction of the church. 'I should have known better than to go inside.'

I was sorry this had upset her so much. It was the first time I'd seen her disconcerted in any way, and curiously it made me feel stronger. We moved on to De Greys for tea and scones.

'My treat.' I pushed away her embroidered purse, and snapped open my wallet. 'A little thank you for all you've done.'

'It's nothing, I told you. Anyone would have done the same.'

She began talking then about London, how she had 'outgrown' it, how she could hear the streets ringing with the marching feet of the Roman legions. Then she folded her arms as if she'd come to a momentous decision about something:

'You know, Vida, I feel I could really settle in a place like this.'

On the way back to the car park we passed Bridge Books.

Rhiannon halted over the reduced stand in the doorway. 'Do you mind if we go in? You can tell so much about a place from its bookshops.'

Of course I didn't mind. I loitered close to the door, leafing through a book about old roses, the luscious photographs making me long for summer. Within minutes she was bustling back down the aisle towards me, her expression heated, urgent. When she spoke it was in the tone of someone trying to break bad news gently.

'Vida, I've just checked out the "T's" in fiction. They don't have a single one of your books. Not even *The Gingerbread House*.'

This was no surprise to me. I explained that it was hardly a current title.

'Vida, you are a local author. If a bookshop can't support its local authors, what is the point? What kind of philistines are they in this place?'

'It's a family business.' I wished she'd keep her voice down. 'They can't afford to stock everything, and David the owner does his best. He organized a book signing for my last book...' I broke off, recalling that mortifying day when only one customer had shown up.

How thankful I was he wasn't behind the counter today, with his affable dusty boiled-egg look, watching his eyes flicker with faint recognition as he tried to recall my face.

'Rhiannon, wait...' She wasn't going to, was she? Oh my God, she was! She was at the counter already, demanding to know if my last title was in stock.

'*The Gingerbread House*,' I heard her say, uttering the title, *my* title, as if it was an incantation, as if it somehow belonged to her, as if *she* was the author herself. 'You must have that one at least.'

David's young assistant stared fearfully at the computer screen, tapping keys. A shy boy, with an inflamed rash pulsating behind a floppy fringe, he muttered apologetically: they didn't appear to have it in stock.

'Is it still in print? We could order it for you?'

'Not in stock? Tell me you're joking. Do you know who this is?'

To my utter mortification, Rhiannon turned to indicate me.

'This is Vida Tremayne, author of *The Gingerbread House*, winner of the Peccadill Prize. You have heard of the Peccadill Prize?'

I hovered speechless while, registering an awkward customer, the poor boy pushed at his fringe. 'I... sorry...'

'And she lives on your very doorstep. She is a local author, and you're very privileged to have her…'

'Rhiannon! It doesn't matter. Please…'

Blithely ignoring me, she went on. 'Look, can you get me the manager please?'

'No!' I interrupted. 'No, that won't be necessary. Rhiannon, I'm going now.'

Since trying to wrestle her from the shop would only create a worse spectacle, I stalked out ahead, hoping she would follow. She did. Although not without some parting threat to the assistant, I was sure.

I didn't wait for her to catch me up. I put on a spurt, hardly pausing for breath until I reached the car. I was already seated at the wheel by the time she caught up.

'Something wrong, Vida?'

She looked quietly triumphant, as if she'd scored a point scaring that poor spotty boy to death on my account.

I laughed. 'Wrong? What could possibly be wrong? You've just humiliated me, made a complete exhibition of me in my local bookshop, thank you.'

'Vida, if I can't speak up for you, then who can?'

'My agent does that job perfectly well'. Actually she doesn't, but I've never mentioned Fee Moody to Rhiannon and have no intention of doing so.

She makes a dismissive humphing sound. 'These people have no appreciation.'

'Rhiannon, forgive me, but my sales, my work, my books are really my business!'

She was silent, infuriatingly superior beside me, like a mother humouring a toddler's tantrum. I plunged ahead into the silence, unable to stop myself.

'You seem to have some, I don't know, some fixation about me being a literary genius. Sorry to disillusion you, but I'm not. I'll admit I once wrote a good book, but that was at my peak, I *peaked*, understand?'

'No, no.' She twists round in the passenger seat to face me. 'The best is yet to come, believe me.'

I slapped the steering wheel. 'You're wrong. If you want the truth, I haven't written for months apart from my diary, and the bloody shopping list. I'm getting old. I'm dried up. Blocked. Do you understand? I am finished as a writer. *There will be no more books!*'

My words were intended to shock her, but in fact it was *me* they shocked the most. No more books. I stared bleakly out through the windscreen, smeary with bird shit and dead fly. Did I really believe that? Was my future really that bleak?

In the brief silence that followed I could hear her breathing. When she spoke it was in the steady reasoned voice of an adult dealing with a juvenile delinquent:

'You say you're "dried up". There's no such thing as "dried up". Dig down deep enough and you'll always find the wellspring; even in the desert, you'll find it. I understand how you feel, really I do, but just answer me one thing. If you had the chance, would you *like* to write again, something wonderful, something the world can't ignore?'

A dry laugh choked out of me, more like a gulp. 'It's what I do, isn't it? It's all I can do.'

'Then, listen to me Vida.' She moved closer, so I was forced to face her. 'This is what I propose. Give me a month, just a month at your house, and I will free you. I promise, in one month you will be working again, you will be writing like an angel.'

'I don't know…'

'One month. But you have to submit yourself absolutely to my programme.'

'Programme. What programme?'

'The programme I've been working on with my students, I wrote to you about it, remember? About removing creative blocks?'

'Oh those.' I sighed, then shifted uncomfortably. Her eyes were so earnest, so compelling. It's hard to ignore someone else's belief in you. Even Jonathan, although he was pleased for me, never had that confidence in my work.

'You have such faith in me. I'm flattered really but…'

'I'm not doing this to flatter you. I just hate to see talent like yours go to waste, that's all.'

I didn't say 'yes'. Not right then. I was still smouldering after that debacle in the shop. She didn't press me further. She turned back to face the windscreen and snapped on her seat belt, as if the decision had been made. Something about this, about her certainty half convinced me as we drove back to the house. By the time we'd pulled up in the drive, I'd made up my mind to accept her strange offer. Such faith is rare. Such friendship is rare. And who else do I have to care?

'Vida!' She's calling now from the kitchen. 'D'you want your drink in the study?'

'No... no, I'm just coming.' I must put this away, and go and be companionable. The Programme will begin in a few days' time, she says. *The Programme.* I have no idea what it entails. I admit to feeling apprehensive. What exactly have I committed to? But, there it is. I agreed to her offer. I said yes. I promised. I hate going back on my word. And anyway, how on earth can I wriggle out of it now?

8TH FEBRUARY
DORY

It's absurd how edgy Dory feels as she waits for Rhiannon to get back from the hospital. She fishes another pecan Danish from its plastic wrapper and gobbles it in a few mouthfuls. Grains of sugar stick to the corners of her mouth, and she licks them away as she types the blurb for Vida's house sale.

The Gingerbread House is a fairytale hideaway, ideal for those seeking rural tranquillity. Too wordy. She hits delete and starts again.

Rarely on the market, early viewing is advised for the Gingerbread House.

No, that's not right either, but there's no way she's going to entrust this task to some yokel estate agent with all the imagination of a lobotomized sheep. She's looked in the windows. She's seen their blurbs and they suck, frankly. Of course, christening it after Vida's famous novel could be a problem. This has always been Vida's private name for the place, but on the title deeds the cottage is simply No. 7 The Thatch, Long Lane. Not an address that's likely to grab any starry-eyed Londoners looking for the dream.

'Sorry, Mother,' she whispers. 'Sorry I have to do this stuff, but someone has to.'

She brushes pastry crumbs from the Boden cable cardigan that looked great on the catalogue models, but does little to keep her warm. If she stays here much longer she'll lose every last shred of style and vanity she ever had. She'll end up barrel-shaped like one of those Russian dolls, layered in bulky hand-knits, Rhiannon-style. Rhiannon. She looks up from the laptop. What *can* she be doing at the hospital all this time? It's seven now and it's been dark since she hurried indoors at four o'clock, after seeing that shadowy cat thing by the woods. Better not to think about that now.

Ten minutes pass before she hears Vida's car reversing into the drive. At last! Snapping the laptop closed, she moves to the Rayburn and pokes at the charcoaled remains of a log.

'Ooof, it's lovely and cosy in here.' Rhiannon comes in huffing contentedly the way people do after a hard day's work, a job well done.

'Hi. How is she? How's Mum doing?' Dory barely glances up as she hefts a fresh log on top of the charcoal, dusting off her palms.

'She's doing fine.' Rhiannon shrugs off her coat, that musty velvet scent thickening the air. It's one of those breezy reassurances that mean nothing. The kind you make to a child, not a grown woman. Dory tries to sound more casual than she feels.

'You've been a long time. Have you been with Vida all day?'

'Yes, pet. Have you been lonely here? It's been such a miserable day.'

'I've been working.'

Rhiannon flops into a chair and scrunches the mass of hair from her face into a butterfly clip. Bereft of curls she looks like an ancient child, fine lines scored around eyes and mouth, like the pattern a knife makes in pastry.

'I'm so pleased you're getting your work done. There's nothing for you to worry about, really. Vida's quite comfortable.'

'Comfortable!' Dory clatters the poker back in its resting place. 'What does that mean exactly? Is she lolling on a heap of silk cushions, eating peeled grapes or something? Sorry, I didn't mean it that way. It's just that hospitals always use that word "comfortable" and it drives me nuts.'

Rhiannon shows no sign of taking offence. She eases her tiny feet out of her boots and coaxes them into the knitted slippers she wears around the house.

'When I say "comfortable", I just mean she's sitting in her chair as usual. Don't worry. Vida's not in any pain or distress. I think there may even be some sign of improvement.'

'How? What do you mean?'

'Well,' Rhiannon frowns into the middle distance, 'I've just been sitting with her and talking, you know. I had a sense of something, some flicker of interest in her eyes. She didn't speak, but I know she understood what I was saying.'

'Do you think so?' Dory relaxes her arms slightly. She's been standing with them folded across her midriff like a barricade. Perhaps there is hope after all. Perhaps she's been too hasty with that blurb. She sighs as she drops back into her chair.

'You're so good to her. It beats me how you can sit in that place for hours on end. I can't think what you talk about to her. I wish I had your patience, I really do.'

Rhiannon shrugs this off, and says she considers it a privilege.

'When Vida comes out of her trance, she'll need someone by her, someone she knows and trusts. Think how frightening it would be to wake up in that ward surrounded by strangers.'

Dory does think. She's right, of course. But surely that person Vida knows and trusts should be her daughter. She remembers the one time she was in hospital herself as a young child. It had been a minor operation on her thumb, which was growing at an odd angle. When she awoke, parched and sick from the anaesthetic, her mother was right there beside her, stroking her arm, holding water to her lips. How old would she have been then? Six? Seven? Vida had sat reading *James and the Giant Peach* to her for hours. And that time when she had the flu and passed it on to Vida. They had snuggled up in bed together for over a week, watching silly programmes on TV and coughing companionably while Dad scurried about with hot drinks and Paracetamol. The memory of this is disturbing somehow. It conflicts with her preferred version of her childhood, grow-ing up with a dreamy, disengaged mother, misun-derstood, and generally sold short. She has to admit that Vida was good when she was ill: kind and nur-turing. Probably she'd been easier to deal with when she was laid low, and not bouncing and whooping about the place.

She tells Rhiannon, 'They used to call me Little Miss Fidget Bum. I've never been able to sit still for more than five minutes.'

She's fidgeting now, shifting from one buttock to the other under Rhiannon's scrutiny. Has she ever tested for food allergies, Rhiannon wants to know? Hyperactivity can be due to sugar intake.

'Oh I don't know. I mean it's not a medical con-dition, it's just what Mum and Dad called "the fidg-ets." Everyone gets restless from time to time don't they?'

Does Rhiannon know just how many Danish Pastries she's scoffed today? She brushes a hand across her mouth to check for a sugar moustache.

'That's why I started on the job in the hallway.' She nods towards the door. She's been waiting for Rhiannon to mention the devastation, but all she says now is, 'Wasn't that a William Morris print?'

'Was it?' She had no idea. She's only got the vaguest notion of who William Morris was after see-ing some TV soap opera about the Pre-Raphaelite brotherhood, which had a rather sexy Rossetti in it. 'It needed brightening up anyway. That wallpaper was creepy. It will be brighter for...' She hesitates before using the words 'potential buyers'; it sounds so cold-blooded, so heartless. 'It'll be brighter for Vida when she gets out.'

Rhiannon makes no comment, yet her disapproval is obvious as she rummages in her bag and begins to unload packages.

'Now, what shall I make us for supper?'

❧ ❧ ❧

Back at home, Dory likes to boast that she never dreams. Or at least she never recalls them. She is one of those people who doesn't need much sleep; in fact she's been known to sit up most of the night doing her accounts or checking emails. Her sleep when it comes is short and blissfully blank on the whole. Only if she has a nail-biting deal on might she dream of houses, their empty rooms opening onto one another in a maze of light.

Tonight is different. She is so tired after lying awake the night before, worrying about Vida that she goes to bed early. Almost immediately sleep grabs her and deposits her in a field of waist-high grass. She looks around her. The grass is dry and yellow as savannah. Above her, the sky is blue as in a child's painting. It's some time before she sees the cat. At first only the tip of its tail is visible, charting a course through the grass ocean like a shark's fin. She watches it for a moment. She watches the tail-tip halt, and then the spiralling twist of the grass as the animal turns, faces her. Only when she sees the prick

145

of two black ears does she realize that if she has seen the cat, then the cat has also seen *her.*

Run! She instructs her legs, but of course they don't move. In dreams it's better not to have legs at all for all the good they are.

At this point she wakes up, and burrows closer to Dan. His bulk beside her is reassuring; she listens to his breathing, the rise and fall of his chest. God bless Dan, wonderful Dan, who has driven down late, and let himself in the back door, and crept into her bed while she slept.

'You wouldn't believe the dream I just had.' She burrows closer. Dan smells different, his usual clean pine-woody scent replaced by something meatier, more robust. She inhales it. It's not unpleasant. In fact it's damn sexy.

'Dan? Are you awake?' God how she wants him, right now, deep inside her. She can't wait until morning. She can't wait another minute. She slides one leg across him. Shrugging off her pyjama jacket she presses her breasts tight against his chest, kneading them into the pelt of thick warm fur. So much fur. How did it get to be so thick, so luxuriant, so abrasive, rasping against her skin? Beneath the fur is something lithe, muscular, primal. But... wait a minute; Dan is blond, virtually smooth. Desire gives way to repugnance. Her body quivers, reels itself free. There is a suction sound, repulsive as flesh parts from fur, from flesh...

She screams. And this time the scream wakes up her properly, and there is nothing beside her but empty space.

'Jesus! Shit, what was that about?' She sits up, turns on the light. The girl in the portrait looks as if she has closed her eyes, looks like someone else entirely.

'Shit, shit, shit!'

She slides her legs out of bed and lights up a cigarette, hands trembling. Her heart is pumping like crazy. She's angry more than anything.

'Fuck you, Dan!' She realizes suddenly that she's clutching one of the cushions to her chest like a baby, and hurls it across the room in disgust. This was the cruellest part of the dream, the illusion that Dan was really here breathing beside her. Now the gap where he should be hits her like a physical ache.

She pulls a sweater over her pyjamas and pads downstairs. This is the one thing she promised herself not to do, picking up the telephone, ringing Dan's mobile, like some feeble needy ditched little girlie, but too late, it's already ringing. Any minute now and she'll hear his voice, 'Yup?' That's Dan's standard answer, a chummy ready for anyone: 'Yup?' He uses it on friends, family and cold callers alike. She's often teased him about his telephone manner, but now she longs for that 'Yup' so much that when a woman's voice answers her heart plummets.

'Yes?' The woman, whoever she is, sounds very pissed off.

'Dan?' She almost whimpers, shocked to think how quickly he's found a replacement.

'Who is this?'

'This is Dan's sister. He left his mobile on the sofa, and I've just got in from my shift. D'you know what time it is?'

Ah, only his sister! She tries not to show her relief, and apologizes, 'Oh, Maisie isn't it? Hallo there. Dan's told me all about you. Sorry it's so late.' There's no clock in the hall, but she guesses it's well after midnight. 'Is Dan there?'

'He's asleep upstairs actually.'

'Oh, but can't you wake him up?'

'Are you Dory?'

'Yes. Yes, I am.' It's more an accusation than question; she wonders what Dan can have been saying about her. She's heard all about his bossy sister Maisie, who is a nurse and lives in Finsbury Park, but she's never actually met her.

Maisie is clearly too tired for pleasantries, for she snaps, 'Hasn't Dan told you? He's staying with me for a while. He told me you'd kicked him out. He's been looking after my kids while I do evening shifts.'

'I see.' Dory gathers herself. There is nothing like a dose of hostility to get the adrenaline pumping again.

She says coolly, 'Look, I'd really appreciate it if you could go and wake Dan, because I do need to speak to him.'

'I'm sure I couldn't wake him if I tried. Dan's totally flaked out, my Chloe is teething and she's been giving him and Ailsa a hard time.'

'Ailsa?'

'Dan's girlfriend. She's staying here too.'

Clearly his sister relishes passing on this news. She fills her in on the details, how Ailsa and Dan have known each other for years, but only recently started going out and she's delighted because they are so good together, and...

But by this time she's slammed the receiver down. She's amazed to find that she's trembling all over.

'Is everything all right?' Rhiannon is tramping down the stairs, wrapping her kimono around her. 'I thought I heard your voice. Is it Vida? Is it the hospital?'

Dory sinks onto the chest by the phone, where Vida keeps the extra blankets. She feels almost too miserable to answer, but she manages to murmur, 'No, not the hospital. Just a private call. Sorry if I woke you.'

'Heh... what is it? What's wrong?'

Rhiannon is bending over her, her face all soft with concern, with understanding.

'It's Dan,' Dory blurts. 'My boyfriend – ex-boyfriend, I mean. He's got someone else. I hadn't expected him to get fixed up so soon. We only broke up before Christmas. We had a row about me working evenings and weekends. Dan doesn't get it. He likes people around all the time, he likes to cook for a crowd, he likes to party. He didn't get that it's not much fun when you have to get up at five in the morning to drive clients from house to bloody house, praying that just one of them hits the spot. I told him to get out. But just now I had this terrible nightmare about him, that he was here beside me, and then he wasn't, it wasn't him, it was some… *creature* lying next to me. I hate this place. It gives me the creeps. I need to get back home. I need to work.'

She can't help herself, the tears are already pumping. She can hear herself snorting and blubbing like some baby.

'Sorry, sorry. It's not like me to do this. I never cry.'

'Shh… shhh… everyone has to cry some time.' Rhiannon's arm is heavy around her shoulders, steering her to the kitchen. She's murmuring something about the stress, the strain of the last few weeks.

'It's shock. You've been bottling it all up. It has to come out some time. I'll make us a hot drink.'

Vaguely Dory recalls Vida doing this, making her cocoa in the early hours, when she came home once crying after being dumped by her first love, Nelson Hayward, at a party. How she had flinched away from her mother's embrace, screaming, 'My life is shit! I don't want any bloody cocoa. Cocoa won't help me, it's for sodding old people!'

She'd been what… fifteen, sixteen? Her first broken heart. And the way Vida looked at her, that pain deep in her eyes.

She finds herself wondering as she watches Rhiannon pouring milk into a pan and setting it on the Rayburn. What would Rhiannon be like as a mother? She seems a natural. Why doesn't she have kids of her own?

Rhiannon dribbles out a couple of pink Valerian pills on the table. 'Take these. Go on. They won't hurt you.'

'Thanks, but I'll pass. I'm not sure I want to sleep after the dream I've just had.'

Rhiannon plonks down two mugs of the kind of milky drink that would normally make her throw up, and sits down opposite. The skin of her upper chest where the kimono gapes open has the tawny look of weathered terracotta. Creases run diagonally from her cleavage as she folds her arms beneath her breasts and leans forward. Beneath the harsh glare of the kitchen light she looks old, older than Dory first imagined. Her eyes are like velvet buttons.

'Dreams are a message to us from the unconscious. Would you like to share it with me?'

'I'd rather not, if you don't mind.'

'It might help to get it out of your system. I work a lot with dreams. It's surprising what we can learn from them.'

'I'd rather forget about this one.'

'You said '*a creature...*''

'Oh please. I can't stand people who go on about their dreams. It's so boring.' She takes a gulp of the drink. 'Anyway, it was stupid of me to ring him. I must've been half asleep. It's over and that's all there is to it. I seem to have a talent for ruining things.'

Rhiannon shakes her head. 'Maybe he wasn't right for you. There could be someone else waiting right around the corner.'

Dory snorts. 'Hah, I've heard that before. And if there is someone, I'll hardly find him stuck down here in the middle of nowhere, will I.'

Rhiannon leans closer, her eyes urgent. 'So why don't you go back to London?'

Dory stirs sugar into the already sweet drink. 'It's not that easy with Mum and the house.'

Rhiannon cuts through her objections with an emphatic shake of her locks. 'It's as easy as packing a bag and driving back south.' She holds up her hands. 'I'm here. I've told you that already. I can be here for Vida just as long as you need me to be.'

Dory can feel herself wavering. She is so desperate to get back to her life, and Vida will hardly know she's not there. As for the house, Brendan Riley could get on with the renovations while she's away. Rhiannon could oversee the operations. She doesn't need to tell Rhiannon she intends to sell it. Not yet anyway.

She sighs. 'I can't go just yet. Harvey's arranged a viewing near Ludlow next week. I'd have to stay and show the clients around first. Perhaps... once I've got that over with, if you're sure.'

Rhiannon smiles. 'I never say anything I don't mean.'

'Well then,' Dory looks at her, 'maybe I will do that, just for a while. Rhiannon, you've been such a star. I know I've been a bit edgy. You probably think I'm an ungrateful cow. Well, I *am* grateful. Quite honestly I don't know how I'd have managed without you.'

Oh Lord, she's weeping again. Rhiannon is coming around the table, pulling her into a hug, patting and soothing.

She mumbles into Rhiannon's chest, 'I do miss her. Mum, I mean. I'm so worried about her. Okay, she hasn't been the most perfect mother in the world. We've had our differences, but I've been mean to her in the past, and now I can't tell her...'

'Shh. Shh,' Rhiannon says, 'of course you miss her. She'll be all right, you'll see. I'll take care of her. Vida will be just fine. And so will you, Dory. So will you.'

Vida's Diary

Tuesday 9th October

Such twilights we've had these past few days! Through my study window the sky is all daubed in gold and smoky pinks and violets the colour of the whinberries we gathered up on the hill this morning. I've snuck in here to catch up with this diary while Rhiannon makes us a tart from our hoard. Funny how I say this, as if it's perfectly normal to have a friend in the kitchen making a pie, yet I still have to pinch myself to prove it's real. Yes, a *friend*. She's turned out to be such good company, my fan. We haven't begun on the Programme as yet. Rhiannon thinks we should delay until I've built up my strength a bit after my illness. That's fine by me. I'm in no hurry to begin, if I'm honest. This past week has been a pleasure. We've talked endlessly about books, naturally. I've also let slip a few things about Jon, the break-up of our marriage and so on. I suppose it's something of a relief to get it all off my chest.

Today I felt slightly guilty about it. It seemed my outpourings were all a bit one-sided. What about *her* life? What about her family, her problems, her goals in life? She always deflects such conversations if I ask. I made a concerted effort this morning to draw her out.

'Did you write stories as a child, Rhiannon?' I asked her. It was a casual enough question. We were threading our way across the sheep tracks through the heather and rabbit droppings, searching for the last of the whinberries. A bedraggled ewe gave us a haughty stare as we passed and stamped one hoof like a flamenco dancer as if in a show of temperament before fleeing to join the rest of the flock. Buzzards wheeled about the Devil's Chair to the north, and I could hear a chiff-chaff cheeping its monotonous tune from a nearby gorse bush although I couldn't quite see it.

Rhiannon crouched low, her hair masking her face.

'Stories? I can't remember.'

I couldn't read her expression, but I sensed she didn't care for this line of questioning. I set down my basket between us, and pressed further. She must have been a bookish child though, I suggested.

'I imagine your mother must have read to you from a young age.'

Even as I said this I realized my theory was flawed. All those bedtime stories and weekly library visits had had little effect on Dory; in fact one might say a reverse effect. But Rhiannon seemed to have little memory of her mother reading to her. I watched as her purple-stained fingers teased the berries from their stalks.

'We could make jam,' she murmured as if to herself, 'but we'll need more than one basket for that. It'll have to be a tart.'

'Do your family live in London?' I asked her.

She straightened with some effort, the way people do when they're carrying too much weight.

'This might sound strange to you, but I find blood ties over-rated. I've seen the damage that families can do to each other. It's friendship that matters.'

The way she said this with an odd blank expression on her face told me the subject was closed, yet I couldn't resist asking, 'But haven't you ever wanted children?'

'No. I don't believe in happy families.' We were silent a moment. She began rummaging through the berries in her basket, but I could tell her mind wasn't on jam. When finally she spoke it was with reluctance, as if I'd wrung a confession from her by trick or torture.

'My mother didn't want children. She told me so many times. She told me how she jumped up and down the stairs to get rid of me when she was five months pregnant. She showed me the varicose veins on her legs, and told me they were all my fault. She thought she was carrying a monster apparently. The devil's child.'

I drew in a deep breath. 'Oh... dear God, I'm so sorry. You don't have to talk about it if you don't want to.'

'It's all right. I don't hold any grudge against her. She was a sick woman. She had undiagnosed schizophrenia for many years. My father abandoned her when she was pregnant, and my grandparents didn't want to know. I had two mothers. There was the mother who sent me off to school in clean socks, with a packed lunch. Then there was the monster who trashed my room, tore up my story notebooks. I never quite knew which one of them I would come home to find.'

'Your story notebooks? Oh, you wrote as a child? But that's so tragic... oh Rhiannon...'

'Stories were my means of escape. Magic, mermaids, fairies, dragons... especially dragons. I knew all about dragons. My mother said they were evil and the only thing to do was burn the evil out of them. We had an enormous bonfire in the garden. The fire got out of control and the man next door called the police. Shortly after that she was sectioned and I was taken into care.'

'Dear God. How old were you?'

'Eleven, I think. Close to my twelfth birthday in fact.'

I was so staggered by this confession I hardly knew how to react. My first instinct was to give her a hug, but she looked so in control it didn't seem appropriate. Perhaps she had lived with this particular demon for so long she'd come to terms with it. From her measured tone she might have been discussing one of her clients.

'I'm so sorry,' I said again.

'There's no need for you to apologize. It's not your fault. But you see now why stories are so important to me. Even the ones that burned on that fire, I knew they were safe inside me, here all the time you know?'

She laid her right hand across her belly, spreading her fingers. It struck me as strange that she did that. Stories came from the heart, didn't they? They were heartfelt. Or that's how I saw it. But maybe for Rhiannon, they came after all from a much deeper place. My eyes filled up at the idea of this child watching her little notebooks reduced to ashes. What an extraordinary person she must be to survive intact.

'I knew I could write more. You know, like Mother Spider, I could spin them from here, from my gut.' Again she fanned her fingers protectively across her middle, almost the way pregnant women do caressing their unborn children. I imagined those stories as skeins of black silk, spinning their intricate patterns out of this woman's pain.

'When I went into Care, my library ticket was the most important thing in the world to me. I read everything I could get my hands on. Those stories, those authors saved my life.' Her eyes locked with mine. 'For me those authors, my favourite writers were my saviours, my friends, you know? That's why I love to work with creative people like you. It's my whole reason for the Programme.'

'But you didn't write any more yourself? I'm just wondering why you didn't become a writer.'

I had a feeling she didn't like this question. The hand dropped back to the basket, and she glanced back at the berries.

She said in a dismissive voice. 'I scribbled some childish poems, that's all. I suppose I didn't have the gift. I was happier to read other people's stories.'

'Your mother... is she still alive?'

'She died when I was in my twenties. That's really all I want to say about her.' She dusted some dried, powdery bracken from her jacket, adding in a brusque tone. 'You understand now why I don't buy into the myth of the happy family. And forgive me, Vida, but can you say your daughter has brought you happiness? I saw how distressed you were after that phone call the other day.'

I was a bit taken aback at this. I'd rung Dory the day before yesterday, and she'd been quite sharp with me. I was upset, but hadn't realized this showed so much.

'Oh,' I said, 'Dory doesn't have a lot of time for writers. She thinks we are all self-absorbed, and selfish...' I laughed. 'Maybe she has a point.'

'Selfish?' Rhiannon clucked disapproval.

'You know, the way we sometimes use friends and family as material. Dory thought I was writing about her, you see, in *The Gingerbread House*. She thought she was spoiled little Hetty Jackson. She wasn't, of course. I made Hetty up entirely...'

At this Rhiannon seized my hand and looked so earnestly into my face I was shocked. An artist should never apologize, she said.

'People are your material, Vida. Nothing and no one is sacrosanct.'

'Well, I...' It was embarrassing standing there in the middle of the moor, hand in hand. I withdrew my hand gently. 'Maybe, but I've never consciously used my family as material. Dory never reads my books, so she wouldn't have known in any case. A friend of hers who read it imagined a likeness and read her out a couple of paragraphs.'

Rhiannon muttered something about my guilt complex.

'Your daughter resents your success. Isn't that the trouble? This could be the source of your block, have you thought of that? Your husband left, and now you're afraid that success will alienate your daughter further.'

'Oh no, I…it's not that… I…' It astonished me how the tables had turned. Somehow or other, she'd deflected the revelation of her dark past, and turned the spotlight on my relationship with Dory.

Rather than dig a deeper hole for myself, I pointed to the rocky outcrop ahead of us in the distance:

'Do you see the "Devil's Chair"? I'd love to use it as a setting, but Mary Webb got there first.'

This interested Rhiannon very much, so we spent the rest of the morning clambering about the rocks and no more was said about Dory, or families. When we got back to the house, Rhiannon said I was looking so well now that in a couple of more days we could start the Programme. I'm pleased, because the more we delay it the more apprehensive I begin to feel, somehow.

Thursday 11th October

The Programme begins tomorrow! I'm scribbling this in bed, because once it gets underway, I'm not supposed to write as much as a shopping list. Just as well Rhiannon gave me what she calls the contract, *after* supper tonight, and not before. I'm looking at it as I write and, well, let's say it's a bit more serious than I'd imagined. I doubt I'd have enjoyed the pheasant, roast parsnips and sweet potatoes quite as much if I'd seen it before. Pudding was chocolate tart and whipped cream, along with the last of the whinberry tart, all washed down with wine the colour of ripe damsons. It was a celebratory dinner, Rhiannon said. I was so touched by her efforts. She'd been busy in the kitchen for hours. As we sat down to eat she raised her glass to me across the table.

'To you, Vida Tremayne. Here's to the last night of the old you! Why don't you say it?'

'Say what?'

'Just say, *To the last night of the old me.*'

To the last night of the old me.' I said it with ironic emphasis. She looked gratified and I suddenly felt like a child learning my lessons.

'You know, this is going to be an adventure. Do you trust me, Vida?'

'Yes, of course I do. We wouldn't be here otherwise.'

'Good. Because you have to *trust me*. I'm saying this now, because I'm going to show you the Programme later on. Some of it might strike you as a bit strange. But we have to keep our end goal in sight, the fabulous book you will write.'

'Oh, that.' I grimaced.

'It *will* be fabulous,' she insisted. 'You have to believe that it will be.' She began talking about how we create our own realities. Believe in success and success follows.

As I tucked into the perfectly crisp potatoes, I felt uneasy about such a one-sided deal and told her so directly. Would she, I suggested, accept any payment from me?

'I can't just keep taking and taking from you, and you've already invested so much time in me. I'd be more than happy to pay. I'm not short of money. *The Gingerbread House* is still selling, thank God, and I'm more than comfortable.'

The idea of money seemed to horrify her; it was almost an insult.

'I thought we were friends, Vida.'

'It's kind of you to say that, but...'

'And don't friends help one another? I consider it an honour to be part of the process. By working with a great novelist like you, don't you see, I can get *inside* the process; I can see what it feels like from the source.'

This was so heartfelt, so genuine, I felt my eyes filling up.

'You've been so good to me, Rhiannon,' I said. 'Well, almost more than a friend, more like a daughter. I really value that. There are so few people I can talk to about work these days. Most of my writer friends have drifted away over the past year or two, even my friend Cindy. You can't blame them. No one likes failure. People get tired of editing the good bits

out of their news, the big advances, the launch parties, the fan mail, the Amazon ratings in case they
make you feel jealous. Even though I'm not at all
jealous, they imagine I must be. Bitter and twisted
is the phrase I think. They think in my place they
would be bitter and twisted.'

Rhiannon reached out briefly to touch my hand.
'You could never be that, my love. And I'm really
glad you've shared all this with me, because it will
help us in the Programme.'

She let go my hand, and began rolling the stem
of the wine glass between her fingers.

'There is one very small request.'

'Yes? What is it? Tell me, please, and I'll be happy
to grant it.'

'I was thinking, an acknowledgement in your
next book, something like... *To Rhiannon Townsend,
without whom this book would never have been written.*
Also in any subsequent press interviews, it would be
wonderful if you could mention the Programme.'

'Well, that sounds fair enough. If there is a next
book, of course.' I tried not to let her see how jolted
I was by this request. Indeed at first I thought she
must be joking. I almost opened my mouth to laugh.
But then I saw from her expression that laughter
would not be in order.

We moved into the sitting room after supper. I've just
begun to notice how comfortable Rhiannon is in my
house now. And so she should be of course, after giving up so much of her time for me. I don't want her

to feel like a guest. I'd rather she made herself right at home. For instance there is only one sofa in the sitting room and an assortment of not very comfortable chairs. Rhiannon took the sofa, stretching herself full length so there was no room for me, propping cushions at her back, and kicking off her slippers. I sat in the Windsor chair by the hearth, my eyes drawn to her bare toes as she dreamily circled her right ankle, this way, that way. She seemed in the mood to talk about herself for the first time. Not about family though. She began regaling me with stories of her travels in Ecuador. How she lived for a while among the Indians, how she drank from some plant called 'The Soul Vine' and conversed with the spirits. She's told me so little about her life so far that I paid attention.

'These people are so in tune with the universe.' She gave me an odd look as though challenging me to disagree. 'You can travel the Astral with the Soul Vine, both lower and upper layers. I've done my share of that. Why are you looking so worried, Vida?'

'Am I? I don't mean to.' Actually I'd thought *she* was looking worried, as if her astral travels had not all been happy ones.

She bent forward, tugging her long skirts over her toes, and said that the Soul Vine didn't grow in northern Europe.

'So you needn't worry. We won't be using hallucinogens.'

'That's a relief.' I tried to make light of it. 'I'm a bit old for tripping out, or whatever they call it nowadays.'

She seemed to consider it for a moment. 'Drugs can be a short cut but they're not without risk. There's no way I plan to put you at risk, believe me. We'll be taking the long way round. The long way round is safer.'

'So, how long exactly will it take?'

That, she said, was difficult to say, although it would certainly be two weeks at the very least.

'A fortnight? Oh.'

'Is there a problem with that? Do you have something booked?'

Something booked. No indeed, I had nothing whatsoever booked. The very thought of those white unmarked spaces on my calendar hardened my resolve. 'No, there's no problem. I haven't got anything planned.' Unless Dory plans to make an impromptu visit, or invites me down there, I was about to add. But that, I knew, was highly unlikely. I cleared my throat. 'Didn't you say something about showing me the Programme?'

She went to fetch it from her room. When she came back she presented it with great solemnity, as if it might be a fragment of the Turin shroud.

'Take your time, Vida, and read it thoroughly. Then when you're ready to sign...' She sat and unscrewed the top of her fountain pen as I read. It's the first time I've ever seen her look uncertain as if she was afraid I might refuse to sign. I studied the single sheet of paper in silence.

PROGRAMME FOR RELEASING THE INNER ARTIST

1) *For the duration of the programme, no books to be read, either fiction or non-fiction. No newspapers or magazines. No television or radio. No computer or emails. Music to be chosen only by the Director at designated times.*

2) *There will be no communication with friends, family, colleagues, the outside world, except in emergencies. Telephone calls to be dealt with by Director. Letters to remain unopened until completion of programme.*

3) *Menus to be chosen by Director, though participant may help with food preparation.*

4) *For the duration of programme, any dreams (daydreams included) to be recorded in notebook and shown to Director.*

5) *Leaving the premises for any reason is forbidden, unless accompanied by Director, on permissible route.*

6) *Writing (except in dream notebook) strictly forbidden. Any other creative activity such as painting for instance, may be chosen at Director's discretion.*

For the duration of this programme, I agree to all of the above absolutely and without reservation. I also agree not to question the authority of the Director, no matter how bizarre her requests may seem.

I trust the Director's judgements and concern for my welfare, and the success of this programme.
     Signature...... Vida Tremayne

I almost laughed when I first read it. I would have laughed if not for her grave expression. Her eyes fixed on the page on my lap as if willing me to absorb every word. She calls it a Contract. Now that I have the Programme... I mean, the *contract* beside me, I must confess some of this sounds a bit daunting. But I doubt we'll take it that far. I had a brief urge to tease her about her title – Director – but decided against it. She takes it all so *seriously*. I begin to think the success of this project matters more to her than it does to me.

So of course I told her it all looked very exciting, and signed my name with a flourish, just as if it was a serious legal document.

Saturday 13th October

I write this in bed at eleven o'clock. Yes, I know. Writing anything other than my dreams is officially breaking the rules of the Programme. But I don't think Rhiannon means me to take them that seriously. In any case I've been keeping this diary for four years now. In the wilderness years that followed the heady days of *The Gingerbread House* it became like a friend to me. And it's become such a habit now it feels downright neglectful to let more than a day or two slip past unrecorded.

So, Day One of the Programme and Rhiannon said we should begin gently with some warm-up exercises. I must admit I felt a bit silly as I mirrored her movements, stroking the air with my hands. But after we'd finished, I did feel more alive, as if something had loosened besides my stiff joints. When I told Rhiannon this, she said it was all about harnessing energy, working *with* it, rather than going against the flow.

After that we had muesli and yoghurt. I'm to keep to a light diet throughout the programme, she says, which is fine by me. I could do with losing some weight, especially around the hips. The first morning was taken up with domestic tasks, like sweeping the floor and ironing. Apparently mindless rhythmic tasks like this are good for stimulating creative flow. After lunch we went into the garden and filled two carrier bags with windfall apples, which took all afternoon to peel and stew down for the freezer.

The only slightly uncomfortable thing was the lack of conversation. It's better if we keep that to a minimum, Rhiannon says, as too much chatter is a distraction. How did she put it? A manifestation of "monkey mind".

'You understand, Vida?' she told me. 'Our inner voice speaks into the silence, and we need silence to hear it.'

I can see where she's coming from, but it's funny how this made me want to talk all the more. Nervous energy, I suppose. Surprisingly I felt so physically tired on that first evening that I didn't miss reading or writing or watching TV, and came up to bed at nine p.m.

Sunday 14th October

Today has been more of the same, except that I woke up this morning to the booming of a great gong from downstairs. As it echoed through the house, I thought I must be dreaming back to years ago, to those seaside boarding houses I stayed in as a child with my parents in the fifties. The dinner gong usually heralded some inedible mulch that I would pick my way through: slabs of damp brown meat and lumpy mash. After a while though I realized it must be Rhiannon waiting for me. I found her sitting cross-legged on the sitting room rug, a great brass bowl nestled in the lap of her skirts. When I commented on it, she told me that a friend had brought it back from a Tibetan monastery.

'It will help us set the right vibration.' She traced the rim with her forefinger, and the bowl hummed faintly as though with pleasure.

I've done a course of meditation in the past, so it wasn't hard for me to let my thoughts drift until they dissolved into a blissful nothingness. There was another session later this afternoon, but that seemed to go on so long, I almost fell asleep. When Rhiannon finally sounded the gong, it felt like I'd been away for years.

I asked her how long the meditation had taken. 'I seem to have lost all track of time,' I said.

Rhiannon said time was irrelevant. Without the artificial constraints of clocks and watches our bodies would find their own natural rhythm. She smiled her rare smile. 'You're doing really well, Vida. I knew you would. I knew you'd be the perfect subject.'

I can tell she's really pleased with me, and childishly perhaps, I *do* like to please. I've come up to bed tonight feeling genuinely rested. It's almost a relief to have someone else take over, decide things for me, dictate my routine. It stops me having to think for myself. All those worries about how to write like Ella de Vile seem to have evaporated. Routine is peaceful. It imposes an order on the day.

I can hear her snoring now. I'd better get some sleep. It's surprising how tired all this makes me feel.

Monday 15th October

Not much to report today. The sun shone this afternoon, and it was wonderfully peaceful just wandering about the garden with Rhiannon collecting more windfalls. I'm beginning to adapt to the idea of silence. No radio or TV. No chat. No newspapers. The world could have ended for all I know. Even the two hours spent preparing the apples has been strangely therapeutic. I take my time, separating the tasks of sorting the maggoty ones from the good, peeling, coring, and rinsing with absolute attention. I suppose it's called "being in the *now*". It did strike me once, as I peeled, that the Kates are waiting for an outline of the next 'Ella de Vile'. That they might call any day now. The realization was like a thump in the solar plexus, but I pushed it aside.

Rhiannon is increasing our meditation periods. We sat so long this evening that my spine stiffened up, but I've wedged the pillow in the small of my back and the ache is easing a bit. She mentioned that in a day or two we'll be working more with visualizations, whatever that means.

We are three days into the Programme, and it doesn't seem as if a lot is happening. If I am truthful I'm not sure this is going to help me to write. I'm not sure if I even care.

Tuesday 16th October

It must be around midnight as I write this. I've been lying here trying to sleep for hours, but it's hopeless. Something happened this afternoon that rocked me a bit. Perhaps writing it down here will help me make sense of it all.

Today began much like the others, with exercises and meditation, a silent prowl around the garden and back for breakfast, which is a thin porridge now we've run out of muesli. Rhiannon seems to have something planned for every moment of the day. I get no time to myself. To be honest I was feeling restless after lunch this afternoon. I had a sudden urge to jump in the car and drive into town. Rhiannon laid out an old sheet on the sitting room floor. Her idea was that we collect acorns and leaves from the garden and form them into a Mandala pattern on the sitting room floor. It seemed like a playschool activity to me. I suppose my heart wasn't in it, but I played along, making a sort of clock face with bits of twig and leaves, my mind wandering to other things. After a while, Rhiannon excused herself, saying she needed to go to the bathroom. She'd been gone a minute or two when the telephone rang from my study and I went to answer it.

'Vida, this is Fee, how are you?'

There was no mistaking the abrasive urgency in her tone. *Fee Moody.* The last person I was expecting. Following on these days of quiet self-absorption, her voice was like a slap round the face. I'd barely had a chance to mutter that I was fine, thank you, before she launched into her tirade.

'Vida, I'll cut to the chase. I've just been talking to Kate, your editor at Nelson and Hargrave. She says they've now had all the submissions for the Ella de Vile series in, except yours.'

'What? But...?' I was struggling to understand what she meant by all the submissions. Fee wasted no time in putting me straight.

'You were supposed to submit a proposal by early this month, Vida. An outline. That was the deal. And I have to say it sounded a damn good deal to me when you've been out of the game for so long. I could hardly believe it when Kate said you'd been ignoring their emails and prompts to meet the deadline. They had three other people in the frame. But they had you down as their first choice.'

'But Fee... I wasn't aware of any of this. It was all very loose, a suggestion... that is...' I was trying to think straight. Had they mentioned that there was some kind of competition? If they had then it had somehow flown past me. Perhaps I'd drunk too much champagne. Perhaps I'd been dreaming, carried away by the flattering words, or perhaps I was just going senile.

Fee hardly let me finished my sentence. She rattled on, unstoppable; how the Kates had me down as de Vile's natural successor. What a pity it was I hadn't grasped the nettle. Perhaps I thought I was *above* writing for that genre, she suggested? By now I was sitting down at my desk. My insides felt hollowed out suddenly. I could barely trust my legs to support me. In the background I could hear the whir of a printer, a girl's voice informing Fee she had an author waiting in reception.

'Tell her I'll be right there,' Fee said. Then, into the receiver, 'They've given it to Isabelle Griffin. She has no problem branching out from Historical, and she's already got a strong fan base.'

'I'm sorry, Fee, really. Please pass my apologies to Kate. I must have misunderstood the situation. I, er... I haven't been very well lately. I may have missed some of those emails.'

Clearly she didn't believe a word of this.

'It's a pity you didn't keep me informed at least. I could have held them off for a bit longer. That's my job after all. No matter. Anyway, must go, I have an author to meet. Sorry to be the bearer of bad tidings.'

There was a brief exchange of goodbyes. Fee was the first to clap down the receiver on me. Only then did I realize that the door to my study was wide open and that someone was standing behind me.

'Rhiannon. I didn't hear you come in.'

She was silent, staring at the telephone. Then, in a disappointed tone, 'Vida, what does it say on our Contract?'

'Contract?'

'The rules of the Programme. The rules that you agreed to and signed only three nights ago. In case you've forgotten, it's at No. 2 – *There will be no communication with friends, family, colleagues, the outside world, except in emergencies. Telephone calls to be dealt with by the Director.*'

I felt almost winded as I tried to take this in. The pasting from Fee was bad enough, but Rhiannon's disapproval was harder to bear. My eyes filled with tears. It was as if I'd betrayed her in some way.

'But you were upstairs when it rang. To tell you the truth I completely forgot about that bit of the Programme. Anyway, it could have been Dory; it could have been an emergency.'

'*Could* have been. So if it wasn't Dory, or an emergency. Who was it? Whoever it was must have upset you. You're as pale as a ghost.'

Her tone softened as she said this. She drew up a chair to face me. She was so close I could smell the garlicky soup we'd eaten for lunch on her breath.

'It was my agent.'

Rhiannon huffed her disapproval. Clearly she didn't think much of agents. She waited for me to continue.

'I haven't heard from her in ages. Fee didn't exactly choose to take me on as a client; she kind of inherited me years ago when Harriet, my first agent, left the company. She's not at all happy with me.'

Rhiannon's eyebrows lifted in query. I told her about the Kates, how I must have mistaken their offer that lunchtime.

'I didn't realize they had other people lined up, that we had to submit a proposal. Stupid of me. I expect she's writing the letter even now, Fee Moody, terminating my contract with the agency.' My throat was aching by now, that painful swelling ache that comes when you try to hold back the tears. I couldn't hold them back this time. I felt too wretched. As my breath shuddered, I was aware of Rhiannon's hand laid flat upon my knee as if to calm me.

'Now you see why it's better to let me deal with calls. This philistine woman has upset you. She doesn't know you like I do, Vida. She doesn't respect you as an artist. All she and people like her are interested in is how much money they can make out of you, don't you see? And now she's undermined your self-esteem and almost sabotaged the Programme when it was going so well.' She seemed angry with herself at this point, saying she wished she hadn't gone upstairs at that precise moment.

'But she's right.' I faltered. 'I don't like her, but she's right. I haven't acted in a professional manner. I've failed to deliver something I promised.

I've failed in every sense, and like it or not, that was probably my last chance to prove myself…'

Rhiannon snorted. Why should I prove myself? 'You'll see when the Programme is completed. You won't be writing like de Vile or anyone else, you'll be writing like *Vida Tremayne*. The way she wrote when she was at the peak of her powers, when she wrote *The Gingerbread House*.'

The title of my old book worked like a charm. I blew my nose hard on the tissue she dangled in front of me. 'Thanks but…'

There was no argument really. Her voice was kind, but stern. I had to trust, she said, I had to trust her completely if the Programme was to work.

'Do you trust me, Vida? From now on, you must give yourself absolutely to the Programme. No more phone calls. No more distraction or intervention from any stupid ignorant people. Can we agree on that and go forward?'

How could I disagree? Her commitment to my cause, her readiness to forgive was a kind of absolution. I could have laid my head in her lap and wept, but I didn't. Of course I didn't do that.

From somewhere up in the woods, the bark of a vixen scythes through the silence. I rub my eyes. It hurts to blink as if they are full of broken glass. I can hardly see to write this page in this light. I should finish this and sleep now. Tomorrow we go forward, she says. A new beginning. And I shall worry no more about the Kates, or Fee Moody or Ella de Vile. From now on I'm going to put all that behind me and put my trust in Rhiannon, in the Programme.

13TH FEBRUARY

DORY

'Was that a train I just heard?'

'Was it? I didn't notice. There is a railway line, but I think it's two fields away. You couldn't possibly hear the trains from the house.'

Dory is showing Roddy and Fay Gillespie around the six-acre garden of a Tudor mansion north of Ludlow. The house hasn't been a huge success. It is, apparently, too old, too dark, and the beamed ceilings are way too low for the willowy Fay. Yes, they had asked for a historic character-property but hadn't realized it would be quite so dingy. Now Dory prays the velvet lawns with westerly views to the Brecon Beacons will save the deal.

'That's hardly the point, is it?' The husband confronts her brusquely.

'Sorry?'

'My wife can hear the train out here. Is she supposed to run into the house and shut all the windows every time a train passes?'

'No, well of course not...' What is this? Why is she under attack over a bloody train? Her smile is beginning to hurt. The wife is explaining her sensitivity to noise. She is one of those permanently blissed-out women that Dory can't stand. But these two are important clients of the kind who have so much money that money is not an issue.

'I understand, really. But I don't think they're all that frequent. I'm sure you'd get used to them after a while.'

'Listen, we're not paying good money to get *used* to anything. Believe me, we'd notice them, okay!' Roddy Gillespie snorts.

'Well, why don't we have a look at the lake?' She plays her trump card, indicating the path that skirts a giant redwood to the glimmer of water beyond. The Gillespies exchange looks of shocked betrayal. There was no mention of a lake.

'I'm sure it's on the particulars I sent you.'

'We're busy people. We don't have time to read *particulars*. That's what we hired you for.'

What's wrong with these people? Most clients go dewy-eyed over lakes. But the Gillespies are concerned for the child that Fay is clearly carrying, her belly proudly butting over her jeans.

'Well, let's have a look now we're here, shall we?' In a mood of bright despair she leads them beneath the redwood. 'I don't think it's all that deep.'

Fay informs her that a child can drown in a mere inch of water.

'Is that so?' Dory tries not to show her dismay. She can feel the deal slipping away from her even as they stand there. Normally she never admits defeat, but somehow she's lost the script. Part of her is back at the house, worrying about Brendan Riley. Should she have trusted him to crack on with the work alone? Supposing Rhiannon comes back unexpectedly? She hasn't told her about the renovations yet. Since she broke down and cried like a baby that night, she's barely been able to look the woman in the face. Okay, Rhiannon caught her at a vulnerable moment, but it was utterly stupid to expose her feelings like that. Yet Rhiannon has been so kind to her since that night, kinder than she deserves. And then there's Dan and this Ailsa woman. Something about the smug togetherness of the expectant couple needles her.

'You could have it drained,' she suggests. 'It would make a fantastic bog garden.'

But the Gillespies are already drifting away, their features set as another train rumbles past.

※ ※ ※

Back at the Gingerbread House she is greeted by the industrious sound of the scraper and the slap of wet plaster.

'Heh, the wallpaper is all gone. Am I glad to see the back of that! Sorry I had to leave you to it.'

The cheery tone sounds hollow even to her ears. She kicks off her suede heels, and bends to pick up some post, aware of the stretch of her skirt across her hips. Riley doesn't appear to notice. She might be invisible. He murmurs assent without looking at her. He is halfway up the ladder, slapping the wet plaster over the walls in swerves and sickle shapes.

'You've got on brilliantly. I bet you're dying for a cuppa.'

As he raises his arms, she notices the dark patches of sweat on his T-shirt, and her throat contracts. His arse is level with her head from this angle, and she can just see the waistband of a pair of red boxers above the combats.

When he comes down to drink his tea, she tells him her plans. 'I've got to go back to London for a while. I'm not sure how long for at the moment. There's never a let-up in my line of business.'

Her mind turns once more to her flat, and she visualizes stepping into its dazzling streamlined space. Empty of Dan it has lost its heart. The balcony is spotted with pigeon shit, the lilies which Dan used to water for her have withered in their pots.

She swallows down the panic and tells Brendan, 'But you can get on with the jobs as we discussed. I've got a friend staying here. Well, actually, she's my mother's friend. She'll be in and out quite a lot, visiting the hospital, but I can leave you the spare key. And here's a little upfront for materials in case you need them.'

He seems reluctant to take the roll of cash she is trying to hand him. 'You said... a friend...?'

'Yes. Rhiannon can supervise, and if there's anything you need...'

He says slowly, 'Rhiannon? Rhiannon Townsend?'

'You know her? Well, of course, you might have met her if you've done work for my mother before.'

'We've met.' He wards off the cash so forcefully, it's almost as if it's cursed. They can settle up, he says, when the job is done.

'But you might need some more paint or something. Are you sure?'

He is sure. She watches him as he tilts his mug to drain the dregs of the tea, noticing the way his Adam's apple protrudes on his neck. She feels so low, so needy. If he were to slap the stupid mug down and pull her into a clinch, she wouldn't exactly pummel his chest with her little fists and threaten to call the police.

'So, er...' she says as he finishes, 'is that all right with you then?'

He barely nods, just compresses his lips. 'You've told her I'm to do the work?'

'No, I haven't, not yet. Why? Is there a problem?'

He nods towards the hall. 'Plaster's wet. Better get on. Cheers for the drink.'

⚜   ⚜   ⚜

In Vida's study she telephones the office to tell Harvey the bad news.

'Sorry, Harve, we've lost the Gillespies. I did my best. But I think we can safely say that house didn't tick any boxes whatsoever.'

Harvey seems unconvinced. 'But it had everything they asked for.'

She tells him about the trains and the lake. 'Never mind them. Listen, have you got any clients lined up for this place yet?'

'But aren't we being a bit precipitous? You said it was a dump. We don't have any clients requesting a "dump" on their particulars.'

'Oh, don't be so literal Harvey, please. It's not a dump. It just needs a face-lift. If you can just whip up some interest, if we can get enough people to fall in love with it, then we could be talking bidding wars.'

'Bidding Wa...euaw...ars? S'cuse me...' Harvey is talking through a giant yawn. 'Tell you what then, sweetie, why don't you email me through a pic of your ma's abode and I'll do my... euaw... sorry, bit of a late night darling, best.'

'Harve, are you on something?'

'Only my ergonomically designed Swedish chair. You know I've got a back.'

'Yes, and I've a pretty good idea how you got it. For God's sake, I hope you're not yawning all over the clients, because that is so unprofessional; we are supposed to look as if we have our fingers on the pulse after all.'

'Darling, my finger is constantly on the pulse.'

'Yes, well, I'd better go, I've got a man here doing some work, and before you get all excited he's just an odd job man, right? He's not in any way shagging material. So anyway...' She freezes; Riley has just walked in the room. 'I'll, er, I'll email through that photo then, Harve... bye...'

She turns. 'Is everything okay?'

There is no sign that Riley heard the bit about "shagging material". Even so it's disconcerting, him just breezing in here like this.

'Sorry, didn't know you were…' He nods at the phone, thus saving himself at least three words. He seems unable to finish his sentences. She senses that this is nothing to do with being shy. Riley is clearly not shy. He is self absorbed, inscrutable, reluctant to waste words. She's met men like him before among her clients, the silent type, looking like something's eating them from inside. Their partners are almost always pretty, giggly child-women. Somehow she can't see this Riley with a partner at all. However, he is not completely un-shaggable. He is perhaps a few inches shorter than she is, but what is an inch or two when you're in bed?

'I just wondered,' he manages finally, 'if there was any plastering needed in here, I've got the mix to use up.'

'Oh, well no, I don't think so. I'll probably leave the decoration in here as it is, once I've cleared up, sorted out all the papers and files and that. I'll have to do that when I get back from London. As you see I've got quite a job on.'

He nods. 'Was she in the middle of working on something?' Wow, a show of interest! She's a little miffed that the question happens to be about Vida.

'Pass,' she shrugs. 'Mother didn't exactly confide to me about her work. Anyway I have my own business to run.'

She's hoping to put an end to this line of conversation, but he goes on leaning there in the doorway, arms folded, his gaze sweeping over the files, and folders heaped in piles on the floor as if assessing the extent of her task.

'Her friend, Rhiannon, maybe they were working on something together?'

'As I said I have no idea. I haven't been able to get up here for some time now.' Something prompts her to ask further. 'When you were here, working on the broken window and everything, was my mother writing? I mean, I know it sounds strange, she was always writing, but Rhiannon said something about her having difficulties, being blocked and so on.'

It's painful having to admit her ignorance of Vida's state of mind to a bloody builder, and she can feel the colour rising in her cheeks.

Riley folds his arms. 'I saw her writing.'

'Oh? What in here? You were working in the study?' She frowns around the room, growing more puzzled. There's something to come, something he doesn't want to tell her.

'Not in here; in the old greenhouse. I saw her when I was lopping the walnut branches, after the breakage.'

'That's a funny place to write, isn't it?' She speaks her thoughts aloud. 'The greenhouse is a mess, the panes are smashed. Someone should pull it down.'

He clears his throat. 'It was a secret. She told me she didn't want her friend to know.'

'Oh?' She puzzles over the childishness of this, if it's true.

'It was her diary. She said she was writing her diary.'

'A secret diary...' She casts around the room again. She didn't know Vida kept a diary, but why not? Thinking about it, it seems a very Vida-ish thing to do. A very writer-ish thing to do. And if so, how many diaries were there, and where are they now?

She leans one hip against Vida's desk and lights a cigarette. 'Did you, er... did you talk much to my mother? I mean did she seem okay to you?'

He nods; it's that kind of abrupt, evasive gesture that men tend to give when things get personal. Clearly he feels he's said too much. He moves towards the door. 'I'd better get on.'

Perhaps her questioning has scared him off. He packs up his tools before it gets dark. There's barely time to thrust her mobile number in his mitt before he takes off, backing out of the drive so fast his tyres are spinning. Charming.

Back inside she notices he's left his newspaper behind. It's the local rag, *The Border Advertiser*. She fingers it with distaste. It's half rolled up, and so badly printed her skin is covered in black smudges. She's about to bin it when the headline catches her eye:

Fresh Alert for Puma after Farmer finds Sheep Mauled
Local farmer John Cadwallader alerted police yesterday after finding two of his pregnant ewes savaged. Mr Cadwallader states that one ewe was still alive but was suffering from such appalling throat injuries he had to have it put down. The other had clearly been dragged from the pasture into the cover of a small spinney which borders the land. Not much was left of the animal. The discovery gives credence

**to recent sightings of a large cat-like creature said
to be stalking the remote uplands. Mr. Cadwallader
said: My family have been farming here for genera-
tions. There's never been anything like this before.
These are upland sheep and I can't keep a 24-hour
watch on them. It's high time this beast was hunted
down before it does more damage. Supposing it had
been a child.....**

Dory stops reading there. She thinks back to the
other afternoon, that shadowy streak she caught
sight of against the tree line. Or *thought* she saw.
Could it have been...? But no, come on, the idea of
wild Pumas roaming the countryside is for psycho-
survivalist types: sad people. It was probably some
stray dog. After all, in a godforsaken hole like this
where the big news is the vicar opening a garden
fete, the press are bound to make a meal of it.

Just to prove she doesn't believe a word, she
wanders outside to the greenhouse. The door creaks
open, releasing a sour smell of old soil and withered
vines. Nothing has flourished here in an age. Ice
fans the inside of the windows. She disturbs some
soil with the toe of her boot and a pale unidentifi-
able insect scurries beneath an old flowerpot. She
shudders. What did she expect? Fragments of diary?
Should she ask Rhiannon about the diaries when
she gets back from the hospital? Something tells
her not to. It's bad enough having to tell her about
the re-decoration works. But even as this worry registers, she wonders at it. Why should she care what

Rhiannon thinks? Okay, she means well, and her patience with Vida's recovery is bordering on the saintly. Even so, it's not *her* house. It's not *her* mother. If she, Dory has to be the villain of the piece, so be it. It won't be the first time.

Outside, the sky is paling into twilight. The birds are silent. She can feel the day retreating like a parent sneaking out of a sleeping child's bedroom, leaving it to the horrors of the dark. A fox barks somewhere. At least she thinks it might be a fox. She hurries back to the house and begins packing her bags ready for an early start next morning.

⚜ ⚜ ⚜

By the time Rhiannon pulls up in Vida's car, it's late. Dory, leaning against the bar of the Rayburn, hugging herself against the cold, feels slightly miffed. You'd think as it's her last night, Rhiannon would tear herself away from Vida's side before nightfall. There are a few things to discuss before she goes, after all. Is she such poor company? It would seem so, judging from everyone's reactions recently. First the Gillespies, then Brendan Riley, and now her mother's friend, people she wouldn't normally give the time of day to, all appear to be taking her totally for granted.

'Heh!' Rhiannon embraces her, as if they haven't seen each other for months. Dory is enveloped in that scratchy poncho thing; she feels Rhiannon's cheek cold through the mesh of her own hair.

She forces a smile. 'Hi. You're late. How did it go at the hospital?'

'Oh, sweetheart, bless you, I hope you didn't wait for me to eat? I meant to get back early as it's your last night, but things got very interesting with Vida.'

'Oh yes?' Her heart flips. 'Did she speak? Did she say something?'

'Well… in a way she did speak, yes…' Rhiannon is maddeningly slow as she removes her gloves, hands Dory a piece of paper.

'What's this?'

'Vida. She's writing again. Dory, isn't that wonderful?'

Dory frowns. There is just one word repeated over and over – AKARA – in different size fonts, capitals, bold, Akara, Akara…

'What's Akara mean?' She feels cold. Her voice is cold. Rhiannon's entranced smile, inviting her to celebrate such a non-event, almost curdles her blood.

'We don't know what it means.' Rhiannon's voice is gentle, humouring. 'But it doesn't have to mean anything. It shows the old impulse is still there. The creative impulse, it's what drives Vida. It means she's connected with some deep part of her old self.'

'But is that all… she didn't say anything?' Dory can barely keep the dismay from her voice. AKARA. What the hell is that to get excited about?

'She didn't need to. A writer writes. This is her method of communication.'

Dory wishes she could share Rhiannon's triumph. All she feels is some nameless dread taking hold, seated in her solar plexus.

'So this is what she's been doing all day?'

'I kept giving her fresh paper, and she kept writing. It was so marvellous to see. Then she got tired of course, so I left her sleeping. But you're not to worry,' Rhiannon consoles her, 'we should take it as a sign that she's on the turn; the start of her recovery.'

Dory wonders aloud, 'I wish I could believe that. I wish I had your faith, Rhiannon. Maybe I should stay on for a bit.'

'Do you *want* to stay on?' Rhiannon's voice is gentle as she flumps down into Vida's rocking chair and kicks off her boots, her body settling into its curves as if it's been made for her.

'It's not a case of what I want. Supposing she needs to talk? If she's regaining some kind of consciousness, I should be there.' Dory knows she is arguing herself out of what she really longs to do, to run, run, and keep running.

Rhiannon rocks back and forth. 'That's your decision, of course, but what about your business? You've worked so hard at building it up. Vida told me how dedicated you are. And if there's any real change in her I'm just at the end of the line.'

'Yes... yes, you are. Thanks, Rhiannon.' Dory is ashamed, the way she actually senses the burden lifting from her. 'You really care so much about Vida's writing, don't you? That must've really pleased her, before she took ill, I mean. I'm afraid I wasn't much use on that score.'

'It's a privilege, I told you,' Rhiannon says.

Maybe it's the prospect of imminent escape, or sheer gratitude she's not sure, but something prompts Dory to confide her feelings. 'The writing annoyed me when I was a kid. I suppose I was lonely. I wanted attention and Vida was always somewhere else, if not physically, in her head, you know. I couldn't even trust her to look after my pet rabbit properly when I went to Paris with the school one time. She left the hutch door open and that was the end of poor Murphy. And then there was that upset over *The Gingerbread House*. I was in my late teens when that came out. Okay, I admit I was a bit stroppy in those days. I accused Mum of using me as a character. Well, you've read the book. You know that obnoxious Hetty Jackson person? I thought that was me, the way she chain smokes and fidgets all the time. I wasn't fooled by the red hair incidentally. It could've been black as your hat, everything else was me, I'm sure of it.'

Rhiannon appears to consider. 'Perhaps Vida used parts of you, almost unconsciously. They do say that the child of an artist is really an orphan.' She leans forward and looks earnestly into Dory's eyes. 'That must have been tough for you, Dory, to recognize yourself like that. I can see how that would hurt, to become material for your mother's book. How did you feel about it?'

Can this be Vida's devoted fan, taking her side? After the wretched day she's had, this crumb of empathy is almost too much.

'Well, how would *you* feel, if your mother used you like that? I felt betrayed at the time. To be honest I hardly spoke to Vida for a month or two. She denied it all of course, and said she'd made Hetty Jackson up. Maybe she did. Probably I was a bit over the top about it, but I was low at the time. I'd just been through a wretched affair with an artist friend of my father's, who was married and promised to leave his wife. Huh. The next one was married too. That's another of my many talents, picking the wrong guy.'

Rhiannon has her professional counsellor face on. It's like waiting for a tap to stop dripping, she supposes. Stay silent for long enough and drip drip drip… out it all drizzles, all the bile, all the resentment, all the hatred and hurt she's been storing up for years.

'The thing that gets me, I mean *got* me at the time, was her lack of understanding about the hard time *I* was going through. It was all about the bloody book, especially when it won the Prize; it was like nothing else mattered. I suppose you think that sounds terribly selfish of me.'

Rhiannon shakes her head. 'You know what, Dory, it doesn't sound selfish at all. Don't mistake me, I adore Vida, but I can see she may not have been the best mother in the world. The writing comes first, always the writing. For a daughter, it's not easy taking second place.'

'Well, I'm not sure about second place.' Dory wonders if she's said too much. 'I mean it sounds a bit harsh. Mum didn't neglect me, as a child, I mean. I expect she did her best and everything. And I haven't been the most brilliant daughter in the world, I know that. It was just...' She looks away and twiddles with the tea cloth, despising herself more and more with every word she utters. 'Well, the Hetty Jackson thing didn't help, you know?'

Rhiannon does know. She understands totally. 'And that's all the more reason why you should get back to your life.' She spreads her hands. 'Don't get me wrong, I love Vida, I respect her both as a person and an artist, but had I been her daughter, well, then, I might feel betrayed, just as you do.'

'Betrayed?' Dory considers. 'That's a bit strong. I'm not sure I feel *betrayed* exactly.'

Rhiannon furrows her brow, as if she's squinting into the sunlight, straining to see the situation as it really is. 'That's very forgiving of you. But there's no reason why you should carry this burden of guilt. You feel in your heart that Vida let you down. She wasn't there for you when you needed her, yet you've tried to be there for her. You've abandoned your clients, and left home when you're still raw from the break-up of your relationship with Dan. You've rushed up here to play the part of the good daughter without a second thought. You feel it's your duty, but it's what goes on in here that matters.' Rhiannon spreads a hand above her left breast to indicate her heart. 'You must go where your heart leads. Don't feel bad about your mother, Dory. This is karma in action. We all reap what we sow.'

Dory blinks. This is quite a lot to take on board. She's never discussed her problems about Vida with anyone before. Now that she has aired them, they sound petty and self-pitying. The business about Hetty Jackson is hardly a major issue. It hasn't ruined her life. These are just niggles, aren't they? Yet Rhiannon's take on it all is a kind of absolution. It's as if her doubts about the relationship are wholly justified. She feels lighter suddenly. Even the fidgets have quietened as she listens to that sorrowful voice talking on about the myth of the happy family.

A thought strikes her. 'Do you ever want to have children, Rhiannon?'

Interrupted mid-flow, Rhiannon looks taken aback for a moment. Kids are not on her agenda, she says finally. 'I've seen the damage families do to one another in my work.'

'What about *your* mother?'

'We're not in touch.' The vague, dismissive tone suggests this is a no-go area. Rhiannon rises, shaking her hair free of her collar, rotating her shoulders. 'You know what, Dory,' she speaks mid-yawn, 'I'm all-in. I think I'll just go on up to bed if you don't mind.'

'No, of course not.' Dory stands with her. She knows it's feeble of her but she can't resist trying for a final reassurance. 'You don't think I'm being self-ish then, leaving you to take charge?'

'Now, what have I just been saying?' A rue-ful smile, head on one side, Rhiannon's embrace convinces her otherwise. 'Look, my love, if I don't see you in the morning, have a good journey won't you?'

Dory blinks back a tear at this. She manages to choke out a thank you. 'Yeah, I will, and thanks again, Rhiannon, for listening to my gripes. Thanks for being such a rock.'

It's only an hour or so later, when she hears Rhiannon's snores reverberating down the passage that Dory remembers; she has completely forgotten to tell her about Brendan Riley coming to work on the house.

Vida's Diary

Tuesday 16th October

I scribble this in bed, by candlelight. It must be around nine thirty. At least I think so. I seem to be losing all track of time. Rhiannon has hidden most of the clocks in the house: she also took my wristwatch with my prior agreement, of course, so that we might fall into what she calls a more natural rhythm. It doesn't help that the bulb has blown in my room, and there are none left in the utility room stores. We can't go out for supplies, Rhiannon says, until the Programme is finished. I tell her the village shop keeps some in stock, but she's resolute.

'Maybe the bulb has blown for a reason,' she says. 'Everything happens for a reason. It may be that our work will go better in natural light.'

She questions why I should need electric light in any case, when bed is only for sleeping and dreaming in. 'You won't be writing or reading after all. Remember the book, Vida,' she says if I question anything. 'Just remember what we are trying to achieve here.'

I am *trying* to remember but it's difficult. The day didn't get off to a good start. I should have been prepared for it, I know, after yesterday's call from Fee Moody. Rhiannon made it quite clear that the Programme was about to shift into a different gear. I can't say I wasn't warned. I agreed to it all. I understood it was for my own good, but somehow I never expected it to be quite like this.

I was so tired this morning I must have slept right through the beating of the gong. It was still dark as I surfaced from sleep. There was a chill crawling along my back, a lightness where the weight of my duvet should be. I opened my eyes to find light washing in from the landing. It took me a while to register her shape, silhouetted at the foot of my bed, standing perfectly still.

'What? What's happened?' I struggled into a sitting position. In my fuddled state I thought there must be some emergency. Someone was ill. A fire. Or maybe Rhiannon had been called away urgently, back to London. The duvet was drawn right back. How did it get like that? I snatched it up around my chin and looked at her. I couldn't believe she'd actually come in and pull back my covers. She wouldn't do that, would she? I must have kicked them off while I was asleep.

'Time to begin, Vida.'

'Is there something wrong? What are you *doing* in my room?'

'Didn't you hear the gong?'

'Gong? No, I didn't. I was so tired.'

'That's why I've come to wake you. Time to get up. If we were in a monastery retreat I would be ringing this at three a.m.'

'Isn't that the time the nuns pray for the world?' Actually the idea of the nuns praying gave me a comforting feeling. I hoped they would pray for me. I said firmly, 'I think six is quite early enough.'

'Remember the Programme?' I saw she had the paper in her hand; she waved it lightly. 'We talked about it yesterday, didn't we, about what happens when rules are broken. About the consequences. You agreed to obey without question.'

'But you can't be…' I'd been going to say 'serious', but of course she is rarely anything but serious. Now in the darkness of a wintry pre-dawn, I felt like saying let's forget it, I'm not playing this game after all.

'Not to obey without question,' I objected in the steadiest voice I could muster. I told her there must be limits. 'Rhiannon, I know we've discussed this, but really, there's nothing on that paper about you coming into my room when I'm asleep.'

She didn't bother to argue. She began reading from the Agreement, the white paper glowing in the grainy half-light: '*I agree not to question the authority of the Director, no matter how bizarre her requests might seem.*'

'But… it's not a legal contract, is it?'

She explained patiently, 'It isn't *legally* binding. But you made me a promise, and you have a moral obligation to keep that promise. You've already broken the rules once.'

Moral obligation? My head spun. Something about her voice, the way she just stood there implacably, made me want to shrink back under the bedclothes.

'This is just…' I tailed off, not knowing how to finish. Perhaps she did, after all, know best. I'd agreed to this experiment, hadn't I? She'd warned me it might seem a bit strange.

I sighed. 'All right, look, if you just leave me to get dressed, I'll be down in a while.'

She nodded. 'I'll wait downstairs.'

Once she'd gone, I pulled on jogging pants and an old brown sweater of Jonathan's with a hole at the elbow. The sweater reassured me. I breathed in its woolly outdoorsy Jonathan smell, and whispered into the silence, 'What would you say about all this, Jon? Do you think this will work?' But of course if Jonathan were here, none of this would be happening.

Downstairs she was sitting as usual, cross-legged on the floor, the Tibetan bowl nestled in her lap. Her hair was woven in a single muscular plait, a thick rope dangling over her right shoulder.

I shuffled my limbs into the required position. 'So, will it be six a.m. every morning from now on?'

She gave me a look then, such a strange look I barely know how to describe it. It was a look that said: *things are different as from today. We're not buddies. We're not confidantes. Don't expect me to make small talk. Everything I do is for a reason.* She didn't need to *say* any of these things; it was all in her look. How can I put this? It wasn't unfriendly exactly. It was just as though our roles had changed. The distance between us was like that between any professional person and a client. I thought of her description – *Director.* The realization that our places had changed so subtly but absolutely was something of a shock.

'I think I've already told you, Vida, that it's better if we keep conversation to a minimum during the Programme.'

'You mean a vow of silence.' I spoke lightly to hide my irritation. I wanted my breakfast. I wondered, had she lit the Rayburn yet? It was still dark outside, and utterly silent.

There was no need for vows, she assured me. 'As we go through the Programme, you will find there's less need for talking.'

There was no breakfast after meditation. Instead I was instructed to clean the kitchen floor: scrubbing it, that is, on my hands and knees. When she issued this instruction I stood staring hopelessly at the terracotta tiles, which are chipped in places, the dirt and coal dust from the Rayburn gathering in the cracks. They've always been a nightmare to clean, although usually I confine myself to a quick swish around with the mop. This early morning task seemed a long way from the peeling of apples and floor sweeping I'd performed thus far. I had to fight back a sense of outrage. Who did this woman think she was, ordering me to scrub my own floor? There was something degrading about it. Was she going to stand over me while I shuffled around like a Victorian kitchen maid in my own home?

'Rhiannon...' I began, 'could we at least have breakfast first? My knees are stiff. They always are first thing. I don't think...'

'Dear, you're not requested to think right now. All you need to know is that this is a *method*. It happens to be a crucial element of the Programme we agreed to. But if I *must* explain further, strenuous physical labour is part of the growth process. It keeps us in touch with the basics, it grounds us. It teaches us humility. Remember Gurdjieff.'

'No, not personally, I don't.' It was her sanctimonious expression that got to me. Fighting an urge to grab hold of her plait and pull hard, I snapped, 'I'm not quite ancient enough to remember Gurdjieff.'

I'd read about him of course, how his disciples slaved away on his Ashram, felling trees and digging wells; how the tubercular writer Katherine Mansfield coughed up the last of her life's blood as she peeled sacks of potatoes, enough to feed the entire community.

Still, Rhiannon stood waiting for me to obey, her arms folded, as if she had all the time in the world. What would have happened if I'd refused to play? I was tempted to make a stand. If it came to a showdown, so be it. But then I thought back to yesterday, how humiliated I'd felt after speaking to Fee Moody. I'd promised to trust her, hadn't I? She wasn't doing any of this for financial gain. She wanted to get me writing again, that was all.

So it was that I sighed agreement, and went to dig out the scrubbing brush from the scullery broom cupboard. We didn't speak. The tiles stung cold through my leggings. My knees were bruised, but at least Rhiannon busied herself at the stove while I worked. I don't think I could have borne it if she'd flaunted her power by watching over me.

With every circular sweep of the scrubbing brush, I comforted myself with the fact that I'm not tubercular like poor Katherine, that this activity, undignified though it seemed, wouldn't kill me. Nevertheless, as I straightened to gaze at my gleaming floor, it struck me that Rhiannon had scored a significant triumph with this little exercise: that we had reached a point from which it would be very difficult to turn back.

Breakfast when it finally came was disappointing: a thin gruel-like porridge, and a quarter of an apple so sour it left my gums stinging. By now it was nine o'clock, and the darkness had thinned to a grey mist which settled over the garden, and the world beyond.

After breakfast I was despatched for a shower, then called back down for what she called a visualization exercise.

It was such a relief to sink down on the sitting room rug that I was only too willing to play the game. The instructions seemed harmless enough. I was to imagine myself in a landscape. I closed my eyes and waited for something to come.

'It could be any landscape you like. A place you know well, perhaps from your childhood. Or a landscape of the imagination...' Rhiannon's voice had a faraway echo as though issuing from a deep canyon. Perhaps that's why the vision that first came to me looked like Arizona. Barren and snake-infested, Arizona has never been on my list of places to visit before I die. But this was surely it, a Georgia O'Keefe landscape of dazzling light littered with animal skulls, and pyramids of sun-bleached bones. No. This was not a place I wanted to go. I realized this must be *her* landscape, not mine. I blanked it out.

As if reading my mind, she began making suggestions. It might be a rocky shore, she said, it might be a desert island; it could be mountains, or forest… or…

Forest then. Maybe I could hide from her among the trees. I thought first of the woods beyond the garden, the scrub of oak and hazel all tussling for their share of the light. Meanwhile Rhiannon had fallen silent. Thank goodness. Suddenly this all seemed ludicrous. Did she really believe this new-age rubbish could help me write? My stomach growled, a distraction reminding me of bodily needs. My mind skipped forward to lunch. If it was soup again, I hoped she'd at least put some barley in it.

How long we sat there I couldn't say. I only know that there was a point when everything changed. One minute I was thinking about lunch, the next I was in the forest. My breath softened automatically. It seemed like I was breathing in harmony with the trees, in and out, in and out, as if I breathed the forest into being. Cradled in the green womb, my senses heightened. Leaves drifted succulent, like silk to the touch; I delighted in their colours, not just green, but every tone and variety of green, gradated through sage, to olive, to emerald.

After a while I became aware of a voice.

'Now imagine a creature has just come onto the scene. This animal belongs here; it is part of your landscape. It is *your* creature. Wait. Just wait. You will know it when you see it.'

I waited. It came all by itself, slinking from the undergrowth, a great muscular black cat with yellow eyes like torches. I wasn't even afraid. Just the sight of it made me stronger. I felt I could run for miles, eat a horse, two horses. My bones were no longer thinning and brittle like crimped pastry edges, but freely oiled and hinged.

'You can open your eyes now, Vida,' the voice said.

I did. It took a while for me to adjust to the room again. My body felt heavier than when I'd left it, so heavy I could hardly move. My hips hurt. When I uncrossed my legs, my bladder was agony.

Rhiannon had her notebook open on her lap; she wanted me to describe the creature, in every detail. I began in a stumbling way, trying to capture the essence of the huge cat. Rhiannon bent her head and scribbled, appearing to write far more than I was actually telling her. When she glanced up from her pad, her eyes glittered.

'This is amazing. I hadn't expected it to show itself so soon. Your totem animal, Vida, is a Puma. Of all the power animals this is the most powerful of all.' She looked at me, head on one side, and I felt the blaze of her approval like an inner fire spreading through me.

'Tomorrow we will go and look for it.'

Wednesday 17th October

I'll scribble this quickly before I blow out the candle. It's only 9 p.m. but I'm so tired I feel I could sleep for years.

There's not much to report. It's rained all day. Too wet to go out and find my "totem animal". She spent hours searching the skies for a break in the clouds so we could go a-hunting. All afternoon she hovered by the front windows, the chink of her bangles against the glass jangling my nerves.

'Does it ever stop raining here?' she muttered once. The rain would make it harder, she said, to find evidence; tracks, spores, tufts of fur and suchlike. Then, after a bit of pacing around, she decided it was wrong not to trust. 'We need more time for you to contemplate. Maybe this rain is a blessing. Once it clears your totem creature will be all the more powerful.'

And so I sat on through the afternoon and twilight in a kind of a daze. Does she really believe that we are going to find an escaped Puma in the woods, just because I thought of it?

The candle is guttering. I can't write any more. I'll have to snuff it out and try to sleep.

18th October

Rain again, all day, torrents blown in on the Atlantic low, gushing down from the hills. Rhiannon appealed to the goddess to clear the skies, but this appears to have fallen on stony ears. Since we can't actually go out and find my totem animal, she wants me to meditate on it continually. We have to do the forest exercise twice a day. I close my eyes to humour her, but really I'm thinking of food: beans on toast and cottage pie, bread and butter pudding and apple crumble and custard; comfort food, nursery food, the kind that warms your heart along with your stomach.

As I write my stomach makes whimpering sounds of complaint. I can't recall when I last went to bed hungry. I think it was on holiday in Cornwall years ago, when Jonathan and I stayed in a B&B miles from anywhere, and the roast tasted of bicarbonate of soda.

I'd give anything for that roast right now. Tonight it was nettle soup. The nettles were harvested by her own fair hands, plucked from my weed-ridden hedge. Her hands were swollen and reddened as she ladled it into my bowl, as proud of her stings as if they were battle scars. A wrinkly jacket potato accompanied the soup. No butter. She sat opposite me at the table, watching me eat, sharing my meagre meal. It's all right for her. There are no signs of deprivation in her easy swaying hips and smug curves, whereas I am all sharp corners and angles. I begin to fear my bones will crumble; by the time this is over, my skin will have crackled like papier mache.

When I mentioned this, she explained that protein is too heavy to digest. 'It supplies the wrong kind of energy for our purposes. We don't want to slow down your system at this stage.'

'Cheese,' I ventured, 'a bit of cheese on my potato wouldn't hurt, would it?' My mouth was salivating at the thought of that strong salty crumbly cheddar that they sell in Cregaron market.

'Westerners eat far too much dairy,' Rhiannon said. Was I aware of the statistics for hardened arteries and strokes in this country? Was I aware that cheese creates an acid residue in the joints? As I sat there meekly cutting up my potato skin into squares to make them last longer, she added that of course I could cut myself a slab of cheese if I wished.

'It's up to you. It's *your* kitchen. I can't stop you from eating just what you like.' She swished the bread around the soup bowl, and lifted it green and sopping to her mouth. When she smiled sadly at me through her green moustache, I felt bad for doubting her. Perhaps she noticed, because she pressed home her advantage at once.

'Honestly, my love, I'm not trying to starve you.'

'I didn't say you were. I understand. The soup is delicious.'

That was a few hours ago. As I write this now, I'm wondering why I didn't just say, okay then, I will just cut myself a slab, thanks very much. It was as if her giving me permission shamed me into abstinence. After all, she's put so much time and energy into this Programme of hers. I should at least try to keep my part of the bargain. This is what I tell myself as I scribble these forbidden words.

Sunday 19th October

Grey skies again, but the rain lightens to a drizzle. We can't put off our big cat hunt any longer, Rhiannon decides. There's a momentum to these things, apparently, and we can't afford to lose the energy we've built up. She stamps her feet into her workman's boots ready for our trek. The gypsy skirts swish as she rests one foot on a kitchen chair to tie the laces. She crams the Alpaca hat with the purple earflaps down over her curls and looks at me as I shrug on my coat, a kind of veiled rapture in her eyes. I think to myself, *she's excited but she's trying hard not to show it. Why?*

'Are you ready?'

Yes, I'm ready. At least, I think I'm ready. It's not until we get outside that I realize how wobbly my legs are.

Rhiannon puffs her cheeks out in the cold air, and instructs me, 'Remember, Vida, all the time we're walking just focus on your totem animal. Think of nothing else. Shut the world out. If you focus, if you believe, it will give you a sign.'

'What happens if it doesn't?'

'It must. We keep looking, until you have your sign.'

'Supposing it takes all night?'

'Then it takes all night. It takes as long as it takes.'

I can't imagine what kind of a sign she's expecting, but I nod agreement. I feel light-headed as we trudge up the sodden slope to where the garden merges with forest. Rhiannon stomps a little behind me, keeping her distance like a Royal Minder.

The gate in the fence is secured with bailer twine. It wobbles beneath our weight as we struggle over. Clearly Rhiannon isn't used to farm gates. Her skirt gets tangled up in the bars, and she spends some time trying to free it. We tramp in silence along the track that snakes through the heart of this place. We used to walk here a lot when we first moved here, Jonathan and I, before we tired of the shooting parties, the doomed pheasant picking their way through the undergrowth like feathered dinosaurs. What remains of the track is slippery with leaf mulch, scattered with rabbit droppings and lead shot. Brambles lasso our ankles as we pass. We have to keep stopping to unravel ourselves from creepers. Every so often the trees are interrupted by small patchwork pastures, neglected, ragged with weeds. We cross a couple of these, side-stepping the stale cowpats, before battling through corridors of pine on the other side. There's a fairly recent plantation here, so dense we're plunged into darkness.

Sometimes Rhiannon falls behind, and I have a sudden childish urge to run on ahead and hide from her, squat down behind a bush somewhere on the higher ground, and look down on her as she bumbles along in her skirts, calling my name. What would she do then? I chuckle out loud to think of it.

It's funny but with every step I take I'm feeling stronger. It's as if out here, I have the upper hand. This is *my* territory.

'Vida...' Her voice fails to carry the way it does indoors, smothered by the overhang of branches. 'Can you slow down a bit, Vida?'

I pretend not to hear. I don't want to slow down. Why should I? Too bad if she can't stick the pace.

'Vida?'

I smile to myself. She's trying to sound calm, like she's in control, but we both know she's not. Not out here. Maybe she *is* in the house. I don't think she's an outdoors person. Her tread is too deliberate, her hips too wide, her breath laboured as she struggles to catch up.

There's a clearing ahead of us, dead willow herb and a murky pool ringed with tall impenetrable rushes. The land around here is boggy, so tread carefully, oh yes, tread carefully, Rhiannon, or you might sink down and disappear forever.

'Vida... can you hear me? Slow down a bit, will you...' Oh that voice, steady, unruffled, murky though like this pool, as if its true purpose is concealed. There are things hiding in the rushes. Creatures. I've seen them. I can smell them too. I can smell *her,* that musty wild garlicky scent of her, and something else, rich and red and salty. Blood. The very thought of it makes me strong, makes me feel I could leap and run through these trees without ever tiring.

'Vida... please! I asked you to wait.'

I turn in time to see her barrelling through a tangle of ash saplings, before she trips.

'Euh!'

She goes down with a thud. I can feel the vibration of it through the soles of my feet, a kind of thrumming. The branches have hooked themselves beneath the hat, and her hair is an angry scribble about her face.

I move closer. I should ask if she's all right, but she said *no talking*. Well, no talking then. Focus. Yes, focus on the totem animal Vida. Supposing I were to jump on her before she scrabbles to her feet? But why would I do that? I shake my head the way you shake water out of your ears in a swimming pool.

When I find my voice, it comes out all strange and sly sounding. 'Be careful,' I warn her, 'there might be snares.'

'Snares?' She looks worried for a moment, hoisting herself upright and dusting herself off. She snatches a backwards look through the trees. 'What do you mean *snares?*'

'Animal snares. The gamekeeper leaves them about.'

'Then he should be reported. Surely that's illegal?' She pauses uneasily. 'How far do these woods go? We must be near a road by now.'

'Are you tired?'

'Not at all.' She looks affronted that I should question her stamina. 'But there's no sense in just hiking blindly on for miles. It's not about how much distance we cover, it's all about intention. Remember, I asked you to focus. Perhaps you should just sit down for a bit. You can focus just as easily on that tree stump.'

I ignore this suggestion. 'It's not much farther.'

'What isn't? We don't have a destination, we have an intention. Vida... Vida...'

I'm ahead of her, plunging into a stand of oaks, their branches strangled by ivy the thickness of a man's forearm. There is a smell here of something going off. It's the smell I remember from Dory's childhood, when she refused to clean out her fish tank. How we used to fight about that! It was a job I hated, sponging off the green slime on the inside of the glass while the fish circled my mixing bowl.

Behind me I hear her breath huffing in the silence. Is she cold or afraid? Both, I hope. Heat pulses beneath my collarbone, as if my blood runs hot.

We can't go home until we see a sign, Rhiannon says. Are the feathers a sign? Every few paces feathers are scattered: pigeon, buzzard, pheasant. I bend to pluck the pheasant feather from the path. As I stroke the blue-bronze filaments, I think of how it would taste, a plump pheasant slowly braised in wine. Or ripped from the bones and eaten just as it is.

We must have been walking for another ten minutes before we find it, a tuft of dense black fur caught in a thorn bush. I stroke the fur in my palm, feeling its springy oiled softness. There is a density about it that surprises me. It does feel thicker, stronger than you would expect from the coat of an ordinary cat. I have to wait for her to catch up with me, raking leaves from her hair, the tiny red threads of veins in her cheeks pulsing with effort.

'Is this what we're looking for?' I hold it out to her like an offering. Relief puffs out of her lungs. She nods. A strange light burns in her eyes. My totem animal has given me the sign, she says. We can now go home.

20th October

Something has changed since our walk yesterday. There's been a shift in momentum, as if we're hurtling towards something dark, inevitable, and there's no turning back. As I write this, the tuft of fur is by my bed. Rhiannon has tied it with red silk thread and placed it in a cellophane bag, like police evidence or some kind of sacred object.

Rhiannon is like someone on the verge of some great discovery. Earlier today I found her in my study, head bent over a book, writing so fast she hardly noticed me come in. When she looked up it was like she didn't recognize me for a moment, squinting. 'Vida? Aren't you supposed to be resting? We have a lot to get through tonight.'

'You're writing,' I said. Just that. It was a statement, not an accusation.

'Mmm.' She lifted her hands from the page and said it was just some notes, nothing important. 'Why don't you rest, my love. Just take a nap.'

'You mean a cat-nap,' I said. I laughed at my own joke, but I could see she didn't find it funny. She twiddled the pen as if she couldn't wait to get rid of me, to write again. *My* study, I thought. What is she doing in my study? But when I looked around the room, it was as if all the words I'd ever written were hovering there, an accusation, the great weight of them making me nauseous. So I left her to it, and crawled back up here to bed.

She has a feverish look tonight, as she clears away our supper of lentil broth. Her cheeks flame crimson and her hair springs about her face like a tangle of old red knitting wool. She turns off the lamps and I have to lie on the floor and close my eyes. She wants me to meditate on my totem animal. The dark is so absolute; I can just make out the shape of her. When she shakes her head, her hair swishes as if it has a life of its own.

'Just close your eyes, and allow it to come to you. Don't be afraid. Remember your totem animal is part of your psyche. It can't harm you.'

In the darkness, the earthy grain of her voice is more apparent. As she leans over the CD player to put on some of her weird music I'm aware of the chink of bangles, the rustle of skirts, and the old garlicky scent of her. Music is playing, the twang of a guitar, pitched taut. Shaman music, she calls it; a yowling female voice accompanied by primal drumbeat, the kind of thing you hear in shops selling Angel Cards and ear-candling kits.

'Don't force it, Vida, just let it to come to you. It may be shy at first.'

It's shy at first. I hope it remains shy. When I close my eyes, strangely enough, I'm thinking of Dory, my Dorothea. Not Dory as she is now, that distant, difficult grown-up Dory, but the little girl scribbling her pictures, crayons gripped in her chubby fist. Dory taking my glasses off, and hanging them loosely on her little snub nose; the shrieks of laughter as she surveys herself in the mirror. 'I look like a teacher, Mummy. Mummy, I look like a teacher, don't I, Mum?'

Why should I think of Dory now? I can't imagine, but it makes me feel sad. It makes me wonder what on earth I'm doing here, lying on the floor of my own house with this crazy music yowling around me, all for the sake of a new book that maybe no one will read.

It's then, just as I'm feeling sad, that it shows itself. It's as if my sorrow tempts it out of hiding. At first there's just the *sense* of it, the sense of something huge and enormously powerful behind the sofa. The curtain which hangs behind the sofa twitches minutely. The animal stench is so strong I want to throw up. It strikes me that I'm laid out here like a sacrifice. At the same time I know it won't harm me. It's part of me, so how can it?

The beast pads slowly into view, as if it's unsure, limping slightly. It lifts one massive paw, and lowers its muzzle. I hardly breathe as I watch it drool. Then it extracts something from the hard pad with its teeth, quite neatly like any domestic cat cleaning its paws after a saucer of milk. Such huge fangs it has! They are long and curved as stalactites; fangs that could crunch a man's thigh bone like candy. Its breath makes a rasping sound as it licks, or is it that violin in the background, rasping, rasping…

'Turn it off now, please!'

Somehow, I can't take any more. I know this is my limit. I'm scrambling up off the floor, fumbling for the lamp switch. *My* lamps, *my* electricity, *my* house, I remind myself.

Rhiannon hovers in the shadows by the bookcase. She's staring at the spot where the beast showed itself, yet I can tell she hasn't seen it yet.

'Did you see something that frightened you? Do you want to share it with me?'

'No. No, I didn't.' I rub my shoulder, pretend it's only the awkward position, the draughts that got to me.

Rhiannon just smiles like she knows better and takes out her sewing. And then it's almost as if everything is ordinary again. We sit in silence, me watching her needle flash back and forth since I'm not allowed to read, until my head droops. That's why I've come up to bed even earlier. It's quarter to nine.

I can still hear the music. It's like something scratching me, deep inside.

21st October

Today she asks to see my dream notebook. My fingers close protectively over my little blue book. 'Is it really necessary?'

'Very.' She seems agitated, as if she's steeling herself not to snatch it out of my hands. 'This is a crucial part of the Programme. You must remember, in the rules.'

'If you must, but they're not very interesting. Just rubbish, you know.'

This is a lie. The thing is I really don't want her to read last night's dream. But she is plucking the book gently from me, smiling.

'Dreams are messages from our unconscious. They are the treasure buried in the empty room. All we have to do is to decipher their code.'

God knows then what she will make of this one. This is my dream:

I am sitting in a train carriage, very excited, because I'm on my way to the Cheltenham Literary festival to give a reading. I have my book in my lap, a title I don't recognize. The cover jacket is bright and glossy, and I look younger in my photo as if a light is shining out of me.

I am dressed to kill in a black fur coat which hangs heavily to my feet. It must be lined with silk, because I can feel it cool and heavy as water on my skin. I am wearing a fur hat too, and tight leather gloves and spiky black stilettos. It's then I realize that beneath this get up I am totally naked. Excitement gives way to shame. Supposing people see the real me beneath? Supposing my coat falls open, and my flesh bursts out like a wiggly white grub from a cocoon?

A man in the carriage is watching me. I think he knows. I try to get up, to walk elegantly along the length of the carriage in my teetery shoes, but the train rocks suddenly, propelling me onto my hands and knees. Then I am down, shuffling on all fours, furs draggling, breasts dangling. I'm looking for something, someone. I'm so ravenous, I could eat a horse.

That's my dream.

Rhiannon's lashes sweep down the page, then she smiles. 'It's happening, Vida. The Programme. It's beginning to take effect.'

23rd October

There were no dreams last night. I hardly slept because of the wind. It blew up some time after we retired to bed as if out of nowhere, hurling itself at the house, so that everything creaked and rocked and groaned. I've always loved the wind. It blows away the cobwebs, my mother used to say. Let's go out in the wind and blow away the cobwebs shall we, Vida? But this wind was different, as if it had purpose, a definite intention. I huddled beneath the covers waiting for it to do what it must. I could hear the thatch creaking and groaning. Jon always worried so much about the thatch. He said a thatched roof was a curse because of the maintenance. Perhaps the wind had come to blow off the thatch and carry it off like a silly hat. Then we'd be like one of those dolls' houses where you lift up the roof and peer down god-like at the tiny doll people, walking them from room to room, sitting them at the table. There we'd be, me and Rhiannon exposed, with only the night sky to cover us.

All the time I was thinking this, the wind raged, retreated, raged, retreated, as though gathering itself for a final assault. There would be an assault, I knew. Somehow I welcomed it. Perhaps the wind would blow us all away, hurl us about, clean up this stickiness, this heavy yellow stickiness I've been feeling following me around.

Where does the Wind Come From? Nobody Knows. I used to love that nursery rhyme as a child. I used to plague my mother over and over, *where does the wind come from, Mummy?* Thinking of my childhood, my mother was like a warm blanket tucked cosily about me. Let the wind do what it must. I was almost falling asleep when I heard the crack. Such a great wrench, I knew at once it was something serious. In the same moment, there was the sound of glass smashing. It was like an explosion. It was as if someone had hurled a great stone right through my bedroom window.

I must have yelled out. She came running, of course, stumbling along the passage in her dressing gown, throwing open the door. 'What is it... what's happened?'

She fumbled for lights, but they flickered just once and went out. I swung myself out of bed and she held up her hand. 'Careful, Vida, mind where you step, there's glass all over the floor.'

I looked. The curtains were billowing right up, and the cold air streaming through into the room. Moonlight picked out the fragments of shattered glass. They looked quite pretty, I thought. You could almost make a necklace out of them.

Rhiannon was stepping gingerly among the rubble, waving her torch. Nearing the window, she traced what was left of the windowpane with her forefinger.

She spoke as if to herself in a kind of breathless wonder. 'The entire pane is gone. There's more energy here than I realized. We must have released something huge for this to happen.'

It could have been a scratch, she went on, the scratch of a paw. It would only take a hairline fracture to shatter the pane. Then, as if remembering my presence, she looked at me. 'What are we going to do? You can't sleep in here now.'

'I don't mind. I like the fresh air.'

'No, you'll catch your death, and there's glass everywhere. I can't sweep it up in the dark.'

I agreed to move to the spare room, although the glass didn't bother me. She'd never have gone back to bed if I'd stayed put.

This morning we saw the extent of the damage. It was the walnut tree that Jonathan always said was too close to the window. He wanted to have it lopped years ago, but I wouldn't let him because I loved its twisty black bark and white spring blossom. The wind must have cracked the main branch and thrust it through the pane.

Rhiannon is not so sure. She holds that it's all connected with the Programme. Apparently releasing powerful energy can cause all kinds of phenomena. She looks slightly worried this morning as she surveys the damage. The main branch is hanging dangerously by just a few threads and could kill someone. All right, she says, we could just board up the window for now, and I can go on sleeping the spare room, but that branch, what to do?

'We could call a man in to fix it.' It seems the obvious thing to me.

She frowns. 'The timing is bad news, frankly. Well, I suppose it should only take a day or two to replace the glass, and lop that branch down. All right, we'll look for someone. Or rather I will. I don't want you getting involved at this crucial stage.'

She goes on about damaging the Programme for a bit. I'm not sure if she's talking about the smashed window or the man who will come to fix it.

18TH FEBRUARY

DORY

The sky over the M42 is gunmetal grey. Dory eases her foot off the accelerator and veers into the inside lane. It's frustrating having to slow down when she's still around forty minutes north of Oxford, but there's nothing else for it. Rain driving in from the west is turning to sleet, and her wipers can barely cope with the spray from the overtaking Lorries. On the CD player, Elbow's *If she says she needs me* is a sibilant hiss. She turns it off, and in doing so, a rush of anxiety floods through her.

This is crazy. She should be euphoric about escaping from Wurzel Land. In another couple of hours, if this weather doesn't get any worse, she could be back home in London. Better still, it would be with Rhiannon's blessing. Yet despite all that stuff about families and karma, she can't shake off the sense that she's shirking her responsibilities. This is what it comes down to.

What's really niggling at her, though, is Riley. Was she stupid to place so much trust in him? Especially when he acted downright weird that day, hanging about in Vida's office, asking strange questions. Supposing he turns up while Rhiannon is still in bed, and starts demolishing the hallway? Okay, she left a note on the table explaining things, but she should have done it face to face when they were talking last night. This is a fine way to treat a person who's been so generous to her.

Dory squints for a Services sign through glancing sleet. The least she can do is to call Rhiannon and warn her. Anyway, it's high time for her coffee and ciggie fix. She noses the car up the slip road, and off the motorway. The service station is ablaze with light. She stalks through the entrance, past the space-invaders, the magazine racks and waxed jackets, heading into the coffee-scented fug. Something about the early hour, the sleet driving in around the glass bowl of the Rest Awhile Café, gives the place a surreal look. She thinks of those horror movies where the zombies turn up in American diners. Here they sit slathering over their fried breakfasts, eyes glazed. A baby in a pink plastic highchair crumbles a wodge of doughnut in its fist and screams at its parents. Grabbing a coffee and a croissant the colour of cardboard, Dory takes them to an isolated table in the corner and stamps out the number of the Gingerbread House.

Damn. There's no reply from the house. She checks her watch. Nine thirty. Rhiannon must have left for her hospital vigil already. But shouldn't Riley be there by now? She'd told him where to find the key if Rhiannon was out, under that boulder by the porch. Oh God. Was she a total fool to do that? What does she really know about this guy?

She gulps her coffee, and winces at the taste, before trying the house again. Nothing. Maybe he's there but just not answering the phone. Or maybe... why did he ask those questions about Vida's work? Why the interest in what some old woman novelist might be doing? She can see him now, the way he staked out his position in the study, arms folded, watchful, like he had every right to be there. Because she was feeling so... well, *needy* that day, she didn't admit to herself how shifty he looked. What's worse is that if anything goes wrong, Rhiannon will be in the front line. That's a fine thank you for shouldering what is essentially her, *Dory's*, burden.

This is ridiculous. She should be ringing Harvey to warn him she's on her way. She should be thinking about her clients. Unable to sit any longer, Dory makes for Smiths and buys up all the property magazines she can find; the designer builds and glossy interiors never fail to inspire her, usually. Trouble is, she's not in the mood. Even as she slots her debit card into the machine to pay, her mind is back in that godforsaken yokel country. Part of her can't just run away. She's sitting by Vida's bed alongside Rhiannon; she's trailing Riley around the Gingerbread House.

She shoves the magazines in the back of her car, and sits for a moment, iPhone in hand. When she rings Riley's mobile she hardly expects him to answer, but he does.

'Yeah...?' The voice is slurred with sleep, or something else, she can't tell. A girl in his bed, maybe. She doesn't know whether to be angry or relieved that he's not at the house after all.

'Brendan, this is Dory Tremayne. I'm ringing from a service station near Oxford. I've just been trying the house and there's no reply.'

Silence.

'I thought we agreed a nine o'clock start today?'

After a pause, he agrees, yes, they did.

'Well. It's actually ten now by my watch. Look, I really don't have the time or the desire to chase you up on this, but I wanted to know how you're getting on. I am concerned, because I forgot to tell my mother's friend about you. I had to leave a note for her this morning, so I....'

'I can't take it on. Sorry.'

'You what? But... I thought we agreed? I did explain that it's urgent. If it's a question of money...'

'No, it's not the money. Listen, sorry but I can't work on your place with her there.'

'*Her?* You mean Rhiannon? But... she knows you; you said she was there when you fixed the window.'

'Yeah.'

'So what is it? If you two have a problem, why didn't you tell me before?'

Through the burble of background interference she hears him mumble that he'd rather not get involved. Involved? Involved in what?

'Sorry, you've lost me. I only want you to strip some wallpaper and repaint the hallway. And if you're worried about Rhiannon, well, she'll be out most of the day at the hospital. You won't even see her. '

'Yeah. She won't want me there.'

'Well, it's not up to her, is it? It's *me* hiring you to do the job. Of course I can't force you. If you don't want it, I'll find someone else. I'm sure there are plenty of people in your neck of the woods who'd be only too glad of an honest day's work.'

He agrees, yes there are, she could try the local Ad-Mag.

'Yes well, thanks. As I've told you I'm on my way down to London.'

'Look,' he cuts in, 'sorry I can't help. You can ask your mother's friend, if you like. She'll fill you in. She'll have plenty to say about me.'

'But...'

He's switched off. She swears silently. What on earth is he on about? Did he have a thing with Rhiannon? Some kind of bust-up? But that's not likely. She gets the impression that Rhiannon doesn't have much time for men. In any case Riley is too Neanderthal, just not her type, even supposing she has a type. Then, horribly, a cold light begins to dawn... there wasn't anything going on between him and her mother was there? Maybe that would explain his interest in the state of her health. That weekend he worked at the house, something happened, something or someone that could have triggered Vida's breakdown. Did he *do* something to Vida? *Say* something? She says aloud to no one... *Oh – my – God...* and as the engine purrs into life, she steers the car left onto the loop road that will take her not south, but north-west to the borders.

❧ ❧ ❧

The thatch of the Gingerbread House glistens pearly against a pewter sky. The snow is already melting, the eves dripping to form ochre-coloured puddles around the porch. The chocolate-box scene does nothing to lift her spirits as she pulls up. It's early afternoon. She should be in her London office by now, commiserating with Harvey over impossible clients, sending out for a Philpot's pastrami and chutney sandwich, catching up with her friends. Although she has to admit friends have been a bit thin on the ground lately. Her clients have always come before friends. And Twitter followers. Oh yes, she admits she's obsessed about those. Somehow or other the real friends have got pushed into the shadows. And as for lovers, well, she has no problem attracting men. It's keeping them that's the problem. Sometimes she thinks that everyone hates her, except Harve, and Rhiannon who appears to love the whole world, and yes… Vida, her mother who she knows at heart loves her, really loves her, or used to before she forgot who she was. Isn't this why she's had to turn around, really? Not out of duty, or even concern about Riley, but some instinct, misguided maybe, that Vida needs her.

Something is different. She feels it the moment she opens the door, the sense of things disturbed, not quite where they should be. Inside, the first things she notices is that the lid of the hall chest is open with blankets hanging out, as if someone's had a good old rummage. The door to Vida's study hangs half open. Her stomach contracts. She's certain she closed it firmly before leaving the house, yet all appears to be in place when she checks.

She flits back through the hall, switching on every lamp and appliance she comes across. Partly this is an act of defiance. Vida has been known to sit writing in the deepening gloom, to be virtually plunged into darkness before getting up to turn on a light. The wintry Welsh daylight hardly penetrates the tiny deep-silled windows in this house. In the front sitting room she switches on the lamps that squat almost organically on every surface like mushrooms, barely dispelling the shadows with their low-watt bulbs and richly coloured silk shades. Something has been moved and it's a while before she can place it: the Arts and Crafts bureau where her father always kept his insurance documents and files on the house, mainly to keep them separate from Vida's stuff, has been shifted slightly out from the wall, and the side drawer where the passports were always kept tugged open. Inside are a few old photos, a Christmas card, a street map of Cregaron, a bundle of National Trust brochures. It's impossible to say if anything is missing. One thing she's certain of: that shifty liar Riley has been here. He must've snuck in early and had a good poke about. But why, and how can she prove it?

She shivers. The house is freezing. Inspecting the Rayburn, she finds a heap of cold ashes. Much as she has sneered at Vida's antiquated heating system over the years, it really is the heart of the house. It never goes out. Rhiannon makes a ritual of keeping it alight. The other night, cradling the logs in her arms as if they were sacred offerings, Rhiannon half jokingly referred to herself as Goddess of the Hearth.

Rhiannon. A chill takes hold of her.

'Rhiannon? Rhiannon are you there?' she calls up the stairs. Vida's car has gone, but that doesn't mean a lot. She has visions of Brendan Riley letting himself in with the key, murdering Rhiannon in her bed. Oh dear God. She'll have to go upstairs and check.

She checks out hers and Vida's bedrooms first, but everything seems in place. At Rhiannon's door she taps, pauses before entering. Inside, she snatches a breath. The sensation of intruding on some animal's *lair* is so strong, the back of her neck where she's wrung her hair into its usual French knot actually prickles. She loosens her hair without thinking. It's oddly comforting the way it spools down over her neck, as if protecting this exposed vulnerable part of her. What makes her think of a lair, she wonders? A lair is where a wild animal sleeps, a den to lie low in and lick its wounds, a refuge from the world. Certainly Rhiannon has made herself cosy here. The bed is rumpled, strewn with papers, books teetering in piles beneath the window. She can't resist browsing the titles: *Exploring the Labyrinth, Sisterhood of the Wolf, Dreams and the Female Experience.* The framed photo propped on the windowsill catches her eye. It's that one of Vida when she won the Prize, beaming proudly for the camera as she clutches her trophy. Dory remembers it was in all the papers at the time. Vida always kept it on her study bookshelf secreted modestly behind a jug of dried flowers. The shawl draped over the chair she also recognizes as belonging to Vida. It's that Mexican one with the glary red and black Aztec pattern that Dad brought back from one of his solo trips abroad. But this is no crime. It's perfectly possible Vida lent her friend the shawl if she was feeling chilly. She sniffs. The scent of Rhiannon's perfume is strong in here… she tries to identify it, that burnt rubbery scent of lilies on the turn. It's the room of someone who has settled in for the long haul, who has made themselves comfortable. But then why shouldn't she? Taking care of the house and keeping watch by Vida's bedside all day is a lot to ask, even of a friend, especially when she's not even being paid for her services.

Still it's something of a relief to close the door behind her. Retracing her steps she goes outside and checks beneath the stone. It's more of a boulder really. Vida always kept the spare key hidden there in case she locked herself out by mistake. Now, as she squats down to lift it, Dory becomes aware for the first time of its shape. Why has she never noticed before? The boulder's curves are voluptuous, haunch-like, sloping downwards to a blunt head-like protrusion. If you made out its shape in the dark, you might easily mistake it for a large cat, haunches raised, head lowered, ready to pounce.

Dory's chest tightens as she lifts it and fumbles, her fingers closing over the cold metal. Yes, the key is in place but that doesn't prove much. And now she thinks of it, surely the stone has moved? Yes, it has definitely moved. She remembers that it was nestling right up by the porch before. Now it's moved a few inches to the right. So unless it rolled all by itself, someone has moved it, and that someone just has to be Riley.

⚜ ⚜ ⚜

Back in the house, all she can think to do is to light the Rayburn, because without it the radiators won't work. What a sight she must look, all huddled in her fake fur, breaking up wet twigs for the fire while a sleety wind smacks at the window, and the chimney flue makes strange sucking noises. If her friends could see her now they'd never believe it. It takes ages for the fire to catch. In fact the house is only just warming up by around five when Rhiannon pulls up.

Rhiannon stands motionless in the kitchen doorway, arrested in the act of unravelling her scarf. So still, she might have turned to stone. In the gloom of the kitchen, her face takes on a yellowish cast. It's weird, Dory thinks, how the pitted complexion looks kind of sexy with that rough tumbled hair; it's a been-around, earth-mother look that she guesses some men would go for.

'Dory... you're back. What happened? Did you break down? '

'No, no, but it's just as well I turned around. I came back and found things not where they should be. Someone's been rummaging around in Dad's bureau, and the study door was open. The key-stone has moved, although the key's still in place, but I'm pretty damn sure it was Riley, the guy I hired to work on the house.'

It's pathetic how relieved she is to see another human being. All this sitting alone and waiting listening to the wind howl has been driving her insane. Now she blurts it all out, the conversation with Brendan, her sixth sense that she should turn around, abandon the trip home, everything.

Rhiannon unfreezes as if in slow motion, unwinding the scarf from her neck. She frowns. 'But are you sure? You say he's been searching the bureau? Has anything been taken? You've checked Vida's study? Her work, her manuscripts, I mean – are you sure everything's in place?'

Dory feels a twinge of annoyance. After all that stuff last night about the children of artists being orphans, Rhiannon's first concern is for Vida's work, always the precious work.

'As far as I can tell it's all okay. I mean I don't have an itemized list of every single scribble Mum ever made, so I can't say. Look, I'm sorry about springing Riley on you, leaving the note and that. I should've told you I'd hired him to work on the house, but we kept getting distracted. He seemed all right at first, a bit surly, but sound, you know. Apparently Mum owed him some money from the work he'd done before, so I paid him for that. Anyway it wasn't money he was after.'

'It wasn't?' Abstracted, Rhiannon plucks the kettle from the hotplate and pours herself a mug of Red Bush.

Dory chews on the end of her finger until it hurts. Rhiannon's perpetual calm can be a tad annoying. She'd expected more of a reaction. It would help if she just shared a bit in her outrage.

'He told me you don't get on. When he heard you were here, he said he couldn't do the job.'

'Hmm. Did he say that?' Rhiannon cradles the mug with both hands, and sups her tea in slow regular sips.

'You know what. I think he was looking for the diaries. When he was here working, the day you were at the hospital, he followed me into Vida's study.'

'I hope you shooed him right out again. We don't want anyone in there, disturbing things. It should be left absolutely as Vida left it.'

'He was hanging around, you know, nosing about, asking me about diaries.' She spreads her fingers on the table top, reassured somehow by the familiar patina, the scratches, the biro scribbles, the waxy bits which have accumulated in the grain from years of polishing.

'Apparently my mother was writing a diary, although why she'd share that with him, God only knows. There's just one thing I can think of...' She hesitates as Rhiannon's eyes flicker up from her cup and rest on hers. 'Supposing she was writing a diary, and supposing there's something in them he doesn't want anyone to see? Rhiannon, I really need to know. What exactly happened when Riley was working here that time? What was going on between him and my mother?'

Rhiannon puts down her mug. 'I don't know where he got an idea about a diary. There *was* no diary. If only you'd mentioned Brendan Riley to me earlier. I had no idea he was back on the scene.'

'But what did he do?'

Rhiannon sighs the way people do when an unpleasant truth is coaxed out of them against their better judgement. 'Look, I'll tell you what I've seen. You need to know, I understand that, but I warn you, you might find it upsetting.'

'Dear God, I can't be any more upset than I am now.'

'It was when he came to fix the window. In a way I blame myself. We needed a workman urgently and Vida seemed unable to suggest anyone, you know, someone reliable that she and your father might have used for jobs around the house before. I found his name in a local ad-mag that was lying about. He seemed all right at first, a bit surly perhaps, but his work was mainly outside of course. I hadn't bargained for Vida's reaction though, the way she pursued him around the garden.'

'Pursued?' Dory tries to take this in.

'This is difficult for me…' Rhiannon hesitates. 'It's painful to tell these things about Vida, because at this point she seemed to be *unravelling*. When I tell you this, I hope you're not going to think badly of her. Remember she was ill. The fact is, she seemed determined to show herself.'

'*Show* herself?'

Rhiannon meets her horrified gaze full on. 'I mean that she'd go out, trailing about after Riley in her nightclothes. I looked through the window to see her leaning over the woodpile, her nightie slipping down over one shoulder, her breasts on display. Well, you can imagine my panic. I had to run about after her, trying to get her to cover up.'

'Oh God…' Dory feels sick suddenly.

'By that time her illness was taking hold. Naturally I warned Riley not to encourage her, that she was unwell, but well, I'm Vida's friend, not her jailer. They spent a lot of time talking. She was rambling by then, so goodness knows what kind of stories she told him. As for the diary, she may have told Riley she was putting everything in her diary, and got him worried. But Vida could barely hold a pen steady at that stage. She'd sit at her desk and scribble away, then I'd go in and find paper shredded all over the house like confetti. She'd write something and rip it up.'

Dory swallows down the lump in her throat. She realizes now the extent of Rhiannon's devotion. What might have happened if Rhiannon hadn't been around? Would Vida have run down the village high street naked, wrestling the local oiks out of their tractors and having her wicked way with them? Her mother had always been a dignified person, old-fashioned. Even Dad used to tease her that she should put more sex into her books if she wanted to sell better. She can hardly believe it would come to this. It's all so sad, and humiliating.

'Are you telling me he took advantage of her, when she was vulnerable and ill? But that's *sick!*' She spits out the word.

'The truth is Dory, I just don't know. As I say, I couldn't follow Vida around the house all day; I couldn't lock her in her room. The work needed to be done, and our friend had to measure and fit the window frame in her bedroom. I didn't catch them in the act, if that's what you're asking me. It may be that nothing happened. My intuition is that he just saw himself having a chance with Vida. Rich lady novelist, going through some kind of breakdown…'

'Rich? But Mum's not rich!'

'*We* know that, but don't forget most ordinary people think all writers are wealthy beyond their wildest dreams. Maybe he saw a handy little meal-ticket, you know, moving in as the live-in handyman, once he'd got rid of me of course.'

'God. Supposing you hadn't been around when the window broke, and she'd called him in.'

Rhiannon says nothing, just spreads her hands.

'But you don't think he actually made a move on her?'

'Let's just say that he didn't exactly look away when Vida was wandering around half-naked. I saw the look in his eyes, even as I was trying to get her to cover up, to get her coat on.'

'But…' Dory struggles to find the right words; the idea of Riley getting a good eyeful makes her nauseous. 'Why would he even be interested in Vida in that way? She's old enough to be his mother for one thing. He must be an animal!'

Rhiannon seems struck by the word 'animal'. She mentions something about animal nature, and how it was released during Vida's illness. Dory notices her glance over towards the window, where the curtain shivers in the draught. It's as if that animal part is out there while Vida sleeps in her hospital bed, roaming free, a separate entity.

'How can I put this? When people have psychosis, a massive amount of sexual energy is released. It's known as the sleeping dragon. We wake it at our peril. It's a risk we take, but sometimes it's worth it.'

This is territory Dory would rather not venture into. 'No, please, I'd rather not think of my mother in that way.' Her hands shake so much she can barely light her cigarette.

'It's hard to think of our parents as sexual beings.'

'It's not that. Well, perhaps it is, partly.' She needs to think a moment. Is she jealous of her mother's power to attract a man who has shown zero interest in her daughter? But no, come on, this is hardly as if

Vida was perfectly sane, and in some sort of relation-ship with a decent man of her own age.

Rhiannon's all-knowing look shatters her defences. 'Sexuality doesn't end with the meno-pause. And Vida...'

'Oh please!' Dory slams her hands over her ears. 'I'm sorry, sorry. It's just a shock. I thought Mum was all tucked up in her office typing her next novel, and there she was allowing herself to be made a fool of with some Neanderthal half her age. Okay, I should have come up more often, I should've checked after Dad left, but I've been so damn busy...'

'Don't beat yourself up, my love. It's not your fault if that man tried to take advantage of your mother. As for being here... well, after what you've told me, about the way Vida used you for her book, I can see you've had issues.'

'But what do you think he's looking for now?'

'I really don't know.'

'No, well neither do I, but I'm going to sort out Brendan Riley. I'm going to winkle him out of his disgusting little pikey caravan and tell him if he ever comes near the house or Vida again, he'll regret it.'

Rhiannon doesn't care for this idea, she can tell. A simple telephone call would be enough. She won't get anywhere by confronting him face to face.

'I know his type.' She gets up and begins rak-ing the coals over in the oven. 'He'll just play the innocent, lie his way out of trouble if you go there. You know, if I were you I'd just get on with on with your original plan and head home. Pick up your life again. Vida can't come to any harm while she's in hospital. She's being well looked after. I'll be right here, and if our friend comes within a mile of the house, I'll call the police.' She's still holding the poker as she says this. It's no ordinary dainty brass poker, but a great curving scimitar of cast iron, with a looped handle. Dory can imagine it would make a good weapon if Riley came calling, and Rhiannon wouldn't hesitate to use it.

Yet much as she'd love to be home, she's turned back for a reason.

'I do appreciate your advice, and your offer, thanks. But I've decided I can't just run out on Mum. I thought I could, but I can't. I'm going to try and see her doctor tomorrow. I'll get her moved closer to my place in London. It's the only way. I'm going to have to put the house on the market to raise the cash for her care. I'll decorate myself if I have to, just tart up the main rooms a bit and leave it at that.'

Rhiannon takes in this information without blinking, just lodges the poker back in its corner. She doesn't say much after that. It's almost like she's offended, as if she thinks Dory doesn't trust her. Or is it that she doesn't like the idea of the house being sold? As she moves silently around the kitchen, putting together a supper of soup, bread and cheese, Dory gives her an awkward pat on the shoulder.

'I hope I haven't upset you?'

'Upset me?' Rhiannon turns, her expression genuinely mystified. 'Why should I be upset?'

'Oh I don't know; my talking about selling the house. I mean it's not going to happen overnight. These things take time, and don't I know how *much* time in my line of business.'

'It's not my business *what* you do with the house.' Rhiannon puts out the bowls for the soup. Her lips twitch as she says this, as if she's trying to keep words back. When they sit down to eat, she comes out with it. What would happen if Vida made a full recovery and found her home had been sold under her feet?

'To be uprooted from the home she loves… don't you think that would be a terrible shock?'

Perhaps Dory should think about that, she suggests, and sleep on it. This isn't a rebuke, a condemnation. She's speaking in that understanding, wise-woman voice as if she's truly trying to help Dory come to the right decision.

Dory agrees she will sleep on it. But she's already made up her mind. From now on she decides she'll play her cards a bit closer to her chest. For one thing, she's not going to tell Rhiannon that she intends paying Brendan Riley a visit first thing tomorrow.

Vida's Diary

November...

There is a *man* here. His name is Brendan Riley. I haven't spoken to him yet. I saw him from the out-house window. He was standing in the garden with Rhiannon, and she was pointing up at the walnut tree.

'He looks nice,' I say when she comes hurrying back to the house. 'He looks like a nice young man.'

She squints at me beneath her brows, and says she's not that concerned about his personality. 'As long as he gets on and does the job. It'll be better if we don't bother him. We'll just leave him to get on in peace.'

She is edgy this morning, though she tries not to show it. I can tell by the way she eats her porridge. Normally she concentrates on every mouthful, now she shovels it in distractedly.

'And incidentally, I've told him not to bother you, not on any account.' Her gaze drifts to the window behind my back. 'It could wreck the Programme. We don't want any interference at this point.'

Don't we? I like the idea of a man around, doing jobs, fixing things, whistling while he works. I wish she'd let me talk to him. It's not up to her to give work-men instructions. It's up to me, surely? Something has happened since the day in the woods. There's a sharp edge to her voice. It's as if it's just happened without my noticing. I have to remind myself now, this is *my* house. I am the Mistress of the House.

'Anyway,' she says, 'let's forget about him, we've got our own work to do.'

She calls it 'work', our meditation periods. I don't want to meditate this morning, I want to go out and find the stranger, introduce myself. But she's having none of it.

'See how you're distracted already. I wish I hadn't told you now. Anyway, he's just going into town to the glaziers and hardware store for materials. Just put him out of your mind, please. We have far more important things to think about.'

That's just it; I don't want to think about those things.

'But I could have gone too; I could have gone with him.' She doesn't understand. I like the hardware store with its mahogany counter, and the man behind it in his coat the colour of brown paper bags, and the woody chemical scent of white spirit and varnish.

'What would you want to go to a hardware store for?' She talks to me as if I'm a child. She even tells me not to be "silly". 'Have you forgotten the reason I'm here? What this is all about?'

It's as if she realizes then she's gone too far, because she drops her porridge spoon, leans across and takes both my hands in hers. It's strange sitting like this. We look like we're performing some peculiar ritual, blessing the porridge maybe? I look down at my hands and see how white they look compared to hers; the skin is dry, not wrinkled yet but getting there, as if it's been crackle-glazed.

'We just need patience,' she says. 'In a few days time, you can go where you like, talk to whom you like. God help us, you're not a prisoner! But if you go off now, it could blow all our efforts, all our hard work will be undone. You do see that, Vida, don't you.'

'Yes. I see. Has he had breakfast though?'

'What?'

'That man. If he's doing jobs about the place he should have a hearty breakfast. Men always like a good fry-up. Jonathan used to like a good fry-up at weekends. I could cook him eggs and bacon. I remember Jonathan…'

'Fry-ups?' She snatches back her hands and snorts. 'Come on Vida, what is all this fuss about a *man*? Men can perfectly well look after themselves. He's here to work. He can bring his own packed lunch, he doesn't need a breakfast.'

It's women of my generation who perpetuate the myth, Rhiannon says, of men being domestically helpless. 'The first whiff of testosterone, and intelligent women like you want to throw on a frilly apron, and get out the frying pan.' Her words run into each other like joined-up writing. Her voice sounds odd, slurry. It keeps fading away so that all I see are her lips moving, her small pink mouth shaping the words, her pointy tongue, her little teeth. Then all of a sudden her voice is back, blaring out as if someone's turned up the volume. It fades, and dies, and blares until I want to clap my hands over my ears.

But it's not the sound of her voice that worries me, it's how she looks. A moment ago, I could swear, she was wearing jeans, and that green and purple shirt, with the cosmic swirling patterns.

Did she just change? A quick change just now when I wasn't looking, just to confuse me? The figure sitting before me is like something out of a Grimm's fairytale. Where did the dusty black skirts come from? And the hood? At first I think she's dyed her hair black and had it permed, but then I see it's a hood of black lamb's wool. The hands that lift the porridge spoon are gloved in cat-skin, flayed tight across her palms like a second skin. The porridge drips crimson from her spoon. I know why. It's made from the hearts of little creatures, still pulsing in the spoon as she raises the mixture to her mouth.

I press my hand to my mouth to stop the scream. A porridge of hearts, and she's eating them live! At last I see who she really is. Why didn't I realize before? She's the witch who lives in *The Gingerbread House*. She's come back to take up her rightful place. Yes, that's it. And if she's the witch, then who am I? And what does she want from me?

'Not hungry?' As she gets up and reaches for my bowl, I notice the fur pouch dangling from her waist. Somehow I know what it contains: dried leaves and bird bones, clippings of hair, and feathers, and owl pellets. No, don't touch me! She is plumping a cushion now for my back: a cushion of hen feathers, russet and coal black.

'Vida, are you all right? What's the matter? You've gone as white as a sheet.'

Don't speak. Don't tell her what you see. If she knows you've seen through her mask, she'll have nothing more to lose. She'll lock you up in her cage and fatten you up like the Christmas goose. I stare down at the table. I don't want to see the red cavern of her mouth, which has swallowed the live hearts of innocent creatures; I don't want to see the fleck of blood on her cat's tongue, curling impudently.

'Take a deep breath, that's right. Breathe in and out, good girl.' Her hand presses on the back of my neck. 'That's better. You gave me a fright for a minute.'

I gave *her* a fright? That's something. But when I open my eyes I see the cosmic swirls are back. Her shirt billows out as she leans over me with the glass of water.

'Here. Drink this.'

I look up. 'What happened to your bonnet?'

Her hand flies to her hair. 'What are you talking about?'

'That costume you were wearing just now, made out of cat fur.'

There's a silence, then she says, 'Vida, I wasn't wearing a costume.'

There's no point in arguing. I know what I saw just now. Unless there's someone else staying here, another woman she hasn't told me about. When I ask her, she says it's possible I'm hallucinating.

'I don't want you to worry about it.' She fiddles with her bangles, pushing them up and down her smooth brown arms, fiddle, twist, as if they're handcuffs and she's trying to work out how to unlock them. 'It's nothing to worry about, really, but it might be best to ease off our *regime*, just for a while.'

Regime? She says this as if it will be a great disappointment to me.

'You know, Vida, I think we've earned ourselves a break. It can all get a bit intense at this stage. Some fresh air, that's what you need, a wander about the garden perhaps? There might be some windfalls in that little orchard of yours. Why don't we have a look?'

"*We*", she says. I'm not supposed to go out there on my own. Later, she takes my arm and we stumble about the orchard, arms linked like a clumsy four-legged beast as clouds pile in from the west. The clouds all have faces, angry grotesque witch faces glaring down at me. I gaze up and up, searching for a kindly reassuring face among the clouds but there are none. There is one cloud which perches over our heads like a puff of black smoke. It has a long low crouching shape.

I point it out to Rhiannon. 'Doesn't that one look just like a cat. See the wispy tail at the back?'

She follows my gaze. 'I don't see that,' she says, but I know she's lying. Then she cries out, 'Oh, look at all those apples just lying there rotting! We could make a crumble! Look, Vida.'

The apples are no good for pies. These trees are too old. Their limbs are twisted, arthritic, drizzling fruit into the long grass. I bend and turn them over, inspect their maggoty contents. They are riddled with wasp holes, rotting, brown. Still they smell good; their skins cool in my hand. At the sound of an engine, I drop them back in the grass. A dirty white van pulls up by the house, and the man climbs out.

'Look, he's back.' I want to say hallo, but Rhiannon steers me back to the house.

'We don't want to distract him. Let him get on with his job, and fix that window before the winter comes, eh.'

I don't think she likes men much.

Next Day

I have spoken to the man, Brendan! Rhiannon knew nothing about it. She had to go into Cregaron for Tampax. Her period had come on unexpectedly, and she was fuming about it.

'Damn! Stupid of me to run out. I don't suppose you've got any supplies, Vida, have you?'

If I have, I can't remember where I put them. Wasn't there some blood a while ago? Dark, old stinking blood the colour of rust.

'Perfect timing, why couldn't it wait a week?' She paces about the house like a jailor. I wouldn't be surprised to see a bunch of keys hanging from her skirts. She doesn't want to leave me, not even for half an hour, she says. I could go with her, but a visit to town would sabotage the Programme.

'If someone saw you and wanted to talk...' It's as if she's arguing with herself, then decides, 'No, I can't risk it.'

She goes on like this for some time, before finally getting in the car. The minute she's gone, I nip outside. The man is sawing up the fallen branch underneath my window. I watch him from a little way off at first, slicing through the knotty limb of wood the way a chef slices carrots. He must've built up a sweat. He's thrown off his body warmer. I can see how broad he is across the upper back, the way it tapers to his jeans where his shirt's pulled loose. Creeping up from behind, I almost giggle. Wouldn't it be funny if I jumped on his back while he's bent like that, and took him by surprise?

When I say 'Hallo,' his body whips round, startled; the saw whines on in his hands slicing at thin air.

'Sorry!' He turns it off. 'Didn't see you coming.'

He lays down the saw, wipes his hand on his thigh and holds it out. 'You must be Vida, the lady that writes the books. Hi, I'm Brendan.'

I'm the lady who writes the books? Oh yes, I am. I want to hug him for telling me this. But all I do is stare at the hand. It's a big square hand, with a ruffle of black hairs on the back. My breath catches in my throat. Silly, but it takes me a while to realize I'm supposed to shake it. Then when I do take it, I forget to let go. I've got so used to *her* hands, her brown emphatic ringed fingers, that this one seems huge. I go on shaking his hand, staring, until he laughs, and gently pulls it away.

He indicates the branch. 'That was some wind that night, eh? Could've done some real damage.'

I agree, but tell him I like the wind. 'It freshens things up, doesn't it.'

He smiles and says it sure does.

I like the way he talks in that deep rumbling voice. He's got an easy manner. It's then I notice there's a deep scratch along his forearm. The sight of his blood makes my heart quicken.

I say he should come inside to the kitchen. 'We've got some ointment somewhere, I'm sure we have. I could put some ointment on for you.'

He smiles and shakes his head. 'Thanks but I don't think your friend would like that. She's asked me to stay outside.'

'It's nothing to do with her,' I tell him. I feel strangely reckless at the thought of her away from this house, in the town, buying her Tampax. 'It isn't *her* house. It's up to me. I'm the one who says who... who...'

'Still,' he says, 'I'd better get on, eh, and make this all safe for you.'

"All safe". That has such a nice warm ring to it.

He is holding his arm to his mouth. He licks the blood unthinkingly, like an animal healing its wounds. Hunger pulses in my throat, and I wonder how I must look to him, standing here in my droopy skirt and wellies.

'Thank you for making it safe,' I say. 'It's not safe here. Not with *her* around. I wish Jonathan would come home. Then I'd be safe.'

'Jonathan?'

'Jon. That's my husband. He lives in France now with his friend.' Suddenly my mind feels completely clear as though I've just woken from a long sleep.

Brendan clears his throat, as if he's a bit embarrassed, the way people are when someone has died and they don't know what to say.

'Don't worry. I've got used to it now. But if Jonathan was back here, he would tell her to leave.'

He's kicking some of the stray logs with the toe of his boot, towards the pile. He looks thoughtful as he glances towards the house. He frowns. 'So, can't *you* tell her to go, if you don't want her here?'

I think about this. Can I tell her? 'The trouble is,' I explain to him, 'we made a sort of a pact. It's like a Programme. I agreed to it, you see. I signed a document. It's to help me write the next book.'

He looks mystified. He opens his mouth to say something but at that moment the car pulls up, and she's calling for me... 'Vida! Where are you?'

At once he rips the cord of the chainsaw again and sets up the roaring. I think he likes me though.

'Coming!' I call out as I head back to the house, 'I was just going to collect some apples.'

23rd October

This morning at breakfast Rhiannon is strangely animated, asking if I'd like to do some painting this morning.

'I found some paints and paper in your study. You never told me you dabbled. Are they yours?'

Are the paints mine? I have to think a while. Then I remember. 'Oh, those. They were Dorothea's. She left them here.'

Dory came down here once to recuperate after one of her break-ups. I bought her the paints. I had this idea that she might paint it out of herself, all the bad feeling. Her face flashes before me, as if it was yesterday, that look that makes me shrink, scornful, exasperated, 'For God's sake Mother, where are you coming from? Is that your answer to a broken heart, a box of bloody paints?'

'I can't paint,' I tell Rhiannon now.

'I don't believe that.' Her eyes try to convince me otherwise. 'Do you think ancient man questioned his artistic ability when he painted on the cave walls? Everyone can paint. It's a natural human instinct.'

She is flouncing about, spreading the table with newspaper. 'You can paint whatever you want, whatever comes into your head.'

'Whatever?'

'You could paint your dreams. That would be interesting.'

Dreams, she says. All right, I'll paint my dreams. It takes me hours, almost all morning to paint her, Rhiannon, in her fur bonnet, eating heartily (hah!) with her staff and pouch of bird bones. Behind her a great black beast of a cat licks its paws. In the bottom right-hand corner a tiny imp figure crouches. It's wearing a pink nightdress. I think it's me.

When I show her, she flinches. 'Oh... that's not... who is that, Vida?'

I like to see her like this, scared, worried for a change. Serves her right.

'I told you I couldn't paint.'

'It's not me, is it? I mean, it's not how you see me?' Her eyes pore over the picture as if she's searching a map for clues to the buried treasure.

I nod.

She looks worried. 'Vida, I'm not evil. I only want to help you. I want to help you to write again, remember?'

Later, after lunch, she says she's got some notes to write up. 'We'll have some Free Time this afternoon, won't that be good?'

Free time? I stare at her, as if waiting for further instruction. As if I can't move from this spot without it. Something agitates at the back of my mind. Something I should do. Something I always used to do with my Free Time. Now I don't like the sound of Free Time, it has a terrible emptiness, a space for weeds to grow and bugs to breed, and terrors to lurk.

Rhiannon lifts her arms from her sides and drops them again. 'Just anything, whatever turns you on, do something you *enjoy*.'

She looks mildly exasperated, as she sidles into my study and closes the door in my face; she looks like a mother running out of ideas to occupy a bored child during the school holidays. I stand staring at the closed door of my study... *my* study. Isn't this the wrong way around? Shouldn't I be closing the door on *her*? Notes, she says, she is writing *notes*. *What about my writing?* My fingers tremble, useless. How do I know she isn't writing a novel? Stealing my ideas? Then I remember I don't have any ideas any more.

Enjoy. Do something I enjoy. I wander outside in the garden, and sniff the damp air. I look around. The man, Brendan, is doing something over by the greenhouse. Maybe he'll tell me what to do? It's odd how everyone seems to know what their purpose is except me. When I draw close, I see he's stooped over something.

A wren lies cradled in his palms, perfect in death.

He looks up at me. He doesn't smile. He looks as if he finds life too serious for smiling.

'They see their reflections and bash into the glass,' he explains.

I peer down at the wren, and gently stroke its feathered belly with my forefinger.

'She probably killed it,' I say. 'She keeps their feathers. She keeps their bones in that pouch around her waist.'

He frowns. 'Who does, your friend, you mean?'

I nod. Suddenly I want to confide in this man. I glance over towards the house, and the windows look back at me, like half-closed eyes.

'She's not really my friend. I thought she was at first. She helped me when I was ill. We picked whin-berries and she made pies. We talked about everything. She says she's not *her* but I know she is.'

'Not who?'

'The woman in the fur bonnet. She has gloves too, made from cat-skin. She makes cushions from the feathers. Not just wrens' feathers. Hens', geese… all kinds.'

He considers a while, then whistles softly. 'Skin and feathers, eh?'

That's all he says, but I find it strangely comforting. Skin and feathers. As if he knows, as if he's got the measure of her.

'This is free time,' I tell him. 'She's in my study now, and I'm supposed to be enjoying myself. I'm writing a diary by the way, but don't tell her, will you, because I'm not supposed to write.'

At this he gives me a long stare that makes me blush.

'Who says you're not supposed to write?'

'*She* does, but she doesn't know about the diary. I'm going to hide it somewhere she'll never see.'

'Is that right?' He retracts his hands from my reach, and says maybe he should bury the bird. I watch him scoop away the loose earth beneath the rhubarb.

'You'd better dig it deep, or the cat will dig it up.'

He looks over his shoulder. 'I didn't know there was a cat.'

'It's a big one,' I tell him. 'It's a big wild cat. A beast.'

He begins to say that there aren't any escaped feral cats; that it's all rubbish got up by the media and I shouldn't worry about it. That's when I hear her calling.

'Vida, Vida, where are you?'

Free time is up. It didn't last very long. I tell him I'll be back later, and he says any time I want to talk he's here. That sounds so nice, so friendly: any time I want to talk.

Later, when it's nearly dark, I look out of the window and see Rhiannon talking to him, waving her arm towards the house. When she comes indoors her eyes are hard with anger, the pupils like darkened window-panes.

'He's taking his time getting that window fixed,' she grumbles. 'So rude too, the way he speaks to me. I've just told him to get a move on.' She pauses. 'You haven't been saying anything to him, have you Vida?'

I look blank. 'We talked about the wren he found. It crashed into the greenhouse and died.'

She stares for a moment, then says 'Oh', and gets on with making our supper.

24th October

It's not even light yet, but I must get this down now, before she comes knocking at my door, wanting to know my dreams. The window is fixed and I'm back in my room again. Brendan's just left me. He was doing the finishing touches to my window, I think; the wood was rotten, he said, and he had to renew the whole frame. I don't know why he was working so late, and in the dark. Maybe she told him to. I was asleep. That's my defence. I thought it was a dream at first, a nice warm, sticky dream, the kind you don't want to wake up from. He came softly as a cat, sliding beneath my quilt, nuzzling, nibbling.

I was afraid to begin with. He was so heavy, heavier than you'd expect from looking at him. I thought he'd crush me altogether, squeeze the breath right out of my lungs. When he stretched his full weight on top of me, my chest squeaked... squeak squeak squeak... I could hear it pitched high like a tiny wren piping. Or was that my bed? The bedsprings were twanging so loud, I thought she'd hear. I thought she'd come running, but she didn't. Thank God, she didn't. His dark curls were in my mouth, my face, smothering me. I'd forgotten what it was like; it's been so long. My body hadn't forgotten though. He stroked my fur; he flicked my feathers until I thought I'd died. I thought I was like that wren lying in his palms, the one that smashed into its own reflection.

Must hide this. I can hear the shuffle of flip-flops, the swish of her gown along the landing. Any minute now and it'll be, 'Vida, Vida, tell me your dreams!'

Well, she's not having this one.

19TH FEBRUARY

DORY

Dory slams on her brakes. She curses. There are bloody pedestrian crossings everywhere in Cregaron. To her right the grey bulk of 'Huffins' supermarket looms like a military barracks. It's school run time. The mothers waddle over the crossing as if the fact that they're pushing buggies and trailing swarms of kids gives them the perfect right to hold traffic up for as long as they want. Dory taps the wheel. She'd like to run them over actually, squash their smug fat arses in their too skinny jeans, drive on and not stop till she gets to London. But she can't. She's going straight from here to the hospital. First, though, she has to confront Riley. She feels betrayed. No wonder he was so concerned for Vida's well being, when according to Rhiannon's dark hints, it could have been *him* who helped to push her over the edge in the first place.

She told Rhiannon this morning that she'd go straight to see Vida. If Rhiannon was disappointed that she hadn't taken her advice and headed back south, she didn't show it. She just nodded and said she'd use the time to catch up with her notes. Dory imagines she means the papers she saw scattered all over the bed. She wonders vaguely what they are, as the last mum clears the crossing. Grinding the gears into first, she lurches away over the speed humps, past the new orange-brick toy-town housing estate, and the recreational Heritage Meadows with their dome-shaped tourist centre. After a mile, the town gives way to fields. She pulls in at the next turning, where a sign says, 'Watch out for Tractors Crossing'.

In the farmyard, monster machines sit idle beside pyramids of car tyres. Everywhere there are bales of fodder wrapped in black polythene like giant sheep turds. She climbs out.

Over by the house, a blonde girl is dragging sheets dripping from the line. To her left, behind the Dutch Barn, she can see the caravan where Riley lives. The girl is looking over at her. Let her look. Who is she anyway? Hardly the townie's idea of the farmer's wife, just another fat-arsed tart, with hair like bailer twine. Probably he's shagging her too.

She turns her back on the farmhouse, and picks her way around the rolls of rusting chicken wire, heels stabbing at cowpats, towards the caravan. The caravan is a heap. Beneath the slimy metal steps are various buckets, a plastic water container, a tin bath, a bit of old carpet.

'Anyone at home?' She knocks briefly, and tries the handle. The door opens on an interior not much bigger than a chicken coop. Just as she'd expected. Stooping her shoulders she takes in a doll-size sink piled with dishes; there is barely any space between the table flap and the bunk opposite.

'So, this is where you hide out.'

He's lying flat out on the bunk, a paperback held at arm's length, obscuring his face. She has to admit he gets top marks for cool. Any normal person would be mortified to be caught in such a dump, unshaven, and with toes poking through their left sock. But all he does is lower the book an inch or two.

'Hey. I thought you were in London.' He hoists himself lazily up on one elbow, looks at her.

'Change of plan. Thanks for asking, I will sit down. Mind if I smoke?' She perches on one of those midget-size folding seats and lights up. 'That blonde girl hanging out washing, is she your girlfriend?'

'What? That's Mart's missus: my mate who owns the farm. Is something wrong? I told you I'm not interested in the job.' He leans over to turn down the radio volume, Van Morrison singing *Ancient Highway*, his growl softening to a purr.

Well, obviously something is wrong. Does he think she came here for tea and biscuits? She takes a pointed look around the caravan. 'This is so cosy, isn't it? I suppose you brought *her* here…'

He looks blank. 'Brought *who* here?'

She snorts. 'Vida. *My mother.* Did you bring her here for a shag? When the caravan's rocking don't come knocking?'

Ah, now he gets the picture! He draws a hand across his face, groans softly. 'What's she been saying?'

'Mother? Absolutely nothing. She's virtually a zombie; what would she say?'

'Not your mother. Her friend.'

Her left hip hurts sitting squashed up on the midget seat like this. She crosses her legs to ease the weight.

'You said it yourself; you told me she'd fill me in on the detail.'

'She told you I was getting it on with your mother?'

'She told me that Vida was already half out of her mind when you turned up to save the day, with your little toolbox, and your Nick Knowles man about the house act. She told me how my mother followed you about half-naked and how you got a bloody good eyeful. Anyway, I'm sure it's all in those diaries you were so intent on finding, every grubby little scene. Mum doesn't need to talk, does she? She's a writer after all, and no doubt you feature heavily in her diaries as the hero. Or should I say love interest?'

He's leaning forward, elbows on knees, shaking his head. 'Wait a minute, you've lost me... What d'you mean "I was so intent on finding"...?'

'The diaries. Is that why you poked about the house when you thought I was safely in London?'

'I what?'

'When I got back yesterday, I noticed it straight away. Someone went poking around the bureau, looked in the study, had a good rummage through the chest. You knew where the key was, so you thought you'd sneak in and have a good butchers. You're lucky I didn't call the police. But I...'

'Hey, hold it right there. I didn't come to your place yesterday. I told you I didn't want the job. As a matter of fact, I was helping Mart put in some new kitchen units. I didn't come within a mile of your place. I'd have to be mad, wouldn't I, with that woman hanging around.'

She barely registers his alibi, steaming on regardless. 'I understand now why you didn't want to see Rhiannon again, after the way you behaved with Mum. She told you to keep your distance, didn't she?'

Her heart races so fast she's sure he can see it pulsing at her throat. What is she trying to say? The coolly sarcastic tone she intended has disintegrated into babble. 'Frankly I don't want to know what you two got up to. It's the taking advantage of a sick woman that I find so distasteful. What is it, anyway, can't you get it on with a normal woman? I mean someone who has all her faculties, who knows how to say no.'

It's awful how she can hear it, the tone of moral outrage in her voice. She sounds like some sexually repressed evangelist, some dried up 'just say no' person, some sad jealous person. Oh God.

He's not even trying to defend himself. He's reaching over to the fridge. 'Want a beer?'

She notices how everything in this caravan is within arm's reach. It's all here, all the essentials except for a loo. She wonders where he goes for that. She imagines the warm steam of his piss against barn walls, trees. No, don't think of that now. Can't he see she's a cocktail girl?

'No thank you. Not at this time of the morning. Anyway I'm driving. I'm on my way to see my mother in hospital, actually.'

It's unbelievable. He's got the nerve to just sit there on his bunk thing, casually pulling the ring tag, taking a long swig.

'I suppose you just lie here all day long swigging that stuff.' She watches him drink.

'I can put the kettle on if you'd rather,' he says easily.

'Why didn't you just tell me you had a thing with my mother when you turned up at the house? Of course she was already off her head when you turned up. Great timing on your part, eh? Crazy, lonely old bird gagging for it, and famous too. I suppose you thought there was something in it for you. I suppose you're one of those people who thinks all writers are rolling in it.'

If only he'd make the effort to defend himself, she wouldn't have to blether on like this. He just sits savouring his beer. Impassivity is a kind of arrogance, she thinks. It's a bloody insult.

When he looks up at her from beneath the fringe of hair, his expression is weary. 'Why don't we take a walk along the river.'

'A walk?' She laughs, outraged. 'Why on earth would I want to walk by the river with you?'

There's that fizzy sensation behind her eyes again, which in a feebler person might mean tears.

He shrugs. 'It gets stuffy in here.'

'I'm not dressed for walking.'

'We'll stick to the path then.'

'Look, if you've got something to tell me, just spit it out will you?'

He looks down at his hands, and twirls the leather wristband around as if it might be restricting his blood flow. 'I'd rather talk outside.'

Actually, some fresh air might be good; the smell of beer and old socks is turning her stomach. Also, if he's going to tell her something shocking about Vida, it might be better to hear it out in the open.

'If we must then,' she sighs. 'But I'm not going on a hike. Ten minutes, okay?'

❧ ❧ ❧

There is one rusting gate between the farm and the Heritage Meadows. Riley plays the gentleman and holds it open for her. The meadows are not real countryside, which suits her well. This is as close to nature as she wants to get; gravel trails skirt reedy pools with their jetties and information plaques. The wind frets the surface of the water, and birds with punk hairdos, which a plaque tells her might be Crested Grebes, glide oblivious towards the rushes.

They turn right and wander aimlessly away from the roar of the main road, towards the river. If her friends could see her now with Riley in tow, what would they think? Her stride is naturally long, with an assured hip-switching bounce; now she has to rein it to in, measuring it to his jaunty Rottweiler's strut. For the first time in years she feels her height as a disadvantage; she feels lonely up here, the gawky girl in the school playground. She has to stoop a little to tune into Riley's voice.

'I didn't sleep with your mother. For one thing I'd have to be a quick worker, wouldn't I. I was only there three or four days. You might find it hard to believe, but I'm not that...'

'Hard up? Go on, say it.'

'I didn't say that. Vida seems like a nice lady. She wanted to talk to me, yeah, because she seemed upset. I thought her friend was meant to be looking after her, like a carer or something.'

A carer. She hasn't thought of Rhiannon as a 'carer' before, but she can see why Riley would imagine that. There's something about the word that rocks her slightly.

'Your mum kept slipping out of the house. She liked to watch me to work, she said.' He shrugged. 'I didn't mind her watching, as long as she didn't get too close to the tree when I was lopping the branches and that. She told me about her husband, and how she missed him. Said if he was around he'd keep her safe, and he'd tell that woman to leave.'

Dory blinks, confused. This is the first time anyone's mentioned her father's absence, and it hurts. Of course Vida must have been missing him terribly. But why would she want to get rid of Rhiannon... her carer, the good friend who was looking after her so well? It must have been paranoia. Yes, that's it.

Isn't that the first stage of disintegration, when the people you trust the most become your enemies?

She resumes her attack. 'Rhiannon told me about Mum following you about half-dressed.'

'Yeah, well that's her version of events. On the last morning I was there your mum came out early in the morning with her dressing gown on, that's all. She told me she'd dreamed of me the night before. I tried to make a joke of it, laugh it off. She seemed like she was crying so I put my arm around her...'

'Oh look, I really don't want to hear.'

'I'm just telling you; that was as far as it went. That friend of hers saw us from the window and came out raving at me like some maniac. The situation there was crazy. I couldn't wait to get the job done and get out. I didn't even stick around for my money. That's why I came back for it later and saw you.'

She's ahead of him on the path before she realizes he's stopped abruptly, and is doing that stone-skimming thing which boys, big and small, seem to find irresistible. She moves on a few paces. Damn sure she isn't going to backtrack and stand beside him while he skims stones, which leaves them at an impasse. He makes no effort to catch her up, just stands brooding over the slick black surface of the pool. The wind is freshening, frisking the rushes, loosening her hair from its French pleat, and reddening her nose.

She clacks back towards him. 'Listen, I didn't come here for a stroll in the park. I came to warn you...'

'To warn me?'

'Your sexual preferences are your own business but...'

'Wait a minute...'

'I don't care who you sleep with, just come anywhere near my mother or the house again, and I'll report you under the stalking laws.'

'Stalking laws?' His mouth crinkles at the edges. It's the nearest he's ever got to cracking his face, as far as she can see.

'I'm glad you think it's funny, because I'm deadly serious. I know your type, you see. You think because my mother's written a few books that she's sitting on a goldmine. More money than she knows what to do with. Well, I can assure you that isn't the case.'

She swings on her heel and heads back towards her car.

'Listen,' he shouts after her, 'if *I* didn't turn your place over, think about who did. Just think about it.'

✤ ✤ ✤

No, she won't think about it. Driving north, back through town towards the hospital, she does everything she can to blot Riley's words from her mind. The interrogation hasn't exactly gone as planned. She'd expected him to be shamefaced, protesting his innocence. Either he's a damned good actor or his hands really *are* clean and the implications of the latter are something she'd rather not take on board right now.

The hospital sign looms out of the mist to her right. As she pulls into the car park, she's aware of a sickly nervous emptiness in her stomach. She snatches a half-eaten Danish from its plastic wrapper on the dashboard and chews rapidly. She chews so fast she accidentally bites the edge of her tongue in the process. It's the sight of those boxy buildings that so unnerves her. The very thought of that ward. What state will she find Vida in? Will Vida recognize her today? Will she be disappointed that she isn't Rhiannon and tell her to go away?

In the event Vida does none of these things. Vida is in her usual chair by the window. As Dory approaches she sees that only her mother's hands are moving in a kind of rhythmic motion, back and forth, back and forth. What is she doing? Close to, she sees what it is. The hands are balled into what can only be described as claws; the nails dug into the chair arms are raking off the horrible brown varnish into long scars. Someone must have cut Vida's nails; they are short and cut square across, which renders the scratching fairly harmless. Even so, it's a sight that makes Dory shudder. She can't help it.

Perhaps she might distract her. She pulls up a chair, rests a hand on Vida's knee.

'Hallo, Mum. Surprise, surprise, eh? It's me today, not Rhiannon. I was going back to London, but in the end I just couldn't leave you like this. I told Rhiannon to take a day off. Are you pleased to see me?'

Is this really her mother? Is this even the same woman who gave Riley the come-on? It hardly seems credible. Just as she's thinking this her eyes lock with Vida's. It only lasts a second, but she'll never forget that look, like a drowning person silently pleading for rescue.

Dory takes a deep breath. 'I've been talking to Brendan Riley just now, do you remember him? You liked to watch him work, you said. Remember he fixed your window when the branch broke?' If anything the clawing grows worse at this. 'You'll hurt your hands doing that. Why don't you rest them for a moment, eh?'

She takes hold of her mother's hands and places them in her lap, shocked by their coldness. As she does so the fingers claw into her palm so hard she cries out. She snatches her hands away.

'That hurts. It's all right. I know you didn't mean to hurt me… it's…' Tears sting her eyes. This is horrible, hateful. Did she do this with Rhiannon? But no, of course not, because Rhiannon gave her pen and paper to claw away on… AKARA… AKARA… Is that what she wants, pen and paper? The hands are back in place on the chair arms. The scrape of nails on the varnish sets her teeth on edge.

'Mum, Mum, can you hear me?' Perhaps it's best not to register this stuff; she'll just act as if nothing's wrong, and try to talk normally. 'I've been thinking about you moving into a nice home somewhere, closer to me, Ham perhaps, or Petersham Meadows? It's lovely there by the river. But we'll need to sell the house first. It's so hard for me, you know, being away from my work all the time. There's only so much I can do online.'

It's odd, the effect of these forced staccato sentences, as if they break down her reserve and free her to speak from the heart. She takes a deep breath: 'By the way, I may as well tell you, Dan and me, we've broken up. He's not living with me any more. He's got someone else. Ailsa. I know you liked Dan, didn't you. I expect you think it's my fault. Well, maybe it was. I've always put work first. But then, so have you, haven't you, Mum. Remember how frustrated Dad used to get when you didn't hear what he was reading from the newspaper and he had to keep repeating stuff.'

Where did that come from? It occurs to her suddenly that while her father was supportive on the surface, the cracks must have been there from the beginning. There was that historic row when she was sixteen, about a trip to Egypt. For some reason he had to take his holidays in May, but Vida couldn't go then. She had a couple of signings to do at local bookshops. It was no big deal, Dad had said. Surely she could cancel them, or move the dates. Vida had been resolute. It was unprofessional to just cancel, she'd said, and perhaps they could go to Devon for a short break later in the year. She remembers her father's snort of disdain at the idea. He'd retreated into a sulk for months afterwards. Vida had gone off to that book signing red-eyed. Later, she'd overheard Vida confide to one of her writer cronies that

Jon didn't really prefer camels to cream teas; he was just being bloody-minded. They'd shut up as soon as she, Dory, walked in, of course, and changed the subject. Whatever the truth of the matter, it wasn't fun to be around either of them. But by then she was spending most of her time at friends' houses anyway.

The realization that her parents were not the devoted couple she's always thought of them as being, to the point where often she felt excluded, is unsettling. What else has she been wrong about? Just how many different versions are there of the past?

Vida's head jerks suddenly, fingers tapping out a rhythm on the chair arm. Perhaps she imagines she's at the keyboard, typing the next book?

If only she could talk all this through properly. Dory is appalled at the sudden sense of loss. She's always preferred to confide in girlfriends than her mother, yet Vida was there if she needed her, a last resort, the person who had been there from the beginning, who knew her faults and virtues better than anyone. Now Vida is gone. She feels as if her entire childhood, her history, the roots of her being have been wiped out. The Dory that her mother knows and cared for is vanished along with her sanity. Is this what growing up really is? They say people don't really grow up until their parents die, no matter how old they are. Well, this is a similar thing isn't it? Her mother has left her to finish her growing up, and now she's freewheeling towards some terrifying oblivion.

'I haven't got any paper, Mum. Is that what you want?' Vida is making a guttural sound, deep from within her throat. The scratching motion is surely growing more frantic, more random. Should she call someone? A nurse? She glances over her shoulder but no one is taking any notice. Well, Rhiannon may sit here all day long, but she can barely tolerate another minute. She pats Vida's hand,

'You just rest. Try and rest, eh? I'll be back to see you again soon, I promise.'

Back in her car she grips the wheel with both hands.

'Oh Mum!' It's a groan, almost a summons, a peculiar longing such as she hasn't felt in years. Not since she was a little girl.

Vida's Diary

Early November

It's so cold in here. I write with an old cardigan draped over my nightdress, scribbling on my knees. It's as if I'm a child learning to write all over again. I'm conscious of how the letters are formed, a nice round O, then Ps and Qs, their tails flicking in opposite directions. I do whole rows of 'g's' with squiggly tadpole tails, like sperm under the microscope. Sperm. I can hardly believe I have a young man's sperm inside me. Every time I go to the loo, I wipe up inside myself and sniff and think of him.

'You look rather dark around the eyes, Vida.' Rhiannon peers at me as I glide downstairs. 'Are you having trouble with sleeping? Tell me, if you are. I can give you something.'

I don't want her 'something'. I want to lie awake all night and think of him, to think and think until I can feel the rough graze of his jaw between my breasts.

I haven't written in here for what, two days, more? I can't even think what the date is. I think it must be late autumn, because Rhiannon has filled all my vases with Michaelmas daisies from the garden, exclaiming over their raggedy purple-pink heads. 'Aren't they beautiful? I thought we'd cheer the place up a bit.' She shivers, rubbing her upper arms and looking over at the door as if someone just walked in. She adds something about flowers attracting angelic energies.

I don't care about the flowers with their musty old lady colours. All I know is *he's* gone. Yesterday I went looking for him, searching every corner of the garden, with her, stumbling along behind me.

'It's no good looking for Brendan Riley. I told you, he's finished the work.'

'You made him go. You had no right to drive him away. It's my house, and I said he could stay... I...'

She stands, exasperated, twisting her hair up in her butterfly clip. 'I don't understand why you're getting so upset about it. He's just some man. He's nothing to you.'

'How do you *know* he's nothing to me?'

'Well, I... he's only been here four days.' She looks at me, disconcerted. 'Did he *say* anything to you? Did he say something to you about me? You must tell me if he did. Vida, look at me. I'm serious.'

She's always serious. She hasn't got a sense of humour, that's her trouble.

'He was my friend,' I say.

She cautions more gently. 'But you don't even know him. You had a chat about the weather, the wildlife one day, that's all.'

'That's all you know!' I fling the words at her. 'It was more than that.'

'How do you mean, more than that?'

'What do you think? We got on. He liked me. I suppose you think I'm too old? Past it?'

'You're not saying... you're not trying to tell me...?' Her face clouds over. 'I knew it was a mistake letting him stay here. It was in the rules, no contact with the outside world. No wonder you look so exhausted. No wonder it's falling apart. It was meant to be a controlled experiment.'

Experiment. The word is cold, without compassion. It shocks me so much, I allow her to lead me back to the house.

That was yesterday.

Today I feel strange, ungrounded, as if I'm drifting out to sea and can't remember when I last saw land. Vaguely I'm aware of her voice trying to tempt me with cake, fried eggs, baked beans, custard and cocoa. But I'm not hungry.

She's given up the chanting. Instead of meditation, she turns on the TV and urges me to watch some American sitcom where people rush in and out of a living room, screeching a lot. The canned laughter hurts my ears. She takes me to the study and tries to talk books. Which ones have I read? Can I recommend anything?

'Would you like me to read to you, Vida?'

I shake my head. 'It's against the rules. It's not in the Programme.'

'Oh well, I've been thinking. We might be able to relax the rules a bit now.' She's leafing through a volume of short stories by Elizabeth Taylor as she speaks. It's one of the old Penguin editions, and the cover is curled and tea-stained in places. It used to be one of my comfort-reads. Not any more. I don't get any comfort from reading. The urge to snatch it from her hands is so strong that needles and pins are shooting up through my fingers, along my arms.

When the phone rings, she jumps, and the Elizabeth Taylor thumps to the floor.

'Oh, the phone. Vida, your telephone. Don't you want to answer it?'

'Not allowed. Not in the Programme.'

'Shall we forget the Programme for now...?' The phone goes on ringing, and she grabs the receiver:

'What? Cindy who? Hang on a minute, please, I'll get her...'

She pushes the receiver into my hand, and I hold it at some distance from my ear.

'Vida! You've been hiding from me. I've been trying to get you for ages.' Cindy's voice all but shatters my eardrum. 'Why don't you answer your emails? Anyway, I've been dying to tell...'

'Sorry I can't talk now.' I slap it down.

'One of your friends?'

'I don't know.' Is she? For a moment I can't think who this Cindy is.

Another Day

Today she says she'll have to use my computer as she has a lot of notes to write up and print out. She doesn't ask if I mind. She pushes past me after breakfast, and settles herself at my study desk. When I follow her in, she gets up, shrugging a shawl around her neck as if she's chilled and says to close the door to keep it cosy.

I know that look, abstracted, not quite in this world. It's how I used to be when I wrote, when I was in the middle of something. When Dory tapped at the door in the school holidays: '*Mu... um... can I have a drink Mum, can you make me a cheese toastie, can you play with me Mum...*?' I'd stare at her without seeing, my senses still tuned to that inner landscape. She'd have to repeat herself until her voice registered as a whine and I could ignore it no longer. I'd blink myself back into the world like some hibernating creature exposed to the light. We used to joke, my writer friends and I, about the caprices of the Muse; how it always strikes at the week before Christmas just when the house is filling with relatives, or at the start of school holidays. But you can't ignore the Muse. You can't. When she comes at whatever time of day or night, you must welcome her in and allow her to lead you wherever she will.

Oh yes, I recognize that expression. I see it in Rhiannon Townsend's eyes as she tugs *my* shawl about her and makes to close the door on me. *My* door.

'I might be a while, Vida. Why don't you go for a walk while the rain has stopped, eh?'

Next Day

She's at my computer again this morning, tap tap tap, her ringed fingers ceaselessly sweeping the keys like mine used to when I was meeting a deadline.

I notice this because the phone is ringing. When I go in, she begins shuffling her notes into piles.

'You'd better pick it up before it rings off,' she snaps.

'But I thought you said not to?' I hesitate to pick it up. It might be that nasty woman Fee something. I know I did something to upset her. Or was it something I didn't do?

'We've relaxed that rule,' Rhiannon says. 'Remember? We discussed it yesterday.'

I pick up the receiver. 'Hallo?'

'Mrs. Tremayne? Brendan Riley here. Sorry to bother you. I just wondered like, how you'd like to settle the bill.'

My mouth falls open. I feel my lips droop. I am speechless. His voice is deep, like the ringing of a great bell; it resonates all the way along my spine to my feet. I wish he would stay on the line forever. I clutch the receiver close to my ear.

'The bill...?'

He coughs. 'Yeah, I, er, left it with your friend. She said you'd settle at a later date, when you were better...'

I steady my voice. 'I'm perfectly well, thank you. How much do I owe you?'

'Who is that? It's *him*, isn't it! Yes it is, I can see from your face. Give it to me, I'll deal with it.' She's ready to snatch the receiver from my hand, but I won't let her.

'Do you mind? This is a private call.'

'Vida, my love, you're in no state to discuss...'

'I enjoyed our chats so much,' I tell him, 'I've been looking for you everywhere, but you're not in the greenhouse. Why did you sneak off without saying goodbye, Brendan?'

'Let me have that!' Rhiannon makes a decisive grab at the receiver, jerking it from my hands. 'Hallo… is that…' She pauses, makes a face, then slaps it down. 'He's gone. I wonder why.'

'You frightened him away.' I pluck the receiver from its cradle again, and press it to my ear just in case, but there's only the line humming. 'He wanted to speak to me.'

She scoffs. 'He wants paying, of course, so I'll get you to sign a cheque in a day or two and we can post it to him. Once we've settled his bill he won't bother us again. Now if you don't mind, Vida, I'd like to get on.'

Next Day

The days pass. I sleep later and later in the mornings. There's no point in going downstairs too early. It's warmer in bed and I can write this diary without fear of her seeing. She doesn't seem to mind now if I don't join her for breakfast. Sometimes she forgets about meals altogether. She grabs a sandwich and eats it at her desk instead. Her desk. Did I say *her* desk?

When I do go downstairs I don't feel right. I feel like a visitor in my own house. She's hardly ever in the kitchen now. Even the Rayburn fire goes out this morning. I go to the study to tell her we need to bring in coal, and she looks up and smiles as if she's only just remembered I live here. 'Morning, Vida. Did you sleep all right, my love?'

I nod. I'm looking at the half-eaten banana lying on the desk with the skin all curled back and browning.

Her fingers pause on the computer keyboard. 'You didn't hear anything unusual in the night?'

I shake my head.

She gets up then and ducks her head to peer through the front window. Outside the sky is the colour of spilled indigo ink. A watery sun glimmers through a gap in the cloud. It looks as if someone has punched a hole in the sky and a tiny bit of light leaks through. It has an unhealthy look. Like an open wound.

'It sounded like an animal, an animal in pain. I wondered about what you said in the woods... the traps the gamekeeper sets. It would be awful if there was an animal caught up there, struggling, wounded and nobody knew.'

When I don't say anything she turns her head and gives me a sharp look. 'Have you been thinking about your Puma lately? I'm not saying you *should* think about it, don't worry. In fact it might be a good idea if you let it rest for a while.'

She moves back to the desk, and I glance at the sheaf of freshly printed papers stacked on the printer.

'What are you doing? Are you writing a novel?'

She lets out a huff of surprise as she gathers stray pages. 'What makes you think that? *You're* the novelist, Vida, not me.'

'I think you are. I think you are using my computer to write a novel. I think the Muse has struck.'

'The Muse?' She stands clutching the papers to her chest, a hunted expression on her face. 'It's my notes for the Programme, that's all. I did tell you. There's so much to catch up on.'

I turn away. If I tried to tug them from her, it would be like wrenching a newborn from its mother's arms.

18th November

I'm writing this late at night, in bed with this book balanced on my knees. I've straightened things up a bit, pulled the covers back up, so I can make a kind of tent out of my quilt. My hand is shaking so much the pen keeps slipping through my fingers. Something happened today, but I'd better go back to the beginning.

I know the date, because this afternoon when I go downstairs she asks me to sign a cheque for Brendan. She smoothes out the bill he's left on the kitchen table, and says she'll get it off next time she goes to Cregaron post office, then we can 'get him off our backs'.

'He's not on our backs,' I say. I wish he were though.

'I'll admit we've kept him waiting a bit,' she says. 'To be honest I've been a bit distracted. I'll go to town tomorrow. We don't want him coming round to collect it in person.'

I wish she'd stop saying 'we', '*we* don't want', as if she and I are of one mind, the same person. She keeps looking over her shoulder, like she can't wait to get back to the study.

I ask her, 'Have you finished writing those notes?'

She gives me an odd look, and says yes, she's up to date with them, thank you. I can't help smiling. She's dried up, that's what it is. The flow has stopped. She's stuck, and now she's wondering what happened to the muse. She's panicking. Some devil in me decides to provoke her. I know just how to touch her sore point.

'You don't like men, do you?'

'Men? Of course I like men.'

'I think you hate men. You're jealous of me and Brendan. You're jealous of him touching me, liking me, wanting to come into my bed.'

She gives me a sad look as though she doesn't want to disillusion me. 'That never happened. How could it have done? He went home every day at five o'clock. I saw him off the premises personally. Thank God I was here to save you making a total fool of yourself! You may have dreamt it happened, and the dream stayed with you. You wanted it to be real. Oh God, don't look at me like that please.' She seizes the cheque and waves it to dry the ink. Then she sighs so deeply it's like a breeze that stirs from some deep undiscovered source. It might even be a sigh of surrender, of defeat.

She collapses into a chair by the stove and rakes her fingers through all that hair. 'You misunderstand my intentions, Vida. But I don't blame you. You're all mixed up. This imaginary affair with the odd-job man, it's ludicrous. It's not even original. It's straight out of *Lady Chatterley*. I should have seen this coming. It can happen when you release the totem animal; you can awaken appetites you forgot you ever had. It's the cat, Vida, don't you see? That's fine, that's normal. I'm not saying there's anything wrong with it. I'm just saying that a man like Brendan wouldn't be the best choice for you right now.'

She gets up and comes over to me, arms open wide as if in forgiveness. I stand stiffly in her embrace wishing she were him, Brendan. There are tears in my eyes. I remember how he took hold of me that day in my garden. It was like I was a tree to be planted, and he was steadying me first, holding me straight.

'I'm sorry I've been neglecting you these past few days, shut away with my notes. It's time we got back on track with the Programme, and decided what to do about you.'

Do about me? I don't like the sound of that. What does she intend to do about me?

I feel quite cold and clear-sighted when I say, 'You were supposed to help me write my next book. But *you're* the one who's writing now, not me.'

'Oh no... no....' She looks genuinely upset. 'You're mistaken. You *will* write again. I'm only writing dull old notes. I suppose if you force me to admit it, some of your creative energy might be rubbing off on me a bit. Creativity is like that. It's *infectious*. Now we need to think about you. We need to tidy up the loose ends and bring the Programme to a close. Your Dream Book, for instance. I haven't even seen that dream you had about our Mr. Riley. When did I last look at that?'

Our Mr. Riley, she says in that sarcastic tone. My dream book, she wants my dream book.

'There's nothing in it. I've told you everything that's written there.'

'In that case there's no harm in me having a look, is there?'

'I don't know where it is. I lost it.'

'What's the point of all these lies when I only want to help you? Now, come on, we'll go together and look for your Dream Book, shall we.'

She takes my hand as if I'm a child and begins leading me towards the stairs.

'No!' I shake my hand free and push past her. 'Not now. I'll look for it. I'll bring it down and show you later.'

'I'd really like to see it now, if you don't mind.'

But I'm ahead of her, into my room, shoving a chair against the door. I snatch the Dream Diary from under my pillow and prod it beneath the mattress. I stand by my bedside like a soldier awaiting kit inspection. There's no lock on my door. All Rhiannon has to do is push lightly, and the chair rolls on its side.

She glances at the chair and smiles. 'What's all this? Honestly, Vida, there's no need for barricades.

Don't we know everything there is to know about each other?'

I fold my arms across my chest. 'No, I don't think we do. I know nothing about you, do I? I don't know why you came here. I don't know anything about your life, your work, or your family. And I don't know what you're writing all day in my study. You've taken something from me, I do know that. But you're not going to take any more. You're not having my book.'

She gasps as if I've struck her, but I stand firm. 'Can you leave now? Can you please leave my room? In fact I want you to leave my house.'

'I'm sorry you feel that way. I'm sorry you don't want to *share* the creative experience with me, when I've only been working for your good.'

I look down and notice suddenly that a corner of the blue dream book is still poking out from beneath the mattress. Rhiannon follows my gaze and sees it too. She holds out her hand.

'You know it would be really so great if you gave it to me voluntarily.'

'Don't!' I hold up my hands as she moves towards the bed. 'Don't take another step.'

It's the first time I've stood my ground. I was afraid before, I suppose, afraid to test her, to see just how far she'll go. It's just as I feared. She ignores my command the way an adult disregards the whims of a child. She lunges forwards, and snatches the book with an air of self-righteous purpose.

A tremble runs through my entire body. I cease to think. I fling myself at her, slamming her into the bedstead. The brass knob catches her shoulders. I think I hear a crack. She groans. You can scent the fear on her breath like something sweet and brackish.

'Vida, no! Please don't be stupid, Vida!'

We tussle. She is big, a big woman, her flesh squashy but powerful under the layers of wool. Her hair tickles my face so I can hardly breathe. So much hair, it blinds me, chokes me. I manage to grab a great hank of it, and yank as hard as I can. My other hand finds its target. Fingers claw through the mass of softness to something hard, something knobbly. I drag my nails deep, deep into her scalp. It feels good. I feel like I'm marking territory, raking my talons down the bark of a tree. Then I make the mistake of grabbing her scarf, and pulling that. That's how she frees herself, unwinding from the scarf like a dancer on *Strictly,* stumbling down the stairs, still holding my book, out of the house, across the garden, then through the bracken which spreads along the northern margins, skirts, hair flying...

I'm close behind her. I can hear my own breath sawing in my ears. She turns, holds out her hands as if to ward me off. 'You can have it back, I only want to...'

Her words die away as if they never began. We both freeze, right where we stand. The forest clamours with birdcalls. Rooks rocketing skywards in vast dark clouds drift like smoke above the treetops, as if panicked by gunshot. They're heading west, already little more than faint black specks against the fading light, like specks of mud on a windscreen. Silence settles upon the forest. The smoky twilight deepens. There's not a breath of wind. Why then is the bracken moving? We stare. The bracken is rippling in one long wave, rolling inexorably towards us. Fronds of golden bronze part very definitely as whatever it is slinks towards us in a stately, unhurried procession. There's no doubt about its direction. The bracken crackles, divides as if bowing to a superior force of nature. Something is in the bracken and it's huge.

'Oh my God.' Her voice rasps beside me.

It reveals itself gradually, head first as the last fronds of bracken part to let it through. I can see its eyes, lazy, intent, the great muzzle, just as I've seen in my visions. The Puma.

'It can't be…' Rhiannon is whispering, my book slipping out of her hands and into the bracken. 'It doesn't… it can't…'

The expression on her face is resigned, like the willing victim of some sacrifice.

'Keep calm, Vida… don't run. We mustn't run.' She's whispering just loudly enough to hear above the swish and crackle of the bracken.

I am calm. I don't feel any fear of my Puma. It is quite beautiful. If it opens its great stinking maw it will speak to me, it will give me a message about him, about Brendan, I'm sure of that. I shall speak to it, and we shall converse in Puma language.

'Calm, keep calm, Vida, just step back quietly, easy…' She's flapping her hand at me, trying to push me, edge me gently back towards the house.

I don't move. The Puma stares at us, and we stare back at her. In that stare there is no past, no future. There is only the present moment. Never have I felt so absolutely alive. I can hear the blood pulsing through my veins, my arteries, pounding in my ears. I exist. I know that now. I am here, alive. I exist. Not as Vida Tremayne, a silly woman who tries to write novels nobody wants to read, but as energy, pure vibrating energy.

I'm aware of something, a human hand seeking mine, fingers entwining with my fingers, cold damp fingers, chunky with rings.

'Vida, my God… don't even breathe.'

It's as if the Puma is making up its mind what to do, then decides we are not worth the bother. In the golden depths of its eyes I see only contempt. It turns almost lazily and with a switch of its tail vaults the fence and vanishes into the longer grass towards the woods.

20TH FEBRUARY

DORY

Dory peels off a glove as she heads through hospital reception. She strokes her fingers across the palm of her left hand. The scar from where Vida scratched it the day before is still raw, pink and angry like an extended lifeline. She clenches her hand into a fist. Please God, let Vida be quieter today.

'I'll sit with her today,' Rhiannon told her that morning. She was already packing goodies into her basket like the matter was decided. 'She might be less agitated with me there.'

'Are you saying she's disturbed by my presence?' Dory had snapped. She didn't mean to snap, but Rhiannon's mother-knows-best act needled her.

Rhiannon seemed taken aback. No, of course she wasn't saying that, but Dory was obviously deeply upset by the attack yesterday.

'It wasn't an attack,' Dory said, 'my hand just got in the way.'

'Well, if you're sure. It's more distressing for you as her daughter, that's all I meant. Whereas I...'

'Thank you, but now that I've made up my mind to stay here until things are sorted, I may as well visit my own mother.'

Okay, that was sharp, but she can't just dismiss what Riley told her yesterday morning. His account of what happened when he worked at the house quarrels with Rhiannon's version of a half-naked Vida pursuing him around the garden. Someone is lying, but who? Dory hardly slept a wink last night for thinking about it. Riley may have his own reasons to lie. She doesn't entirely trust him, but it would be so much more convenient to demonize the local Mr. Fixit guy, because the alternative is just too awful.

※ ※ ※

'Excuse me; are you Mrs. Tremayne's daughter?' The staff nurse accosts her as she passes the nurses' station at the ward entrance. 'Would you mind having a little talk with Dr. Saleem before seeing your mother?'

'What's wrong? Is she worse?' Her mouth has gone dry.

The staff nurse says not to worry. 'There hasn't been much change since yesterday, but the Doctor would just like a chat, that's all.'

Dory thinks back to the interview a couple of weeks ago. Probably he's going to ask her to visit more often. She flushes as he rises to shake her hand.

'How do you think your mother's getting on?' he asks her.

'Well,' she clenches the scratched hand in her lap, 'I'm not sure. I came yesterday and she seemed worse, as if she couldn't keep her hands still. It was...' She isn't going to mention how Vida scratched her. They might step up her drugs, or bundle her into a straitjacket. Do they do still such barbaric things in modern hospitals? It may or may not be coincidence that just as she envisions the straitjacket, a piece of the Maple and Pecan Danish she gobbled en route dislodges itself from a tooth and catches in her throat. She coughs. She can't stop coughing. She coughs until her eyes stream with tears. 'Sorry, sorry...'

The doctor pushes the tissues towards her. Probably he thinks the coughing is a sham, to hide the fact that she's crying.

'Thank you.'

She blows her nose, and swallows back the irritation.

Dr. Saleem tells her that yesterday was not a good day for her mother.

'She has been a little restless just recently. It's not unusual in her condition. We had her quite heavily sedated until two weeks ago when she showed signs of recovery. There seems to have been a lapse in the past few days. We have been trying to adjust her medication. You understand, too much stimulation could undo our good work so far.'

'Yes, of course.'

'We think that the writing may have upset her.'

Writing? It takes her a while to make the connection. 'She's been writing? Oh, you mean that scribble, that word she writes over and over?'

The psychiatrist's serene manner has a tranquillising effect. How can she say what's on her mind? How can she say, 'Look, I want to know, is my mother totally, officially, irrevocably off her trolley or what?'

If she's to sell the house she needs to have Power of Attorney, and there is no way she will get this without a full medical report on Vida's mental incapacity.

'Please tell me the truth. There's no chance of my mother ever writing properly, of ever being normal again, is there?'

She steels herself for the answer, a cold clenched feeling around her heart. A length of tissue emerges from the box on the desk. Just think of all those other relatives who have broken down in this room! She resolves not to be one of them.

Dr. Saleem spreads his hands, and clasps them again in a gesture of impotence.

'It's too early to say, I'm afraid.' He launches into an explanation about the menopause, how the hormonal changes can make women vulnerable to breakdown. All the time he's talking, she imagines how it might be to feel the caress of this man's damp brown eyes upon her, his gentle voice prizing out her secrets like oyster pearls. Her mind drifts as she imagines what Dr. Saleem would be like in bed. Then she thinks of her mother and Riley.

'Sorry, what did you say?' She flushes.

Dr. Saleem is waiting for a response.

'If she is pushed too much now, well, it could be counter-productive.'

What does he mean, pushed?

'Sorry, I'm not with you.'

'It's come to my notice from the ward staff that she has a regular visitor, her niece I believe, who urges her to write all the time she's awake, brings her paper, holds the pen for her... it's a little early for that. We have tried to talk to her visitor about it. The problem is that we are gradually weaning her off the sedation, and trying some new drugs. The crucial thing is to keep her calm at this stage.'

Her niece! What niece? *Rhiannon.* He's talking about Rhiannon.

She says as if to herself, 'You've tried to talk to her? But she... she didn't mention this to me.'

'Hmm. The staff nurse says that your cousin became a little defensive when challenged. She appears to think the writing will help release something. You understand that any interference with medical procedure, no matter how well intentioned, could be dangerous for your mother.'

Dory is still digesting that word 'cousin'. Suddenly Rhiannon is not just a friend, but related. She is family. A blood relative. She tries to swallow back her shock.

'Oh, I understand. Yes, absolutely. I'll have a word with her.'

He nods, satisfied, and looks at his watch. She stands up in something of a daze. It's horrible to think of Rhiannon refusing to listen to the staff, pushing Vida to write, endangering her recovery. How could she be so stupid?

She coughs. 'I must ask you, how long do you think this will all take? I have my work to get back to, you understand; I need to make long-term arrangements for her care.'

She can hear her voice rising in mild hysteria, okay, but there's no need for the tissues, which he's pushing tactfully towards her. She's not crying, just on the brink of insanity.

'You understand, there are no guarantees in the territory of the mind.' The man's eyes brim with sympathy. If she wants, he says, they can arrange for Vida to be sent to a hospital nearer to Dory's home. She will have to see the Ward Clerk and fill in the necessary forms.

'But you know, your mother is doing as well as can be expected in here. It may not be wise to move her just yet. Why don't you have a little think about it, hmmm?'

※ ※ ※

Back at the Gingerbread House, the kettle simmers on the hotplate. All is quiet, orderly. There's no sign of Rhiannon.

'Anyone at home?' Dory checks the sitting room, Vida's office; she shouts up the stairs. Hearing a muted cough from Rhiannon's room, she raps twice and walks straight in.

'Oh, Dory... you're back early. Is everything all right?' Clearly Rhiannon is taken aback to see her. She's sitting up in bed; a newspaper spread open in her lap. Her face as she turns to greet Dory is puffy in her nest of hair. She explains, 'I thought I'd come back to bed after you left, have one of my lie-in days.'

'Lie-in days? Are you ill?'

Dory can't help noticing how quickly she slides the newspaper beneath a purple folder as if she doesn't want her to see what she's reading. It's the latest edition of the local rag again. Not Rhiannon's usual fare, unless she's developed a sudden interest in sheep sales and the Young Farmers' social calendar.

'No, no, I'm *never* ill. But sometimes we need to just *stop*, you know. I thought I'd just catch up with my notes.' She pats the folder, and tweaks the fluffy throw she carries around with her like a child's comfort blanket. It nestles around her neck, blanketing her ears.

Notes. God knows what they're about, and Dory's not going to ask.

Dory says, 'Vida was fast asleep. They've sedated her quite heavily so there was no point in hanging around.'

Rhiannon shuffles stray pages into the folder. She looks perturbed. 'I don't like the sound of that. She'll never get well if they keep drugging her.'

'I told you yesterday the state she was in. I showed you the scratch. Dr. Saleem called me into his office this morning. He says that encouraging her to write has set her back quite a bit. She's in a highly agitated state. They're going to have to increase her medication again.'

Dory can see Rhiannon bristle as she prepares her defence. She speaks in the sorrowful whine of the morally righteous. 'But don't they see she *needs* stimulus. Those drugs aren't helping her; they're just creating a new dependency problem.'

Dory comes to the point. 'Rhiannon, why did you tell the staff you're Vida's niece?'

Rhiannon sighs. 'I should have told you, I'm sorry. I said I was Vida's niece because they asked me about my relationship to her. You were in London at the time, and if they'd stipulated next of kin only, well, Vida would have had no one at all.'

At this reminder of her absence, Dory feels a stab of guilt. Her fingers unclench. The white lie seems reasonable under the circumstances. Probably she's too ready to think the worst.

'Okay, well it's not that I'm so concerned about, but the writing. I know you've been trying to help, but you can see their point. They're the experts. The writing can come later, when she's completely well. We can't risk upsetting things. It was terrible to see her in that state yesterday, scratching the chair arms over and over like some kind of animal, until her fingers bled.'

'*Experts.*' Rhiannon picks up on the word, giving it ironic emphasis. 'Dory, I understand why you'd want to trust the "experts" but it's a bit naïve. They don't want Vida stimulated. They want her to stay nice and quiet because it's less work for them.'

She begins to expand on staff shortages and the state of the NHS, but Dory doesn't want to hear this now. Somehow or other, Rhiannon is shifting the blame. She hasn't apologized. She hasn't promised to obey Dr. Saleem's request. Her arrogance is astounding.

'Yes, well that may be so, but I think it's better if I take care of the visiting from now on.'

Something she can't interpret clouds Rhiannon's face, as she shifts her knees beneath the coverlet.

'I see. Are you saying you don't want me to visit Vida again?'

Dory swallows. She folds her arms across her midriff. 'For the time being, yes, I am saying that.'

'If you think that best...' Rhiannon keeps her voice steady, but her flushed cheeks give her away.

Dory makes to leave, avoiding eye contact, saying she's going to catch up with some work.

'I'll be in Mum's office if you want me.'

Once she's pulled the door closed, she breathes more easily. Still she hasn't got to the real point; she hasn't asked Rhiannon how long she plans to stay. She hasn't suggested that maybe it's time Rhiannon thought about getting back to her own life. Why not? It's not like her to chicken out. God knows she's had some difficult clients to deal with over the years and she's not afraid of some straight talking. So why then did she sidestep the issue? Is it because there is something almost pathetic about Rhiannon, in her desperate need to be needed, to be of service? It's hard, too, to forget how she listened when Dory first came back, how she empathized with her over Vida, the loss of Dan, the hugs and homilies, not to mention the soup.

'I'm a nurturer,' Rhiannon once told her. 'It's why I'm here, to nurture people. That's why I nurtured Vida's talent.'

Hasn't Rhiannon nurtured her too? Wouldn't it be damned ungrateful to chuck her out because she's tried to encourage Vida to write, and introduced herself as a niece? Maybe Rhiannon has no blood ties of her own, so needed to invent one.

But there's something more. Something that doesn't add up. Something niggling at her. How is Rhiannon paying the bills? How is she paying rent for that flat of hers? She's not earning any money while she's lolling around here. Unless she has private means, of course. But she doesn't look the type to have a rich daddy bank-rolling her. And what about her post? Surely someone, that neighbour who was looking after the cat, would be forwarding her bills at least?

Back downstairs in Vida's study, she flips open her laptop. It's come to her suddenly that checking out the flat might be a good idea. In fact why didn't she think of this before? You can learn a lot about a person just by googling 'Street View'. A broken gate, dustbins on view, a tatty windowbox can tell you volumes.

Where did Rhiannon say she lived in Palmers Green exactly? She remembers asking the name of the street that first afternoon. Rhiannon had mumbled something, a name she didn't recognize at the time; Faringdon Avenue, that was it. She types it into GoogleSearch. Nothing. Maybe she's spelled it wrongly. She types it in with two 'r's'. Still nothing. After trying every possible spelling variation of Farringdon, she tries moving slightly north to neighbouring Southgate. Still nothing. There are it seems heaps of Farringdon Avenues, right across London, but not one of them is in, or anywhere near, Palmers Green.

So, if Rhiannon has lied about her address, where does she live? Does she even have a home of her own to go to? Her skin prickles with impatience. Should she go straight back upstairs and confront her with the discovery? No, she reaches for her cigarettes instead. Better to bide her time. Be sure of her facts before she goes steaming in with accusations.

⚜ ⚜ ⚜

Later, when she goes to the kitchen to make herself a drink, she notices the newspaper Rhiannon was reading is scrunched up in the log basket next to the Rayburn. Well, fire-lighting is all that rag is good for. Despite this, some instinct drives her to fish it out of the basket. She smoothes the scrunched-up middle section of the paper and spreads it on the table.

It's another Puma story. This time the sighting has been reported by a young couple driving home from a party in the early hours of Tuesday morning.

'It just slunk out from the trees by the side of the road and strolled in front of us, like,' the driver was reported as saying. *'We caught it in the headlights, and I don't mind saying it gave us a turn. It looked straight at us. It was massive. Well. Lucky I didn't hit it like. I just slammed my brakes on in time...'*

The report added that the driver swore he hadn't been drinking, and that police had investigated the scene but had found no tracks and nothing to substantiate the sighting.

At the thump of footsteps from upstairs, Dory hurriedly screws up the paper and shoves it back in the basket. Puma stories. Total rot. Handy for filling up newspaper space at this time of year, she supposes, when there's nothing much else going on. But why is Rhiannon so interested? And why is she shivering, even as she hurries back to the sanctuary of her mother's study, her hands cradling the steaming mug.

Vida's Diary

Some time in early December

A journal should always have a date. You don't know where you are without a date. I know that it's winter, of course, because it's cold and dark almost all the time. The house even smells cold. There is a log pile by the back door, but I keep forgetting to put logs on the fire before it gets too low. I think we're in December. Have we had Christmas yet? There's no one to ask so I'm not sure.

I would ask that woman who was staying with me. She'd know, because she seems to know everything. But she's gone. She said she had to go and help out a friend for a bit, that I'd be all right, wouldn't I. She gave me a big hug and then she was gone. Something happened but I can't quite remember what. Did we have a fight? There was a cat, a big one, I seem to remember that. I keep checking she's not hiding somewhere: under the bed, in the cupboard beneath the stairs, behind the plum tree. I think I hear her humming... *for I am the wife of the carpenter...*

Strange it doesn't feel like my desk any more. Even my chair now seems knotty and unyielding, as though it's adjusted its shape to accommodate *her* curves. She's left her imprint on the seat, buffing the patina of old pine smooth with her gypsy skirts. She was here every day towards the end. Writing... writing... what was she writing?

I have no curves. The bones in my bottom dig into my seat as I wriggle, trying to get comfortable. I don't feel secure. The chair is like a capricious horse who wants its old mistress back. Any moment now it may buck me right off. My back aches with the cold. I wish I had a cushion to sit on. Hen feathers are good, especially if they are russet and black.

The phone rings a lot but mostly I don't answer. When I do pick up I hold the receiver some distance from my ear, as if I might catch something. Today when I pick up there's a voice shrilling at me.

'Vida! How are you? You sounded a bit upset last time I rang. Some strange woman kept answering and making excuses. Was it your P.A? I'm thinking of getting one myself, someone to deal with the fan mail, you know, someone to chase off the stalkers and handle the press; what a pain that lot are…'

I'm trying to think: Cindy, Cindy, who is Cindy?

'Listen, I must tell you about Belinda Arden, remember that mousey little thing at our Authors' Society do? Can you believe she's been shortlisted for the Orange Prize? Darling, it's dross! I read the manuscript because she wanted my opinion, then totally ignored it, I might add. I mean, there is no justice in this business, is there.'

I agree there isn't. No, no justice. I've never heard of Belinda Arden. Have I?

Then *her,* that woman, my fan I think, Rhiannon someone… the woman who sat in my chair, at my desk.

'Vida? Are you all right? I've been worried about you. I hated to leave you like that, but you understand I couldn't stay after our... well, our disagreement. I just wanted to say, don't try to do any of the meditations without supervision. It's not safe. I mean...' She pauses. 'Especially not with your totem animal. Do you understand, Vida? Whatever you do, *don't try to make contact with it.*'

I don't say anything, I just go on standing there holding the receiver to my ear, waiting. I'm not sure what I'm waiting for. It seems rude to just put the receiver down. Then she says, 'Vida... I don't like to ask this, but are you writing again?'

'I'm writing my diary,' I tell her, 'only I keep forgetting what day it is. Such a nuisance. You don't happen to know the date, do you?'

'Your diary?' She's quiet for a moment, then she says in this nice, kind, calm voice, like a doctor talking to a child, 'I didn't know you kept a diary, Vida.'

'My journals. I never miss a day. It's my record, you see. You have to keep a record, otherwise you forget everything that's happened. I'm getting a bit forgetful. It's such a nuisance when you can't remember what day it is...'

Still she doesn't tell me the date. She starts talking about a Programme, was I keeping the Journal then, because I really wasn't supposed to. I don't know what she's talking about. That's when I put the receiver down. When it rings again, I take it off the hook and leave it there.

Next Day

Something is not right, not as it should be. This morning I find myself standing in the old greenhouse, which is choked with dusty tomato vines. The windows are all iced up. Spiders scuttle over my feet. I can't think how I got here, or why.

Then I remember: I'm supposed to be writing. Didn't I used to have a routine? Nine to midday every day, clackety clack, never stirring from my study, except to make coffee. Or was that years ago, when Jonathan lived here?

I wander into my study and mooch around. The bank of typing paper glares up at me from my desk, dazzling blue-white like a snowfield awaiting footprints. I sit at my desk, examine rubbers and pencil sharpeners, and sort paper clips into neat piles. I feel like I'm a child playing in a parent's office. I doodle on the pad, hideous faces growing out of my pen, jeering at me.

Somewhere deep inside, I hear a voice, slow, husky, insistent: '*The Programme will free you, Vida, you need to break through the blocks. You can do it, Vida.*'

She said that novels would drip from my pen faster than I could write them. I would spin tales as the princess spun gold out of straw. Now I can't even organize the words in my head. I write my name. Vida Tremayne...... Vida Tremayne.....Vida Tremayne.. It looks like the name of someone important. I don't think it's me.

Today when the phone rings I ignore it. I can't be bothered to dress properly. Dishes pile up in the sink. A strange dog comes and sits at the back door, and I throw it scraps. When I try to stroke it, it growls and trots off up the track, as if I am not the person it has come to see, and is disappointed.

I thought I heard the whine of a handsaw from the edge of the woods earlier. I stumbled outside in my dressing gown and called his name.

'Brendan? Brendan, is that you?' Nothing.

Indoors, I look in the mirror and see a stranger. What is her name? She looks like that old woman in the fairytale who lives in a hovel made out of gingerbread and eats little children for supper. I thought that was *her*, Rhiannon, but maybe it's me. If it is me, then I'm too old for Brendan Riley. He's found some lusty girl with firm flesh and the same taste in music. That's how it should be.

Early December

It seems strange, there was a time when I didn't hear from Dory for weeks: months would pass and never a word, or she was always out when I called. Now the phone rings almost every day. She sounds exasperated. She thinks I sound odd. She wonders if I am well, and have I seen a doctor lately?

'I wish you'd speak sense, Ma. I've got a big deal on right now, I can't just up sticks and rush up the motorway.'

I tell her I don't expect her to do such a thing, that I'm perfectly fine.

'Well, why don't you get the decorators in and cheer the place up? Why don't you have a valuation done? I don't mean to nag, but the market is hot right now, and believe me, I should know.'

Do I want to sell this house? Dory seems to think I do. Where would I go?

In the event, Dory decides for me.

'Listen, Mother, I've gone ahead and set it up with a local agent. All you have to do is open the door to him, and offer him a nice cup of tea. Don't say too much and whatever you do don't point out any of the million of jobs that need doing. Just let him make up his own mind, all right?'

So today, a young man from Nisbett Fox comes to take particulars of the house. He doesn't seem to mind about the lack of white paint. He is very taken with the study.

'So,' he says, 'this is where it all goes on then? The novel-writing? This is where you do the novel writing?'

'Yes, yes, I...' I hate to tell him, not any longer. While he flicks his tape measure and scribbles notes, I flip the page on my desk facedown. I don't want him to see my doodles, like hieroglyphics, gargoyle faces.

'You'd be surprised what a good selling point it is.'

'I beg your pardon?'

'The novel writing.' He begins to tell me about a Grace someone, a famous novelist, whose house just sold for fifteen thousand over the market price.

'Mind you, she's passed away. That tends to give extra cache, if you know what I mean.'

I nod. I hope he doesn't hear it, the cat snuffling, prowling. I don't want to frighten him, this nice young man with the rash on his neck, and the blunt northern vowels. His voice is so reassuring, I think of asking him to stay here, move in as my lodger. He is exactly the sort of man I need about the place.

No, that's not entirely true. I'd prefer that other one, Brendan, the one who crept into my bed. But I have a feeling he's not coming back.

'Would you like a cup of tea?'

'Sorry, love.,' He does that thing some men do, bending his arm at the elbow to free his watch from the crisp shirt-cuff. 'Better get on. Two more to see after this.'

'Oh, never mind.'

'Yes, like I was saying, Grace Selbourne? Have you heard of her?'

'I don't think I have.'

'Passed on two months back. Her daughter wanted to sell up straight away. Couldn't stand the memories. Buyers are going to preserve her study, sort of a shrine. They were fans apparently. Bit of a waste of reception space if you ask me, but mine is not to reason why.'

'Indeed.'

Icy fingers stroke my spine. I flash-forward into the foggy horizons of my own future, and feel the void opening up before me. I do wish he'd stay. As soon as his car vanishes out of the drive the house fills with whispers. Draughts snuffle beneath the doors. They sound like an animal breathing.

When I come back in here to my room, I find the sheet of paper I was scribbling on smudged with what look like paw prints. I hold it up to the light, the paper trembling so much in my hands I can barely make out the words I've written. It doesn't matter anyway. There's hardly a sentence that isn't obliterated by prints. The creature has been in here, I know. Huge pads have walked right across my desk, trailing a bloody feral scent. Is it looking for me? In the night sometimes, I hear it howling. It sounds so lonely.

Mid-December

Dory rings next day. She has spoken to the young man at Nisbett Fox already, and his valuation, she says, is a joke.

'So we won't be requiring his services, I said... Mum... are you there?'

'I think so.'

She sighs. 'What d'you mean, you think so? For heaven's sake, Mother, haven't you been to see Dr. Philbin yet? Look, I'm worried about you; I can't keep dropping everything and hurtling down to the back of beyond to check you're all right.'

'No, I don't want you to. I'm fine.'

'Sounds like it. Hold on a minute, what was that, Harvey?' There is some urgent discussion in the background, phones ringing, a buzz of voices and laughter. When she comes back on, her voice is thin and rushed:

'Look, I've got to fly, but I'm going to ring and make you an appointment with the doctor myself. I'll call you back and let you know the time. And just be sure you get yourself there, okay?'

So this is why I'm here this morning, in Dr. Philbin's waiting room, watching a small child with a snot-caked nose trying to eat a Lego brick from the play box. The child distracts me. Dory was that size once. I can hardly believe it. The child gives me a curious look and offers me the Lego, saliva-smeared, still attached to her mouth by a string of dribble.

The gesture touches me, reminds me who I am, who I was.

I smile at the girl. 'What's your name?'

But the mother gives me an odd look and snatches away both Lego brick and child. I adjust my hat. Maybe it's the hat she's wary of?

I'm trying to remember what I'm doing here. Is it a sore throat? Is it that knee joint which cracks slightly when I go downstairs? What? A sick panic begins to gnaw at me. What am I going to tell the doctor? He'll think I'm a malingerer, a time-waster, when there are genuinely sick people coughing around me, shuffling about on sticks.

In fact, it's not Dr. Philbin at all but Dr. Mapston, who is young and wiry, wearing old man's spectacles. When he asks me what the trouble is I manage to stammer that I'm having problems sleeping.

He nods knowingly. 'And, are you still having your periods, Vida?'

I have to think. Am I? 'No. They seem to have stopped.'

More nodding. He reels off a list of symptoms: do I have hot flushes, cystitis, headaches? Am I depressed?

'Depressed? Yes. I think I'm very depressed. I think that's my trouble.'

Everyone gets depressed, don't they? Depression is quite normal. Why does he just sit there, though, silently gazing at me, his eyes mild and anxious behind his glasses? Suddenly I want to tell him everything. But can I trust him?

'I've been on edge,' I admit. 'I keep thinking...'

'Yes?'

'Well, I keep thinking I think I *see* things. You know, like dreaming, only in the daytime.'

The soft eyes sharpen with concern. He asks if I have any history of mental illness. He consults my notes thoroughly. Then he checks my glands, peers into my eyes, asks me to stick out my tongue.

'Any dizziness at all?'

'No. No dizziness.'

He returns to his desk. He seems relieved.

'I see you're an author by profession, Vida.'
He smiles. 'Perhaps you've been over-working your
imagination a bit.'

He concludes finally that my problems are
menopause-related. He recommends HRT patches,
supplemented by sleeping pills.

'Come and see me in a month's time. I don't
think you need anti-depressants. What you're feeling is perfectly normal at this stage of your life.'

The Cregaron road is dusted with a light wet
snow as I drive home. The trees throw up their
branches against a bleached sky, a black scribble,
like hieroglyphs, like a message. I think I read
the word BEWARE. My knuckles are white on the
steering wheel. It's up here somewhere, that creature. Didn't we, my fan and I, go searching for
signs?

There's a lay-by up ahead. I know it well. People
walk here in summer, along the footpath, past the
forestry commission hut, through pinewoods dark
as velvet. The urge to pull in here is so strong, I can't
deny it.

There's no one about. I step out of the car, and
breathe the air sharp in my lungs. There's a bristling
at the back of my neck.

'Puss… puss… puss…' I call to it.

A pheasant rattles out of the undergrowth,
unwieldy, like a child's wind-up toy, a thing made
from clockwork. I lick my lips. I think of the pheasant, its blood and red wine pooling on my tongue.

It feels right up here. I'm not afraid to come face to face with the cat. I think it will be like coming face to face with myself.

Later

The phone keeps ringing and ringing when I get home. In the end I pick it up. Dory is shouting. She must think I am deaf.

'Mum, did you see the agent? What about the doctor? What did he say? Listen, I know I said Dan and me would be away staying with friends in Oxford for Christmas, but that's not likely to happen now.' She breaks off, and I hear the click of her cigarette lighter. 'So, I could come by to see if you're okay but don't go faffing about making mince pies for me or anything. I hate the things and I haven't been eating much lately anyway. What d'you think? Would you like me to drop in?'

'Couldn't Dan come, though?' I say. 'Dan would like mince pies.'

'No, I just told you. He's gone, Mother, do I have to spell it out?' She sounds nasally, as if she has a bad cold. Smoking won't do it much good, I want to tell her. I'm trying to understand what she's saying to me, something like 'We're not together any more! Look if my company isn't good enough for you just say so. Do you want me to drop in or not?'

'Drip in?'

'No. *Drop...* I said *drop in.* What are you ON? You're not on the G and Ts already, are you?'

I think she must be making a joke. I start to laugh. But perhaps I go on laughing for too long, because then she keeps telling me to stop in a cross voice.

'Sorry,' I say. 'Sorry, Dorothy...'

'Dory, not Dorothy, don't tell me you've forgotten my name now. I am your daughter, Dory, remember?'

'Dory, that's right. I was thinking of Dorothy who lives in Kansas and her house blows away in a tornado and she goes to see the wizard.'

'Dear Christ, Mum! What's with the Yellow Brick Road stuff? Look, you're seriously beginning to worry me, Mum... Mum?'

I take a deep breath. 'Will you please excuse me, Dorothy? I have to go and feed the cat now.'

I have made up my mind. I won't answer the telephone ever again.

20TH FEBRUARY
DORY

Dory buttons her cardigan to her neck. It's the finest cashmere, warm enough to bring her out in a sweat normally, but Vida's study is like a tomb. She types her password onto her laptop and hugs herself, rubbing her upper arms to warm her blood. Through the window some half-hearted snowflakes are fluttering dizzily about. The online weather forecast for the area when she checks it out is flashing an amber warning. Snow. Terrific. That's all she needs.

Had she been alone in the house she might have worked in the warm kitchen, but Rhiannon could haul her arse out of bed and come tramping downstairs any moment. If only she'd take the hint. What's the point of her hanging her around any longer? Can't she see she's overstayed her welcome? Any normal person would be packing their bags and slinking off back home.

She must focus. She's neglected her blog these past few days, and that's not good enough. She chews on the end of her pen. Some blather on downsizing might be timely. She begins typing:

Is your empty nest feeling a tad draughty now the kids have flown? Fed up with heating all those empty rooms? Tired of dusting a lifetime's clutter? You're not alone. At Tremaynes' we've noticed more and more clients looking to simplify their lives and downsize. The good news is that you don't have to exile yourself into the wilds with only the crows for company. The trend these days is for apartments in the London villages such as Marylebone, or St Margaret's where the boutiques and street cafes create a lively buzz. Why not drop us a line and tell us exactly what you're looking for. It's our pleasure to take the load off your back, and see you through this crucial phase of your life. Moving is always a big step. But this is one step you'll be so glad you've taken!

What a load of twaddle. Dory grimaces as she types in the exclamation mark, and despatches the lot to Harvey to put on the site. She checks the web mail for queries and there are just two, one with a check-list of must-haves that runs to two pages. She's about to attend to this, but the cold must have seeped its way to her brain. It's ridiculous. So now she has to sit here and freeze, while the lodger installs herself by the Rayburn for the rest of the afternoon.

She casts around for that hideous bristly tartan rug thing Vida sometimes used to spread over her knees when she was working. Then she remembers, she last saw it in the back of Vida's car.

❧ ❧ ❧

Outside in the strangely metallic light the snowflakes look more serious. Ducking her head, she darts over to where Vida's car is parked slightly askew beneath the Poplars. Looking at it now, she feels that strange pang of loss. She almost smiles. Her mother's devotion to her ageing KA has always been a family joke. Still, old banger it might be, but she's never noticed that scratch on the paintwork before. She fingers the scar, which runs all the way from the left back wing to the bonnet. It looks angry, deliberate, as if some yobbo has keyed it in the parking lot. If it happened recently Rhiannon said nothing about it; but then…

Dory goes round to the back and opens the boot. The tartan blanket is here all right, draped over something bulky. Whipping off the blanket is a thoughtless act, performed in a second. Too late to put it back in place again. Too late to pretend she hasn't seen what it's been hiding. She stands motionless, staring. It's just a heap of books with identical hardback covers in a dull shade of blue, yet she might have uncovered a nest of vipers the way she feels. These are not just any old books. They are notebooks. Journals. She lifts one and reads the white sticky label – *Vida's Diary – May – August 1995*.

So Riley was right about Vida writing a diary. What else was he right about? She glances automatically up towards the front bedroom window. The curtains are still half drawn, but Rhiannon might show her face any moment. She might look down and see Dory standing there, arms stacked with Vida's diaries, the diaries Vida was supposed to be too weak, too confused to write. Why would she deny all knowledge of them and then hide them? Well, she's about to find out. Dory closes the boot as quietly as she can, and creeps back to the house to fetch her coat.

❦ ❦ ❦

Five minutes later and she's pulling her car into the empty car park at the Stiperstones. The Bog Visitor Centre is little more than a wooden hut. She reads the sign: 'Closed until May'. In all these years it's only the second time she's been here. Her parents insisted on dragging her up to see the Devil's Chair the week they moved into the Gingerbread House. Duty performed, nothing Vida could say would ever induce Dory to join her on a walk up there after that, even though it's only ten or fifteen minutes climb from the cottage. She recalls her mother's efforts to persuade her. Would it have killed her to come just once with Vida? Would it have hurt to listen to Vida rabbiting on about Megaliths and Iron Age barrows and some fusty old Victorian novelist, Mary Webb, who set all her novels here? Now she's finally up here and it's too late. All she has left of her mother are a pile of notebooks stacked on the seat beside her. She's not sure why she's come here now. It just seems a good place to be sure of avoiding Rhiannon, and she can't bear the thought of going back to the house just yet.

Jabbing a cigarette between her lips, she squints through the windscreen at the snowflakes. Against the drifting white, the sheep look dirty, mangier than ever as they pick their way over the boulders. There is too much of *nothing* here, she thinks. The vastness of moor is relieved only by the craggy outline of the Devil's Chair to the north. The outcrop glitters like sugar frosting as the snow begins to settle.

Shrugging herself closer into her wool coat she shuffles through the book pile to find the latest entries. It's hard to know where to begin. The first journal she plucks out is all nature notes, and stuff about other writers Vida knows or has known. She flicks impatiently through descriptions of woodland tramps, birdlife, even a recipe for blackcurrant jam. Dory digs deeper into the pile. Then she has it. She knows instinctively without even looking at the date – September of this year – that this is it, where it all begins. There's something different about the hand-writing on the opening page, a wavering, an uncertainty. Whole paragraphs have been crossed out and rewritten. September then... She stubs out the cigarette, pulls up the collar of her coat and reads.

It's some time before she looks up again. When she does the land is stippled white. It's stopped snowing for the moment. The sky deepens to indigo as daylight fades. She checks her watch. Four p.m. She's been reading for one and a half hours without stopping and her feet have turned to ice. There's more to come, but she's got as far as the *Programme*, far enough to confirm her suspicions about Rhiannon. One thing for certain, she can't go on reading here in the dark. She has to go back to the house. She needs to read all of it, before she takes action.

❧   ❧   ❧

Rhiannon is in the kitchen when she gets back. Through the half-closed door, she can hear the hum of a play on the radio, the clink of cutlery. Only yesterday, this might have consoled her. Not now. She heads upstairs, but not before the kitchen door tugs open.

'Dory?' Rhiannon stands there, sleeves rolled up, her plump forearms dusted with flour. 'I thought I'd make us some gingerbread, do you fancy some with a cuppa?'

'No thanks. And I'll pass on supper. I'm not hungry.' Had she not discovered the journals might she just have fallen for that old homey, momma bakes apple pie act? She doesn't trust herself to meet Rhiannon's eye as she dismisses her kind offer. Once their eyes lock she won't be able to stop herself, and she needs to be sure of her facts before the showdown.

'I'll be in my room, working.'

Rhiannon calls something after her, but she decides to ignore it.

Dory doesn't go down to supper. She'd rather starve. It's around eight when she hears Rhiannon's purposeful tread on the stairs. The wonky floorboard on the landing creaks as she pauses outside her door. She must be seriously worried by now.

317

There's a gentle rapping. 'Dory? Dory, are you in there? Is everything all right?'

She holds her breath. This is how it must've been for Vida when the Programme was in full swing, scribbling in her bedroom by candlelight, dreading a visitation from the Director, from *She who must be obeyed.*

Rhiannon moves on down the hall. Let her interpret her silence however she likes. A few moments later and there's a gushing sound from the pipes, the bump and grind of ancient plumbing. That bloody woman is running a bath! Just picturing her idly soaping all that complacent flesh, using up a whole tank of hot water after the damage she's caused, sets her teeth on the edge. She takes the opportunity to sneak downstairs to refuel. The empty kitchen hums with Rhiannon's presence. The gingerbread, dark and sticky and smelling delicious, sits out on a plate covered with a chequered tea cloth. There's a note beside it telling her to help herself if she gets hungry. Dory bites her lip as her stomach purrs. No thanks. Too late to sweeten her up, she'd rather drink arsenic. She settles for Marmite toast and tea and spirits it away to her room.

Back in bed, she reads, her heart growing heavier with every page. The diaries make for uncomfortable reading. By the time she gets to the section about the Puma, about Riley climbing into Vida's bed, something she's now convinced is Vida's fantasy, the pipes are quiet. But for the rumble of Rhiannon's snoring, the house is wrapped in the deepest silence.

Dory reads on until her eyes feel sore. Some time around midnight, before she can finish the final entries, her eyes grow heavy. She drifts off to dream that Dan is back at the flat dishing up a meal for a strange woman, who is not her. Then she sees that the woman is her mother, and the two of them are laughing about something but they won't let her in on the joke.

⚜ ⚜ ⚜

She awakes to a clatter from downstairs. It's seven thirty. No time to dress. She tugs a big sweater over her pyjamas, scrambles downstairs to the kitchen.

'Good morning! Have you seen the snow? It's absolutely gorgeous.' Rhiannon doesn't look up as she speaks. She carries on, calmly packing her wicker basket with items for the invalid: a carton of pineapple juice, a box of violet tissues, and yes, the blessed gingerbread. Surely she doesn't think Vida's going to eat that? She's dressed to go out in her velvet coat, and sheepskin-lined boots.

'Did you sleep well?'

'No, actually I didn't sleep well at all. What exactly are you doing?' Dory struggles to keep her cool. If she loses control, she loses her authority. Rhiannon will play the part of the older, wiser, forbearing mother figure and wait patiently for the tantrum to subside. It's the role she plays to perfection.

She considers her options. She can hardly call the police. There's nothing in the diaries to indicate that this woman's hold on Vida is a criminal matter. What would a court of law say? They'd say that Vida was a weak woman who allowed herself to be manipulated by one of her fans, and the whole sordid affair would become public. No money has been taken, no jewellery or personal possessions, at least not off the premises.

'I'm just off to the hospital.' Rhiannon is patting a tea cloth over the goodies, all solicitude as if she is tucking an infant into its cradle. 'Is there anything you'd like me to take to Vida?'

'No, and if there is I'll take it myself. I've already told you, you're not going to see Vida. You won't be seeing my mother ever again.'

They are facing each other across the kitchen, opponents, as if assessing each other's strength. Stand off. Dory observes the change in expression, now that the mask is dropped. How come she didn't notice this before, the hard intensity of Rhiannon's gaze? She knows from the diaries that Rhiannon is not afraid to fight for what she wants. If she was prepared to wrestle an older woman weakened by lack of food just to read about her dreams, she'll have no compunction about tackling the younger, stronger, ungrateful daughter.

'I read the diaries,' Dory says, 'or rather I read that last volume. You know the journal you swore Vida couldn't have written? I don't know where you found them eventually. In the hall chest maybe, or the bureau, it doesn't matter. You hid the whole lot of them in her car just to make sure no one else got there first. What were you planning to do, light a nice big bonfire? No, don't answer that, please. It's because of you my mother is ill. I don't understand what your game was exactly. All I know is you destroyed her, and now you want to pack up your little basket of goodies and go hospital visiting. Do you really suppose a slab of gingerbread can compensate for the damage you've inflicted? Or do you just go to gloat, is that it?'

Now that she's started, she can't stop. Rhiannon just stands there taking her punishment. It's infuriating the way she makes no attempt to defend herself, to interrupt. At the same time she hardly appears shamefaced. You'd think she would be protesting her innocence by now but no, there she stands patiently waiting for Dory to run out of steam. When Dory falls silent she nods. It's as if she's taken all the accusations on board, digested them thoroughly and found them wanting.

She speaks in a gently reproving tone, the way a teacher might speak to a wayward pupil. 'If you read the journal, Dory, you'll know how lonely your mother was, how depressed she was...'

'Yes, and you took full advantage of the fact.'

'I wanted to help. Who else was there for Vida? I was hoping I wouldn't have to say this, but how often did you visit, or even telephone?'

'You what... but that's none of your business.'

'True, but I was there when Vida did take a call from you. I think it was something about not coming up for Christmas, wasn't it? When she came off the phone, she was fighting back tears.'

'Don't give me that!' The accusation hits hard. She's almost winded by it. It's true she could have made more of an effort. But that was then… and now is now. She recovers herself. 'And in any case, didn't that suit your purpose perfectly? You didn't want me in the way, did you? You don't want me now. You've been pretending to be my bosom buddy, oh yeah, but all the time you've been trying to get rid of me, pack me back off to London ever since I arrived, and no wonder. You're so nice and cosy here, aren't you? Nice comfy bed, hot baths at the drop of a hat. What I want to know is where are your friends? What about your work, your so-called 'clients', God help them? Do you actually have any clients, Rhiannon? Do you have a life? Don't you have a home of your own to go to? Well, if you do it's not in Farringdon Avenue, because I looked it up and there isn't one in Palmers Green, is there.'

Rhiannon smiles a disappointed smile.

'You know if you've read the last journal, it wasn't all about me. Vida felt let down, abandoned by her only daughter.'

'Oh come on, we're talking about *you* here, what *you've* done. I may not be the greatest daughter in the world, but I didn't send my mother to the loony bin, you did that all by yourself without any help for me.' She pauses. 'Who are you anyway, Rhiannon? I mean *who* are you really?' She half dreads the answer to this question, especially when Rhiannon stops to consider.

'Since you ask, I suppose I'm just someone who appreciates the sheer force of creativity. I understand what drives people like Vida to create. It's the kind of gift that can be either a blessing or a curse. Sadly, with your mother it had become a curse.'

'Meeting you in that café was the curse, your demented Programme was the curse. She'd have been better off joining the Moonies. There should be a law against what you've done; in fact I'm sure there is. I'm speaking to a lawyer friend about it later today...'

This is a bluff; she doesn't have a lawyer friend, indeed the idea has only just occurred to her. She pauses. Why discuss this any further? She doesn't have to justify her relationship with her mother; this is none of Rhiannon's bloody business. She should just get rid of the woman.

She takes a step forward. 'Listen, I'm not going to argue with you any further, just leave please, now. Just pack your bags and go. I'll call you a taxi. Can you be ready in ten minutes? What are you doing... get off me!'

She is unprepared for this, the hand clamped on her upper arm as she turns to leave the room, the hiss of words in her ear. 'I've listened to *you*, Dorothea; now please have the goodness to listen *to me.*'

It's not a fight, not yet, but it could so easily degenerate into one. She musters her steeliest tone. 'Please don't talk to me about "goodness". Now take your hands off me please.'

It isn't enough. She doesn't back off. Fingers, ringed and chubby, bite into her flesh. A vision comes to Dory of the diary excerpt, Rhiannon plucking the dream book from Vida's hand, the unseemly, terrifying physical tussle. She looks into her opponent's face and sees it distorted, all pretence at complacency vanished. For the first time it crosses her mind that this woman could be psychotic.

'I won't ask you again. Let go of me now.' Some instinct keeps her voice steady. *It's the way you should speak to an animal,* she thinks, *a dog you're not sure of.* Unflinching, she looks straight into Rhiannon's eyes, matches her will to hers. The pupils of her small hazel eyes are wholly opaque. Supposing, just supposing this crazy woman has a knife tucked into her skirts? Would she use it? She imagines the headlines… **Daughter of novelist, found murdered in mother's house**… But the grip loosens. Rhiannon withdraws. She looks thwarted, almost wounded as if Dory has dealt her a physical blow.

Released from the grip, the spell is broken. Dory feels the adrenaline charge, like the sugar rush of a dozen Danish pastries, carrying her out of the room and up the stairs to Rhiannon's room. She shouts back, 'Okay, if you won't go quietly, I'll help you pack your stuff!'

Action is all that matters now. Hardly thinking, she grabs at everything, clothing, books, slippers, pens, hurling every trace of the mad fan into the two overnight bags on the floor. Overnight? Huh, that's a joke!

Rhiannon is close on her heels. Vaguely Dory is aware of her protests, that oh so reasonable tone that drives her wild.

'You can't do this, Dory. Vida is my friend and I'm here at her invitation. This is not your house. You have no right to tell me to leave, Dorothea.' Dory swivels around in time to see her gathering up papers.

'What's all that stuff?'

'It's a manuscript.'

'So where do you think you're taking my mother's manuscript? I'll have it back, please.' She holds out her arms.

'No. I'm afraid you can't have these.' Rhiannon hugs the papers to her breasts.

The nature of her adversary is slowly dawning upon Dory. She tries to reason.

'Look, Rhiannon, we're two grown women; at least I think we are. We can stop this right now before something happens we'll both regret. Just give me Vida's papers, please.'

'They're not Vida's papers, they're mine.' Rhiannon speaks in the assured tones of one who knows she's in the right.

'It looks very like a manuscript to me. What was it? Something Mum was working on, something new? What are you planning to do with it exactly?'

Rhiannon shakes her head. 'You have no right to this, or any of Vida's work. You don't understand about creativity, you never did. You resented your mother all your life because she was happily absorbed in her own world. The problem is, Dorothea, you've never grown up. You can't bear to think of Vida as an individual. You can't bear to think of her as a talented woman, with fans, admirers. Did you ever go to any of her book signings, her launch parties?'

Dory snorts. 'She hated launch parties. Anyway I wasn't asked.'

'Did you ever read anything she wrote, apart from her diaries, that is?'

'I told you I don't read fiction.' Why bother explaining herself to this psycho?

'No, but I bet she admired all *your* painting efforts, didn't she? I bet she was always there to cheer you on. She was so proud of you running your business. She honoured you as an individual, and you treated her with contempt.'

There is no ducking this blow. It's all true, isn't it? Dory almost shrinks from this reflection of herself, as if from a cruelly revealing mirror. Contempt is too strong a word. But it's true; she never went to the launch parties, never read the books. She only ever thought of Vida in terms of her shortcomings as a mother.

'Give me those!' She can't stand any more of this. She makes a lunge for the papers. As they scatter about the room Rhiannon bends to retrieve them.

She puffs, the now desperate tremulous tone in her voice unmistakable. 'You don't understand, it's not Vida's work, it's mine. It's *my* novel.'

Dory reels back. The silence sifts between them like snow.

'*Your* novel?'

Rhiannon slumps onto the bed. In a defeated voice she explains. 'I wanted to be like Vida. I wanted to understand how the creative mind works from the inside, the whole process. It's a kind of alchemy. It's about turning the base metal to gold. I wouldn't expect you to understand.'

Rhiannon isn't exactly sobbing. Even in extremis that's not her style, but she's as close as she'll ever get, Dory thinks.

'I was a writer once, you know, as a child, I wrote stories, hundreds of stories in little notebooks. I used to bind them with red knitting wool, design my own little covers. I always wanted to be a writer when I grew up. But then they all got burnt, you see, destroyed. That didn't stop me reading though. I didn't just read books, I consumed them, I *devoured* them. I wanted to see how they did it, those authors I loved, like Vida. You have to live with an artist to understand. You have to get right up close and inhabit them, worm your way inside their heads, the way novelists inhabit their characters. The creative impulse is a mysterious thing. I set myself to unpick it, to unravel it piece by piece. That way I could learn how to put it together again. Vida was blocked. If I could unblock her, I thought I could free myself. It worked for a while; at least I thought it did. But I seem to have run out of steam. I haven't got her gift.'

What is this, a confession? Some kind of play for sympathy? If so, it's not working.

Dory bends over the bags. 'Yes, well, this is all very interesting, but there's a law of copyright, isn't there. I don't know much about the creative spirit you keep raving about, but I do know about plagiarism. Anyway keep your manuscript if you must.'

The sound of bags being zipped has a note of triumph, of finality. Game over.

'I'll carry your bags to the hall.'

Rhiannon pads to the door behind her. 'You understand nothing. You can get rid of me, but not the creature we released. It's out there, Dory. It's your mother's muse. It's the Beast.'

She shudders. She's not going to listen to this madness. She's already dialing the number for the taxi.

In the end it's surprisingly easy. The snow hasn't begun to lie yet, and the taxi driver arrives promptly. Rhiannon pushes out of the door without a backward glance. Dory leans against it in case she changes her mind and comes back. She waits until she hears the purr of the taxi engine fading into the distance. Can she really be gone? Her knees are trembling.

'Bloody good riddance!' She wipes tears from her eyes with her sleeve. She goes back upstairs, rejoicing in its emptiness. Only when she enters her own room does she see the journal lying open on her bed, right at the final entry.

Vida's Diary

Christmas?

This morning I heard the carols on the radio and remembered Christmas. The cards have started to arrive, names of people I can barely remember and no longer see. They lean drunkenly together on the mantelpiece above the Rayburn, or flutter down into the coal bucket where I leave them to make a good blaze. Some of them are still addressed to Mr. and Mrs. Tremayne. One that arrived this morning said:

Dear Vida and Jonathan, wishing you both a very Happy Christmas and all good wishes for the New Year!

Jonathan and Dory always used to take care of the decorations. I looked around the house and realized: I don't even have a tree. It all looks so dreary, as if no one is living here at all.

I remembered then that we always kept the decorations in the cupboard on the upstairs' landing. I could hang up some tinsel perhaps, for when Dory arrived in two days time. I felt I should make an effort; otherwise Dory would start nagging me about seeing the doctor again.

So I went upstairs. I opened the door of the cupboard and breathed in its musty scent. Jon always said we had mice in this cupboard. I could see the droppings like nuggets of black liquorice, and a roll of old wallpaper minutely shredded. There was the battered shoebox with the baubles and tinsel spilling out. I began pulling at it when I noticed the folder. It was wedged beneath the biscuit tin where I keep

the old birthday and Christmas cards I'm too sentimental to throw away. I pulled it out. It was just an
ordinary cardboard folder, coloured charcoal, quite
thin. It must, I thought, be one of mine, some old
writings I'd meant to throw out. I've been so careless lately. Maybe it was something good, something
I could recycle. My heart beat faster as I opened it
up. Inside were just a few pages. A first chapter, that
was all. I read the heading:

***Totem by Rhiannon Townsend – Work-in-
Progress-1st Draft-October***

I read the words again, silently at first, then
aloud as if trying out the title on someone. I shrank
back on my heels. Everything in me slowed. I could
feel my blood thicken, even as I feel it now, churning like cream in my veins. Rhiannon Townsend.
My fan: the woman who swore to help me write
again.

I read on, on and on down that page and the
next one. The words burned so bright, leaping
like flames from the page, so dazzling, so alive with
energy I feared they might catch fire. What was the
story about? I don't know. It doesn't matter. I only
know that I haven't been able to write like that in
years. Maybe at my height, as they used to say, ***Vida
Tremayne is at the peak of her powers***. Compared
to these bright words, I saw what poor things mine
are.

I took the folder downstairs and burned it on
the fire, every page, until it was ashes. I sat shivering
until the fire went out. She took it from me, I know.

She took my gift. She stole my Muse. She wanted to become me, and now she has.

Next Day

This morning when I wake up I can't remember for a moment who I am. I have to instruct my legs to move, to slide from beneath the covers, to walk me over to the mirror. A mad grey ghost stares back at me.

'You are Vida,' I tell the ghost. '*You are Vida Tre... tre... Tremayne.*'

The ghost opens her mouth wide. I clamp my hands over my ears. I think she will scream and when she does the glass will shatter into millions of fragments, the way my window shattered.

But then she speaks in a hollow voice. '*Who am I?*'

'You are Vida, of course.' I'm getting annoyed now.

'But who is Vida Tremayne?'

I don't know the answer to that. I pull on clothes, and go outside to feed the cat. Outside is like a speeded-up film, trees swaying like dancers, wind frisking clouds across the sky until the whole world seems to spin around me.

'Puss... puss... here pussy... pussy here... look what Vida's got for you...'

I found the lamb chop in the freezer. It's still frozen but the cat won't mind. Still it doesn't come. It's shy, I think. Or maybe it's gone off with *her.*

'Breakfast, pussy!' The cold knifes into my ribs, the wind blasting right through me, as if I'm hollow. I stagger about the garden; such a vast garden it seems, surging up and up towards the dark quiff of trees. The trees groan, throw up their branches as if in surrender. I'm waving the lamb chop. It must be here somewhere. When I look into its eyes I shall know. I shall know then who I am.

Dec…

I write this at my kitchen table. How did I get here? How did the kitchen get into such a mess? My kitchen is littered with dead birds, feathers flutter down, bones are picked clean. I am dressed in my furs: fur coat, fur hat, fur bolero, fur mittens. The mittens are making it hard to write these words. I have to clutch the pen in my fist, so then the letters grow and grow. They score great rips in the page. Nice clean white pages, all in shreds and tatters. I am so cold. I can't get warm. I am shivering, whining deep in my throat when I hear the key in the door. A voice calling out in the hallway. 'Mum? Mum, are you there?'

I think I can hear a woman shrieking.

'My God, what's happened to you? What the hell has happened here?'

In the hall, someone is picking up the telephone.

21ST FEBRUARY

DORY

The radio forecaster is speaking in that apologetic voice as if the weather is his fault personally. Wintry showers are expected for East Wales and the Midlands, he says. He speaks as if breaking the news of a disaster. Dory barely registers the words "accumulations" and "drifts" as she wanders from room to room of the Gingerbread House in a haze of cold blue light.

She should be euphoric. She's triumphed, hasn't she? She's managed to bundle psycho-woman into a taxi along with all her possessions. She's even paid the driver to take her to the railway station and watched from the window, eyes glued to the back of Rhiannon's stiffly averted head as the taxi bounces over the potholed drive and turns into the lane. Yet it feels like a hollow victory. Words have been said; wounds inflicted. She feels a stab of longing for Dan, his silly jokes, his comforting arm around her shoulders. Is that feeble of her? It's the lack of that shoulder to cry on that makes her want to crumple, and cry little girl tears into those violet tissues still stacked in Rhiannon's visiting basket.

The only thing that stops her doing so are the words *Travel Disruption*, followed by *Power Cuts*. This is East Wales, isn't it? She rouses herself to look out of the window. Good God, this is all she needs. The snow is already beginning to settle, falling swift and silent around the house. She could be snowed in alone at the Gingerbread House, cut off from the outside world, rationing her cigarettes to two a day.

Pounding upstairs to the bathroom she spritzes her eyes with cold water, patting them dry enough for a hasty makeup job. It's nowhere near up to her usual standard, but it'll have to do. It's not just about beating the blizzards to get in supplies, but she needs to see Vida before the snow gets any worse.

⚜ ⚜ ⚜

It's lunchtime by the time Dory gets to the hospital. Dinner trolleys rattle past, wafting an unpleasant medley of cottage pie and antiseptic. The fluorescent lighting burns her eyes, still raw from all the crying. A pain jags at her left temple. She dreads to think what she must look like, but who cares in this place?

She scurries past the drawn curtains halfway down the ward, from behind which issues a strange hooting cry. It's a yearning, haunting note, hardly human, more like a migratory bird coming into land. No one pays the slightest attention.

Vida is two beds along at the far end. The horror of the situation strikes Dory afresh as she comes upon her mother. She edges closer. Vida's eyes are closed but this is no normal sleep. This isn't repose. It isn't rest. Vida looks old, truly old. Her features are set as if in concrete, the lines deepened, as if she's grappling with some terrible thing on an inner level no one can reach.

Dory draws up the chair, grateful to have something to collapse on. Her knees are still feeling oddly weak after this morning's fight.

'Mum? Mum, it's me again, your daughter, your only beloved daughter. Huh. Joke, Mum. Can you hear me… can you…?'

'I shouldn't bother. She can't hear anything.' A woman with a missing front tooth and tightly cropped grey hair sidles up to the foot of the bed. 'Out for the count, she is.'

Dory ignores her.

'Good job too,' the woman rants on. 'All that howling and growling, keeping us awake all night.' She jabs a finger to her head. 'Thinks she's a cat. Mad. They're all mad in here.'

This is too much. She's had enough of mad-women for one day. She hisses with all the force she can muster, 'Sod off, will you.'

Surprisingly the woman does. You shouldn't tell sick people to sod off, but God, this is too much to take in after the morning she's had. Her stomach knots. Her mouth is dry. She doesn't know whether to cry, or shake Vida even more senseless than she already is.

She thinks back to that dream she had about the cat in her bed. She's tried hard to forget it, but it won't let go. It links in with what she's read in the diary extracts, the totem animal, the porridge made of live hearts, the sex scene with Brendan Riley. It's all a fairytale, isn't it? A fairytale that she's somehow become a part of. She almost laughs. Throughout her life she's resolutely avoided being caught up in Vida's imaginary world, and now here it is coming to get her.

'Mum...?' She speaks softly, in a pretend gentle simper. Does she really want Vida to wake? Supposing she should wake not as Vida, but as the Puma with a slow growl? Asleep, Vida's face is just human: sad and strained, but human.

Dory whispers close to Vida's ear, 'She's gone now, your friend Rhiannon. I finally got rid of her. How's that for good news? You won't ever have to put up with her again. Looks like you're stuck with me now, eh?'

No response. She presses on regardless. 'I have to ask, that stuff you wrote about Brendan Riley, the man who came to fix your window, you didn't really have sex with him did you?'

Vida's expression doesn't change. Her breath catches, that's all. She turns her head on the pillow. It's odd to see her hands just lying there, the fingers idle; it's odd to see her without a pen in her hand. She still wears her wedding ring, Dory notices.

'Those things you wrote about me, how I must have... hurt you. I'm sorry.' Dory glances down into her lap. 'I had issues; I don't deny that. I wish we could have talked, before... before you, that is... I thought you had your work, always your writing. The thing that really got me was how happy you seemed in your own world, how contented. You didn't get why I was so angry most of the time. But now I see we've got more in common than I thought. We can't help doing the things that drive us.'

Vida's eyelids flicker just a fraction. The fingers of her right hand twitch momentarily. Dory pauses. Is it really possible that her words have finally reached Vida, at least on some level no one understands? Encouraged, she presses on with her confession. 'And then there was all that upset over *The Gingerbread House,* your character Hetty Jackson. I know, I know, it's such a sore point; we've never spoken of it since. We had that terrible row. I refused to come to your launch party. You didn't know this, Mum, but Dad pleaded with me to come. He even bribed me, said he'd pay for me to go on a design course I was interested in at the time, but that infuriated me all the more. I couldn't get it out of my head that you *used* me, you see. I know now it's no excuse, but I was low at the time. There I was just turned eighteen, just left school with one pretty crap A Level in Art and Design, and living in this grubby little flat in Westbourne Park. I refused to go to university much to the dismay of you and Dad, because I wanted to be with him. Remember? Mikhail was supposed to be moving in with me. It was meant to be our place together, my first grown-up place as a proper couple. Then he announced he couldn't leave his wife. That was about the time you presented me with the proof

copy of your splendid book. You said something like,
'I know you hate fiction, Dory, but it would please me
so much if you would read this. I think it's the best
thing I've ever done.' So, I made the effort. I read
it, even though my heart was breaking for Mikhail,
and I knew I couldn't cry on your shoulder because
you and Dad had warned me against him in the first
place. And then, a few chapters in, I found her, I
began to recognize myself in dear selfish, spoilt little
Hetty. I see now she could have been anyone, but
at the time I wanted to punish you. It wasn't just
Hetty. You had all these people adoring you, your
readers, and Dad of course supporting you, escorting you about the country to readings. You were a
couple. And I was alone, wondering what the hell I
was going to do with my life...'

Dory falters. Even though her voice barely rises
above a whisper, her throat aches with emotion.
She's hardly looked at Vida while she's been talking. Now she does. Vida's eyes are open. Unfocussed
but open. Her hand flaps gently as if she's trying to
signal something. Instinctively Dory reaches out to
clasp it. There is no scratching this time, but neither
is there any responsive tightening of fingers. Vida's
hand appears to shrink in her clasp as her eyes close
again.

Dory withdraws her hand. She reaches in her
bag for the card she found tucked inside one of the
older journals. She must have made it when she was
about eight. She remembers folding the midnight-
blue sugar paper, inscribing *Happy Birthday Mum,*

love from Dorothea XxXxXX in her new gold pen. She remembers shaking a whole plastic tube of glitter on it.

Now there are flakes of glitter on the sheet. 'I don't know why you kept this. Well, anyway. I thought you might like to see it, when you wake up.'

She leaves it, lying on Vida's stomach. Vida lies so still it looks like a burial offering.

❄ ❄ ❄

Outside she can barely see for the whirl of white feathering down from the sky. The sky is the colour of choked-up phlegm. It's an absence of colour, the colour of depression. Dory can't think why they call depression "the blues".

As she crosses the car park, loneliness hits her *thump* in the solar plexus like a dead bird crashing into a windscreen. Always there have been friends calling, colleagues, admirers, and hangers-on, lovers. Now she wonders how many of them were real? How easily they've vanished from her life. Easy come, easy go. Out of sight, out of mind. All those friends who know she's buried away down here, how many have bothered to ring to ask if she needs support? She imagines the gossip around dinner party tables: 'Haven't seen Dory in ages, is she away somewhere?'

Then the sidelong looks, the low scandalized voices. 'Didn't you know? It's her ma. She's cracked up, completely round the twist, darling.'

There will be some sympathetic murmurings. 'Poor Dory,' someone will say. The conversation will falter for a nanosecond before someone mentions the difficulty of getting a table at Jamie Oliver's. She wouldn't blame them. Who wants to talk about breakdowns, or sick mothers, anyway?

She stalks towards her once lovely car, with its collar of mud, and shit-spattered windscreen, and dead leaves adhered to her sidelights.

Who would miss her? Vida would have. Of all people her mother would feel her death more keenly than anyone. That's the nature of mothers, isn't it? But now, she doesn't even have a mother to worry about her. Rarely has she felt so absolutely alone.

Her mobile rings. She ducks into her car and fumbles for it. Dan? It's a forlorn hope and a stupid one. Why would Dan break his silence at this very moment, just when she needs to hear his voice so badly, when she needs to tell him, to pour out the dreadful scene back at the house. That would be just too convenient, wouldn't it? It would be like one of her mother's novels.

'Good news, darling! I've found them.'

Harvey. The mental shift from the institution car park to her bright plant-filled office is almost too great.

'What?' She struggles to engage her brain. 'You've found what?'

'Not what, darling, *them,* the buyers for your mother's abode, of course.'

'Buyers?'

'Well, excuse me for being a tad precipitous, but my sixth sense tells me it's the perfect match. Sophie and William Lucas. He's in marketing, sick of the rat race; wants to write The Novel. Sophie is a *Creative*, does amazing things with papier mache, you should see…'

'Harvey, wait a minute. Before you go any further, what have you arranged with them?'

There is a silence in which she can feel Harvey deflating. He says in an aggrieved tone that he's merely doing as instructed.

'You did tell me to whip up interest among the clientele. You emailed me pics of the outside, remember? Charming if you like that sort of thing. Sophie and Will have fallen in love with it. They don't even care what state it's in, so you can call off that hairy dwarf builder or odd job man, whatever he is. You won't have to do a thing. Anyway, I just wanted to check with you about the viewing. ASAP, I hope, because they are absolutely foaming at the mouth, bless them. I told them tomorrow.'

'Tomorrow? No… I'm sorry, I mean that's terrific, but could you hold them off for a bit, just for a week or two? I have to apply for power of attorney before I can do anything.'

This is true. She wonders why she's delayed for so long these past weeks. It's not like her to dither. She thought for a moment back there that Vida might be showing signs of recovery, but that's a faint hope. Vida's condition is worsening by the day. She's serving no purpose here. Like it or not, she's got to take hold of the reins and get this house sorted.

Harvey sighs. 'I'll do my best, but you know what these *Creatives* are like. We don't want to dampen their ardour.'

'I don't care how creative they are, I don't care if they want to weave their own sandals out of willow bark.'

'Willow bark?'

'Ray Mears did it on that Bushcraft thing.'

'Mmm… sounds like fun.'

'There are problems, Harvey. My mother… well, my mother… well, anyway, I'm not in a position to show buyers round now, simple as that.'

'I see.' Harvey sounds piqued. 'So what shall I tell them?'

She hesitates. 'Tell them there's a giant Puma on the loose if you like.'

'Puma? Darling, you're joking.'

'I wish. The country round here is full of them. People keep them as pets. They escape from zoos. They breed. Didn't you know? It's not all Red Kites and leeks in these parts, you know.'

The Puma is no laughing matter, but just talking to Harve about it shrinks it to pussycat size.

'By the way, Harve, before you go, you haven't seen anything of Dan, have you?'

'Not a whisker. What's wrong? Has the hairy dwarf scared him off? Look, sweetie, I'd love to stay and shoot the breeze, but I've got two viewings to handle this afternoon, and I'd better get on to

Sophie and Will straight away. Oh, how am I going to break the news? They'll be gutted.'

'Sorry, Harve. Look, just hang in there a bit longer. I'll be back as soon as I've made arrangements for my mother.'

He's gone. She doesn't blame him for despairing of her, after all the pressure she's piled on. But Vida may yet come around. She'd so much rather have Vida's understanding, her blessing.

There's someone else she needs to speak to. She keys in Riley's number and Orange answer tells her the person she's calling is not available and to leave a message. She keeps it short and sweet.

'Hallo Brendan, it's Dory Tremayne speaking. I accused you of going to my mother's house the other day, and well... turning the place over a bit. I was wrong. I'm sorry. Well, that's all I wanted to say. Cheers.'

⚜ ⚜ ⚜

It takes around twice as long as usual to drive from Cregaron to the Gingerbread House, mainly because she gets stuck behind one of those lumbering council Gritter lorries. Ridiculous. Snow can't settle that quickly, can it? She's used to London, where it evaporates as soon as it touches the pavements.

Yet already the lane to the cottage is pure untrammelled white. She slows the car. It's not that deep, not yet, but she's rather not get stuck in a ditch after the morning she's had. Two magpies desert their lunch at her approach, their black-and-white tail feathers gleaming in the soft light. She feels her front wheel bump over part of a mangled rabbit, its blood pooling crimson in the snow. The magpies, with their huge curved beaks, make her think of Rhiannon for some reason. She should be on the train to London by now. But... just supposing she isn't? Supposing she got the taxi driver to drop her at the end of the track, and crept back to lurk in the bushes until she saw the dreadful daughter drive away. She might still be here skulking in the shrubberies. That axe by the woodpile would come in very handy, wouldn't it?

The front wheels of the car spin as she negotiates the slight incline of the drive. When she presses the accelerator the engine groans in protest. She has to reverse and try again before pulling up by Vida's car beneath the poplars.

Someone is here. Climbing out of the car, she hears it, a clear unmistakable clanging sound from around the side of the cottage. She freezes. That's where the dustbins are kept, under a terrible old Perspex-roof lean-to that Vida should have knocked down years ago. She immediately thinks of Rhiannon. Rhiannon is back, like the bad fairy. She's prowling around the house, looking for a weakness somewhere to gain entrance. Did she really believe she'd got rid of her? That she'd get off so lightly?

There's a stick lying beneath the hedge, hefty enough to use as a weapon. She grasps hold of it as she sidles around the corner to the back.

'Hey! Hallo? Who's there?'

There is someone bending over the dustbin, but it's not Rhiannon. The sense of relief is so great it's somehow shaming.

His back is towards her as he replaces a dustbin lid. At his feet lies debris of food waste, and rubbish she's gleaned from the study: fan letters, old bills...

'What are you looking for exactly, Brendan?'

He swivels round, holds up his hands as if she might shoot him dead, or attack him with her stick.

'I got your message, so I thought I'd call by.'

'Oh did you? So where's your Land Rover?'

'I pulled into the lay-by.' He indicates the pull-in further down the track. 'Thought I'd check if she was here first.'

'She's gone.'

He nods as if he's already guessed this.

'I couldn't get an answer at the front door, so I came round the side of the house. Looks like something took a fancy to your dinner last night.'

Now she sees it. It's the remains of the lamb's liver she'd found buried in Vida's freezer. Only the polythene pack remains, streaked with blood, black globules scattered like beads on the concrete standing. The stuff must've bled as it defrosted, wafting its irresistible scent even through the thick plastic of the bin. Only a sliver of meat remains.

'Not my dinner.' She shudders. 'I don't eat offal. I'd rather starve than eat something's internal organs, thank you very much.'

As she says this, it hits her that Vida had always been fastidious about meat, only eating a little chicken occasionally.

'Whatever it was knew you had liver on the menu.'

'Whatever. A fox,' she snaps. 'I suppose it was a fox.'

They are both staring at the bins, as if whatever it was is still in there. He shakes his head. 'A hell of a fox to overturn something like that. Mrs. Tremayne… your mother said something about a cat, a big one.'

She snaps, 'I'd rather not talk about what my mother said or didn't say, if you don't mind.'

He holds out his hands. 'No problem. Mind if I come in and wash?'

'I can't stand people who say "no problem" all the time. There's always a problem. There is no such thing as *no problem*. But come in anyway. You can't go off covered in blood like that, you'll be arrested.'

⚜ ⚜ ⚜

He doesn't use the bathroom with its soft towels and pastel soaps, but prefers to bend over the cracked butler's sink in the utility. He lathers his forearms with that rough carbolic stuff that's strictly for men, the black hairs springing up through the suds. She can't help noticing. Most of the men she knows these days are fussy about their toiletries. Even Dan likes pampering, aromatic shaving oils, herbal shampoos.

In the kitchen she slips out of her coat and sits at the table. She puts her head in her hands. Isn't this proof? Proof there is a cat out there. Her mother's seen it; the mad fan has seen it. According to Vida's diary entry, it was on the verge of attacking Rhiannon. Some might say a pity it didn't. But supposing she'd gone out to the bins last night and seen it, the liver dangling from its chops like a great tongue? Seen its yellow eyes staring.

'So where is she?' Riley comes in rolling down his shirtsleeves. He drags out a chair from the table and sits heavily.

'Oh yes, *do* sit down.' Sarcasm is her default mode, but it seems lost on this man.

'I told you, Rhiannon's packed and gone. I called her a taxi. She should be on the train to London by now.'

'What time did she leave?'

'Oh I don't know; what does the time matter? It was this morning some time. Two or three hours ago. I'm just relieved to be rid of her.'

Riley frowns. He's one of those men who doesn't sit comfortably. He hunkers forward on the hard chair, forearms resting on knees, as if relaxing is agony to him. In that sense he's a bit like her, she thinks. He looks as if he's ready for action at all times.

'Something wrong?'

'Only that if she got to Cregaron Station two hours ago, she's not going anywhere. The line south's blocked. I know because Mart's old lady was going to Cardiff for shopping and she had to call Mart to come and pick her up again.'

'But... surely a few inches of snow wouldn't block the line that quickly, would it?'

He shrugs. 'Didn't you see the news last night? They've got six-foot drifts down Hereford way.'

Damn. She pictures Rhiannon stranded at the station, considering her options. She could put up in the Cregaron Hotel; that would be the sensible option. Or the station is only six miles to the west, so she could... but no, she dismisses that thought from her mind. Even Rhiannon isn't crazy enough to wade back to the Gingerbread House through this lot. Is she?

Riley says it for her. 'She could be knocking at the door any minute now.'

Clearly he doesn't realize quite the effect this has on her; she sits on her hands, partly to warm them, partly to stop reaching for a cigarette. Her chest feels weirdly tight, and all this bloody smoking isn't helping.

'No' she says firmly, 'no way will she darken this door again. We had a serious row. Actually it was more like hand-to-hand combat. I told you about the diaries. I found them hidden in the boot of Mum's car. Perhaps she intended to burn the lot, who knows?' She pauses. Part of her longs to pour it all out, confide in someone about the Programme Vida was subjected to, but she's not sure Riley is her man. What does he know about psychology, about creative blocks, about how writers live? And if he did get a bit too familiar with Vida... well, that doesn't bear thinking about either.

He sits locking and unlocking his fingers now as if it helps him to think.

'She's done a lot of damage.' Dory finds herself transfixed by his hands for some reason; she'd rather look at them than at his face right now. 'Anyway she won't be going anywhere near Vida from now on. Brendan... about that cat... I don't suppose, well, this sounds crazy, but you haven't heard anything about a big cat on the loose in these parts, have you? I mean, you know those sightings you hear about sometimes? There hasn't been anything in the local media, has there?'

His hands unclasp and rest on his knees at this. No, nothing. There was something a while ago up on one of the farms to the west of Offa's Dyke. There was talk of some maniac releasing a pet Puma, but no one's ever got a picture of it.

'You're thinking of the mess out there,' he says. 'It could've been anything; sometimes badgers get hungry this time of year. They're strong buggers, they are, strong enough to knock a bin over.'

He rumbles on a bit about the habits of badgers, and how they differ from foxes and so on. Once she might have dismissed the countryman's patter as boring, but she finds it strangely soothing right now. The deep rumble of his voice touches her; she feels it like buds unfurling in her lower spine, like those Japanese flowers that Vida used to give her as a child, that you put in water and watched them float.

He's saying something now about it being nature, and how townies tend to scare easily. The careless insult misses its mark. Yes, nature, she thinks: *nature*. She says almost dreamily, 'There was a lot about this… beast in the diaries. My mother saw it apparently, and Rhiannon…'

He snorts at this. 'Townies! Sorry, no offence like, but people come from the towns and they imagine all sorts.'

'Yes, well perhaps you're right about that.' She won't give any more away; he thinks she's fool enough already.

'You read the diaries then?'

The question takes her unawares. The blissful tranced sensation in her lower back evaporates in second.

'I had to, didn't I? I know it's bad to read people's diaries, but I had to know what triggered the illness. And yes, it's all there, enough material to send anyone round the twist.' She pauses. 'Then there was all the stuff about you and her. I won't go into the gory details. That's one accusation I'm not taking back.'

She watches his face closely for his reaction. If it's true he won't be able to look her in the face. Sure enough, he lowers his head. Rakes a hand through a kink of damp fringe.

'Look, she might have got the wrong end of the stick. You know, I might have let her think there could be something between us.'

'No. Please. And how might you have given her that impression, pray tell?' She hugs herself as she always does against the cold, or maybe to stop from breaking in two.

He glances up at her, a look of resignation in his treacle-dark eyes. 'She was cold and crying one day, watching me work, so I put my arm around her and gave her a cuddle. Don't look at me like that. I know it was wrong of me. She kept going on about your dad, how she missed him and that. I felt sorry for her that's all. Then of course, her keeper came looking for her and she put two and two together and made eight, like.'

Dory absorbs this unpleasant vision in silence. Can't he see that she could do with a cuddle herself? Or maybe she's just not cuddly enough, maybe that's it.

She murmurs, 'I see.'

What else should she say? If she attacks him now he'll think she's jealous, and the last thing she wants is another fight. He fixes her with that level look, like he's trying to make up his mind about something.

'It was a cuddle, that's all, like you'd give to your mum. It was what she needed. She made to kiss me, and I realized she'd got the wrong idea. Look, I didn't have to come here and tell you this to your face. I just wanted to put the record straight. I don't know what her Ladyship said about me, or what your mother wrote down, but that's all there was, honest to God. Don't worry. You don't have to throw me out, I'm leaving.'

He gets heavily to his feet.

'Wait a minute.' She stops him. She doesn't want him to go. He may not fit the bill as a stopgap lover, but God knows she needs some kind of a friend. 'Just tell me this. If you were Rhiannon Townsend, and you couldn't get on the London train back home tonight, where would you go?'

'If I was Rhiannon Townsend...?' The corners of his mouth twitch, the nearest he's come to a smile.

'Yes,' impatiently, 'there are no trains south, you're freezing, practically snowed in and you've got unfinished business with someone. Someone you've been forbidden to visit. Someone you feel you've still got a hold over.'

He stares. 'You think she's at the hospital?'

'Yes, I do.' She thinks back to Rhiannon's ramblings earlier. All that stuff about living with the artist, sharing their every thought and feeling. The vision she has of Rhiannon hovering over Vida's bedside makes a quick cuddle from the odd-job man look like small beer. It's Rhiannon she's concerned about. Something inside her knows that Rhiannon hasn't finished with Vida yet, snow or no snow.

'Brendan, did you really like my mother? I mean, really?'

He shrugs. 'I told you. I explained.'

'Yes you did, forget it. It happened, but if you want to help Mum I really need you to help me now. How does your Land Rover cope with snow? Could you get me down this track and drive me to Cregaron, to the hospital? I need to speak to

Rhiannon Townsend, and I think I know just where to find her.'

It's slow going back down the track but the main road is still passable. They pull up outside the hospital at just after three thirty. It's nowhere near dark yet, but the density of the falling snow creates a strange half-light of blue tinged shadows. The few trees that screen the car park boundary droop in submission under the weight of snow. The hospital flooded with brilliant white light, the flashing blue of an ambulance pulling up outside A & E, the trickle of visitors heading back to the car park, bundled against the cold, look somehow unreal, a snapshot picture as if already they are fading into history.

'Can you wait for a bit? I shouldn't be long,' Dory is halfway out of the door, the minute Riley turns off the engine.

The hospital corridor to Vida's ward is familiar enough. Each and every time she steps into it she's aware of that strange sensation in her stomach, like a chasm opening, as if her internal organs have caved right in. Her heart is jittery, the muscles around it clenched and ready for whatever dreadful thing she'll find. It's the same sensation this time, only multiplied a hundred times. What will she do when she finds Rhiannon? Will she have to wrestle her off Vida's bed, drag her away kicking and screaming? But when she reaches the ward, Rhiannon isn't anywhere in sight. Neither is Vida. A nursing assistant is making the bed; the starched new-laundered sheets smell faintly rubbery as she goes about the chore, tucking in corners as if it's a military operation. All ready, Dory supposes, for the next patient.

'Where is she?' She almost grabs hold of the assistant's arm. 'Where's my mother?'

'Mrs. Tremayne?' The girl looks almost frightened. 'Sorry, we moved her to the side ward. She was making a bit of…'

Dory doesn't wait for her to finish the sentence. The idea of Vida shut away in a side ward with her limpet-like fan in attendance is too awful. She hurries down the length of the ward to the bay where patients who are too ill or too disruptive are usually placed. There are only two side wards. She tries both. In the first, a pale girl sits holding hands with her boyfriend. In the second, the bedclothes are pulled back, but Rhiannon isn't here after all. And neither is Vida. Vida is not on this ward, nor any other. It soon emerges that Vida is nowhere to be found in this wing of the hospital. There is nothing left of her mother but the plastic tumbler of water on her bedside table.

Vida

I am dying. Isn't this what they say it's like, the hurling through bright white space into infinity. I must not open my eyes. Keep them shut, that's it, or be blinded, dazzled. I am burning out like a star. In a moment I will be nothing but cosmic dust. I will remember nothing.

I wait for oblivion. No Thing. That's what heaven is, I think, oblivion. But instead, a bump... bump... bump... and the creaking of wheels beneath me. I must be alive after all. There is no pain when you're dead, not pain like this. Bolts of pain spearing up through my feet, legs, the length of my spine, as we bump and grind and swish. Not heaven then. Earth. I am still on this earth.

A voice at my back, jerked out between puffs.

'Are you all right, Vida my love? We're just going for a little walk. Your favourite place, remember, where we picked the berries?'

Do I know her? She smells of old skin and vellum and menstrual blood. Her heart pumps like an infernal machine, its workings clogged with black oil. When we judder to a halt my head tips back.

'Sorry. I should have got the taxi driver to bring us further up the hill. He made such a fuss about a bit of snow.'

Snow. That's what it is. Icy wet bursts on my eyelids, but I won't open my eyes. I refuse to open them and see where I am.

'Not much farther,' says the voice. 'We'll find a sheltered spot for you, shall we? In a moment those wretched drugs will wear off, and you can wake up properly. It's for the best. You'll see I only mean the best for you, despite what everyone thinks.'

I am swaddled tightly in hot scratchy wool, only my eyes and the tip of my nose scorched by ice. The rush of air is deafening. I can feel my lungs inflating like those great bellows that blacksmiths used to use. I want to scratch but my fingers are encased in mittens. I am all muffled like a mummy.

'Wait a minute, let's just fix your hat. Don't want you catching pneumonia, do we?'

Can she hear it purring? I can. I can hear the soft pad of its feet as it follows our scent. I can feel the heft and spring of muscles, the salt meaty cat scent of it.

'Puss, puss…'

We jolt, and nearly tip forward over a knuckle of rock. 'Did you say something, Vida? Did you speak?'

Her breathing tickles my face. Her breath is like stale cheese.

No, no, no. Not speak. I won't open my eyes and look at her face. I won't. Let me be. Let me be No Thing.

'You know it's following us, don't you. This is its terrain. That's why I had to bring you out here. It would never have dared come to the hospital. And what would we… what would I have done then? We need it to create, don't we. We need it to write again. I haven't written anything since you went into hospital. Did you know that? Not a word.'

Up... up... the air thins. The cold intensifies until it is bright burning pain. Snowflakes on my eyelids stream like tears. Only my tongue is on fire, aflame with hunger, dulled by the taste of porridgey mush, mashed potato and mince.

Pump pump goes her heart. I am being rocked, now pulled, now pushed in my wheeled chariot.

I hear a sigh. 'We're here, Vida. Now let's see if your Puma will come, shall we?'

DORY

The wheel-chair tracks are clearly visible in the snow. A few yards past the Gingerbread House they swerve erratically up towards the Stiperstones.

'Dear God, they surely didn't get that far? What can they be doing up there in this weather?'

Dory pictures her mother rocking sideways, steered by her crazy disciple beneath frowning overhangs of rock.

She murmurs to Riley, 'I knew Rhiannon was weird, but I really didn't think she was that far gone.'

'I could've told you,' he grunts. 'In fact I *did* tell you. If you'd just listened, it would have saved us both a whole lot of trouble.'

She's about to retort how sorry she is to put him out, but now is not the time for bickering. Her mind is fixed on Rhiannon. On what Rhiannon is capable of. Just how insane do you need to be to kidnap someone from a hospital bed? The galling part about all this is that she'd felt on that final visit to Vida's bedside that she might have been on the verge of a breakthrough. The way Vida had moved her fingers as she spoke it was almost a gesture of acknowledgement. Now this. It could blow every-thing. It could set Vida back months… or worse… She clenches her fists on her knees.

'Can't you step on it a bit, Brendan?'

But Riley has bumped the Land Rover to a halt in the farm gateway.

She looks sideways at him. 'What are you doing? Why are we stopping here?'

His expression says it all. He's not going any further. He's had it with crazy women. He wishes he'd never got involved in this mess. He wants to be safely home picking his toenails in his rusty old caravan.

He says, 'We should've waited at the hospital. You know that, don't you? We should've waited for the police. Suppose we find them up there?' He jerks his head in the direction of the bleak white nothingness beyond the windscreen. 'What are you planning to do, exactly?'

She rakes her hair with her fingers. 'I can't believe you're bottling out. You heard what the invalid taxi driver said, that he'd brought Vida back here, that her "niece" told him she was taking her home for a short break. They could be anywhere; they could be just around that corner. I couldn't just sit in the manager's office twiddling my thumbs, answering a lot of stupid questions while a psychotic maniac takes my mother for a walk on the wild side.'

'I'm not bottling out. We should've waited,' he repeats, stubborn. The thing is she's knows he's right. But it's not *his* mother, is it.

'Okay, look, thanks for bringing me this far.' She makes to open the door. 'You can go home. You don't have to come with me. It's not your problem.'

He grabs hold of her elbow. 'Oh yeah and what am I going to do, just leave you here alone to wrestle that wheelchair off a complete nutter? And then what? You're going to sling your mother over one shoulder and carry her back in the snow? Use your head, will you, this is one for the cops. The medics will know how to handle it. They'll give her a shot of something to keep her quiet. Rhiannon, I mean.'

'Oh, like a tranquilliser dart, I suppose?' Even as she says this, her heart jolts. A tranquilliser dart. Actually that could be a good thing to have about her person right now. 'You don't get it, do you. I don't want some bumpkin plod butting in before the thing is finished.'

'Before the thing is finished... what thing?' He's exasperated now, gazing through the steamed-up windscreen as if for rescue.

A few days ago she might have enjoyed a bit of rough stuff, now she yanks her arm free of his grip. 'The thing that she started, Rhiannon. The cat thing.'

'Oh that. Jesus!'

❧   ❧   ❧

She doesn't know if he'll follow as she clambers out of the vehicle. She doesn't care. She concentrates on every step, boots scuffing snow back into the tracks, head down through slicing wind. It's a good ten minutes tramping up the lane, until rounding a bend, the desolation snatches her breath away. There really is nothing here. Not a rooftop, not a friendly light to cheer the heart. The moor spreads out before her, featureless but for the fuzz of gorse bush, the odd stunted hawthorn, crazed branches black against fallen snow. Only the tumbled slabs of rock are softened, their flanks lightly dusted as if with a sideways roll of chalk. It's stopped snowing for the moment, that's something. Dory looks around. As her breath condenses in the cold air, she remembers she's left her ciggies in the Land Rover. This is a blow, when she could do with a good puff to give her courage.

She glances over her shoulder. No sign of the Land Rover, or Riley. She senses she's passed an invisible line. Riley won't cross it. It's not his place. At first she thought it would be good to have a bit of muscle along, but this is not a situation that calls for brute force. No, it calls for something altogether more intuitive, something essentially *feminine*. It's between her and Rhiannon now, or rather, between her, Rhiannon and Vida.

And there she is. Dory catches her breath. Black Rhadley Hill looms to her left, a great hulking lump of a hill. The way it humps out of a flat plain, isolated from the rest, reminds her of a child's drawing. At first she thinks it might be a finger of rock or standing stone close to the summit. But no, the figure is clearly human, a distant flame blazing scarlet alongside a scrubby outcrop of trees. If that's Rhiannon, where is her mother?

For a moment she stands there trying to assess the situation. Just how crazy is Rhiannon? Is she mad enough to… but no, why would she bring Vida here to kill her? She loves her, doesn't she, in her own twisted way?

She pushes through the gate, beneath the sign that says not to walk dogs here because it's a site of scientific interest. It's a slow, gently curving track: gentle enough to make pushing a wheelchair just about possible, but you'd have to be damn strong. It would be tough enough pushing a child in a push-chair, but a fully grown adult?

The tyre marks zigzag haphazardly, crossing back on themselves. Even this light covering renders the stones lethal. Bracken claws through powdery accumulations. They remind her of human hands, withered, raised in a futile gesture, the hands of someone sinking into a quagmire never to be seen again. She stamps them underfoot in her haste. Her boots skid and she stumbles more than once.

'Sod it!' She's not cut out for this. Her idea of exercise is clacking about shopping malls. She's not designed for heroics. Pausing to gain her breath she glances towards the summit. Rhiannon has seen her. It's creepy the way she just stands there watching her progress from above. Probably she's willing her to break her neck.

'This is no place for you, Dorothea!' As soon as she's close enough, Rhiannon calls out.

Dory murmurs under her breath, 'Tell me something I don't know.' But where is Vida? Her eyes sting with tears of panic as she scans the hillside.

Above her, Rhiannon looms into focus, looking ever more like a Russian doll, all bulked up in her layers, snatching her hair back behind her ears. 'You should go back home. Run on back to your busy little life.'

'I haven't come here to fight with you,' Dory says, pulling her boots free of a deep pocket of snow beneath a rocky ledge. 'I've come to get my mother.' It takes a huge effort of will, but she manages to keep her voice steady. This is the way you deal with nutters, she thinks: humour them if necessary, but be firm.

As she draws level with Rhiannon the wheelchair with Vida huddled in it comes into view. The relief of finding her mother alive is almost too much. For a moment she's speechless. Winded from the climb, she can only stand, gulping in air like a goldfish.

That wheelchair looks none too secure. Rhiannon has wedged it against a fist of quartz rock, slightly above where they're standing now. There is no tree cover on the summit. Vida sits entirely exposed to the elements. Dory has no idea what lies on the other side of the hill. From this vantage point, all she can see beyond the wheelchair is sky.

'Will you please move out of the way?' She's trying to nudge past, but Rhiannon blocks her path, unmoving.

'Where do you think you're going?'

'You know where I'm going. Just move please.'

Dory thinks fast. The only way to reach Vida without wrestling her adversary to the ground is by backtracking and picking up a sheep track, which ascends steeply to the right. But her knees tremble at the thought of this. She can't even go up to the top rung of a stepladder without feeling wobbly.

She calls out, 'It's all right, Mum. Hang on in there. I've come to bring you down.'

'*It's all right Mummy,*' Rhiannon mocks. 'Dorothea has come to rescue you.'

Dory's heart skitters oddly. The quiet derision in that voice has given her a jolt. It confirms her deepest fear. Rhiannon is not just a bit obsessive, a bit warped. She is capable of anything. Absolutely anything.

Now she says, 'Don't you think it's a bit late in the day for the loving daughter act?'

Dory manages to keep her cool, brushing snow from the sleeve of the coat. Brushing off the taunts. Don't show her you're scared, she tells herself. You never show an animal you're scared. She hopes Rhiannon can't scent her fear as she says, 'I don't want to fight you again, Rhiannon. We've been through all this. The police are at the hospital. They'll have spoken to the taxi driver. They'll be here any minute. They'll charge you with abducting a sick vulnerable person and endangering her life. You don't really fancy a spell in prison, do you?'

Rhiannon blows air through her lips, a pffft of scorn. 'And when they come I shall tell the truth.

That I brought Vida here for a walk in her favourite spot, because I thought it would help to bring her back to us. No one prevented me leaving. The wheelchair was with the others in reception. The invalid taxi was waiting on the forecourt. The driver didn't question me. I made sure she was well wrapped up against the cold...'

That steady, lecturing tone, almost as if she is taking the moral high ground, is too much. Dory shakes her head. 'You need professional help.'

Rhiannon is silent a moment. Then, 'What are you trying to say?'

'I'm not *trying* to say anything. I'm stating a fact. You are one sick lady. It's not Vida who needs to be hospitalised, it's you.'

Dory regrets this immediately. Rhiannon pounces, her eyes glinting. 'You think I'm the same as my mother. You're just like the rest of them. You think it's genetic. You think I've inherited her psychosis. Well, you're wrong!'

'Hah... what is this? I know nothing about your mother.'

Rhiannon eyes her for a moment. She says in a quieter tone, 'Go home, Dory. It won't come with you here.'

'What won't come?' She glances over her shoulder. 'Oh you don't mean...?'

She follows Rhiannon's gaze to where a straggle of wind-crazed hawthorns sprout almost horizontally from a ledge some way off to the right. She blinks. It's easy to imagine things in this light. They call it snow–blindness, don't they? Black spots and streaks dancing in her eyes, shadows sneaking across a white canvas.

'Stay quiet! We don't want to spook it.'

'Spook what? There's nothing there.'

'You don't understand,' she says in that tight, manic voice, 'and I wouldn't expect you to. But I'll tell you anyway. It's a Puma. It's her Power Animal. It's an integral part of her psyche. She needs it to write again. And so do I. I need it, and I won't be happy if you scare it away.'

Just in time, Dory remembers her vow to humour the woman. 'Okay, well what if we just take Vida back down the track? The Puma's more likely to be on the lower ground where there's more cover, isn't it? Where there are more trees.' Recalling the passage in the journals she says, 'Isn't that where you found the tuft of fur, in the forest?'

Dear God, now she's playing the game too, she's beginning to doubt her own sanity.

'No, no, *not down, not down.* It's a mountain creature. From up here it sees everything.' Rhiannon isn't falling for this one.

All right. She'll have to do it the hard way. Sidestepping Rhiannon's outstretched arm she makes for the summit. The wind whips up the lying snow, flecking the air with minute blobs, like egg-white flying from a whisk. Vida's wheelchair is creaking gently as she draws closer. And then Vida's head is up, craning around to see where she is.

'Mum?' She can't stop herself calling out. 'Don't try to move, Mum, you'll fall. I'm coming!'

Vida is struggling to extricate herself from the chair. Her head is bowed, mumbling to herself. It's only as Dory stumbles closer that she sees just how precarious the wheelchair is, secured only by the brake, tilted at a jaunty angle. Rhadley Hill is deceptive. From the summit, the northern flank flattens to an almost vertical drop.

Rhiannon has huffed up behind her, panting her orders. 'Leave it where it is. I positioned her there for a reason.'

Ignore her, that's the best thing. Ignore her and she'll go away. She busies herself tucking the blanket back around her mother. 'It's all right, I'm here now. Let's get you home, shall we.'

Wheeling this thing back downhill won't be easy, but she's got to try. She jabs the brake free with the toe of her boot.

'You're not taking her.' Rhiannon stamps her hand upon one handle of the wheelchair. For a brief moment they wrestle like two small girls fighting for possession of a doll's pram.

'Get the fuck out of my way!' Dory grasps the handles and tries to heave the wheelchair around. It won't budge. But then Rhiannon's grip loosens. Her voice softens, all breathy with wonder. 'Wait. Vida, look, it's here! Your Power Animal has come.'

Dory turns to follow her gaze. The sun chooses this moment to shine briefly and she squints, half-blinded into the silver light. A sleek black shape is emerging from the cover of hawthorns. Or is it? It's a movement, no more than that, a patch of darkness streaming in the shadows beneath the trees. She stares. Funny how her brain stills, stops calculating at this point. Her body takes over. Rarely has she felt so alive, every cell in her body primed alert, ready. Beyond the wind, she can hear the pulpy thud of her heart. She is intensely aware of her internal organs, all pumping away and doing their stuff to keep her alive. How fragile human beings are! She's never realized this before. No claws, no prickles, no scent glands to repel enemies, just a brain, a tongue to talk you out of trouble, a pair of legs to carry you to safety. You hope. Then, thank God, the sun vanishes behind a skein of cloud. The dark patch is gone. There is only the cobalt cross hatch of shadow cast by branches on snow.

Beside her, Rhiannon says as though to herself, 'Did you see how beautiful it was? With a creature like that, you could do anything.'

Vida must *still* see something. She's reaching out a hand, making encouraging sounds of affection as if to a pet pussycat.

Dory gazes at the outstretched hand. Vida is stirring at last. She's talking. Her first words in weeks, or almost words, and wouldn't you know it, they're for an animal that isn't even there.

Rhiannon is gabbling away in that urgent mad whispery voice. 'She can see it. She's talking to it, listen! It will save her. I knew it would save her.'

'There's nothing there,' Dory says. 'There *is* no animal.' Or if there was anything there, it's gone. She tries not to think about those newspaper reports she's read.

But Vida has stopped beckoning. She twists her head to look straight at Rhiannon. She speaks: real, intelligible words, albeit in a voice rusty with disuse. 'It's not *your* creature. It's my Muse and you stole it. You stole my words, and now I can't find them anywhere.'

Dory's first instinct is to grab Vida by the shoulders, give her a little shake, wake her up properly to the real world. But something holds her back. Rhiannon stands unflinching. Yet there's no mistaking the hurt in her voice. 'That's not quite fair, Vida.'

'You stole my fire. I saw you writing and writing in my room, in my study. You stole my words...'

'You've been sleeping a long time, Vida.' Rhiannon gathers herself. 'You're confused after all the drugs. When you wake up properly you'll thank me. I risked everything for you.'

'You left me with nothing.' Vida grips the arms of her wheelchair. Her hair has turned almost white in the past month, Dory notices, tufts of it draggling out of the fur hat.

'Mum... take it easy, it's okay.' She tries a calming pat on the shoulder, but she might as well not be there. Vida's attention is fixed solely on Rhiannon.

Rhiannon says, 'I forgive you, Vida. You're not well. But if you remember you had nothing left to say that was worth hearing. Perhaps the world has heard all it needs to from you. It's my turn now. Time you faced the facts. I'm younger than you. I've got the energy to commit. I can take over where you left off.'

'Heh, wait a minute,' Dory says. 'Take over what, exactly?'

She glances over her shoulder to the road far below, or at least where the road used to be before the snow covered it. Where the hell are the police? Where's Riley? If only someone, *anyone* would come, even some yokel dog-walker would be a welcome interruption.

Rhiannon's eyes stray towards the wheelchair, as if she plans to grab it any moment. 'Keep out of this, Dorothea. You're a corporate puppet, you know nothing about Creatives.'

'Huh. And you do?'

'More than you know. I've worked with creative people for long enough. I've figured out what it is they have. I've released it, haven't I. If I could work with this... force... I could write something the world needs to hear.'

'Lucky old world. Personally, I can't believe I'm *hearing* this shit.' Dory grips onto the wheelchair as if to support herself. 'I'm sick of listening to your drivel about bloody writing. There's more to being creative than words on the page. At least Vida had a child, didn't she? She had me.'

'Biology!' Rhiannon sneers. 'Biology isn't Art. Any fool can give birth.'

'Still, you haven't managed that, have you? That Earth Mother act is a sham. You've never created anything except misery as far as I can see. You've never brought a child into the world. And let's hope you never do, God help it. You're not a creator, Rhiannon, you're a destroyer.'

'Dory?' Vida seems to notice her for the first time. She sounds mildly surprised, rather than shocked. 'Dory, what are you doing here in the snow? Why didn't you tell me you were coming? '

It's the moment she's been waiting for. This may be her last moment but she might as well make it a fine one. She crouches in front of Vida, grasps her knees beneath the blanket.

'Mum. Hallo. You're back.'

'I am? But where have I been?'

'I'll tell you when...' She breaks off. Vida's gaze is fixed on something beyond Dory's shoulder. Rhiannon. Dory swivels around. From below, Rhiannon's face looks strangely ancient, the flesh beneath her chin loosening, her mouth twisted, her strangely pitted skin like one of those papier mache masks they made as kids at Halloween.

'Oh but this scene is so touching, the mother-daughter reunion. Vida, I beg you don't fall for the devoted daughter act. She only wants to get you back in hospital again, she wants you sectioned, put away for the rest of your life, so she can get on back to London and forget all about her poor mad old mother...'

'Shut up! Leave us alone, for pity's sake. She doesn't need this.' Dory feels tears of hysteria rising, but she must get a grip if she's to save Vida. If she's to save herself, come to that.

'You know what will happen, don't you, Vida? You'll grow old and die in an institution, and no one will ever hear of you again. Is that what you want? Remember, it was me, it was *me* who got you out of that hospital. Not her.' Rhiannon's eyes glitter unnaturally bright as she speaks; Dory thinks she can see something "other" in them, something not quite human.

Crouching like this is not a good idea, she suddenly realizes. Huddled in front of Vida's wheelchair she's in the submissive position, an easy target, a pushover. She tries to heave herself upright. It's a fine time to get the cramp. Her toes curl under, useless, as pain needles her calf. Mustn't cry out though. Mustn't show any sign of weakness. Vida meanwhile is making unintelligible sounds as if she's trying to reason things out. Rhiannon takes full advantage.

'Do you know how many times she's visited you, Vida? I could count her visits on one hand. She was all too happy to leave it to me, scurry off back down South to her precious clients. It's the clients that come first, isn't it, Dory? Always the clients. It was me who brought you the soup, remember, it was *me* who looked after you when you were ill.'

Vida is twisting her hands together, her lips working as if she's trying to speak. But nothing comes out.

'Don't listen to her, Mum. It's not true about clients, I came back, I came back because I was worried about you.' Dory tries desperately to stamp life back into her leg.

Rhiannon laughs. 'Oh yes, she came back because she wants to sell the house, Vida, your lovely cottage, the Gingerbread House. She's already started stripping off the wallpaper. She's called in the decorators. She's been to see the estate agents. Did you know that, my love? She wants to sell it so she can pay for your long-term care and forget all about you.'

Dory gazes at her. 'You really are evil, aren't you.'

'It was *me* who found you your Power Animal.' Rhiannon peers over towards the hawthorns. 'And now she wants to scare it off. Just as well it doesn't scare easily. It's coming back. Look over there, it's coming.'

Like a fool Dory falls for the oldest trick in the world. She turns to follow Rhiannon's gaze. In her mind she can see it already, the body low slung, the paws scuffing the snow, the tail flexed, the lips curled back in a snarl. She's only turned her back for a second. That's all it takes. And then she's down. Face down, spitting snow from her mouth, blinking it out of her eyes. It takes a while to register the fact that Rhiannon has actually pushed her. She should have been prepared. She should have been ready, but she hoped against hope it wouldn't go that far.

'You pushed her, you pushed Dorothea over. Stop it! Stop it now. Stop it at once!' Vida's cry is oddly authoritative suddenly as if they are two naughty little girls squabbling over a toy. As if Rhiannon is a nasty child invited to tea.

'You should be on *my* side, not hers,' Rhiannon says. 'I'm hurt, Vida, to be truthful. I've gone to all this trouble to rescue you. I've been like a daughter to you.'

'Dory's my daughter, Dory. I only had one daughter...' Vida's voice weakens. She is pleading, pitiful, as if she's only just woken up to the danger they're in. She must get up. Fight if she has to. She straightens her arms and draws her knees forwards into a squatting position. She twists her head to look up at Rhiannon.

'Rhiannon, stop. You're only making things worse for yourself. We can stop this right now. We can get Mum safely back down the hill, and pretend this never happened.'

Might as well talk to the mythical beast, to the monster for all the impact she makes. There is no great cat advancing on them. Only a woman in a red poncho, hatred in her face, hair fizzing wild beneath a woollen hat, in her right hand a branch of dead hawthorn, ermine-tipped. Beneath the pure white innocence of snow, Dory knows there will be spikes. Dear God, she wouldn't really... would she? She reaches out, intending to grip Rhiannon's ankle and pull her off balance, but the ankle is stoutly booted. And Rhiannon is ready for her. The other boot stamps down on her outstretched hand.

'For God's sake, Rhiannon...!' She can't help screaming, the pain is so great. Her fingers are surely broken. Tears fill her eyes. Her life reels before her in back-to-back episodes: the men, the clients... the life that she's been so impatient to live, to reap the rewards of, and now she won't have a chance. What a stupid, stupid way to die, on a hill in the middle of nowhere, attacked by a madwoman.

'Interfering little bitch,' Rhiannon spits above her, boot still grinding down on her hand. 'Heartless little cow. Couldn't keep your nose out of it, could you? Lucky to have a good kind mummy. Should think yourself blessed, but you didn't want to know, did you. Not until there was a house in it for you. Then you bring that pervert Riley into the house. Felt like a good fuck, did you? Did you get it then? Did you waggle your bony little arse in his face then? Rubbish, I knew you were rubbish the minute you stuck your nose in the front door. I saw you, eyeing up your inheritance...'

'Please, please stop...' Dory whimpers. She can hear Vida screaming, yelling something from the wheelchair, calling her name. The more Vida cries, the greater the pressure of Rhiannon's boot seems. It's as if Vida's cries aggravate her even more. Vaguely Dory wonders, if she is to die, what then will happen to her mother?

With a great effort, she wrenches her face from the snow. 'You're right, I'm rubbish. I'll go. I'll go back to London now. Just let me get up... let me...'

'Let you what? You'll tell on me, won't you? You'll tell them I'm mad, and they'll put me away like Vida, like my mother.'

'No, I promise. I won't... I...' But it's too late. Above her, Rhiannon stands, magnificent in her way as she wields the branch like a cudgel, a goddess bringing down plague and pestilence.

The scream seems to come from a long way off. It ricochets around the hills like the cry of a great bird, one of those Red Kites Vida was always raving on about. It's the scream of someone plunging to their death. Yet there is no sensation of falling. She screws her eyes tight shut ready for impact. It fails to come. Seconds pass. It takes her a while to realize her hand is freed. Gently she flexes her fingers sheathed in the fine black leather glove she'd bought in a sale from John Lewis, although why on earth should she think of that now? Her little finger hurts like hell though when she tries to bend it. From close by she can hear a strange mewling sound, almost like a cat. Perhaps if she just lies still, she'll be okay. She'll play dead. She won't open her eyes. Strange that Rhiannon's gone so quiet. In fact... slowly, slowly, she lifts her head free of snow, strains back her neck. She's still lying in the same position. But she's alive. Yes, very definitely alive. How come? The first thing she sees is the wheelchair, empty of Vida, teetering for a moment on the fist of rock, before plummeting out of sight over the edge.

'Mum?' She crawls towards the rock that marks the summit, and forces herself to gaze down into the void. The wheelchair has somersaulted, wedging itself upside down in a crevice, where it lies with wheels spinning. A few feet below, a body is sprawled: face down on a ledge, one arm flung sideways. The wine-red coat is almost the same colour as the blood pooling beneath. Rhiannon.

What happened? She struggles to her feet, turns. Behind her, her mother is bent almost double, using that branch as a prop to lean on.

Vida looks at her. 'I had to. She wouldn't listen to me. She was going to hurt you. I couldn't let her do that.'

The world has slowed, it seems to Dory, almost to a halt. Her mother must have freed herself; she must have rammed the wheelchair into Rhiannon from behind. Just in time. She sees it now in slow-motion replay, the buckling of knees, the floundering forwards. Gone.

For a while neither of them can speak. Then she grips Vida's elbow. 'Can you walk? You've got to walk, Mum, we've got to get out of here.'

But Vida with her stiffened bones and her wasted muscles can only lean on her and sigh. It's as if she's used up the last of her strength.

Dory is so occupied urging Vida to walk she almost doesn't hear the car. But then she sees it. From this height, it looks insignificant, a toy police patrol vehicle, lights flashing as it threads its way through the hills either side of the road. Roaring upfront is Riley's Land Rover. She wants to weep. God bless Riley. He didn't abandon her after all. He must've gone back to get the Landy and led the police here.

'We're up here... look... here!' She waves her free arm. But they've stopped anyway. The relief as they spot her is so great, her hold on Vida slips and her mother falls quite gently to her knees.

TWO YEARS LATER

Vida's Diary

Saturday 29th September

A brand new journal. It may be childish but I
never get over the thrill of starting a new one.
The covers creak slightly as I open them. I inhale the
scent of frost and pine needles, the way a Christmas
tree smells when you first bring it home. The ink
flows juicily from my pen as I write the date – *Saturday
29th September.*

Keeping a diary is good therapy, they say: a con-
fessional for the lonely, a way of making sense of the
world. I don't know about that. Once I vowed I would
never write another. I wouldn't need to. I swore this
to Dory that night we tossed the old journals into
the flames. We made quite a party of it, me, Dory
and Brendan Riley, raising a glass around the bonfire, the night before I moved from the Gingerbread
House. I thought, or maybe I imagined, that the
journals actually squealed in the flames as if they
were alive, the shiny blue covers buckling in the
heat. It was as if all those words I'd poured from my

heart were crying out to be heard. I watched as my old self shrivelled to ashes. It was a kind of purification, a statement of intent that from now on things would be different.

And they *are* different. Really they are. Here I sit at the window of the flat Dory found for me. My flat is a stone's throw from Wimbledon Common, which is my bit of the countryside now with its network of footpaths, its briars and bridleways. I can see over the backs of other houses, narrow strips of gardens, concrete and hot tubs, trampolines, swings, washing lines and conservatories. The flat is all fresh white paint, oatmeal carpet and one of those pebble-effect fake fireplaces, with a candle and sconce in the fake hearth. Everything here is cheerfully fake. There are no corners for shadows to gather in. This suits me perfectly.

I don't miss the Gingerbread House. Not at all. There were too many dark corners, memories, places I didn't want to go. Dory helped me shut the place up and we left it to that young man from Nisbett Fox to show potential buyers around.

That final month in Cregaron Hospital had seemed interminable. I kept telling them I was well enough to leave, that I didn't need their medication. Dr. Saleem was surprised at the speed of my recovery. When I emerged into the daylight it was early spring. Dory drove me home, and even the dull bottle greens of the conifer plantations and the khaki coloured hills were all sparking to life in paint-box hues. I mentioned to Dory that I might take up watercolour, and she groaned and said, 'Let's just concentrate on getting you moved first, shall we, Mum?'

What would I have done without Dory? I can't pretend it's all been mother-daughter shopping trips and recipe-swapping. But Dory insisted I stay at her flat while we waited for the house to sell, so she could keep an eye on me.

We were both scratchy with each other; on edge. Of course I was relieved that my kidnapper survived. I couldn't have lived with the knowledge that I'd killed a person, even in defence of my own child. She – I can't bear to write her name, or even to speak it aloud without feeling I've invoked a curse – escaped with mild concussion and a fractured collarbone. No doubt the bones mended. Her mental state is another matter.

'So what does she actually get?' Dory fumed when we finally got news that the Crown Prosecutors had decided against a trial. 'It was kidnap and assault, for God's sake! That should warrant a hefty sentence. So she's got a history of mental illness. Well, if she's been in an institution before and a danger to the public, why did they let her out in the first place? They'll give her another two or three years in a nice cosy unit, weaving raffia fruit bowls or whatever they do in one of those places and everything's fine.' She broke off, and glanced away embarrassed. I think she'd forgotten that I was in "one of those places" only recently. The only difference being that it wasn't a secure unit.

After that we rarely mentioned her. She wasn't so much the elephant in the room but more like some large exotic cat curled between us on Dory's white leather sofa. We preferred not to waken her, to tread on her tail, but she was there all the same. Sometimes we'd skip around the subject. The minute we got too close we'd both fall quiet, and I knew Dory was seeing it again, the spinning wheels, the blood pooling in snow. I knew she was thinking the same as me. Just how long would they keep her in for?

Poor Dory. I don't doubt that like me she suffers flashbacks, along with the physical scar, of course. The scar sits just above her left eyebrow where the rock grazed her in the fall. She's grown a fringe to hide it, but when she's tired and brushes her hair back from her face, it grimaces at me, red, angry, like a tribal mark on her pale skin, and I have to look away, I feel so sick. What might have happened that day, if I hadn't…?

❈ ❈ ❈

The cottage sold within a month, and I'd moved into this flat by early summer. Dory wasn't sure at our first viewing.

'What d'you think? I've seen roomier rabbit hutches, but the price is good for the area. And at least you won't be able to take in any dodgy lodgers.'

I laughed. But it wasn't funny. That was the closest we'd got to mentioning her since the news from the Crown Prosecutors. It's strange, I sometimes think, how she brought us together again, only in her absence to elbow her way between us. A trauma shared is not as many think a lightened one: quite the reverse. I'm sure it was as much a relief to Dory as me when I moved out.

I never told Dory about the letter that turned up in my pigeonhole about a month after I moved in here. Rather it was a jiffy-bag package, labelled with handwriting I didn't recognize. Richard and Sally Lovell who bought the Gingerbread House had forwarded some mail. Enclosed was a little note hoping that I was settling happily into my new home as they were.

I stood in the lobby downstairs, light sifting in gold and turquoise shafts through the stained-glass fanlight, shuffling through the post, in a hurry to get out for my walk. There seemed to be nothing of consequence, not at first: a flyer on next year's Cregaron Arts Festival, a seed catalogue, a reminder that my subscription to the local Garden Society newsletter was overdue. A small envelope was tucked in amongst this lot, thin blue cheap paper you could read through if you held it up to the light. Except I didn't hold it to the light. The handwriting was enough. *Her* handwriting, but a strangely shrunken, painstaking version, as if by making every letter fairy-sized it might lessen the blow, might slip into my hands unnoticed.

For a while I stood there gaping at it, unable to move. Just a letter, I told myself. I could throw it away, shred it; I could burn it, pretend I'd never set eyes on it. Yet I couldn't pretend. *She* may not have found me, but her letter had. Its very existence was an assault, an invasion of my sanctuary. The writer might be locked away in a secure institution, but this was proof she hadn't let go of me, not yet. Just a letter, but it had the same effect as if she'd sprung from the shadows and grabbed me around the neck.

. I sank, trembling, onto the bottom stair, thankful there were no neighbours there to see me. After a while I found the strength to tear the envelope into shreds, and disposed of them in the paper recycle bin.

What she had to say I could only guess at. An accusation? An apology? A rambling treatise about the goddess? Or maybe, even more disturbing than any threat, a request for me to visit her, some deluded attempt to continue our friendship.

The first thing I did when I finally got my legs to carry me upstairs back to my flat was to ring the Lovells. I thanked them for forwarding the mail, but told them to please not to bother in future as it would only be junk. After that I changed my email, just in case she had access to a computer. Even with these precautions it took a week or two to be able to check my post without my heart going into overdrive.

❧ ❧ ❧

Dory had been right about the flat, of course; it is tiny. There's no room for a study, but that doesn't matter. I never intended to write again. That part of my life was over, or so I thought. I'd donated most of my library to charity before the move to London. Fee Moody was long gone. There had been a letter awaiting me when I got out of hospital, announcing that she was cutting back on her client list and wishing me well for the future. Dory had read the letter over my shoulder and snorted, 'What a bitch! Still, you won't be needing her any more, will you.'

I assured her I wouldn't, that from now on I intended to live a bit, take up painting, perhaps, try an exercise class, buy a bike to ride on the common.

Dory looked at me doubtfully. 'Can't quite see you on a bike, Mother.'

It was in the autumn of that year that I began writing again. It began as scribbles; observations, vague jottings in notebooks, a way of keeping myself amused on my wanderings, the way some people take their knitting or sketchbooks everywhere with them. Gradually the notebooks began to pile up. Soon I was writing on the train, in gallery cafes, on a bench in Trafalgar Square, by the pond on the common, anywhere but home. It felt right to be out in the open, among dog-walkers, tourists, mothers with toddlers in pushchairs. The idea of hunching indoors over the computer was suddenly abhorrent to me. Why shut myself away from humanity in order to write about them? Anyway, it wasn't serious writing. But the fragments had other ideas. They took on a life of their own. They began seeking each other out, forging neural pathways, vivid web-like tentacles probing connections. A pattern was taking shape. Almost without my noticing, I had the book that sits beside me on this desk: *The Retreat.*

'It was only a bit of fun,' I told Cindy on one of her visits. 'It's about this religious cult full of eccentric characters, where the leader comes to a sticky end. I suppose it was my way of working her... you know, out of my system.'

'But what are you going to do with it?' Cindy said. 'You can't just stick it in a drawer, Vida. In fact I forbid it.'

The next thing I knew Cindy had told Hugh, her agent, about me and that was that.

❧ ❧ ❧

Looking around my room now, I can see I may have to move again. It was a squash bringing friends back for a celebration after the Reading yesterday. Oh yes, I have friends. Frances, and Tarek and Vivienne who belong to my local Book Group, and David, my downstairs neighbour, whose Springer Spaniel I take for walks on the common when he's away, and Cindy; they all turned up to give me some moral support, bless them.

Dory came too, bringing a new man who looks much older than her, with shaggy dust-coloured hair and chin stubble and a battered suitcase of a face. I could see Dory fidgeting in the front row and glancing at her watch from time to time. I couldn't help smiling to myself as I read an extract from *The Retreat.* Some things never change.

Dory sidled up to me when the signing began. 'How long d'you think this'll take, Mum? Only Fergus and me are supposed to be somewhere.'

We both looked at the size of the queue, snaking around the shop, and I shrugged. 'I have no idea, love. You go on. There's no point in hanging around.'

'Would you mind?' She folded her arms and looked around impatiently. 'It's not my scene really, all these literary types.'

I waved her away with a grin, and went on signing. To be truthful I never expected this reaction. I wrote *The Retreat* to make sense of a dark time, to bring it all into the light. The critics who slated me some years ago are now struggling to find superlatives: '*The natural successor to "The Gingerbread House",*' said one. '*Vida Tremayne is at the peak of her powers,*' said another. A cliché, perhaps, but who's complaining?

Still my triumph is tinged with an edge of fear. Naturally there's the usual disclaimer in the preface. *All characters are entirely fictitious and not based on any living person etc etc...* Despite this I worry slightly when *she* is still very much alive. I couldn't help thinking of her as the readers shuffled forwards in the queue, clutching their copies of my book. Beyond their heads, I could see through the plate-glass window, the dark street, rain slanting silver in the glow of the street light. Once I glanced up and thought I glimpsed her, the flash of her cranberry coat, the mane of hair, the hard velvet button eyes seeking me out. It struck me that maybe in some horrific, curious way, her so-called Programme had freed me after all. My hand trembled very slightly as I scribbled to Yasmin or Tracey or Carol, with all best wishes from *Vida Tremayne...*

❀ ❀ ❀

FOUR YEARS LATER
A SALON IN NORTH
LONDON

The girl, Zoe, is the chatty type she dreads. Has she got any holidays planned? What does she do for a living? Where does she live? The answer to the first question is no, she doesn't actually care for holidays. To the second she responds that she is a Life Coach, which is true enough in a way. The girl is clearly clueless as to what a Life Coach actually does, as she dabs away with her brush, commenting in a baffled tone, 'Really? That sounds interesting.'

Yes, she agrees silently, *it does*. It's also pleasingly vague, open to interpretation. Quite unlike the new name she's given herself. Penny Marshall. It's taken her a while to settle on that name and she's pleased with it. It's the name of a bank clerk, or the next-door neighbour who takes in the post or feeds the cat. A good, reliable, English name. The kind of name that goes with digestive biscuits and weak tea.

To the third question she replies in a manner that precludes further questioning. Actually, she's not from around here, she tells the girl. She lives in the country and is in London visiting a friend. In fact the hostel that the mental health social worker found for her is just around the corner from the salon, next door to the council offices, a seventies-built concrete horror with coffin-sized rooms and echoing corridors. The fact that it's dire doesn't worry her too much. It's only temporary, after all. If she plays her cards right, she'll be on her way to Oxfordshire any day now.

Zoe settles the polythene cap over her head, lays down the pasting brush. 'Would you like a coffee while you're waiting for the colour to take?'

'No, I'm fine thank you.'

Beige-blonde is a dramatic step. Zoe approves. Zoe says she wishes all her clients were that brave. She wishes Zoe would pipe down, just go and leave her in peace. She glances down at the purplish-crimson curls on the floor. Detached from her head they are lifeless, dead plant material. The look she's opted for is sleek, gamine, a spiky fringe to offset newly acquired cheekbones. She lost a lot of weight while she was at Ransome Hall, at least two stones, the food was so appalling. She's bought herself new clothes, too: sharp, structured, black. It's a worthwhile expense despite the fact she has no job yet. She thinks of it as an investment.

'Can I get you a magazine?'

'No, thank you. I have my book to read.' She pulls it from her bag, lifts it to her face, signalling the end of the conversation.

'Oh, what's that you're reading then? *The Songbird's Secret.*' The girl peers over her shoulder. 'I don't think I've heard of Elizabeth Carey. Is she any good?'

Is she any good? She shudders at the chirrupy voice.

'Yes. I believe she is.' She must keep her voice steady. Keep the smile stitched in place. Too good for *you*, she wants to say, but must hold back. She is just an ignorant young girl. What does she know?

Thankfully the phone rings in reception, and the girl trots to the desk to answer it. She sighs, smoothes the cover of her book. The author peers up at her, silvered waves, and jaunty earrings. She isn't fooled by the image. She's looked deep into those eyes, sad eyes behind half-moon spectacles. The smile tilted at one corner, tremulous. For twelve years the woman has languished, forgotten. Clearly it was providence coming across this copy of her book in the Hospice Shop. She'd turned at once to read the author bio on the back flyleaf: *'Elizabeth Carey lives deep in the Oxfordshire countryside with her two cats, Romy and Remus.'*

It's interesting how much a single paragraph can reveal about a person. No mention of a husband, or children. Just cats. Perfect. Of course she might have moved on by now, but she always trusts her senses in these matters. No, this woman is the type who puts down roots, knotty, solitary, knuckling into the red Oxfordshire soil for the long haul. She is still there, buried away with her out-of-print books even if the cats have passed on. There's no website and Elizabeth's far too modest to waste her time on Twitter and the like, but making contact is no problem. She can always send her letter care of the publisher.

Elizabeth Carey gazes up at her, her eyes pleading. *Not long now,* she silently assures her. As soon as she gets back to her room, she will finish her letter to dear Elizabeth. While she sits there waiting for her colour to take, she writes it in her head:

'*I am only sorry that I didn't come across your novel before, but you know, I do believe it's a case of when the pupil is ready, the Master appears. The right book falls into your hands at the right time. Serendipity.*'

❧ ❧ ❧

ACKNOWLEDGEMENTS

Every novel needs its champions and cheer leaders. I'm indebted to Kathryn Price of Cornerstones for her insightful reading which proved a turning point for this book.

Helen Bryant of Cornerstones, together with my agent Nelle Andrew believed in this novel long before I did. Thanks to Yasmin Standen of Three Hares, Vida's testament will now be heard.

Writing pals are precious; I couldn't manage without Eve Seymour whose wit and wisdom keeps me just about sane in an insane industry. Heartfelt thanks also to Jean Bendell, friend, confidante and the best listener in the business.

Finally thanks to my husband Terry, sounding board and solace, and especially my daughter Mia, also a writer, for her keen eye and invaluable support.

⚜ ⚜ ⚜